The Last Druid

Book 1: Life

The Last Druid: Book 1 Life © Nei Nguyen 2021 – Cover by Lino Sero – Map made with Inkarnate

Introduction Year 512 of the Shattered Age

Northern Glacier

Saizho Furbarst Erjehart

Sei'un Han'ei The Golden Hills Mount Amun A'Va

Yusozhan Titan's Fall

Wulan Azuna Apricum

Sorrow Shards

Evenmoor

Western Gulp

The Desecrated

Howling Peak

Garstan Ysek

Illith Islands

Introduction   Year 512 of the Shattered Age

The Greying North

- Kajrst
- Mul Kowuhr
- sni
- Īse
- Zæchnæ
- Dead Forest
- Eria Mountains
- M'rantor
- Ævesta
- Edurn
- Othelron Ruins
- Frigid Sand
- Ætina
- Flumium
- Mul Tarum
- Ruins of Valandor
- ompi
- Orchran
- Blade of Mortia
- Mul Nordihr
- Mortia's Strand
- The Island Nation of Imirra
- Teda
- Mortia's Hand
- Imirrian Sea

Year 512 of the Shattered Age

CHAPTER 1:

Being a bard, it was important to read the crowd's mood, or even predetermine if a tavern was going to be a decent stage. If you weren't going to make a profit, best keep to yourself.

Being a *hungry* bard, one didn't have much of a choice

Eyes downcast, Darya pretended to tune the strings of her lute, avoiding all the wary glares she was getting. Small as she was, even with her padded shoes, showing defiance would not be smart. She had taken the time to tame her wild golden brown curls, shone the buttons of her best tunic vest, and even lined her hazel eyes with charcoal. Most importantly, she had spent three of her last five coppers to perform here.

Darya was not going to let all that go to waste.

There shouldn't be a need to bother with any introduction tonight. Some light music to soften the mood, then ease into more rousing performances would be a good plan.

Darya cleared her throat.

"O' 'Vasni was his Home

Where the stallions roam

Where the wind soars hi-"

The song turned into a yelp when a mug was smashed at her feet.

"Simmer down, drunkards!!!" The tavernkeep, a burly man with an aggressive-looking mutton chop shouted over his bar.

Darya winced. Tough crowd. But she would be starving *and* sleeping in the fields tonight if she didn't make back at least those three coppers. So the young bard forced her scowl into a smile.

"Perhaps some ambient music would soothe your weary souls. Just kick back, relax, and-"

"Would ye just shut it??? Ain't nobody 'ere 'ave shite fer ye!"

Another smashed mug. The tavernkeep barrelled out from behind his bar, rolling pin waving dangerously. He was about the size of two grown men, so the crowd shrunk back immediately, except for a few tipsy patrons who were just looking for a fight (or a beating.)

Knowing that even her stubbornness wasn't going to produce a single copper here, Darya grabbed her things and dashed for the door. Before she could burst through however, someone grabbed her elbow. Startled, Darya twisted around and was ready to smash whoever's face in with her lute, when she was met with a pair of mismatched eyes and a bewitching smile.

Time seemed to freeze.

"Something for your trouble."

Melodic, echoing, yet softer than a whisper. A wink. A warm coin slipped into her closed fist. And the person was gone in a flick of a blue cloak.

Darya stumbled outside, bewildered. Heart thumping, she slung into the nearest alley before daring to peer into her hand. Hazel eyes widened.

Gold! Shiny new gold! Without even a speck of dirt on it! Dazed, Darya took an experimental bite, and her soul soared as the metal gave. Quickly, she closed her palm over the coin and shoved her fist inside her tunic.

If she paced herself, this could last for far more than two whole months on the road! And might even be enough for a travel beast, with plenty left to send home!

But first. *Food.*

Darya practically skipped towards the market square. It was late, but she managed to catch the baker before he closed down, who was kind enough to give her half a stale loaf for her last two coppers. Darya wasn't foolish enough to brandish her gold just yet. Carrying around a bag of money after dark was asking for trouble. As her eyes wandered a bit further down the square, where a bruised thief was chained to the pillory, she decided that trouble, in this lovely town named Edurn, was *not* something she wanted.

Safe to say Darya did not want to double back to the last tavern. So she walked to an inn on the other side of town instead. It was tempting to buy a full hot meal, but she settled for just a cup of cheap mead and a room. That still left her with ninety-eight silvers and eighty coppers. Plenty for anything she could think of for now.

Settling by the hearth, Darya took her time with her dingy meal, listening to the crowd now that she could afford to.

This place was a lot less hostile than the other tavern. People seemed exhausted mostly, and the loudest bunch was a group of three by the bar, among them only two were contributing while a hooded third nodded along.

"Nobody knows Caldor snuck into his house until he said something."

"Caldor? Or the Count?"

The first speaker said, leaning in conspiratorially, "Count."

Oh? This conversation seemed interesting. With luck, maybe Darya could get enough materials to spin it into a somewhat exciting tale. Discreetly, she scooted a little closer as the man continued.

"He has no proof though, but Caldor didn't say anything, so they put him in the stock."

"But the Count's girl fell ill on the night he said Caldor snuck in."

"That's no proof."

"Could be, if Caldor..."

The man trailed off, making a vulgar gesture. The second man smacked his hand, hissing, "Sam!"

"Sorry, sorry!" Sam shook his head, "But it coulda happened!"

"They have not held a trial for Caldor, though." The hooded figure finally said, voice clearly feminine. Refined, whistling like a song despite being just spoken words.

A chill ran down Darya's spine.

That voice! That was the same voice as the person who gave her the gold! In her shock, Darya almost missed it when a fourth person chimed in, this time from a different table.

"One less mouth to feed. It's been hard enough around here anyway. At least people'd get some entertainment before they'd riot over food."

The hooded woman tilted her head, "It is not fair when the Count has a full storage and vault spilling with money when his people are starving."

"Ain't nothing anyone could do about it," Sam shook his head again, "he has armed guards. Money-bought fighters. Caldor probably wanted to do something about it. Look where he is now."

"But is he not the only one here who knows the way through the Dead Woods?"

Silence followed the woman's words. At last, Sam shrugged.

"We'll make do. His herbs are too expensive these days.

A person laughed, "Well, at least we still have horse-piss beer that'd knock you out after one pint!"

Raucous laughter followed, another round of drinks ordered as cheers echoed all around.

Unlike the others, Darya had forgotten her own mug, eyes glued to the mysterious woman. And it seemed Darya was noticed as well, for a gloved finger was brought to a shadow of smiling lips. Darya could have sworn she was *winked at* when the two patrons sitting next to the woman slurred their words and succumbed to the alcohol, knocking their tankards off of the bar.

The innkeeper yelled over their heads. As the commotion picked up, the hooded woman slung away and out of the door.

Darya wanted to smack herself. This was probably a terrible idea. But she followed the blue cloak anyway.

The market square was empty now. With nary a light on aside from those flickering behind windows, Darya tried her hardest to keep to the shadows, one hand holding her bags away from her body so they would not make a sound.

What in the world was she doing? Darya couldn't explain it. Was she grateful for the coin spared? Yes, but that should *not* be enough to pull her into the night, in a stranger's town with a bag full of money.

There was just something alluring about the woman. Something *terrifyingly exciting* in the way she moved without a sound. In the blue-and-green gleam of her eyes and the smiles that promised all the secrets of the world.

So Darya followed. Hoping that this would not lead to her end.

Her heart dropped to her stomach when the hooded figure stopped by the pillory. Slinking behind an empty stall, Darya watched as the woman exchanged quietly with a posted guard. The guard spat, his sneer visible even in the darkness.

That was until glimmers of gold coins dropped into his open palm. A harsh laugh barked out.

"Why waste me time diggin' a hole when I can make a good coin?"

Turning to the stock, he unsheathed his sword. Darya clasped a hand over her mouth, preventing any noise from escaping. It wasn't like she had not seen deaths and executions before, but this was too sudden!

However, the guard only smacked the flat side of his blade at the thief's legs, getting a grunt in return.

"Didn't know guards now double as slave traders too."

The thief, who Darya realised was the infamous Caldor, got a kick to his side for that. There was a bit of a scuffle, before Caldor was tied up, hands behind his back and handed to the woman at the end of a rope.

"We never saw each other, you hear?" The guard snarled at the hooded woman, who inclined her head, before they went separate ways, with the woman and the thief heading straight towards Darya.

Frantic, the bard curled flat on the ground, making herself as small as she could manage. But for some cursed reasons, she *had* to sneak a peek.

Just in time to see and *hear* Caldor popping his own joints to slip out of his bonds.

It was sickening, and surely as painful as all the Gods knew, but the thief didn't even flinch as he ripped through his tattered pants and pulled out a dagger from his inner thigh, slick with his own blood. Despite his injuries, Caldor swung at the woman's back with the ferocity of a mad dog.

However...

Her movements were entirely too fast to see. Darya's eyes could not follow, but before neither she nor Caldor knew what was happening, the hooded figure had the thief pinned down under her foot

Startled, Darya's breath hitched.

Again, in a melodious voice that was both enchanting and frightening, the woman spoke, "I merely seek a pathfinder. If you find my offer less than what awaits you back there, I have no qualms returning you in chains."

Winded, Caldor could only let out a wheeze in response. The hooded woman tilted her head, almost birdlike in motion.

"Yet it seems my endeavour might not have started out as smoothly as I thought it would."

Darya thought her heart gave out when she was suddenly looking into mismatching blue and green eyes.

How did she move like that?!

"Hello, little bird."

This close, Darya caught a glimpse of it. A thin scar, stretched by her smile, as her gloved hand closed around Darya's nape.

The world went black.

CHAPTER 2:

Darya woke up facing a fire.

Her first instinct was to scream.

"Oh, shut it."

The chilling, melodic voice hit her like a bucket of cold water. Darya squirmed, tried to get up, rolled around uselessly before she realised she was tied up like a lamb to slaughter. So she screamed again. Only to gag when her mouth was suddenly stuffed with cloth. The hooded woman smiled as she patted Darya's face none-too gently.

"There. Much better. Now."

Blue-and-green eyes trailed away. Darya's followed. Caldor was running away. The mysterious woman let out an exasperated sigh.

"Great. See what you have done?"

She stood, holding out one hand. Something hummed under her breath, too quiet and too foreign for Darya to make out.

It seemed tonight was a night of unpleasant and downright horrifying surprises.

Dirt and rocks flew up, swirled in the air for a brief moment, before whistling forward and attaching to Caldor's legs. The thief went down with a dull thud.

Every hair on Darya's body stood on ends. She was sure she threw up a little.

Magic.

There was a slightest wrinkle to the woman's scarred brows, "More complications. Great."

Slowly, those unsettling eyes trailed down Darya's face, "I cannot have a songbird singing about this now, can I?"

Among everything she was feeling right then, *fear* was definitely the most prominent. Darya's eyes almost popped out of their sockets as she shook her head, her muffled begging unable to escape the gag.

This was going south too quickly.

"Hey!" Suddenly, Caldor snapped, "You leave the girl alone! She has nothing to do with this!"

"Hoh?" There was amusement to the woman's tone. The dancing fire reflected eerily in her eyes. She tilted her head at

Caldor, "She is already plenty involved. No thanks to herself, I might add."

"She's innocent!" Stubbornly, Caldor spat, "Leave her out of this!"

"Said the man who abandoned her at the first chance he had."

"Wouldn't you??"

As they went back and forth, Darya curled to herself. Using her thumbs, she managed to pry the cloth out of her mouth. Gasping for breath, Darya was about to utilise her bard-tongue and negotiate her way out of this mess, when sharp mismatched eyes landed on her.

"Please don't kill me!" Was all that came out of Darya.

Pale lips quirked up to a smirk. The woman crouched down, a long, gloved finger tipped Darya's chin up. This close, she could see it clearly. A scar, jagged and ugly, went down from the woman's hairline, crossed her left green eye, and disappeared under her chin. Wisps of midnight hair framed her angular face, a stark contrast to pearly white skin. Almond-shaped eyes were curtained with dark lashes, bright even though they were shadowed with her heavy hood.

She was beautiful. Dangerously, *inhumanly* so.

"I am no murderer." The woman's voice was soft like a caress, "I only need to cut your tongue out."

That immediately broke whatever enchantment her beauty had cast over Darya. Fear rolled painfully in her stomach, but something else also simmered to the top.

"Then I'll write down what you did!"

The woman's smile glimmered like a knife, "Then I'll chop off your hands."

"I'll write with my teeth then!"

"Then I'll pull out every single one of them."

"I'll... I'll learn to write with my feet!!!" Darya shouted. Terror had turned her desperately stubborn. Stupid, too. "Point is, I'll bring you down if you hurt me!!!"

An eyebrow raised. The woman inclined her head and studied Darya, devoid of emotions. Ice dropped into Darya's stomach. She went and did it, didn't she? Grandmama Clarince would dig her corpse up and kill her again if she ever heard of this. And her poor, sweet little Sara, who was going to-

A peal of laughter escaped the mysterious woman. Chiming like silver bells, it was both mesmerising and unnerving.

"Amusing girl." She spoke, strange eyes gleaming, "I can see why you are a bard. A poor one, but entertaining nonetheless."

"Uh... Thanks?" Darya blinked, even though her heart felt like it was going to explode with anxiety, "Does that mean you won't ki-, I mean, maim me?"

Another chortle, before a gloved hand moved to her nape. Darya tensed, expecting to be knocked out again. Instead, the woman grabbed the back of her tunic, and pulled Darya into a sitting position. Dizzied that her panicked tactic worked, she watched in a daze as the hooded woman went over to Caldor, and hauled him towards the campfire.

She picked up a grown man as if he weighed nothing.

Knowing she would pass out if she tried to think about it too hard, Darya finally took a look at their surroundings. And did a double take.

Somehow, they were at the edge of the Dead Forest, the infamous stretch of dead woods that surrounded the western base of the Eira Mountains.

Twenty miles away from town.

How the ... *How* did the woman get them here? By herself? On the same night? They were still on the same night as she bought Caldor and Darya got unfortunately tangled into this mess, right? *Right???*

Darya stared at the hooded woman, dazed, as she pulled a kettle off from the fire.

There was no travel beast around. No cart or caravan. There wasn't even a *road* nearby as far as Darya could see in the darkness.

"I would offer you some tea, but that would mean I have to untie you, and forgive me if I have no reason to trust either one of you yet."

Caldor snorted in response. Darya stared on, still bewildered.

Whoever this person was ... she was clearly magical. And magic... well, it was supposed to only exist in legends. Myths that Grandmama Clarince used to tell on quiet nights. Wild stories. Tall tales. Something that disappeared after the age of wars. Something *people like Darya* were not supposed to see in a lifetime. Not something that just happened so casually it might just be another tool in this woman's bag.

And did she say *tea?* As in actual tea leaves and not the common herbal imitation?

Just who was this woman? *What* was she?

Feeling braver that the hooded woman didn't seem like she was going to go on a killing spree anytime soon, Darya dared to speak.

"I... uhm, I'm Darya, by the way."

Caldor gave her a warning glare. Darya ignored him. The hooded figure chuckled over her steaming mug.

"Charmed. I am Luunaiwel."

Darya blinked, "Huh, I've never heard such a name before. Where are you-"

"You used magic." Caldor jumped in bluntly. Darya rolled her eyes. So much for that warning glare. "*Witchcraft...* We're going to be killed for some kind of weird ritual. You are going to sacrifice us, aren't you?"

Sipping from her cup (ceramic, Darya noticed), Luunaiwel didn't seem at all fazed, "Nonsense. I have already told you, I am simply looking for a pathfinder. You will be paid well for your service after the job is done... And, of course, if you swear to secrecy."

Caldor narrowed his eyes, "You're going to kill me if I don't agree."

"I am not going to kill you," Luunaiwel repeated, as if she was speaking to a petulant child, "I would simply move on and find another way. Though I would suggest you do the same if that is the case, since you do have a target painted on your back."

Translation: Why would I need to kill you if you already are a dead man?

Darya could practically *hear* Caldor's seething rage, but he didn't retort to Luunaiwel's taunting tone. Good. He had no tack or whatsoever. Not that she had much of it, Darya had to admit, considering how she came to be here.

Still.

"Why would you need a pathfinder?"

"Curious, are you not?" Luunaiwel hummed, the fire danced once more in her eyes. Darya started to suspect that was not a reflection, "There is an herb patch, a *wild vegetation* within this forest. Rumour has it only Mister Caldor here knows the way."

Darya's eyes fell to the thief as he growled, "Leave it alone. Don't you have enough money already?? With all that shiny gold of yours?"

Luunaiwel scoffed, "Fool. What I am looking for is beyond what any money can afford."

Caldor didn't seem all that pleased, "If you are looking to take all the herbs, the whole town will die. That's the only source of medicine we have without having to go to Īse!"

Luunaiwel tilted her head, gaze piercing and cold, "Then they have signed their own death sentences when they chained you up to die."

"I was going to get away!"

"Hoh? To do what?" Luunaiwel taunted, smirking at his building rage, "Bring back the herbs for free? Become a starving vigilante?"

"What do you know, you crazy witch!"

Darya lost interest the moment Caldor started yelling. She turned to the trees, whose dead barks were white as bone, with empty, gnarled branches reaching out to a sky that no longer nourished them. She wondered what the forest looked like before it had become... well, *dead*. Darya had wandered around this region, never quite this far, but enough to hear stories.

The trees had a mind of their own in the Dead Forest, they said. Sometimes, the skeletons of what once was moved in the shadows, creating a maze that no living creature could ever escape.

The shadow itself was alive, too, weaving among corpses of trees and rotting remains of those who were foolish enough to enter.

Here, with the fire casting moving shades around them, it was all too easy to believe those stories.

Hold on... *moving.*

A red eye blinked back at Darya.

"Gaaahhh!!!"

A Withered, a creature of twisted flesh and cursed blood, leapt into view. It was almost humanoid in structure, its elongated limbs ending with razor-sharp claws. But where the head should have been was a stump, with a single blood-red eye and a gaping maw.

This was no story. This was the stuff of nightmares.

Darya tried to hobble away with her bound feet. Caldor tried to do the same, but fell once more due to the rocks still encasing his legs. Luunaiwel didn't seem all that concerned.

"Ignia." She whistled.

Their firepit turned blue. Lashing out in tendrils, they snatched at the pouncing Withered mid-air, wrapping around each of its legs. The creature's screech was ear-shattering, and Darya found herself on the ground by Caldor, desperately trying to cower from the fight. The blue flames engulfed the Withered, hissing as it *ate* the creature, flesh, bones and all.

Another whistle, and the flame retreated, innocently crackling as if it didn't leave behind a trail of monster soot. As if it wasn't still a seething blue.

Shaking, Darya couldn't help but stare, unable to make a sound.

The force of the spell had blown back Luunaiwel's hood. Against the light, two large, pointed ears jutted out behind braided midnight hair. Pierced with jewels that shone like starlight, the silhouette was unmistakable, even though Darya had never seen one before in her lifetime. Nor any other humans, even those older than her Grandmama, she was sure.

The tales left enough of an impression.

Luunaiwel was an *elf*.

CHAPTER 3:

Five hundred years had passed since the war ended. Five hundred years of irreversible damage and untold strife.

They said it wasn't the Great War that wrecked most of the havoc, but it was the event that ended it did. The Shattering it was called, a terrible magical showdown between an elf Warlock and a human Dragon Priest that tore the world apart. The war ended, because the land never recovered.

They said something terrible happened in the aftermath of that final battle. The very fabric of the world was ripped asunder, resulting in the barren wasteland that made up most of Ardent. Once abundant forests were reduced to creaking, bare bones. Crops could never grow, harvests were barren. Livestock was always starving or turned rabid. The weather turned wild, years of drought followed by years of flood. Rivers became toxic with strange minerals. Wildlife either dwindled or grew so hostile that humans became the prey.

The suffering was blamed on the creatures that wielded magic beyond human's capabilities. After all, wasn't it an elf who had a hand in destroying their lands? Wasn't it a Dragon who started the Great War, a War that pitched all races against each other, and resulted in a dying world?

Humans remembered dragons raining destruction from the sky. They remembered the elves, swift and silent with mountains of bodies behind them after every conquest. They remembered eyes, sharps and gleaming like cats' in the darkness. They remembered blades that could cut water and magic that could lay a kingdom in ruins. They remembered deadly beauties, and smiles that glittered with fangs. They remembered elegant silhouettes in the moon's shadow, accentuated with pointed ears, whose appearance would always follow with blood.

Elves were terrifying agents of Death, powerful and unstoppable, a force that painted nightmares with red. It was a fear etched into human's consciousness, like the urge to flee when faced with a fearsome beast. A fear that never turned dull with time, despite the elves' apparent disappearance.

And Luunaiwel was one of them.

"She's an *elf!*" Caldor's terrified whisper broke Darya out of her stupor, "She's going to kill us!!!"

"Oh, by all the Celestials known and loved..." Luunaiwel rolled her eyes, clearly had heard him, "For the last time, I am *not* going to kill you. I need you to do something for me, so killing you would be counterproductive now, would it not?"

Caldor's eyes were wild with both terror and rage, "You'll kill us once you're done with whatever heinous sh- OW!!"

Darya, having had enough of the thief, took matters into her own hands, literally, by shoving the bound portion of her wrists into Caldor's fool mouth. The moron tried to head-butt her, which Darya narrowly avoided, hissing.

"Just shut up! You're *not* helping!" Heaving out a breath, Darya tried to adjust her thoughts.

What was an elf doing here, on this side of the Eria Mountains?

After the Shattering, the elves retreated far into the mist-woven East. The only entry to their lands was blocked off with an impenetrable wall, running from the mountains to the churning sea. The gates were forever closed, so none could enter and none could exit. So forbidden that the Elvendom became a place of myths, where horrors were locked away and history could only recall echoes of its once greatness.

But here Luunaiwel was, standing bemused before Darya. An elf with blade-tipped ears and eyes that captured all light in the darkness.

Swallowing, the bard spoke, very aware that any word she said could be her last, "I have a feeling you hate repeating yourself."

An airy chuckle bolstered what little courage Darya had gathered, "Correct."

"Right. You said you're going to pay him to take you to this... vegetation, right?"

"Yes." Luunaiwel hummed, tilting her head to regard them with mismatching eyes, "Let us say... twenty gold coins? For his service."

Darya's eyes bulged. *Twenty gold?!* That was enough for someone to buy their own land and lord over it. Enough to buy *a new life*. Enough to-

Caldor trying to swing at her head cut off Darya's inner rambling. She glared at him before turning back to the elf.

"Judging by how easy that came out of you, how dangerous this is going to be for us and how highly you spoke of this herb patch," Darya trailed off, eyeing the fire between them warily, "thirty gold, you let us go after we're done or no deal."

Luunaiwel tilted her head again, unblinking. Her gaze was cold and terrifying, but Darya stubbornly held the gaze. Even Caldor had gone still.

"You are better as a negotiator than a bard." The elf chuckled, "I will let you go after a secrecy vow. Deal."

Darya let out all the air in her lungs in one go. Offering Luunaiwel a tentative smile, "Not sure if you're complimenting me or insulting me, but thanks." She then turned back to Caldor, "I'm going to let go, but you have to stop yelling, alright?"

He glared at her. Darya rolled her eyes. This was probably the best she was going to get. And let him go. The man sputtered, spitting like an angry cat. Darya sat back on her haunches, waiting for him to shout again.

But Caldor only grunted, "I am *not* fine with this."

Grinning, Darya smacked his shoulder, "Friend, I have a feeling you are usually not fine with most things, but we can't always have what we want in life."

He gave her another baleful glare. Caldor finally turned to Luunaiwel, shaking his head distrustfully.

"Doesn't seem like I have a choice."

Grinning, Luunaiwel huffed. Wet tongue darted out, running slowly over her *sharp* canines.

"Do not be frightened. Or did your mummy tell you a big scary elf would suck your blood as a child?"

Caldor growled. Darya cut in before more arguments could start and ruin the sweet deal she just got.

"Oooookay! So! What are we going to do now?"

Mismatched eyes turned to her, Luunaiwel mused with a finger under her chin.

"Do not be so hasty, little bird. I have not figured out what to do with you yet."

Darya blinked, "Wait... what?"

"Just let her go." Caldor grumbled. Darya stared at him, incredulous.

"Excuse me? I just got you a great deal! The least you could do is pay me back!"

Luunaiwel raised an eyebrow, "And do you honestly think I would just let her leave after all that?"

Desperate and afraid, Darya turned back to the elf, "Do you need... I dunno, a squire or something?"

Her answer came in the form of a slow, cat-like blink, "A squire?"

"Yes! To carry your stuff and help along the way." Darya tried to gesture as best as she could with her bound hands. She wasn't going to *just leave* after so much money was offered. Rightfully, she should be more scared, but Luunaiwel didn't seem like she was going to kill either Darya or Caldor. Well, granted, Luunaiwel needed Caldor for something, but Darya was a liability. But...

"Are you bloody serious???" Caldor looked like he wanted to smack her. Darya probably should smack herself, too.

"If anything, she is amusingly stupid." Luunaiwel muttered. A sigh, "A secrecy vow is easier to make with all parties present. At the end of a journey. Come along, but I will neither hire nor pay you."

Darya opened her mouth, but Caldor elbowed her in the ribs. They proceeded to engage in a glaring battle. Ultimately, Darya conceded, looking away. She was fortunate enough to stay alive. She still had most of the money Luunaiwel gave her back in Edurn. Being greedy would only get her killed.

She knew better.

Welp, at least Luunaiwel was nice enough to not take Darya's belongings away.

Luunaiwel's crisp clap brought their attention back to the elf.

"The night is still young. I believe we have three hours left before dawn. Shall we, Mister Caldor?"

The thief narrowed his eyes, "You did your research."

"But of course I did." From behind her cloak, Luunaiwel unsheathed a blade. Longer than a dagger, but shorter than a regular sword, needle-pointed and covered in etchings that Darya couldn't read. The elf snipped their bindings, and undid Caldor's rock cuffs with a snap of her fingers.

Rubbing her wrists, Darya glanced at the forest, uneasy, "We're going in there? In the dark?"

"That's the only way to do it." Caldor grunted. Sighing, he felt his tender wrists cautiously before turning to Luunaiwel, "I can't go in there unarmed."

The elf smiled, tossing Caldor's dagger to him, still crusted with blood, "I trust you know not to be foolish, Mister Caldor?"

He grumbled, but said nothing. Caldor started towards the woods, back rigid with a limp to his steps. Luunaiwel gestured for Darya to follow him, doused the campfire with what was left of her tea, before completing their sad little trail.

The forest smelled of death and dread.

Every fibre in Darya's body told her to turn around and run. But that would be foolery. Luunaiwel was being lenient because Darya was entertaining *and* because ultimately the elf was getting her way. Darya wasn't going to test her luck any more than she already had. Still, she sped up to walk alongside Caldor, since it was difficult to see in this dreadful darkness.

And it was easier to cope when she wasn't alone.

"How do you know where to go in this pitch blackness?"

Caldor's steps didn't stutter, but he didn't answer her either. Unless an annoyed grunt counted as a response.

"Why, the stars, of course." Somewhere behind them, Luunaiwel spoke, her unnaturally high and low voice was even scarier here.

It did nothing to curb Darya's curiosity, unfortunately.

"What do you mean?"

"Out on the open sea, where the night is an endless nothingness without a single marker to show the way, voyagers used the stars to navigate."

Instinctively, Darya looked up. The sky blinked back at her, glittering with a million tiny lights. Entranced for a moment, she stumbled over a root. Flustered, Darya cleared her throat.

"I wonder why the townsfolk didn't learn how to do this if the herbs are so important to them."

"It's not that simple," this time, Caldor did answer, "Star charts change with time and require too much effort to keep track of. You can only travel here at night and you need to be able to fight. People are either too uneducated or too scared to try. The trees *do* move. It's not a myth. Something in the soil scrambles them before dawn and after midnight every day. There is never a clear path."

Darya made an impressed noise, "Who taught you this?"

Caldor gave her a baleful glare over his shoulder before doubling his speed. Muttering about grumpy people and their prickly attitudes, Darya kept her mouth shut in favour of keeping up.

Luunaiwel was the one who spoke next, much to the bard's surprise.

"I am pleased to know that some humans are still well-versed in the arts of astronomy. I thought this knowledge is forgotten on this side of the world."

"Knowledge is power," Caldor snorted, but didn't slow down, "in this world, the more you know, the easier it is to survive."

"Perhaps," Luunaiwel hummed, thoughtful, "but I cannot say I agree. Sometimes knowing too much can be a double-edged sword."

Darya thought Caldor would react hotly to that, but his response was quiet. Almost regretful.

"That's how I got into trouble in the first place."

Unable to contain herself, Darya asked, "What do you mean?"

"None of your business."

Darya stuck her tongue out at his back.

They travelled in silence for the next hour, or so Darya thought. It was difficult to tell. The forest had worked her nerves to a jitter, with its rustles of leafless branches and mournful creaking of long-dead trees. She tried to talk to ease her anxiety, but was hushed by both the elf and Caldor. In an effort to calm to herself, Darya tried to guess her companions' age range. But she couldn't even begin in Luunaiwel's case. Elves lived for thousands of years, or so went the stories. Luunaiwel looked to be a woman in her late twenties, but she could easily be twenty thousand years old.

Caldor was probably in his late twenties or early thirties. If he wasn't bruised, filthy and always as angry as a prune, he would have been a fine-looking man, with his dark hair and dark eyes. Tall, muscular but on the lean side, he could have made a decent, honest living if he didn't turn to thievery.

Still, didn't the people at the tavern say there was no actual proof of Caldor breaking into the Count's house? And that he was never put on trial?

Darya knew she wouldn't get anywhere if she asked outright. Regardless, this was another tick to her endless curiosity, and she filed the thought away for later inspections.

By the second hour, Darya was just shy of busting out the lute to chase away her stifling nervousness. Fortunately, it did not come to that, and the bard was beyond relieved when Luunaiwel decided to break the silence.

"The locals could not be more wrong. The forest is not dead, it is very much alive."

Caldor spoke before Darya could, "This place's name isn't to describe the trees."

"Indeed."

Unable to keep herself quiet, Darya asked Luunaiwel, "What's your plan with the herbs?"

"That depends on what I find there."

"Why do you need Caldor if you also know how to read the stars?"

"Because I do not know where this patch is," Luunaiwel spoke slowly, as if Darya was dense, "and I hardly have the time to scour the entire forest."

"I thought elves are immortal."

"True immortality does not exist."

Darya opened her mouth, but Caldor suddenly stopped, forcing her to dig her heels so she wouldn't crash into him. His next words made her insides scramble.

"We are being followed."

Luunaiwel's voice was *cheerful,* "For a while now."

Oh, by the Gods!

"Are there more Withered?? How... How are we going to shake them? And why aren't they attacking???"

"Do you *want* them to?" Caldor was exasperated. Then irritated, "Normally, I would have the means to keep them away. Can't do that now since I was dragged out of town with only rags on me. I'm a bit *unprepared.*"

Darya almost punched him, "Why didn't you say anything?!"

He glared at her, "Figured witch lady over here could keep them off, since she was so insistent on barging in. They probably haven't attacked because she smells weird."

"Rude." Luunaiwel hummed, but she didn't sound at all offended. Something rustled behind them, and this time Darya gave up on her dignity, one hand gripping at Caldor's elbow and the other around her pathetic travel dagger.

Meanwhile, Luunaiwel's voice was of pure glee.

"Fascinating. There are at least a dozen of them here, and they have yet to attack."

"A dozen?! Luunaiwel, please tell me you can deal with this!"

There was a smile in the elf's voice, "But I do, fortunately for you, little bird. Duck."

Darya needn't be told twice. Not when the *light* was so blinding.

Around them, the Withered screeched. Like nails scraping against a skillet, the noises they made were grating as they stumbled around, screaming as the light burned them. As her eyes adjusted to it, Darya finally dared a look.

Standing over them was Luunaiwel. In her hand was a staff, gnarled like the roots of an ancient tree, polished into fine ebony and inlaid with many gems, rough but purer than crystals. The light it gave off was like the summer sun, both warm and scathing in all its golden glory. Heavy cloak opened to reveal a willowy figure, encased in thin metallic sheets of armour and a belt of blue sapphires, each stone as big as Darya's fist.

Luunaiwel was glorious. And *terrifying*.

Around them, the Withered's screeches faded to nothing, either had escaped or died. Luunaiwel dimmed her staff to a white glow, looking smug.

"You two may get up now."

Caldor wasn't pleased, "You could have done that since the beginning! What were you waiting for?? One of them to pounce?!"

Luunaiwel smiled benevolently, "It is crucial to observe your enemy before you strike. Why provoke violence and death needlessly?"

Caldor snarled, "Those creatures are *worse than dead*, and you know it! They are abominations!"

He stopped, sucking in several breaths to calm himself down, "Whatever. Let's just get this done and over with."

As much as she disliked Caldor's proneness to anger, Darya had to agree with him, but didn't dare voice herself as they resumed their walk.

Not much was known about the Withered. People said they used to be living creatures. Humans, wildlife, *other living things*, that were twisted by remnants of broken magic lingering in the earth after the Shattering. The Withered were driven by a ravenous hunger, sometimes resorting to cannibalism for survival. Their flesh, patched, hairless and ashen, was poisonous to consume, and whoever unfortunate enough to eat it would turn feral in insanity, before succumbing to death. They were afraid of sunlight though, as demonstrated by the elf, as thus couldn't leave their shaded territories, and sensitive to certain sounds and smells.

Well, at least they were fended off. For now.

"How long till we get there?"

"Almost." Caldor grunted, mood even fouler than before.

Knowing that she shouldn't prod at him, Darya slowed to walk between Luunaiwel and Caldor. Mumbling under her breath, "We should at least have some torches …"

"A sound suggestion," the elf seemed overly pleased, "however, firelight tends to attract the Withered to their prey, unlike sunlight."

Darya had half a mind to ask why, but kept quiet instead. After that attack, even her curiosity was curbed. The bard didn't know whether she was relieved or scared when the sky finally turned pale. The sun meant they weren't going to be attacked by Withered, but it also meant Caldor couldn't see his stars anymore.

There wasn't any warning however, when Caldor suddenly disappeared behind a column of rock.

"Caldor!"

Startled, Darya ran after him.

She was greeted instead by the greenest sight she had ever seen in her life

CHAPTER 4:

Embraced in a circle of white stones was a garden.

No, *not quite*, Darya told herself.

The greenery here grew in abundance, wild and healthy, covering a surface that was as big as a town square. There were some leaves she recognised, most she couldn't. All were soft-bodied plants, swaying in the wind. Some were vines, crawling upon rocks and up to broken columns along the perimeter. Some were in bloom, violet, white and yellow, little gems that gleamed in the morning sun.

They were *alive*, thriving even, like nothing Darya had seen before.

"Beautiful, is it not?" Luunaiwel breathed, kneeling to cradle a small leaf in her palm.

Darya nodded, dazed, "I've never seen anything like this before. Not even our stuff at home could grow like this. They grow, but never *this green* … and they need so much coaxing."

Luunaiwel turned to look at her then, scarred brow rising, "You could grow herbs at home?"

Even Caldor's eyes were on her. Darya flustered at the attention, "A little bit. Just the basic stuff. Sage, thyme, chives... Rosemary is the easiest to grow. We have a decent bush for years now..."

"Hmm." That was all Luunaiwel said before her eyes went back to the green patch before them. Darya couldn't have sworn something shifted in the elf's stare, but she didn't dare ask.

It was rare, being able to grow something as fragile as herbs. Back in Darya's old village, people often praised her for her green thumb, and it gave her household a good, steady income for some time.

"Thank you for taking me here," Luunaiwel said, rising up to smile at Caldor, "now that the main part is done, I would like to perform the secrecy vow. Your payment will be made after."

Immediately, Caldor narrowed his eyes, suspicious, "What does this... *vow* entail?"

The elf produced a blue ribbon from under her cloak, "It is fairly simple. We tie our hands together. You swear that you will never mention my name nor my existence to anyone. I pay you, and we all part ways."

"Just out of curiosity," Unable to help herself, Darya spoke up, "what would happen if we break the vow? Not that I have any intention to, but I was hoping I can make this adventure into a tale, and I don't want to step on any toes, so..."

She trailed off when Luunaiwel smirked. A gloved finger tipped Darya's chin up, and the elf's face came inches from hers. This close, Darya could count each individual lash, and see that Luunaiwel's eyes weren't just typical green and blue. They were opalescent, with specs of colour dancing in the irises, not unlike the stars.

"Why," Luunaiwel's whisper broke goose bumps all over Darya's skin. Her grin was cold, glinting with the hint of a fang, "it would not be pretty, of course, little bird. Thorns will grow out of your throat, invisible to others, but oh-so very real. They will tear at your neck, shredding your flesh and clawing at your insides until you drop dead."

"Hey," Caldor snapped, pulling Luunaiwel's eyes away, "you didn't say anything about death!"

She smiled, as if she didn't just give a painfully descriptive speech about their possible deaths, "It is a guarantee. Peace of mind and all that. But you would not have to worry about the penalty if you have no intention to break the vow."

"Why would I want to put my life in danger on something as flimsy as a witch's words??"

Glancing between the elf and Caldor, Darya asked tentatively, "As long as we don't mention anything about you or say your name to anyone, right?"

Luunaiwel smiled, "That is correct."

Darya sighed, "Caldor, we knew this was going to happen. She wants us to keep a secret."

"She didn't say anything about us *dying* if we don't, though!!"

How did this guy become a thief anyway, when he was both so loud and so tactless?

"You were *so sure* she was going to kill us anyway if we didn't comply," Darya pointed out, "I mean, the way I see it, it's pretty fair. She doesn't trust us to keep her secret, so she puts a guarantee on it. Wouldn't you do the same if you could?"

Caldor seemed like he wanted to argue. But he snarled at the ground instead, "Fine. As long as the condition is if one of us breaks the vow, the other doesn't have to die."

"That can be arranged," Luunaiwel chirped happily, "hold out your left hands. Palms up."

The elf had the tips of their fingers touched as they stood shoulder to shoulder, then looped her ribbon around their hands three times. She pulled out a rose carved from wood, and balanced it on top of their fingers.

"I should be using the common tongue," Luunaiwel hummed, then winked at Caldor, "Peace of mind for you,"

He glared at her. She gave him an airy chuckle. Then her expression shifted.

"Bind of Thorns. Seeds of Truth. Under the Rose, a Vow is Born."

Maybe it was just a trick of the light, but Darya could have sworn Luunaiwel's eyes glowed for a split moment, and her angular face seemed just ancient as the broken pillars around them.

A piece of lost history.

The illusion was broken the moment Luunaiwel smiled at them, fangs flashing, "Now swear. Swear that you will not mention my name nor my existence to anyone outside of this glade."

Darya blinked, "I swear."

After some hesitation, Caldor followed, "I swear."

"Under the Rose, a Vow is Born. Child of Thorns, Your Seeds are Sown."

Darya didn't know what she was expecting. A tingle perhaps? Some pain? Glowy magic? But all she felt was the ribbon tightening for less than a second.

Luunaiwel seemed satisfied enough though. She pulled the ribbon free and dropped a pouch into Caldor's still open hand.

Luunaiwel stepped away, in a swish of blue cloak, "Your payment, as promised. You are now free to go."

Caldor raised an eyebrow at her, before peering into the pouch. He huffed, "Can't go back until nightfall. We'll stick around until then."

Luunaiwel inclined her head, "Feel free. As long as you disturb neither me nor the plants."

Darya thought the elf would immediately dive into the herbs she had been talking so much about. Instead, Luunaiwel skirted the perimeter, took off her boots in elegant strides, and placed them neatly beside a collapsed fountain. Next came the cloak. Under the sun, her armours were blinding, polished to perfection and gave off a pearlescent shine. The sapphire belt was equally bright, supporting two hip bags. One by one, Luunaiwel's plates came off, until only a sleeveless leather tunic, gloves and breeches were on.

    Darya almost looked away for modesty, when she realised every visible inch of Luunaiwel's skin was inked. Woven together, intricate and delicate, they were nothing like the crude etchings Darya had seen on fighters or the occasional sailors frequenting dingy bars. No. The tattoos on Luunaiwel were both like arts and scriptures, in shapes and languages Darya could not understand, but also couldn't help but being mesmerised.

    When Luunaiwel's gloves came off though, it was a different story. The skin on her left arm was all but melted, burnt beyond recognition, along with remnants of smeared ink. It was horrific, like a discordant note to a masterful arrangement, the arm did not seem like it could belong to someone so beautiful and mythical like Luunaiwel. Yet, there it was, a testament to how long and how dangerous the elf's life must have been.

Fearful, Darya averted her eyes, and turned her attention to Caldor instead. He was rummaging under what must have been a sitting bench once. Knowing she ought to leave Luunaiwel alone for now, Darya approached the man. Caldor had pried off a loose rock, and pulled out a small trunk hidden inside a shallow crevice.

Noticing Darya, Caldor huffed, "I come here often. Never know when I have to stick around for the day."

He tossed a small packet at Darya. Tentatively, she opened it, revealing some hard tacks inside.

"Thanks," she said, going over to sit down on the ground next to him as the man threw on some clothes that weren't tattered and bloodied. The crackers were tasteless and could probably break a tooth, but not the worst thing she had eaten on the road. Darya didn't realise how hungry she was up until that moment.

"There's water in that fountain," Caldor grumbled, "it's clean. Don't know how it stays running, but safe to drink."

Mister Tough-guy wasn't that much of an arsehole now that he got some decent clothes on, isn't he? "Huh, good to know. Didn't expect to see something so nice thriving in such a place."

"Didn't expect to come here under these circumstances, but here we are."

Darya chuckled, "You got me there."

Something, *a few things*, clinked next to her. Glancing over, Darya almost dropped the biscuit she was chewing on.

Five gold coins!

Speechless, she looked up at Caldor, who looked away.

"Your cut. You did get me a pretty good deal, after all."

Darya grinned at him, all teeth, "Thank you!"

Yep, definitely not an arsehole. Humming a happy tune, she scooped the coins into her pouch, toes tingling in excitement.

Caldor sat down next to her, carefully felt around his dislocated wrists. The noise when he popped them back into place probably would never fade in Darya's scarred memory. Grunting, and ignoring Darya's slack-jawed stare, Caldor grabbed a biscuit for himself. For a long moment, they sat there, two strangers in a companionable silence, trying to proceed whatever it was on their minds.

Naturally, being a bard in trade, Darya spoke first, "Say, Caldor... You're not really a thief, aren't you?"

He flicked a crumb away from his shirt, "What makes you say that?"

"Thieves don't try to help people," she said a-matter-of-factly, "they save their own skin first. Take money and goods whenever and wherever they can. With you being the sole herb trader in town, I don't think you're poor enough to risk everything and do something as outrageous as breaking into the Count's house."

He shrugged, "Maybe I got greedy."

"You would have asked for more gold then, when I successfully negotiated with her," Darya gestured at Luunaiwel, who was now rolling her braided hair up into a bun, "you wouldn't have given me the coins, because you didn't need to."

Caldor snorted, "Your nosiness will get you into trouble."

She flashed him another grin, "Already did. I'm not as scared of you as I'm scared of her, so I'll take my chances."

"Maybe you should be. I was trained in Apricum."

Darya's eyes widened, "Whoa! You're a Knight???"

Apricum was well known for their militant might. The best fortress in all of Ardent, they said. Most boys dreamt to go there to just be squires, many never got the funds to. The Knights there were the most elite, going on to serve Kings and Queens and Nobles all around the world.

No wonder Caldor knew something as fancy as astronomy.

"In training. My studies were cut short."

"So you're definitely not a thief. How did you get chained up anyway?"

Caldor grimaced at her, "You were supposed to ask why my studies were cut short. Not this."

"Well, it's a bit irrelevant right now, isn't it? I'm a bit more interested in recent events."

He narrowed his eyes, "You should have been a town crier instead of a bard, then."

Darya shrugged, "Tried it. Hated having to stand at one spot all day. It's bad for the throat too, you know."

Caldor gave her a disgusted snort, "Uh-huh."

She nudged him with her shoulder, "Don't judge! I'll have you know I tried my hands at lots of professions before I settled with this." Shaking her lute at Caldor's face.

He raised an eyebrow, "How come?"

Despite knowing Caldor was trying to divert from the original topic again, Darya didn't call him out on it. He was just as stubborn as she was, maybe more. Pushing would just get him all defensive again.

Besides, Darya had nothing to hide. And she rather liked talking. Talking was healthier than the hostile silence they had the night before.

"My family needs the money," she said earnestly, "my parents passed away in a fire. Grandmama Clarince became blind, and my sister Sara has been ill ever since. Breathed in too much soot, the physician said. She was lucky to be alive."

Caldor seemed taken aback, "I... I'm sorry."

Darya was used to the reaction. She never held any punches, "It's fine. A lot of people got it worse than us. Half the village was gone. The fields were ruined, and we had no means to rebuild. So we all moved to Flumium, trying to survive. We still have a tight knit community, but it's not like anyone is more well-off than the other, you know? Everyone has to do odd jobs to survive. And we rely a lot on each other. Cecil mostly stays home with her mum, so she draws water for my Grandmama when I'm away, for example. Agnes can't work in the mines, so he delivers coals for everyone instead."

Darya went on, telling Caldor about her neighbours. She didn't think he cared all that much about her babbling, but it was nice to fill the silence with chatter. Following Luunaiwel's example, Darya shucked off her boots, stretching her blistered feet into the soft earth under the plants. She sighed in satisfaction. This felt nice.

"Didn't you say you can grow herbs? Wouldn't that help with the monetary problems?" Caldor cut in, tired of her monologue.

"Well, it's still hard to grow. Flumium is a city over a river, yes, but the water isn't that great for farming, because of the mines. You have to purify the water first to even wash anything, and it's such a pain. Expensive too. We have enough to sell to our neighbours, but that's not enough for medicines."

"So you became a bard."

She shrugged, "My dad used to play the lute, so I learned to when I was a little girl. I can't sing as well as mum could, but I manage."

Caldor raised an eyebrow, "Why not stick around the city then? They have far more taverns and inns to perform than the countryside."

"Are you kidding? The competition is tough! Nobody is going to let a sixteen-year-old country bumpkin play for them when they can just hire someone professional and has been doing it since before I was born!"

Caldor blinked, "I've never thought about that. Being a bard is tougher than I thought."

Grinning, she tapped his shoulder, "Thank you! You're the first person to say that to me!"

"I have no qualms in admitting facts."

"Not a lot of people can do that. Though you were pretty adamant about Luunaiwel killing us when she clearly isn't going to."

Caldor narrowed his eyes, "That's different. She has magic. And she's an *elf.*"

"And we know nothing about elves aside from centuries-old tall tales." Darya rebuked, knowing that he would argue on that. The man folded his arms, scowling.

"You're a bard. Shouldn't you believe more in tall tales?"

"Unlike with religions, I don't have to believe it to sell it."

Caldor went quiet, studying Darya for a long moment before he spoke again, "I'm having a hard time deciding whether you are actually smart or dumb."

She grinned at him, "I will take that as a compliment, thanks."

It looked like Caldor was about to say something, but a jangle of bells pulled both his and Darya's attention away.

Luunaiwel had changed her clothes. A blue gown that seemed like it was woven out of gossamer and moonlight. It was transparent, showing every well-defined arch of her body and the tattoos that curled around them. She wore the same sapphire-inlaid belt, the gems spilling over a sharp, pale hipbone. No jewellery adorned her, saved for her earrings and a circlet of silver, woven like branches into her updo. In her right hand was her staff. In the other was a thurible, intricately etched just like her inks, each chain had a cluster of bells. White smoke brimmed over, wrapping her whole figure in a veil of mist.

Luunaiwel was no longer the mysterious and dangerous figure Darya blindly chased after. She was now regal and mystical, like the Dragon Priestesses in myths long forgotten.

As if her feet did not touch the ground, Luunaiwel glided onto the green carpet. Thurible swung free with every step, a fragrant curtain was woven around her. The bells accentuated every movement, light swathes of gossamer fluttered as if they were her wings. She was mercury, dancing with grace incomprehensible by any mortal, with eyes gleaming so bright they rivalled the stars. The plants swirled with each of her movements, joining her in this magical ritual that only they could understand.

Darya could have sworn she heard music in the air.

It was... indescribable.

Eyes drawn to the rhythm and mind bewitched by the melody, Darya didn't know when she had stood up. She didn't know when she had stepped into the garden, feet on cool soil. She was unhearing to Caldor's call, nor did she feel when vines started to climb up her legs. She was unseeing when her gaze met Luunaiwel's, and she didn't react when the elf's eyes widened in startled surprise.

Darya didn't feel it when she fell, when the green seemed to open and swallowed her whole.

CHAPTER 5:

It was the smell of rain that woke her.

It was earthy. It was fresh. It was nothing she had ever experienced before.

It was pitch darkness around her, but if she squinted, she could see glimmers of something out there.

Stars, perhaps?

No.

True to her nature, Darya reached out, curious. Something smooth, cool on the surface but warm from the core met her hand.

A red gem blinked at her. Knowing. Familiar. Thrumming with *life*.

Images rushed into her mind. Unstoppable and *refreshing* as a mountain stream.

Green.

Sprouts and saplings and shrubs and bushes and trees. Forests and plains, green as far as the eyes could see. Hills and mountains, rustling with evergreens. Kelps dancing under lakes, moss covering stones, foliage growing abandon on paths no feet ever tread.

Everything was *alive* and *green* like nothing Darya had ever seen.

There were no barrens where nothing moved but dry dust. There were no empty fields where carefully cultivated seeds cracked under the unforgiving sun. There were no withered forests, where woods were bare as bones and cursed creatures lurked in their shadows.

The images were of a world Darya had never known, *a world that once was*, before her time.

The world before The Shattering.

It was so beautiful, it brought tears to her eyes.

Overwhelming. Breath-taking.

There, too, was pain. Searing pain, as if every inch of her skin was cut into. Twisted pain, as if all her veins were punctured. Crushing pain, as if all her bones were broken. Mind-numbing pain, is if it was eating its way out from within.

But amidst the pain, there was hope. The will to survive. The will to see the light again. The will to grow.

The will to live again.

Sobbing, she curled to herself, the red stone over her heart. Feeling the warm pulse. Pushing into it for a way to soothe all this pain.

"It hurts." She cried.

It hurts.

She closed her eyes. Wanting to sink back into darkness. Wanting the pain to stop.

Something warm wrapped around her nape.

Darya gasped.

And into the sunlight she woke.

Her vision was filled with Luunaiwel's shining eyes and Caldor's pale face. The pain was but a memory. Still it throbbed at the back of her mind and in her heart. The child in her crumbled, and tears streamed down her cheeks as she threw herself into Luunaiwel's lap, bawling. A hand carded through her curls, calming and gentle.

"I do not believe my eyes." She heard the elf mumbled, but Darya hadn't the mind to ask what Luunaiwel was talking about. Darya cried to her heart's content, until her voice was hoarse and she had no more tears left to shed.

Nobody said anything until then.

"Are you alright, Darya?" It was Caldor who asked.

Now coherent enough, she sat up and away from Luunaiwel, embarrassed by her outburst, "Y-yes... Yes, I think so, I... So-sorry and uh... thanks..."

"Anytime, little bird." Luunaiwel's smile was smooth as always, "What did you see?"

"What did you do to her?!" Caldor was quick to snap, dagger in hand.

"Cap it, chivalry," Luunaiwel drawled, her high voice almost a hiss, "I did not do anything to her, she heeded a call."

"What is that supposed to mean, witch?!"

Knowing Caldor might do something stupid if she didn't say anything, Darya put a hand on his chest, "It's alright. Just... calm down for a bit... Let-let me think."

Thankfully, Caldor did shut up, but that didn't stop him from glaring at Luunaiwel. Sniffling, Darya pushed herself up and towards the fountain. Just as Caldor said, there was water in the chipped basin. Clean, sweet, cold water.

Darya submerged her head.

It was refreshing. The water calmed her down, flushing away the remains of blistering pain lodged at the back of her mind. Darya counted to twenty, blew out a cluster of bubbles, and stood upright again. Wiping her face, Darya brushed back her hair, took one deep breath, and turned to face her companions.

"I don't know if I can describe it as *seeing*," she said, more to Luunaiwel than to Caldor, "it's like... memories and emotions being poured into my head."

Luunaiwel tilted her head, "What memories did you see?"

"Green," Darya swallowed, "lots and lots of *green*. How the world once was. Healthy with life and rich with minerals. Ah!"

Something warm, a bit *too warm*, pulsed over her heart at those words. She clutched at her chest. Darya startled when she felt a hard lump through her tunic.

What in Vita's name happened to her?

Luunaiwel was in front of Darya in the blink of an eye. A cool hand placed over Darya's, the elf carefully pried the girl's hand away. And peeled open Darya's collar.

Luunaiwel gasped, repeating herself in surprise, "I do not believe my eyes."

A bit panicked, Darya looked down as well. Her eyes widened.

There, in the middle of her chest, laid the red gem Darya had seen in her vision. It was embedded into her skin, glowing softly and warm to the touch. There was no blood, and it fused seamlessly over Darya's heart, lying there like it had always been a part of her.

"I am not going to attack you."

Oh, *shit.* Caldor was still here. Probably freaked out, terrified or angry. Or all three, judging by how shaky his voice was, "But what in the name of the Ancient Five have you done to her, *elf?*"

For once, Luunaiwel was mystified, "I did nothing to her."

She looked up at the sky, thinking for a moment, "We still have about four hours left before nightfall. Enough time for preparations and a quick chat. Please, excuse me."

Luunaiwel danced away from Darya and went for her neat pile of discarded clothing. As the elf changed out of her ceremonial garbs, Caldor strode over to grab Darya by the elbow, dragging her to a different edge of the clearing.

"Are you sure you are alright?" Caldor whispered under his teeth, "What's the deal with that stone... Do you want to cut it out??"

"I'm alright, I don't know and that's probably a bad idea," Darya answered in one breath, rubbing her eyes, "four hours left... whoa, have I been out for that long?"

Caldor narrowed his eyes, "Yeah, the plants... I don't know. They just sort of rose up and wrapped around you. And snatched you down under."

Darya's eyes widened, at a loss for words.

Caldor spat, "I hate to admit it, but if *she* didn't grab you, you probably would have sunken under all of that. Not to say that this hasn't been her plan all along."

"If this was her plan, then she seems pretty shocked by all of it." Darya ran a hand through her curls, grimaced at the melting grease clinging to her fingers. Right. She hadn't the time to get the stuff out of her hair since that botched performance yesterday.

Yesterday... Even thinking that was strange. It felt like a whole week had passed since Luunaiwel gave her that coin in the tavern. So much had happened.

"Thanks, Caldor."

The man blinked, "For what?"

Darya chuckled, "You tried to defend me, even when you didn't have to. It was my fault I got tangled in this to begin with."

He stared at her for a moment, then diverted his eyes, "I took an oath before my training. Never leave the defenceless undefended. Never face wrongs with ignorance. And I wasn't much help, so don't thank me."

Somehow Darya doubted that his training was cut short. His moral compass was at least on course.

"Well, still, *thank you*. It's the thought that counts. Grandmama Clarince always says that." Darya said earnestly, patting his elbow.

Out of the corner of her eye, she saw Luunaiwel approaching. Blinking, Darya tugged at Caldor's shirt, whispering quickly, "Let's just hear her out, ok? I want to know about this as much as possible. Please don't get mad or interrupt randomly."

Caldor didn't look pleased, but he nodded regardless.

Luunaiwel was all wrapped up in her cloak and armour once more, and there was no laughter in her mismatched eyes, "Darya, what you just went through was an initiation ritual to become a novice Druid."

The girl tested the word on her tongue, "A... Druid? What's a *Druid?*"

"A Druid is one who tends to nature. Someone who helps trees and foliage grows, aids wildlife, and tends to the earth and wild elements. Among other duties."

Darya gaped at her, "Whoa whoa, *what???* You're saying that I can do all that??? I can do *magic???*"

There was a crease on the elf's brows, "In a sense. But their line of magic is more duty-oriented than any other magick-user. A Druid's role is to seek out life and *encourage* it to grow, using magic given to them by the earth."

That sounded far too simple, "How is that different from me growing herbs at home? Aside from the magic part and it would be my job, that is."

"The difference is, little bird," Luunaiwel wagged a finger, eyebrow raising, "with proper training and resources, a Druid can start a forest all on their own. Not overnight, mind you, but over the course of a few short years, which is remarkable for any single individual to achieve."

It didn't sound like that at first, but when Darya factored in the time and effort to grow and keep a single herb plant alive, then yes, that was incredibly remarkable.

"Alright, so I'm a Druid now," the word still sounded weird on her tongue, "how did *that* happen? You said a chain of events, right? Did you plan this?"

"I assure you, I did not mastermind this event, flattering that could have been." A hand under her chin, Luunaiwel hummed, "Mister Caldor, correct me if I am wrong, but you have taken other people this glade, and there have been others before you who came here, yes?"

Caldor was reluctant to answer, "Yes. But nothing like this ever happened."

Luunaiwel tilted her head, "But of course."

To Darya's surprise, Luunaiwel sighs. Her shoulders drooped, and she mumbles something to herself that sounded intelligible. The elf then shakes her head, "Perhaps Mister Caldor is right. In a sense, this might have happened because of me."

Caldor frowned, but he refrained from yelling, "But?"

"Ah, he uses his head," Luunaiwel smirks, but speaks before Caldor could lose what was left of his temper, "I did not come here with the intention of creating a Druid, nor did I expect to find one."

"Then … what happened? Or what do you think happened?" Timidly, Darya asked.

Luunaiwel's smile softened a little, "As you both know, the world is dying. Patches of land that are thriving like this in the wild are rare. I came here, upon hearing the rumours, hoping to learn the reason of its existence, perhaps encouraging it to grow more with my own magic. However, as I tap into the life force of this grove, it must have awakened something else."

Darya's hand goes to her chest, cupping at the stone. Luunaiwel's smile widened.

"This is a most incredible event. And here I thought I was only going about with another mission, but I stumbled upon a fresh Druid instead."

Of course Caldor was distrustful, "And what kind of mission was that?"

Luunaiwel winked at him, "A self-assigned mission. As the earth's veins were cut after The Shattering, which ended the Great War, I am seeking to re-establish the connections among all the remaining earth pulses."

Darya blinked, "I don't follow..."

"Of course not." Luunaiwel patted her head, "That is a lesson for later."

"Huh?"

"But I assure you, I have no plans in initiating a Druid when I set foot upon your miserable town." Caldor growled, but Luunaiwel ignored him, "Druids went into extinction after the Shattering. With the connection to the earth severed and many of the groves destroyed, the last Druids of old were not able to tap into their powers. Most went insane and died, the rest withered away with age. There had been attempts at creating a new generation, but the earth was unresponsive. They gave up after two hundred years."

"That's... That's so sad!" Darya exclaimed.

Luunaiwel grinned, "Well, there is no longer cause for despair, because here you are. I have done a lot of things over the course of my long life, but bringing a new Druid into this dying world is a first."

"Hold up," Caldor cut in, pointing at Darya's chest, "you still haven't explained this thing."

A gloved hand stretched out, hovering above the blinking gem on Darya's chest, "Ah, yes. May I?"

Darya nodded. Luunaiwel traced along the seam of where skin and stone met. Something warm pulsed within Darya. The touch hadn't been painful like she thought it might be. The skin around the stone felt... normal, if not somewhat tingly. The stone did, however, pushed into her as Luunaiwel prodded it, giving Darya a vivid image of it clicking against her bone. She gave an involuntary shudder, which had the elf drawing away with a whispered apology.

"I had not seen one of these for so long... This is a Heart Stone. A seed of the earth," Luunaiwel said, her voice gentle and awed, "every Druid has one. It is a piece of the earth pulse itself, formed and tempered in the most ancient of Nature's magic, and gifted to a new Druid. It helps the Druid in possession establishes a connection with nature and gives them the magic needed to carry out their duties. This seed ... must have slept here for centuries. I can sense the vast powers it has cultivated within."

"Wow..." Darya's own hand came up to touch the stone when Luunaiwel stepped away.

This was...

This was a lot to take in.

All her life, Darya thought magic only existed in myths. Something that disappeared ages ago. Now, in the course of two days, not only she had witnessed magic used by an *elf*, but now *she was part of it.*

"I need to sit down." Darya said, out of breath, and dropped onto her rump. Caldor's eyes darted between her and Luunaiwel, caught between concern and distrust.

He probably wasn't going to defend her all that much now, considering his distaste for magic. Caldor had been dealing with all of this much poorer than Darya was.

Magic, huh?

"So... what now?"

"What do you mean 'what now'??"

Darya rolled her eyes at Caldor, before turning to Luunaiwel.

"Being a Druid is important, isn't it? Since I'm the newest one to be made after so long... So what to do now?"

"That depends on what you would like to do." She hadn't expected that from Luunaiwel. A long speech about how Darya *must* embark on some kind of quest to restore the earth, yes. Every story she was told … had been telling about heroes of the past would continue on like that.

Darya didn't think she was being given a choice.

The elf tilted her head, eyes dancing with light, "A new Druid granted to the world is a cause for celebration. It means the earth is ready for a new generation to walk this world, to replenish it. To bring life back once more. It means it might even be possible to raise more Druids now."

Luunaiwel paused for a moment, staring at Darya, unblinking, "However, if it is alright with you, would you let me study your relationship with the earth? At least for a few months? So we might have a chance at bringing more like you into this world and revitalise the lands. If, after these few months end, you would like to continue your journey with me, we may discuss the possibilities then."

"I..." Darya hesitated.

She shook her head, and then looked into Luunaiwel's mismatched eyes, "It's going to take a while for me to wrap my head around this. But yes... yes, I can deal with that much for now."

Frowning, Caldor cut in, "You're not going to do anything weird to her, aren't you?"

"As far as I am concerned, Mister Caldor," the elf's eyes glimmered dangerously despite her ever-smiling lips, "you are not her keeper, and she is old enough to give consent."

Caldor didn't back down, "And she's also too naive for her own good. Or 'amusingly stupid', in your own words. None of us has any reason to trust one another, you haven't given us a reason to trust you yet, and if she does agree to go with you, there is no guarantee you wouldn't pose a threat to her."

Luunaiwel's smirk was sharp as a knife, "Cautious, aren't you?"

"Thanks. Had my fair share of experience."

Tiredly, Darya raised a hand to grab their attention "How about I pick the course of the road for now? I have things to take care of first before whatever Luunaiwel plans to do with me. And I think I can decide in the meantime whether she is trustworthy or not."

Caldor gave Darya a bewildered look, "Are you bloody serious???"

"Mister Caldor, if you are so concerned about her safety, will you not accompany us?"

Both humans turned to stare at Luunaiwel, taken aback by the suggestion. The elf shrugged, nonchalant.

"A supervisor, of course. To advise and watch out for Miss Darya's interests."

Stumped, all the anger seemed to drain out of Caldor. He glanced at Darya, then away, "I can't do that."

"Oh? Does a *dead man* have some prior arrangements elsewhere?"

He seethed at the smug elf. But instead of arguing with her, Caldor turned to Darya, "Someone is waiting for me back in Edurn. I... made a promise to that person first. I would have seen this through if it wasn't for..."

Taking pity on him, Darya patted his arm, "It's alright. I'm not your responsibility, you know? Knight Code or not, you do what you gotta do."

Caldor still seemed torn. Mismatched eyes darting between the two humans, Luunaiwel suggested, "How about another vow?"

"Another of those thorny horrors?" Darya raised an eyebrow. Luunaiwel chuckled.

"Another one, yes. But I will be making the vow this time. To protect you from harm and teach you what I can, until my knowledge is no longer of service."

That sounded fair. "Alright."

"And Mister Caldor would be our witness."

He was immediately suspicious, "And you will be the only one affected by the penalty?"

Luunaiwel smiled, "But of course."

They stood in a small circle again. Shoulder to shoulder, finger to finger. Luunaiwel pulled out a ribbon, this time green, wrapped it around their hands, and placed her wooden rose on top of it.

"Bind of Thorns. Seeds of Truth. Under the Rose, a Vow is Born."

Eyes glowing, Luunaiwel hummed, her voice echoed like afternoon bells.

"I, Luunaiwel Narquelion, First of her Name, Last of the Othelris, vow to protect Darya, Grandchild of Clarince, Bard of Flumium, First Druid of the Shattered Age, until the first cycle of her apprenticeship ends. With Caldor, Knight of Stars, as our Witness, I call upon Mortia, Queen of Death, as judge and executioner, should I fail this Vow."

This time, there was a tingle of something, sparked from the ribbons around their hands. It tightened, longer than the last time. The Heart Stone pulsed with warmth upon Darya's chest. Strangely, it felt like approval.

"Under the Rose, a Vow is Born. Child of Thorns, Your Seeds are Sown."

Darya let out a breath she didn't know she was holding when Luunaiwel pulled the ribbon away.

"That was fancier than last time."

"An Archmage's vow to an Apprentice Druid is no laughing matter, little bird. Must get all the details correctly, else it would not be pleasant," she then turned to Caldor, "here, keep this, Mister Caldor. If it turns black, it means I have failed to uphold my vow. If it curls into itself and forms a rose, it means the conditions are met and the vow has ended."

Caldor flipped the strip of fabric around on his hand, eyes narrowing before pocketing it, "You did get *all* the details down."

Luunaiwel tapped at her own ear, "Forgive me, but I was born with much better senses than a human's. The glade's silence did not help."

The sky started changing as they spoke. The sun was setting, spilling gold over green and over the bone-white trees surrounding them. It was an unsettling reminder. Soon, they must plunge into the darkness and trek through a maze infested with Withered.

Darya asked, knowing the answer and dreading it, "It's almost time to leave?"

Caldor confirmed with a grunt, as he went to pick a few small white flowers, "They know we're here. They'd be gathering right after sundown for a hunt. It's always like that."

Darya gulped, staring at the shadows under the trees, "Would they pounce us here?"

Luunaiwel pulled up her hood, her bright eyes followed the dying light, and "They have not been able to raze this glade to the ground yet, because of the protection spells woven deep into the stones and soil of this place. The same magic that scrambles the trees and keeps flora growing. Nothing corrupt may set foot here, least it desires excruciating pain."

"That's a relief." Darya said, but that only intensified her desire to not make that journey through the woods.

"Alas, our presence here and the ritual performed must have roused a crowd. The road ahead shall be more treacherous than the last."

Caldor swore under his breath, "Are you saying that we'll have to deal with more than normal?"

Luunaiwel smiled at him, "Much more, Mister Caldor. I would say a whole nest of them is gathering now. Why," her ears twitched, and there was a feral glint to her eyes, "I can *hear* them converging around us even now. Moving under early shadows and rabid with hunger."

Caldor swore again, and went back to his stash. When he stood, in the former Knight's hands was a gleaming longsword, well-polished and deadly.

Darya whistled in appreciation. Caldor grumbled, "I was hoping I wouldn't have to use this."

"Same." Luunaiwel tilted her head, "Considering we will be heading to a densely packed forest, such a weapon can be compromising."

Caldor snarled, "Bring it, *elf.*"

She grinned at him, fangs and all, "Whoever has the least kills must buy the winner the finest casket of wine in town."

For once, Caldor grinned back, "Deal."

CHAPTER 6:

Their mad dash through the forest was disorientating.

Before the last rays of the sun disappeared, Luunaiwel gave them a beaming smile that bolstered no courage whatsoever.

"I can maintain the light no more than a quarter hour at a time every one hour. The trek through the forest takes three hours if we do so with leisure. Two and a half if we run. I will use the light in three bursts: When we start, when we get half-way, and when we are at the edge of the forest."

Darya was instructed to stay in the middle of them, with Caldor leading and Luunaiwel at the back. Armed with just her travelling dagger, the bard felt awfully under-equipped. Especially when they headed out, she could see just *how many* Withered were lurking in the shadows.

The sight alone was terrifying. The mass of disfigured creatures hissed and clicked their teeth at them, clambering over one another to get close. Sharp claws ripped out chunks of woods and dirt, pale flesh stretched over muscles and bones. They were desperate for a hunt, desperate to feed. Only to screech when their beady eyes met the light from Luunaiwel's staff.

"Their eyes are sensitive, you see," the elf explained, chipper as if they were taking a stroll down the street instead of being chased by spawns of shadow and death, "when they are exposed to sunlight, they would feel immense pain, and would try to claw their own eyes out to stop that pain, killing themselves in the process. Rather messy, but saves us time."

"I'd rather not have heard that, thanks." Darya said, shuddering.

Things got nasty the moment Luunaiwel started dimming her light. Whatever left that wasn't hurt at the beginning started circling, unseen in the darkness beyond what they could see. The sounds of gnashing teeth and growls filled the air, getting closer and closer.

"The valerian should keep them away for a bit. They hate the smell." Caldor grunted, lighting up torches as Luunaiwel's staff flickered away. Before they began, Caldor had rubbed the white flower all over their clothes, except for Luunaiwel who politely declined. Darya could *smell* why, though. Valerian stunk, unlike what its delicate appearance might suggest. It stunk like sweaty laundry that hadn't been washed for *months*, then dragged through dirt and thrown into the stables.

But it was better to stink than to be eaten.

It was rather fascinating, seeing the Withered averted Caldor and her to attack Luunaiwel. Darya was afraid for the elf at first, but then gave up on that as Luunaiwel seemed like she was having the time of her life. Sword in one hand and staff in the other, she was a whirlwind of destruction. There would be a crunch of smashed bones and broken flesh if a Withered met her staff. If it met her sword, it was a whistle of metal, slicing through the creature as if it was lard, and a hot splatter of blood that smelled far worse than the valerian oil on their clothes.

"Mister Caldor," Luunaiwel called, gleeful with her kills, "I do believe you are falling behind!"

Caldor snapped, whirling his torch around to fend off a Withered that got too close, "Just wait until we get half-way! You might get your face bitten off by the swarm."

"I dare them to try," Luunaiwel cackled, slamming the butt of her staff onto an incoming creature's head, brutally smashed it through, "it has been a while since my blood last sang in such excitement!"

Caldor muttered something about crazy elf-witches, before driving his long sword through a Withered.

Darya thought they were both crazy.

Luunaiwel was one thing, but Caldor, despite knowing what it was like to go through this place, yet still continued his travels back and forth? Just from two trips, Darya had seen enough of pale, blistering skin, snapping maws and manic blood-eyes for her whole sixteen years of life. No wonder no other townsfolk wanted to learn how to get here by themselves.

The further they went, the bolder the Withered became. The group's speed had slowed down significantly as a result. Caldor had to fight incoming attackers off, and Darya didn't know much else to do besides cowering between him and Luunaiwel, shaking dagger held like a lifeline. This was definitely *not* what Darya was warned about she set out on her journey. A ruffian or two, a few drunkards, occasional uninvited troubles... yes, but this was absolute *madness*. Nobody in her neighbourhood would ever believe her if she told them.

"Luunaiwel! Can't I use some kind of magic to help???"

"Afraid not, little bird." Luunaiwel's voice rang clear above the chaos, "Druidic magic is not meant for combat. That was why many of them carried melee weapons or had a familiar back in the days."

She paused for a moment, slicing a Withered in half, "Ha! What do you know? That is another lesson!"

That sucks arse, Darya thought, but she didn't dare say.

As if she could read Darya's mind, Luunaiwel chuckled, "All in due time. I promise if you would like to learn how to fight, then you will be taught."

Another swing of the blade, another Withered fell dead.

"But now it is not that time."

Luunaiwel was confident that they would live to see another day. And since the elf had vowed to protect her, Darya knew she shouldn't be afraid. So she kept her head down, was relieved when Luunaiwel's staff came ablaze once more, giving them a much needed breather.

"Damn elfish stamina." Caldor cursed, wiping sweat off of his brows.

"Wait until you get in bed with one." Luunaiwel winked. Caldor made a scandalised noise. Darya giggled, breathless and a bit delirious.

They covered as much ground as they could with the elf's light. However, when Luunaiwel's staff dimmed, the Withered seemed reluctant to attack again.

"Reckon we scared them to half-wit?" Caldor asked, wary. Luunaiwel hummed.

"They are already half-wits. No. They are either slowing down to eat their own kins' corpses, or they are waiting for more to come. Either way, we should hurry."

Neither Darya nor Caldor had any qualms against that. Darya just wanted to get out of here in one piece. Unfortunately, they didn't make it far before something stopped them. A sound, *thunderous,* crashed in the distance, and seemed to only get louder.

"What was that???" Caldor stood rigid. Luunaiwel tilted her head from side to side, listening.

"Hoh," she blew out an airy chuckle, looking positively *delighted*, "they have a Gargantuan."

"A *what?!*"

Her eyes turned sharp, "*Run.*"

Luunaiwel needn't tell them twice. Not when the frightening sound grew louder and the ground under their feet shook with it. Caldor doubled his speed, Darya hurried after him. Luunaiwel had given up on being at the back, she was flying left and right on their flanks, cutting down any Withered that came too close.

"Not fast enough." The elf said, no hint of laughter in her voice.

Above all, that scared Darya the most.

The thundering sounds were now creaking with fallen trees and roots being ripped out of the earth. The Withered screeched, scrambling away from their path, *away from the noises.*

Whatever a Gargantuan was, it sounded like it was right behind them.

"Darya, hold this."

The poor bard stumbled when Luunaiwel's shining staff was shoved into her hands. The elf skidded to a stop.

"Keep running," Luunaiwel said, and split her needle-like sword into two thin blades, "the light should hold for another quarter hour."

"What about you???" Frantic, Darya stopped too, only to be pulled away by Caldor. She was glad he did, because what came flying out of the shadows next would have crushed them both if they were still.

It was big, ugly and grotesque. With arms the size of tree trunks and fists the size of boulders, it decimated everything on its rampage, sending fragments of dry wood and dirt flying everywhere. Its head seemed to have melted into its giant chunk of a body, gaping mouth drooping down its chest, each tooth a yellowed spearhead.

Yelping, Darya held Luunaiwel's staff high, hoping it would be deterred just like the Withered were. But this creature, *the Gargantuan,* wasn't, and she realised her mistake almost immediately.

It had no eyes.

Growl thick, as if its throat was clogged with mucus, the Gargantuan swung its meaty arms around, batting blindly at where it could hear its prey. Caldor and Darya scrambled to their feet, but the shaking ground made it difficult to stand, and the shattered trees around them didn't help.

Oh, Gods above. Darya felt her heart turned to stone. They were going to die here.

Luunaiwel's battle cry pierced the night.

Head on, she charged at the Gargantuan. It roared back, a giant fist came down to crush the elf. She rolled to the side, then stabbed both blades into the creature's flesh, and used them to vault herself onto its arm. Black blood pumped out, smelling of tar and rotten eggs, as Luunaiwel yanked out her swords. Howling, the Gargantuan swatted at her, but missed by a hair when Luunaiwel slid up its arm. Having punched itself instead, the creature screamed in both rage and pain. Its bone was crushed, puncturing through putrid flesh.

Luunaiwel wasted no time. She hopped onto the other side, dragging her blades along the Gargantuan's pale hide as she ran, spilling forth even more blood and screams. The creature shook itself, in hopes that the elf would fall off, but she dug her sword into it again, this time in the chest. With her other blade, she slashed at its gaping maw.

Darya almost threw up when a twitching tongue and a piece of pruney lip fell to the ground.

The Gargantuan tried to take a bite at Luunaiwel, thrashing in desperation. She made incredible leaps and bounds around the towering monster, almost a blur in the darkness. The Gargantuan's mountainous size was now a fatal disadvantage, for it was too slow and too clumsy to catch something that was faster than the eye could follow. It spun round and round, one arm dragged uselessly on the ground and the other swatting in a crazed frenzy, unable to touch Luunaiwel.

Darya had a distinct feeling that Luunaiwel was *toying* with it.

As the Gargantuan made a blind attempt to head-butt her, Luunaiwel leapt to its meaty shoulder, legs either side of its stumpy head and swords raised high.

"Ralach sa Amun, Pult!" Sparks of lightning came to life, weaving around her gleaming blades as she plunged them into the Gargantuan's skull.

Darya was sure she would never forget its scream, convulsing in death as Luunaiwel fried its brain. It thrashed for what seemed like an eternity, before the elf pulled her swords out, jumping away. The giant corpse went down with an ear-numbing thud, filling the air with a rotten burning odour.

"Disgusting. That was probably one of the nastiest smells I have ever come across. Top twenty, at least." Luunaiwel snorted, wiping her swords on the Gargantuan's body.

Then, she looked up, meeting Darya and Caldor's gawking stares, "What are you idiots doing? Keep moving."

And they did, speechless. It seemed the show of power had scared off the remaining Withered as well, for they could hear the creatures scurrying away. Even when Luunaiwel took back her staff and snuffed out its light, none dared to attack.

Darya would have been terrified too if she was a Withered. By the Gods, she was terrified now as it was. Luunaiwel wasn't just any ordinary magick-user, not that having magic was *anything ordinary* to begin with.

They exited the Dead Forest without any further incident, and Darya almost collapsed out of overwhelming relief. In the distance, they could see the town's lights, tiny and flickering. Reachable, unlike the stars above.

"This is where we part ways." Caldor told them. His eyes were trained at the town though, and there was something haunted in his expression, "Darya, I wish you well. Elf... I owe you a barrel of wine next time we meet."

She grinned at his scowl, fangs and all, "I will hold you to it."

"Wait, aren't you going to town too, Caldor?" Darya was disappointed that he would no longer accompany them. It was childish of course. He had no responsibility over her, she even said so herself.

Caldor shook his head, "Not like this. There are things I need to take care of, and it would be easier for all of us if I do so alone."

Knowing that there was no convincing him otherwise, Darya nodded, "Alright. Take care of yourself."

"You as well. Don't get your nosy nose into more trouble." Caldor took a few steps away, along the edge of the forest, "You take care of her, elf. So long."

"See you!" Darya waved, hoping dearly that they would cross paths again. Caldor turned away, and soon disappeared into the night.

"Well, then," Luunaiwel smiled down at Darya, "we would best be on our way."

They reached town by sunrise. Darya was surprised that she didn't have to stop and rest, but she supposed she did have a long nap back at the glade, however that was. And Luunaiwel said she only needed sleep once every four days. Which was slightly terrifying in Darya's opinion. Sleeping was one of the luxuries they were still allowed in the Shattered Age. Not being able to do so or at least enjoying some resting time was beyond her.

On the other hand, they still needed supplies. Luunaiwel also left her travel beast back in town. She insisted on purchasing Darya one, just to shorten their travel time.

"You keep the money you have," said Luunaiwel, as they browsed through the selections, not that they had much to choose from, at the market, "you will need it eventually."

Darya wasn't going to argue. She was beyond ecstatic when they walked away with her own mount. A dun-coated mare, with two black front socks. She was a gentle one, a bit thin according to Luunaiwel, but who wasn't these days?

"I have to think of a name for her." Darya said, giggling when the horse nosed at her head. The neighbour kids and Sara would flip when she showed them this one!

"Names are important," Luunaiwel agreed, "give her a fitting name, for she will be your companion here on out."

They got some dried meat and some hard tack, a couple of saddlebags and a travel cloak for Darya, before heading back to the inn where this all began. Darya waited outside while Luunaiwel went to pay her overdue, still giddy over her mare, and listened to the stable boys' gossip with one ear. They were talking about the Count's daughter apparently, who was sent off to her arranged marriage the day before.

"What a shame. She woulda been able to stay if she wasn't so reckless."

"Pah!" One of them spat, "I woulda get my first ticket outta here as soon as I could afford to. Them spoiled brats sure know how to kick up a fuss."

"Sides," a third one chimed in, "the Count probably wanna cover up everything. Y'know, after that whole mess with Caldor."

Darya's attention honed in on that immediately, leaning just a tad forward to catch whatever else they might say.

"Yeah, can't have the Lord know precious Metzania's been defiled by a common thief, eh?"

They broke out into raucous laughter, before being shooed off to work by the innkeeper. Darya had half a mind to ask what that was about, but Luunaiwel emerged from the stables then, leading out a malla and leaving Darya speechless once more.

Mallas were rare creatures, with long and muscular legs that ended with thick, opposable claws that allowed them to travel any terrain with ease. The dwarves bred these hardy creature to ferry goods up treacherous mountains, both as mounts and guard beasts. Mallas were expensive to maintain. Darya had never expected to see one outside of Flumium.

Then again, she had never expected to see an elf either.

Luunaiwel's malla had a russet coloured coat, golden eyes and a strong, swishing tail that could crack rocks. Its belly and feet were covered with reptilian brown scales, thick and glossy. The fur was longer around its round snouts, perfect for burrowing as mallas were omnivores, with a pair of majestic curved horns protecting its skull.

Shaking herself out of a daze, Darya asked, "Whoa! It's majestic!!!"

Luunaiwel winked, slinking herself onto the glorious beast's saddle, "My friend here is Tuura. Now, where to, little bird?"

Blinking, because she hadn't anticipated being the one who'd decide where to go, and mentally berated herself because that was part of the arrangement. Darya gave it a quick thought.

"Is it... I mean, I want to go back to Flumium, if that's alright."

She wanted to deliver the coins to her family as soon as possible. Besides, maybe on the way, she could think of what to do with her current situation. Luunaiwel talked about lessons, maybe she would know how to teach Darya to be a real Druid?

The elf's smile glinted under her shadowed hood, "To Flumium, it is."

With a tug of the reigns, they kicked off, embarking on a journey that Darya couldn't help but be excited for.

CHAPTER 7:

"I cannot teach you True Druidism, little bird, for I am no Druid," Luunaiwel had said when Darya inquired about the "lessons" she spoke of, "however, I can teach you the basics of being a Druid, magic and train you in the arts of combat, if you so wish."

What kind of idiot would say no to that?

They spoke a lot on their travels during the day. It made the dry, scorching mid-year sun more bearable, and the barren road ahead less depressing. Even the cold nights seemed less hostile when they camped.

"A dagger is not a preferable weapon for a Druid, as it is too close-ranged." The elf said, balancing Darya's only weapon on the tip of her finger, "The goal is to keep your opponent as far away from you as possible, so you may inquire for help from the elements around you or your allies."

"So I'm running support."

Luunaiwel nodded, handing back the weapon, "That you are. The preferred weapons for Druids were staves, one-handed swords, and maces. Some even employed archery in order to keep their distance. But since we have no other weapons right now, a dagger will have to be made due."

Darya asked, "Would that interfere with my weapon usage later on if I choose to change it?"

"No, as we will stick to the basics for now. Hand to hand combat," Luunaiwel smiled, "besides, knowing how to use more weapons is always advantageous. You cannot be too sure of what you might find on the way."

"Will I ever be able to fight like you did with that Gargantuan?"

Fangs glinting, Luunaiwel grinned, "Most probably not. Humans do not possess the same athletic capabilities as elven-kins do."

"Aaaaw..."

Luunaiwel chuckled, ruffling Darya's head, "Do not be disheartened, little bird. That should not stop you from trying to achieve the best that you can. Now, square your stance."

While more knowledgeable than any scholar Darya had met, Luunaiwel was not as gentle. She was detailed in her instructions, demonstrating to Darya what she needed to know.

Like how to crush someone's airway with a shove of her palm.

"Hand to hand combat is a necessity. Unlike weapons, they cannot be disarmed. Unless someone did so *literally*."

The elf circled around Darya, fixing her posture. Luunaiwel taught Darya to always keep her balance, and what to do if certain situations arose.

"There is no use trying to fend off more than two attackers at once. Run, when you are outnumbered and outpowered. False bravery only leads to a foolish death. If you have no choice but to fight, lead them to a closed quarter, where they would be forced to fight you one on one.

Always be aware of your surroundings. A stray rock or a sharp branch can keep you alive or kill you. Always be resourceful. Never think too much when you are being attacked. Let your instinct take over."

Darya huffed, "So … fight like a street rat who is caught by other street rats after scoring a nice loaf of bread?"

Luunaiwel's eyes glittered with amusement, "Essentially."

Two more nights passed until Darya asked, "Aren't you going to spar with me? I know I am a novice, but I heard it's better to have a sparring partner."

"Well, for one," Luunaiwel drawled and, before Darya knew what was happening, her feet were swept, knocking her prone, "your core is not balanced. Two, I might injure you beyond recognition. Elvish strength is not for show, after all."

Groaning, Darya stood, dusting her pants, "Point taken."

"We can spar once we move on to mock weapons. I am sure we can find a stick or two."

They both looked out at the barren land ahead. Darya snorted in disbelief.

They hadn't been able to find firewood since they left town. That was five days ago. Their only source of light at night was Luunaiwel's oil lantern, their food was dry rations and hay cakes for the mounts. This wasn't an uncommon occurrence. With most of the world deprived of vegetation, having woods to burn was a luxury. Darya guessed Edurn could afford hearths and such only because they could harvest wood from the Dead Forest.

Elsewhere, people had to rely on drilled oil for light at night, mined coals, or going to bed as soon as night fell.

As Darya marvelled at one of the gold coins during dinner, she noticed there were thick runes etched along the metal's seam.

"This is a dwarfish coin, isn't it?"

"Oh yes, yes it is," Luunaiwel hummed from where she was leaning against Tuura's curled form, "pretty, are they not?"

"Yes … Do you deal with them often?"

"As often as I can. They are, after all, the most excellent merchants and crafters in all of Ardent."

If there was one thing Darya learned about her companion, it was that Luunaiwel always eluded from speaking about herself. The elf could go on and on about one topic or the other, but never anything personal, always cleverly diverted the flow to something else if asked. And Darya hadn't dared to ask Luunaiwel anything too direct, yet.

That wasn't to say any of Luunaiwel's topic-of-the-day was boring. As a bard, Darya was naturally drawn to the tales she heard, and was fascinated by how an elf such as Luunaiwel perceived the common myths. It was much easier to follow her story compared to Grandmama Clarince's, as Luunaiwel encouraged Darya to interrupt and ask any questions any time she'd like.

"To further your understanding." as the elf said.

On their seventh day of travels, Luunaiwel told Darya about the Gods' origins. But she called them "Celestials" instead, and did not put a name to any of them, unlike the stories Darya was told.

"The Celestials came from the Deep Beyond," Luunaiwel hummed, "throughout the eons of their existence, they are known by many names and many faces. But to them, they are only the facets of what they represent.

It is difficult to say who came first, Time or Darkness. Time likes boasting that there was no existence before him, but then Darkness would smile and remind him why their kind call their place of origin the Eternal Night.

Next came Light, with eyes of starlight and a crown of moonbeams. The true Herald of ages to come.

From her came the Twins of All that Are: Life and Death. The All-Mother and The One Who Takes. They remain two ends of the spectrum, forever opposite till the End Time.

They, Darkness, Time, Light, Life and Death, would make the Original Five."

Darya blinked, "The Ancient Five, as we call them."

"Correct." Luunaiwel smiled, "The dwarves call them the First Council, and the Dragons regard them as Creator-All. But they are essentially one and the same."

"So they are the ones who created our world?"

Luunaiwel tilted her head, "Not quite. You see, the Original Five are nomads. They traverse the universe, looking for suitable worlds to shape and mould to their images. Well, at least to Life, that is."

"The Goddess Vita?"

"As you know her. In a perfect world, Life would be a Creator, hailing forth its prosperity and abundance. And, if her creations do not fail her, the Celestials would be granted with those who worship them. Should she fail, and that world turned into a ravaged rock by Death, they would move on, with Life's tears trailing their path, and Death's smile to illuminate the way."

Darya winced, "That's brutal."

"It is," the elf chuckled, then continued with her tale, "as Time trickled along, Life sought to hone her craft. She recruited and shaped the Elements to be her helpers, and was disappointed when they turned too wild to be controlled, a set of double-edged blades that served both Life and Death. Both malleable and dangerous to Life's more sentient mortal children.

In Life's frustration, War was born, and the child has proven to be her most terrible creation yet. Disgusted, she cast War aside, only for him to be recruited by Death."

"Is that why Bellum is always portrayed as a young boy?" Darya asked, thinking about the statue and inscriptions she had seen at Fumium's Holy Temple.

"Yes, and no. He is often portrayed as a child because war is like a child throwing a temper tantrum. Usually provoked by manners too insignificant to a nation as a whole, chaotic in practice and exhausting in the aftermath."

When it was put into words like so, "That makes sense."

"Yes. Where was I? Ah," Luunaiwel snapped her fingers, "to prevent the climbing mortality rates, the Original Five held a council, and Harmony was proposed to be their next creation. However, unlike anything before him, to create Harmony would require a balance among all, including the Twins of All that Are.

Naturally, they failed on their first try. Thus came Discord.

Harmony was born at a great cost. As the Celestials set their sight on another destination, across many, many universes, Life vowed to make the next world her best work of all."

Luunaiwel paused, tilting her head, "In your language, that world was called Asylum the Golden. Where Nature and its creatures flourished. Where civilizations grew with the trees, where Light was abundant be it day or night. Ivory towers embraced in jade canopies, waterfalls glittered with gold and every breath was infused with the Elements' purity. The people were beautiful, intelligent and free of illnesses. Asylum was a masterpiece, the best Life had ever shaped."

"That sounded beautiful." Darya said. The elf chuckled.

"It does, does it not? But nothing good lasts forever." Luunaiwel cast her gaze around them, to the endless barrens where nothing could grow. Her mismatching eyes were far away, like she was seeing something that was not there. But the elf quickly refocused and smiled at Darya.

"Asylum the Golden was Life's pride, and she had wanted it to last forever. But then, her twin sister, Death, and Darkness joined in matrimony, whence Love was born."

Darya did a double take, "Huh? So Mortia and Tenebrum got married, and gave birth to Amare? In our stories, it was Vita who created Amare from starlight and blessed the world with her powers."

"Not in our tales," Luunaiwel chuckled, "Death and Darkness's union gave birth to Love. Threatened by this, Life was convinced, by none other than Discord, that her twin's marriage was a direct display of opposition. Hatred, Deceit and Fear were born from this incident. Sought into Life's mortals, her perfect world was soon doomed."

That was terrible, and a whole different narrative from the stories Darya knew. The Holy Temples would surely be enraged should they ever hear of this.

Luunaiwel continued, "They moved on, but with the Seeds of Discord deep within Life, all her creations onward were destined to fail. In turn, Life grew to hate Death.

When Harmony was unable to reverse the damage done, the solution arrived in the most unexpected source. Love stepped forward in Death's urging, and aided Life in fixing her broken creations. Untrusting of Death's child, Life watched her newest world closely, even walking amongst her mortal children at times, heedless of them stumbling upon her divinity."

The elf grinned at Darya, "As thus, our world Ardent came to be."

Darya clapped for Luunaiwel, returning the grin, "That was... fascinating. Although I'm sure I'd be stoned to death if I dare to tell this version in the taverns."

Gods above, Darya would get an earful if she ever dared to talk about this in front of her neighbour Marge. Grandmama Clarince wouldn't be taking too kindly to it either.

"Understandable," Luunaiwel nodded, "the younger the race, the more impressionable they are. The Ancient Ones thrive on worshippers."

"What about elves? Do you worship the Gods?"

"We do not. We pay respect to them, as they made the foundation of this world. But we do not worship them, neither do the dragons, not in the sense that humans and dwarves do."

That was the first time Luunaiwel spoke directly about elvish customs. Feeling lucky, Darya decided to push it.

"What about the elements? I heard you invoke the Goddess of Fire's name, Ignia, the night we met."

"Sharp," Luunaiwel winked, "but no. There are multiple facets to an element, and multiple whom of which an element is invoked. Yes, Ignia is associated as your Goddess of Fire, responsible for all fire in your culture, but for the rest of us, *Ignia* is a bit... complicated and simpler than that. Ignia is the element which is responsible for man-made fire, fire that sparks unnaturally, and fire that lights the hearth. So on, so forth. Fire sparked naturally, by lightning for example, a natural disaster, would be Ambustio, the equivalent of your God of Storms."

That was long-winded, "What difference does that make?"

"Not much for a normal person," Luunaiwel said, then rubbed her forefinger and thumb together, and breathed *"Ignia"* to them, creating a flickering, dancing dot of blue flame, "but for a magick-user, it is *everything*. You must always know the source of your magic, where it comes from, for not all magic comes from within and is often borrowed from the world around you. Did you notice what happened when I used magic?"

She snuffed the wisp out with a snap of her fingers.

Darya mulled over the question, "The first time, you used magic to attach rocks to Caldor's legs. The rocks are already all around us. The second time, when the Withered attacked, you used the campfire."

"Correct. I use the elements around me, invoking the connection I have already established, so it would not drain my own magic reservoir."

"Alright, I can follow that," Darya nodded, "what about the light from your staff and your lightning swords, then?"

"Ah, what they are would be magical artefacts," Luunaiwel patted her hip, where her sword sat sheathed, "with the right components and the right enchantments, after years and years of forging and reforging, you may infuse elemental magic into them."

"So objects can actually carry elements?"

"It is more like a housing situation," Luunaiwel wagged her finger, "but do not think of them yet. They are incredibly rare to come by. Can pay for two kings' ransoms, usually kept under locks and keys, and mortally dangerous. I suggest learning and mastering the basics first, before even thinking of any artefact."

Darya couldn't help it, "So how did you get *two?*"

"They come with the job, unfortunately. Ha, lucky for you, since you did get to look at them and even touch one!"

Not willing to divulge personal information again. But Darya wasn't about to push it with Luunaiwel. Vow or not, she did *not* want to piss the elf off.

"Aw, chin up," Luunaiwel chirped at Darya's scowl, "we should be at Flumium in three more days. You will get to see your family soon."

That brightened Darya up immediately, "Yes! We'll get to see Sara and Grandmama Clarince! I can't wait! They'd be happy to see me! And you! Grandmama makes the best soot cakes in the world, you'll see!"

Luunaiwel smiled at her enthusiasm, eyes glittering, "I can hardly wait."

CHAPTER 8:

It was nice to be back to Flumium after so many months on the road. In the sense that it was where her family and everyone she knew lived.

If Darya had to be honest, she didn't think the Great City upon River was all that great. Perhaps it was once great before they came, or a couple hundred years before that, but certainly not now. Built over the river Flumin, at the southernmost of the Eria Mountains, Flumium's means of trade relied solely coal.

There were so many mines and so much coal in production, it seemed to coat the very air with a grey-black cloud. The river was dark, and everyone from children to elderly were always smeared no matter how they scrubbed themselves. The very streets were covered in soot, with houses and walls blackened as if someone committed arson on a regular basis. No matter how hard they tried to dull the noises, the entire city always vibrated with constant clink clangs of pickaxes against stones.

Mul Tarum funded the city, of course. Who else would need that much coal? The dwarves needed it for their strange machines and ways of life under the mountains, and only they could afford to fund such huge operations. Quarter yearly, they traded money, along with supplies and occasionally mining equipment via a rail track, guarded by a small army of dwarves, going back and forth from Flumium to the dwarfish city Mul Tarum through an underground tunnel.

Most people came here to work at the mines. Almost everyone who survived back in Darya's old village did. She, Grandmama Clarince and Sara only moved with them because they didn't know where else to go. Darya was only ten back then, and Sara was four. For a few years, Darya used to bring water to the miners per day, for four coppers and a half. It was hard work for a child, it didn't pay well, and it wasn't safe either. Accidents happened in the mines, and with how many tunnels they had, even seasoned miners could easily get lost.

Grandmama Clarince forbade Darya from going back after she got stuck underground for two whole days. Thinking about that incident still gave Darya the chills.

They entered Flumium through the north western bridge and sent their mounts to the public stable. As they walked along the Flumin, Darya had the same mixed feelings she always had every time she returned. A slight distaste, for the city itself and the mines, and an expectant happiness to see her family.

Today, she was concerned about how well they would receive Luunaiwel, too.

Before they approached the city, Luunaiwel redid her hair so it would artfully hide her sharp-tipped ears with intricate arches of braids. She was beautiful, of course, but the hairstyle only made the elf look more highborn than she already did, scars and all.

Darya thought there would be a cover story for their meeting, since she was rather sure the vow would prevent her from introducing Luunaiwel. Well, not exactly, but it wouldn't end pretty, according to Luunaiwel.

The elf just smiled and told Darya to act normal as she "will handle it". Darya had no choice but to agree.

Her family lived at the edge of the city, by the river where the rest of their villagers stayed. The houses were small, built with rock and mud as the poorest of the poor all were, a few feet away from the river and propped against the stone steps that led to the streets. It was dark and wet and dank, but Darya couldn't help smiling at the familiar faces, and got nothing but smiles and friendly cheers back.

"Auntie Marge! Hey!!"

The robust woman waved, "Darya! Back finally! How was your trip?"

"It was tiring, but I did some good work ... Uncle Ralf! How are you? How is Cecil?"

"Fine, fine! She keeps askin' about you! Mighty eager to hear about your travels, I bet!"

Darya laughed with him, "I'll drop by later! I miss her too, gotta thank her for helping Grandmama!"

"Don't mention it, kiddo."

"Ay! Darya! You're back!"

"Hey they, Agnes! How's the family?" Darya returned the shoulder clasp, grinning at the lanky boy.

"They're good! You're back earlier this time! How was the trip?"

"Mmhm! I went all the way to Edurn though, so it's still the furthest I've gotten so far!"

Agnes' blue eyes widened, clearly impressed, "For real? You gotta tell us all about it!"

"Definitely!"

There was no shortage of welcomes. Everyone seemed happy to see Darya back in one piece, and though they were curious about the stranger following her, they politely didn't ask. It was another trait that Darya adored about her community. Despite being tight-knit, they weren't nosy. Though she suspected since there weren't many of them, news travelled fast, so there was no need to pry. Everyone would know about everything eventually, without having to impose.

At last, they stopped at a creaky door, with the handle chipped and hinges uneven. Luunaiwel chuckled under her hood.

"You are popular with the locals."

Darya shrugged, still grinning ear to ear, "They are all friends! Ready?"

"After you."

Taking a deep breath, Darya pushed the door open and stepped inside.

"Grandmama Clarince, Sara! I'm home!"

"Darya? Darya, is that you?"

"Grandmama!" With long strides, Darya came to embrace her tiny Grandmama, almost knocking her over, and reached down to hold her sister's shaky hand on the bed.

"Darya!"

There wasn't much in their home. A stove, creaky and stained with age sat in one corner. Two odd chairs, one missing half a back, leaned against a table that had seen better days. In another corner was a few chipped pots where her scrawny herbs grew, tucked at the end of their single, patched up bed where Sara lay.

Mist blurred Darya's vision. She was home.

"I've missed you guys so much!"

Luunaiwel quietly closed the door behind her. Grandmama Clarince perked up.

"Oh? Do you have someone with you?"

Though blind, her ears were excellent, and she was sharp despite what her age-weathered body might say. Before Darya could speak though, Luunaiwel stepped forward, gloved hand placed gently upon Grandmama's.

"Forgive my intrusion, milady. My name is Luna, and I am Darya's travel companion."

Clarince turned her hand to hold Luunaiwel, "Oh, my, what a polite young lady! Just Grandmama is fine, dearie, everyone here calls me that. How nice, how nice! It's so rare for Darya to bring home a friend."

"The first time." Sara giggled from where she was, only to be interrupted by a string of chesty coughs. Clicking her tongue, Darya propped her sister up in one well-practiced motion and poured the girl a glass of water. Still, Sara coughed for another full minute.

Despite being at an age that she should experience some growth spurts, Sara was incredibly small. Due to her lingering sickness, she could never soak up enough sun, nor could she play with the neighbours' children. Sara was so frail, a strong wind could blow her over, and she would cough her lungs out before she could walk to the market two streets away.

"So-sorry about that, Miss Luna," Sara rubbed her eyes, smiling, "my name is Sara. You're so pretty, miss Luna!"

"Why, thank you," Luunaiwel offered the girl her other hand, "what a charming young lady you are! Darya, you never told me your sister is so much better-behaved than you!"

Darya elbowed the elf, as her grandmother and sister laughed, "Hey! I'll have you know it's all just for show! She's a little rascal, that's what she is!"

"I do not believe that one bit. And just Luna is fine, darling." Luunaiwel winked at Sara, who giggled again. Grandmama Clarince smiled up at Luunaiwel, gums and all.

"Where are my manners... sit, sit," she said, pushing Luunaiwel towards the chairs, and only sat down at the edge of the bed when she heard the elf did, "Darya, get her something to drink, would you? We don't have much to offer, but as long as you stay in Flumium, consider this place home!"

"Thank you, mil-Grandmama. I truly appreciate it," Luunaiwel turned to Darya, "you might not be as well-behaved as your sister, but you definitely got your enthusiasm from you Grandmama."

"Yep, everyone says so." Darya agreed easily. Something warm bloomed in her heart, and it wasn't the Heart Stone. Seeing her family again, especially when they and Luunaiwel got along so well, made her happy.

"How did you and Luna meet, anyway?" Innocently, Sara asked.

Oh yes, so happy it almost gave her a heart attack. But Luunaiwel slotted in without a beat.

"We met at a town up north, Edurn. Darya was giving a very exciting performance. I have always had a love for tales and myths, so naturally, I must strike up a conversation. Since I have some business down in Mul Tarum, I figured I would keep Darya's company on the way to Flumium."

Grandmama Clarince was impressed, "Oh my... Business with the dwarves? Do you mind if I ask what you do for a living?"

Luunaiwel smiled, "Not at all. I am a historian, and I am working on a commission for a Lord in A'Vasni: composing a book about towns and cities situated along the Eria Mountains."

Smooth.

Grandmama Clarince seemed beyond impressed, "A historian! No wonder you're so well spoken! I hope Darya can learn a thing or two from you!"

She had *no idea*.

"I hope so too. Oh, Grandmama," Darya almost tripped over herself, coming to hold her grandmother's hand, "I actually... This trip, I actually made a lot of money! Enough to move us to a better place!"

The old woman was surprised, "Are you sure, Darya? That must be a lot of money... Have you been eating well?"

"I am, Grandmama! It should be able to afford Sara's treatments too!"

Clarince was bewildered, "What? How much did you... What did you do, Darya?"

Blinking, because she did *not* expect that question at all, "I... uh, I got really lucky, I guess..." Trailing off, Darya glanced at Luunaiwel for help.

There was a frown on Grandmama's face now, "Darya, did you do anything bad?"

"No! Of course not, Grandmama!"

"Don't lie to me, Darya!"

"Oh, come off it," Luunaiwel finally decided to come to the rescue, *thank the Gods,* "Grandmama, this girl was just shy. She thinks she is undeserving."

Clarince turned her blind face to where her guest was sitting, confused, "Undeserving?"

"After meeting her, I thought her tales were most excellent, but of course she was not being paid enough for them, performing at common taverns and inns after all. So I used my contacts and introduced her to a few regional Lords. She did not get an invitation right away, but a Count, who was having a parting-banquet for his betrothed daughter and was short on entertainers, agreed to have Darya in. From what I have heard, she made quite a fortune that night."

Grandmama gasped, shaking Darya's arm, "Is that true, Darya??"

Darya fought back a grimace, because she hated lying to her Grandmama, but there wasn't much of a choice. Besides, Luunaiwel already did almost all of the lying, anyway.

"Yes, Grandmama. I don't feel right about it," because she didn't. She almost died for the gold, after all, "but money is money, right?"

"Oh," there were tears on her grandmother's face, and Darya was alarmed, until she was gathered into a shaky hug, "oh... Darya, I don't know what to say..."

"There, there, Grandmama," Darya smiled, rocking her back and forth, "it's alright. We'll be fine. Sara will be fine. I promise."

Unexpectedly, Grandmama gestured at Luunaiwel, "Come here, come here, dear girl. Oh, I don't know how to thank you..."

For a moment, Darya thought Luunaiwel would decline, but she rose from her chair, and enveloped both Darya and Grandmama Clarince in her long arms, making sure to reach down one hand for Sara to hold. She kept the bulk of her body against Darya's back, hiding her full armour.

"Do not fret over it, Grandmama," Luunaiwel said with a smile, "good people ought to be rewarded, so I was taught. I am sure Darya would have made it big, with or without my interference."

After the tearful moment, Grandmama insisted that Darya go and get them something nice for dinner, as there were so many causes for celebration and now that they could afford to. Chuckling, she agreed, leaving Luunaiwel behind to chat up her family.

Whistling a cheery tune, Darya headed towards the market district. Everything opened after dusk till dawn in Flumium, as opposed to from early morning till afternoon elsewhere. This was due to the miner's shift, making the city mostly deserted during daytime. There weren't many shops, but most owners being dwarves, as thus the food was of higher quality.

If one had the money that was.

For once, Darya could afford something fresh, and she couldn't believe she was actually thinking of getting a *property* on top of that. She didn't know how expensive a house would be, but she did overhear some merchants buying lands with a few gold coins some time ago, so Darya hoped they could afford something decent with what she had.

But, as she hauled around a nice chunk of ham, a fresh loaf of bread and even some root vegetables, Darya saw beggars lurking in alleyways and thought, *what about the others?*

All Grandmama Clarince ever knew was her community. They were all she and Sara could rely on, especially when Darya was away. What were they going to do if they moved? Darya couldn't ask Agnes or Cecil to run back and forth like that. And she was sure they wouldn't be able to afford a servant after buying a house, and she knew Grandmama wouldn't agree to it even if they could.

To make matters worse, Darya couldn't stay home. They wouldn't last long without her income. And what about Luunaiwel? The elf would probably be unhappy to stay, vow or not. Darya didn't think it would be fair to ask more from

Luunaiwel, the gold *did* come from her, after all. Then there was that whole Druid business...

Forlorn, her hand came up to touch her chest, where the stone laid under her tunic, pulsing quietly with a reassuring warmth.

"Young miss, would ya like to have yar palm read?"

Startled, because she didn't realise she had stopped in the middle of the street, Darya blinked down at a woman. Glazed eyes, red-rimmed due to all the coal dust in the air, stared up at her under a moth-eaten head wrap. Gnarled hand reached up, shaking with fatigue, over disfigured legs, poorly concealed by a ragged blanket.

The streets were where people went, when the mines weren't kind to them.

Taking pity on the poor woman, Darya smiled, "Sure, why not."

Shifting all her purchases to one hand, she offered her free one. Thanking her, the woman reached up...

And flinched the moment their skin touched.

"Y-you... you... You!" The palm reader stammered, eyes wide, lips shaking. Before Darya could ask, the woman stood, hobbling away as fast as she could, as if she had seen a ghost.

That was strange.

But it wasn't the first time Darya had seen someone with erratic behaviour in this city. People tended to see all kinds of things down in the mines.

Darya certainly had.

Before she headed back though, she decided to scope out some of the neighbourhoods. A place near the river would be cheaper. The richer folks couldn't stand the smell, and it would be close to the community, so Grandmama and Sara wouldn't be alone. Some houses were posted for sale, but she wasn't sure the owners would be too happy discussing prices with a kid. Darya estimated a house would fall around four gold coins, some more, some less. It was expensive, but even if they bought one, there would still be plenty leftovers for Grandmama and Sara to live on for half a year without being frugal. It was reasonable enough. Whatever else Darya might make on the road with Luunaiwel, she could send home then.

Darya came back to Grandmama Clarince and Luunaiwel sitting on the bed with Sara, the elf reading to them from a book. Both her sister and grandmother were entranced. Whether by the story or by Luunaiwel herself though, was debatable. But it didn't matter, because when Sara waved at her, sickness all but forgotten, warmth rushed through Darya's entire being.

"Luna is telling us a story about a Princess that fell from the stars," Sara said, green eyes sparkling with awe, "have you heard that one?"

"No, but I'll make sure she'll tell me later."

Luunaiwel chuckled, voice rich, "There will be time, little bird."

Darya's smile widened.

They had a simple dinner. Ham and bread and boiled vegetables, or in Sara's case, a soup broth with a hunk of bread. It was probably the best dinner they had ever had under this roof, not only because of the food's quality, but also because of the sheer happiness Darya felt at that moment. Even Sara was more animated, doing her best to impress Luunaiwel with all the stories she heard from their neighbours. Darya poked fun at Sara here and there, bickering in good humour as Luunaiwel chimed in with her usual witty quips. Grandmama Clarince was content to listen, laughing like Darya hadn't seen her laughed since her parents were still alive.

It was a good evening.

When the city fell into a quiet lull of humming production, Darya cleared the table, then brewed a kettle of rosemary tea, the only luxury they had on a daily basis. After tucking a knackered Sara into bed, Darya brought steaming mugs over to Luunaiwel and Grandmama.

"Thank you, my child." Grandmama said, murky eyes wet, and Darya knew she meant far more than just for the tea. Ducking her head, she teared up a little.

"Anytime, Grandmama."

Luunaiwel smiled at both of them, "Thank you all for your hospitality."

"No, no, thank *you*," Grandmama reached over to hold Luunaiwel's hand, "it's so lovely having you here, dear girl."

"It is lovely to be here," Luunaiwel patted her wrinkled fingers, "though I must say, I am afraid I have some business in town early in the morning, so it might be best for me to secure a room at a nearby inn should I wish not to be late."

Grandmama seemed disappointed, but she understood the underlying meaning. There was no way their tiny hut could accommodate another person, and there was no way Grandmama would let a guest sleep on the floor.

"I see, I see... Would you visit us again then?"

"But of course," Luunaiwel said, "I must discuss with Darya on whether or not she would like to journey with me to Mul Tarum."

"Mul Tarum? My... But Darya doesn't have any paperwork to enter... would that be a problem for her?"

Grandmama Clarince was rightfully worried. Coming from where Darya was, she barely had a residency permit in Flumium. The dwarves were notoriously strict about entry to their hidden city. It was as good of a time to speak on this matter as any.

Luunaiwel tilted her head with a smile, "The Lord I have business with is a generous one. He would not turn down my companion. That is... if Darya would still like to accompany me?"

Darya didn't know how to respond to that. They hadn't exactly discussed their next steps after Flumium. But it seemed like her Grandmama had other ideas.

"I'm sure she would love to join you then, dear Luna!"

Incredulous, Darya blinked, "I am? But Grandmama-"

"Hush, Darya," Her grandmother reached for her hand, which Darya immediately took, "it's not every day you get to visit a dwarfish city! Besides, after all Luna has done for you, the least you can do is help her on the way!"

Darya sighed, wishing dearly she could just tell her sweet grandmother what was truly going on.

Chuckling, Luunaiwel interjected, "Oh, no, no. There is no rush for her to decide. My business here in Flumium will take at least a couple of days," turning to Darya, "in the meantime, I shall be staying at the Rowdy Rooster."

With some final exchanges, Luunaiwel bid Darya's family a goodnight, and disappeared behind the door.

"What a fine lady that Luna is"

Biting her lips so she wouldn't tell her grandmother anything damning, Darya huffed out a laugh, "That, she is."

CHAPTER 9:

Funny how one's perspective could change after certain life-threatening events.

Well, Darya couldn't say travelling on the road like she did was anything safe, and she had her fair share of scuffles growing up. But running away from a small horde of Withered and a terrifying encounter with a Gargantuan did change how she looked at things.

The young Bard was wary of her family's living situation. Grandmama Clarince wasn't getting any younger, and the narrow strip that they called a street was a breadth away from tragic accidents. Thank the Gods neither Grandmama nor Sara had gotten into trouble while Darya was away.

Thus, her determination to find a more appropriate abode for her family solidified. After making sure there was enough food for the day, Darya resumed her hunt for a new home. Plenty of people, mostly older folks, were looking to move to quieter towns like Pompi or Īse, so finding a property wasn't a problem.

No, the problem lay elsewhere.

Darya had prepared for the day by dressing up in her performing clothes. She even wiped herself off, and did her hair. Still, with her short stature and her young face, it was truly difficult to get anyone to consider her inquiries seriously.

People would open their door with expectant smiles, only to scowl and shoo Darya away as soon as they realised it was a ratty teenager on the other side. This continued on past midday bells, and at that point Darya was so fed up with her fellow townsfolk's attitudes, she gave up.

Heading towards the Rowdy Rooster with curses under her breath, Darya's mood was further soured by the merry jangle coming from the inn. Normally, Darya wouldn't be so petty about another bard's performance, but seeing someone performing so freely in Flumium only reminded her about how easy they got it here. These bards and performers didn't have to drag themselves ragged on dangerous roads for meagre coppers, never had to worry about the family they left behind.

Deep in thought, Darya didn't realise she was blocking the entrance, and was rudely shoved to the side by a miner.

"Outta m' way, y' moron!"

Stumbling into a bench, Darya bristled, but knew better than to pick a fight. In a better part of town or not, this inn was still filled with off-shift miners, each of them easily three times her size.

So, despite her stewing anger, Darya righted herself with a huff, and scanned the crowd for a familiar face. Sure enough, she spotted mismatched green and blue eyes in a corner, a scarred eyebrow rose in silent questions. Sighing, Darya made her way there, and sat at the empty spot by Luunaiwel.

"I did not expect to see you here so early."

Darya wrinkled her nose, "My morning plans didn't go according to plan."

"Oh?"

With another sigh, Darya recalled her failed endeavour to Luunaiwel in frustration. The elf listened from under her hood, nodding in quiet understanding at the angry tirade. Darya grew more animated the longer she talked, unmindful of the looks she was getting from nearby tables.

"-and she called me a *street urchin!!!* Can you bloody believe that???"

Sympathetically, Luunaiwel patted her shoulder, and flagged down a server for a meal with her other hand, "That was highly uncalled for, indeed. I suppose it is difficult, looking for an estate when you are so young."

"I'm not looking for an *estate*," Darya grunted, "just some place that functions like a house and won't threaten to collapse if I close the door too hard."

"Would you like help? I do not mind negotiating. However, I must warn you that I am rather terrible with my spending habits."

Cocking her head to the side, Darya peered at Luunaiwel's smiling face with narrowed eyes, "I was getting that impression... Who in their right mind would be willing to spend that much on a random wayfinder?"

"The destination was far more valuable than money" the elf raised her flagon at Darya, "but I suppose you are right. I probably should keep a tighter lid on my purse."

They went silent when the server brought out the food for Darya. Egg-stuffed black sausage slathered in dark gravy, and a skewer of grilled pork livers. Luunaiwel had bought her the most expensive items on the menu.

"You didn't have to." The bard said, but dug in much vigour and gratefulness anyway.

Luunaiwel muttered, "Everything else sounds mortifying. Forgive me, but I am not going to depress you more with a meal of sheep lungs."

Darya shrugged, chewing through a juicy piece of liver, "You gotta eat whatever to survive. It's not like Flumium is abundant with resources. Personally I'd have been fine with sheep lungs."

Luunaiwel made a disgusted face, "Each to their own, I suppose."

The conversation halted for a bit as Darya worked through her meal. The performing bard's music filled the silent gap between them. Begrudgingly, Darya had to admit that the man, however garishly dressed, was good at his trade. He made lute-strumming look like an art. His iron-soled boots clapping on the floor substituted for drums, and his voice was obviously well-trained.

Darya would never be able to compete with that.

Feeling steadily gloomier, Darya turned to Luunaiwel, "It'd be great if you could help me talk to some sellers. Do you... uh, do you need compensation?"

The elf seemed amused, "That would be a bit pointless now, would it not? The money you are using did come from me, after all."

She had a point, "Well... Is there anything I can do for you? I don't feel right taking advantage of your generosity just because I'm a... well."

Luunaiwel's eyes glinted at Darya's awkward shoulder roll, "If you insist, then there is something you may assist me with. I would like to sightsee Flumium properly, as all my previous visits were rather brief."

Darya blinked, "That's all? Yeah, I can do that. Just let me finish this, and I'm good to go."

"Oh? I thought you would want to secure a property first?"

"Eh. I already knocked on all the doors I liked today. Best let them forget about me first before we try again."

Tilting her head, Luunaiwel chuckled, "As you wish."

When they exited the Rowdy Rooster, Darya was stumped. Flumium wasn't known for its legendary structures like Garstan, nor did it boast regal military forces like Apricum. It was a city... yes, but it was also just a glorified mining town.

"What do you want to see in particular? Do you want to see the mines? The rail entrance to Mul Tarum? We have a small port for trading ships coming from Pompi and, uhm..."

Luunaiwel was amused by Darya's fumbling, "You mentioned a Holy Temple?"

The young bard blinked, "Oh, yes. That. Seriously? You want to see Flumium's Holy Temple?"

There was a twinkle in the elf's mismatched eyes, "Is there anything else to see?"

Darya grimaced, "That's a good point. Let's go."

They continued up the street from the Rowdy Rooster, and into the richer part of town. The houses here were built on the hill slopes that connected to the side of Eria Mountains, two to three storied and looking like a desperate attempt to escape the soot clouds that encompassed Flumium. Flumium had one Lord, a Duke by the name of Edgar, and his mansion was the grandest thing in this city, aside from the temple. Darya made sure to point it out for Luunaiwel.

"I see." She raised an eyebrow at the estate.

For a Duke, his house wasn't as gaudy as some of the noble's Darya had seen on her travels. His fences were stacked rocks, and the gate was wooden, enforced with iron. It was an obvious dwarfish design, probably commissioned from Mul Tarum. Duke Edgar had a front yard and a few squares of back garden, though it was debatable whether he could grow anything in there or not. The building was a standard structure seen all around Flumium's merchant district, rectangular with three stories, just much larger in size and also included a separate servant quarter at the back.

"I wanted to try and be a servant when I was a kid." Darya suddenly said, peering up at the house with a nostalgic smile.

Luunaiwel made a small noise, "Let me guess... the pay is better than working in the mines?"

"That, and the people who came from there always dressed so nicely. Always so proper," Darya wrinkled her nose, "but the Duke only recruits older people to be his servants, and they all have to be from Flumium."

Luunaiwel gave her a crooked smile, "I do suppose he has to create job opportunities for his own people. Besides, if you had become a servant, then we would have never met."

"I'm still not entirely sure if it's a good thing or not." Darya said jovially, to which Luunaiwel chuckled.

"How to perceive it ... it is entirely up to you."

The Holy Temple was only a short distance away from the Duke's estate. And one could recognise it right away, not just because of its tall bell tower, but also because of the flock of beggars outside.

Carefully, Darya tugged Luunaiwel past grabby hands and despaired moans, and into the quiet sanctum of the Temple.

"The Monks aren't allowed to turn away people," Darya felt she had to explain, flustered, "it's... I don't know what to say. But..."

"There is no better solution for them, is there?" Luunaiwel's voice was gentle. Looking away, Darya sighed.

"No. There isn't."

It was a dilemma. Flumium was fair in payments for its workers. Some might say the miners here had it better than most cities. But if something unfortunate was to happen...

They didn't have the physicians nor the medicines available to treat those who were injured in the mines. So those who couldn't recover were tossed to the side, to roam the streets for scraps that others could barely spare. With time, they withered and wasted away, forgotten and replaced by the next wave of unfortunate souls. It was horrific. And Darya could only be grateful that she made enough so her family wouldn't be the same. She wouldn't know what to do otherwise.

Pushing those depressing thoughts aside, Darya turned her attention to the great hall of the Holy Temple.

This building was the oldest architectural site in Flumium, built an age before the Shattered years, before the Great War, even before the city was established. The inside of the Temple wasn't as decrepit as the outside, because it wasn't charred and soiled by coal dust, and the Monks tried their hardest to keep everything clean. But the stains on what must have once been white marble flooring and the cracks along support columns showed the Temple's age. Despite best efforts, it was evident they didn't have the funds to maintain the sanctum.

There were Monks walking on the Temple's ground, all dark-robed and quiet in their duties. Respectfully, Darya kept her distance and led Luunaiwel into the Holy Hall, the Gods' Home in the mortal realm.

Along the walls were statues of the Minor Gods and Goddesses, each with their names carved into the stone base at their feet. While time had whittled down the sharpness of their features, it was still astounding how life-like they looked and how masterful the craftsmanship was.

Glancing over, Darya saw Luunaiwel contemplating the deities, wearing a placid expression under her hood. The elf-mage regarded each statue carefully and, with a leisurely pace, made her way around the room. Luunaiwel stopped with a tilt of her head when they were in front of Tempesta, the Goddess of Weather. A faint smile bloomed on her lips. Curious, Darya tried to decipher what the elf found so funny.

Like the other statues, this one's craftsmanship was just as excellent, from her flowing robes to her intricate hairdo. As the Governess of Weather, Tempesta was given dragons wings, and a staff mounted with the symbols of the sun and moon. However, unlike the rest of the Pantheon, there were visible, deep cracks all over her, some were mended with gold, creating metallic veins on her alabaster skin.

"They said there was a revolt a few decades after the Shattering," Darya said, "people were upset that the weather turned so cruel, so they broke down this statue."

Luunaiwel smirked, "They blamed her for it?"

"That's what the Monks said," Darya shrugged, eyeing some robed figures across the hall, "apparently there were offerings and prayers made, but obviously the weather didn't change."

Luunaiwel scoffed, and her mouth curled into that faint smile again, with pity and disgust glimmering in her eyes, "Of course not. The one who governed the weather was not your Goddess, but the Dragons. Quite difficult to do so when they were hunted to near extinction, though."

It took Darya a moment to let that sink in. Even after it did, she still didn't know how to respond.

Darya had never been religious. Sure, she knew all the myths and scriptures forward and backward like any good bard did, but she never prayed to the Gods nor did she strive to present offerings to the Temple every end of the year. But Grandmama Clarince was a believer, as thus Darya was taught to respect the Gods.

Luunaiwel's flippant comment about how one Goddess in the pantheon left Darya with conflicted feelings. Especially when the elf had told Darya stories similar to her own religion. Especially when said Goddess was said to be dragons instead, when Darya grew up being told dragons were the most fearsome and ruthless beasts, and would have drowned the world in flames had they not been erased.

But, did it matter?

Looking at Luunaiwel, who had walked off to the next statue, Darya decided that, in her now suddenly too complicated life, it really did not. Just two weeks ago, Darya was blissfully unaware that magic still existed. Now, not only she had seen it in action up close, she was travelling with an apparent Archmage. And, supposedly, Darya herself had magic, if the warm stone embedded on her chest was of any indication.

The same stone that she had been trying very hard to ignore, but was now part of her body.

With a sigh, Darya followed Luunaiwel to the main alcove, where the Ancient Five sat on their thrones. On the highest chair was the Goddess of Light, Illumien, with her Orb of Starlight and benevolence in her marble eyes. To either side of her, there were Vita, the Goddess of Life, and Aevum, the God of Time. And at the bottom, hand in hand, were Mortia and Tenebrum, the Goddess of Death and the God of Darkness.

For some inexplicable reasons, Darya's gaze was drawn to Vita. Leaning upon an ivory arm, the Goddess' smile was distant. Despondent. Hair draped over her shoulder, loose waves spilled under a crown of flowers. Her eyes were framed with delicate lashes, dewy and faraway.

Luunaiwel's eyes moved from one statue to another, lingered just a little longer on Vita and Mortia, before turning to Darya.

"Thank you for showing me around. This has been... enlightening."

Blinking at the elf's choice of words, Darya shrugged, feeling a bit uncomfortable, "It's nothing. I'm just glad I can help you with something. Is there any other place you'd like to visit?"

Tapping her chin, Luunaiwel hummed, "Nothing in particular... Does Flumium have a library?"

"There's a library here, but only the Monks have access to it. They only read the Holy Scriptures on the first day of the month and the last day of the year for masses, but that's about it."

"Ah, shame." Luunaiwel clicked her tongue. After a moment, she pulled out a gold coin and flicked it into the offering bowl before the Ancient Five, then left with a swirl of her cloak. Throwing a grimace at the coin, Darya ran out after Luunaiwel.

A contingent of knights ... or at least armed men on horses, marched past the church outside. Like everything in Fluminum, they were all covered in coal dust, grim-faced and dour. These men were tasked with peacekeeping within the city, but they stirred up more dirt than anything. Everyone here was either too busy, too tired or too poor to think much else other than their own survival.

Oh, well ... at least they provided something to look at.

Without much else to do and a lot on her mind, Darya followed Luunaiwel to the communal stables. Their mounts were in a stall together, cramping quite a bit for space and chewing on the saddest hay Darya had ever seen.

Wordlessly, Luunaiwel snatched up two brushes and handed Darya one. In companionable silence, they worked through the travel beasts' coats, dusting them and untangling matted hair.

After a quarter of an hour, Darya couldn't keep quiet any longer, "So about Mul Tarum... Are we really heading there?"

"That entirely depends on you," Luunaiwel said without turning to look at Darya, "Mul Tarum is an option, but also just to ease your Grandmother's mind. Where we go from here is entirely your choice, as per our agreement."

Darya went quiet. For a while, between them, there was just the sound of Luunaiwel's brush through Tuura's mass of fur.

"You said you were on a self-assigned quest when we met, right?"

"That is correct."

"Let's say we're still on that same quest. Where would you go next?"

Luunaiwel hummed, "I was planning to go to Evenmoor. I started my journey from Mul Nordihr, so going back to Mul Tarum would not be ideal for me."

"Oh, alright."

"However," The elf turned around to face Darya, leaning back against her malla's flank, "it might be beneficial for you to visit Mul Tarum."

That was unexpected, "How come?"

Luunaiwel tilted her head, "You as you are, can be equipped with knowledge and training. Both can be acquired by visiting the greatest halls under the mountains."

"But you said you only want to study me, right?"

"That is true, but in order to do so, I must get you to an environment that is suitable for you to thrive," there wasn't even a second of hesitation in Luunaiwel's answer, "again, it is your choice as to where we are going next. You do wish to take care of your family before setting out again, yes?"

Slowly, Darya nodded.

"Then do so. We do have time. You can decide on where to go next. It does not have to be any of the places I suggested. But leave, only when your mind is free of worries for your family. It is both your sake and theirs."

It was dark when she parted with Luunaiwel. Darya felt a headache incoming on her way to the market. Planning for a journey was always her least favourite part of travelling. Usually, Darya skipped that by following nomadic tropes, only leaving when she got enough to sustain herself.

Well, sustainability wasn't going to be a problem this time around.

Darya didn't know whether she should tell her family about her status as a Druid or not. She didn't think they would understand. Darya herself didn't know enough to explain it to them either.

Perhaps it was best to keep it a secret for now. Safer that way.

Darya could ask Grandmama and Sara where she should go next. *After* Mul Tarum, she would say. While Grandmama was under the impression of Luunaiwel leaving for Mul Tarum, she didn't have to know the elf would follow anywhere Darya would go. And Sara was always excited to help Darya deciding on her next destination, as the girl also wanted to travel one day. That could be their next destination. Or they could skip Mul Tarum altogether and went wherever first.

Darya's hand moved to her chest without thinking.

It wasn't like she was too anxious to become a Druid. Putting it off for a while wouldn't hurt anyone, when nobody really knew about it.

With that decision in mind, Darya felt lighter as she purchased dinner for her family. And some flour, too. Darya did promise Luunaiwel some soot cakes made by Grandmama.

On the way home, Darya thought of a list of what to do. Luunaiwel had agreed to meet up with her in the morning to help negotiate. Darya didn't doubt that with the elf's respectable demeanour and her own thriftiness, they would be able to secure a good deal. Waiting for whoever agreed to sell them the place to move out would take a good few days, and in the meantime, Darya could prepare her family with-

Her line of thought stilled with her steps. The splashing river was still the same, so was the thundering sounds of productions, stirred by creaking wagon wheels and distant shouts by the market. But the corner round the uneven path down the bank was empty. No Auntie Marge trying to make one last sale of woven flax, no Agnes skipping down the path after his shift was over.

Something was wrong.

Every nerve in her body screamed for her to run away, but the fear for her family triumphed, and Darya found herself rushing forward, heart hammering in her chest.

On the steps down to the river bank, Darya almost fell to her knees.

There was so much blood.

There were so many bodies.

Bodies of *those she knew.*

No...

Nononononono...

Darya didn't know whether it was her thundering heart that blocked her throat, or if it was her fear that rendered her speechless. But as she ran, desperate and crying, she couldn't make a sound. Praying to whatever God or Goddess that was listening to spare her family.

She almost slipped and fell multiple times. Boots soaked with the blood of her neighbours, of those she had known since she was a child. But she pushed on, frantic.

Please...
Pleasepleasepleasepleasepleasepleasepleaseplease...

But when she reached her home, Darya crumbled.

The door was smashed in. What was left of their meagre belongings lay in a pile of rubble, the only thing left standing was the bed, which had collapsed halfway.

And... *there was blood.*

Breaths hitching into crazed sobs, Darya rushed in and dug, with her bare hands, heedless of splinters and sharp rocks.

"No... Please..."

Tears broke when her worst nightmare came true.

Below what was left of their home, lay Grandmama Clarince. Unmoving. Unbreathing.

Darya screamed.

This wasn't supposed to happen.

Darya was supposed to buy her grandmother a house. She was supposed to have a better life. *She was supposed to live.*

It wasn't supposed to be like this.

Darya screamed. And screamed. And she would have kept screaming, if a tiny voice didn't stop her world.

"D-Darya?"

Snapping around so quickly her neck popped, Darya let go of Grandmama and scrambled over to the collapsed bed. The tears made it difficult to see, but she dug and dug, until she could just make out Sara's pale shape, curled up in the furthest corner.

Darya's heart nearly fell out of her chest.

"Sara!"

Trembling, she pulled her sister out and into her lap. There was blood on Sara's forehead, but she was conscious, though terrified.

"There were... There were s-so many p-p-people, they-they," poor Sara blubbered, clinging onto Darya with all the strength her frail body had, "there we-were... so m-much screa-screaming!!! Da-... I-I-... Grandma-... told me to hide, bu-but I-I h-hit my h-he-head and-and..."

"Alright, alright..." Darya hushed her, rocking back and forth. She kept her back to Grandmama, blocking the view away from Sara's eyes. The last thing they needed now was for Sara to have an attack.

She needed to do something. She needed to get Sara to safety first before anything else. Darya swallowed. Her throat felt like it was paved with gravel. Her head was heavy, and her heart wrenched in so much pain, it could have bled right out of her chest.

"Sara, honey, I'm gonna need you to close your eyes, alright?"

Sara immediately clenched her eyes shut. She was too scared to ask questions, trusting only her big sister. With a shuddering inhale, Darya lifted Sara's tiny form up into her arms.

It took her every ounce of power to not look back. Tears burned in her eyes, Darya clutched at her shaking sister and ran off into the night.

CHAPTER 10:

To say Luunaiwel was surprised to see her and Sara would be an understatement. Stumbling into the Rowdy Rooster, all Darya could manage was a few simple words, in the midst of her gasping panic.

"Our neighbourhood was ruined!"

The cold fury emitted from Luunaiwel could hail forth another winter. But the elf was quick to devise a plan, just as Darya had hoped.

Luunaiwel told Darya to go hide under the south east bridge with Sara. The elf threw her cloak over the girls, and told Darya to be careful to not let anyone follow her. The elf escorted the sisters down the streets, saying she would be grabbing a few essentials before re-joining them.

Darya didn't know how long she sat there, under the bridge hugging Sara. They were both shaken, but alive, *thank the*

Gods. Sara's breaths came out wheezing, high whistles in her throat and chest, threatening for an attack.

Wrapping herself around the last of her family, Darya burrowed her face into Sara's hair, and tried her hardest to not cry.

How could everything go so wrong so quickly?

Something tumbled into the river, startling both sisters. Shaking, Darya pulled Sara impossibly closer. It could have been a rock. Could have been someone throwing trash into the river.

Could have been *someone's body.*

She had seen it, *she had seen them*, when she made a mad dash to escape the carnage. Faces of people... people Darya knew... Agnes and Cecil and Marge and Ralf and...

Dead.

They were all *dead.*

"Darya?"

"Yes?"

There was a pause. A slight tremble passed through Sara's body.

"Where's Grandmama?"

Darya's tongue turned to stone.

The image of Grandmama Clarince, lying crushed and blood-soaked under the debris of their home flashed in Darya's mind.

How could she answer Sara's question? How could she tell her little sister that their grandmother was gone? And that she didn't even know *how*, or *why*. Or *who* would ever commit such a terrible crime.

And it wasn't just their Grandmama... it was their whole community too...

Darya shuddered at the too fresh memory.

Before she could find an answer for Sara, another voice rang out.

"Darya."

She jumped into a defensive stance, only to immediately crumble in relief when she realised that it was Luunaiwel.

"I have the mounts. We need to ride through the night. I will hold onto Sara. It is not safe to stay here."

Numbly, Darya followed Luunaiwel up the sloped bank, to where their mounts were waiting. The elf took back her cloak and wrapped it around Sara, lifting the girl onto the saddle.

"Wai-wait," startled, Sara cried out, "What about... what about Grandmama??? What ab-about *home???*"

There was something unreadable in Luunaiwel's eyes when she glanced at Darya. The young bard looked away.

"Your home is no longer safe, little one," Luunaiwel spoke, her voice gentle and lulling like a song, "we must get you both to safety first before thinking about anything else."

Sara opened her mouth, clearly wanted to argue, but Luunaiwel put a gloved hand over her head.

"Sena."

To Darya's astonishment, her sister's eyes rolled back, before she slumped down into Luunaiwel's arms.

"What... what did you do?!?!"

Luunaiwel adjusted Sara into a more comfortable position, "Relax. It is but a simple sleeping spell. We would not be going anywhere with her struggling."

Numbly, Darya nodded.

They set out into the night.

Half an hour on the road, the cold wind sobered her up a little, and Darya found herself asking, "Where... Where are we going?"

"To Mul Tarum. I have a friend there who will help." Luunaiwel said, nimble fingers wrapping up the shallow cut on Sara's forehead. Darya's heart throbbed painfully at the sight, so she looked away.

After a moment of silence, the elf spoke again, "Darya, did you talk to anyone about being a Druid?"

She flinched, "N-no! Of course not! I wouldn't... *I would never...* I didn't have the time to and even... even *I* know it would be stupid to throw that around!"

Luunaiwel finally turned to look at her, blinking slowly.

"I believe you," Darya felt strangely relieved at those simple words, "did something strange happen then? Anyone followed you?"

"No... I mean... I spent the whole day with you. If there was anything weird, you would have noticed before me, and..." Darya swallowed, stopping herself from rambling more, "no, uh... No. Nobody followed me either."

She kept her head down, thinking about it for a moment.

"But there was this... there was this woman, a beggar. Yesterday, when I went to get food from the market. She offered to read my hand, but she started running the moment she touched my hand. So that was pretty... uh, strange..."

"Well, *shit.*"

Darya's eyes widened. She had never heard Luunaiwel swear before. The elf looked positively livid, and Darya shrunk into her saddle, terrified that Luunaiwel might direct that glower at her.

"I was careless," the elf growled, "I did not expect *one of them* to be so far down south. I should have."

"One of... one of *who?*"

"The Night's Hand," Luunaiwel shook her head, letting out a frustrated sigh, "this is a lot to take in. And you are in too much shock right now to process all of it. I promise I will explain once you have calmed down."

The elf turned her head, eyes narrowing at the darkness behind them. For a long minute, there was only the sound of hooves and talons beating on the ground, and Darya didn't dare talk.

"We will be followed. We *are* being followed," Luunaiwel said with such conviction Darya felt sick, "we cannot ride at full speed in the darkness, and we will need to stop eventually, so I can have a better look at Sara's conditions. They will catch up to us at this rate."

"Luuna-Luunaiwel... why are they doing this?? Was it because of me??? Wha-what are they going to do to me???"

Mismatched eyes met scared hazel, "I sincerely hope we will not find out."

Darya didn't know what to say to that.

"I suppose it is best to head to Mul Tarum now."

Darya's shoulders trembled, "But … you need... you need special paperwork to get into the city, if you're human … Are we... Am I and Sara going to be alright going there? You said you have a friend, but we don't have any paperwork... Well, we *did*, but everything was inside the house, and even if we had them we still don't-"

"Calm down, little bird," Luunaiwel smiled at her, the first time she did since they got away from Flumium, "request for entry will be granted. As long as you are with me."

Luunaiwel sounded as confident as she ever was. Not for the first time, this grounded Darya. Clenching onto her reigns, Darya swallowed around a lump in her throat.

"So, what's the plan?"

"We ride until sunrise. It is not ideal, but we would put some distance between us and whoever is chasing you. We won't make it to Mul Tarum, but we can take refuge by the side of the mountains," Luunaiwel patted the side of her malla's neck, who grunted in response, "Tuura will lead us there. He can see, hear and smell better than any hunting beast."

"Huh, I didn't know that. Guess mallas are pretty awesome, aside from looking majestic and being stronger than horses."

"They are." Luunaiwel smiled, "Not to mention Tuura is one-of-a-kind."

"How come?"

Luunaiwel put a finger to her lips, winking, "All in due time. Now. Tell me more about Sara's conditions, so I might have an idea on how to help her."

"Well," Darya glanced at her sister, face still pale and breaths still shallow, "she's always been sickly since the fire. It's why she's a lot smaller than her age. The physicians we've seen all said she breathed in too much smoke and ash. They think there is something wrong with her throat and lungs, and it would be best to take her somewhere with fresher air."

Moving to Flumium didn't help at all, but they had nowhere else to go.

"I couldn't take her on the road either. She, uh... She would get these attacks? That she can't breathe during them and she would be ... not cough, but wheeze. It's also difficult for her to breathe through her nose sometimes... most of the time, and her nose is always stuffed. It's better today... well, *yesterday*, but usually she has to blow her nose a lot."

Luunaiwel went quiet, thinking. Darya watched her, hopeful.

"There is not much I can do to help your sister now. However, my friend might. We still need to take a rest stop, especially for Sara, discuss what will happen and proceed from there. Sounds good?"

Darya nodded, "Alright... Thanks, Luunaiwel..."

"Anytime, little bird."

There wasn't much conversing after. Darya was exhausted, physically and mentally. Luunaiwel told her to try and catch a nap, she wouldn't let either her or Sara fall. Unfortunately, Darya hadn't trusted herself on horseback yet, plus she was too worried and anxious to sleep. Thank the Gods, Sara hadn't woken up since they left. Darya still didn't know how to talk to her sister about what happened. She wasn't ready to think about it, didn't think she ever would be. So she did her best to ignore all thoughts but counting the time her horse's hooves hit the ground.

Dawn was cold. As much as Darya wanted to keep on riding, she halted to a stop when Luunaiwel did. The elf was right. The mounts needed rest and it would be better for Sara to sleep undisturbed, spell-induced or not.

"You should get some rest too." Luunaiwel told Darya once they laid her sister down on a sleep roll.

"I can't even if I wanted to."

"You will need your strength on the road. Do not be stubborn." But Luunaiwel didn't push her further than that. Darya appreciated it.

The elf checked Sara's pulses, under her eyelids and her mouth. She changed her bandages, wiped down her face and hands, and then bundled Sara up under a travelling blanket.

Through it all, Darya sat on the side, knees curled up under her chin, hugging her legs close.

She felt utterly *useless*.

She hadn't been able to do a thing. Wasn't there when the attack happened. Wasn't there when her family needed her most. She was flouncing around Flumium, without a care in the world.

Oblivious.

But truly, what could Darya possibly have done? These Night's Hand Luunaiwel spoke of, they came to kill. What was she going to do, throw a lute at them? Wave her pathetic dagger around? No, she would have been dead. Just like everyone else.

If it wasn't for Grandmama's quick thinking, then even *Sara* might have been-

"-rya. Darya!"

She snapped back in focus, staring cross-eyed at Luunaiwel's gloved hand, waving in front of her face.

"Oh, sorry. What were you saying?"

The elf sighed, "You need to get some sleep. You look like you might pass out at any moment, and we cannot have that."

Darya looked away, "I won't be able to. If I do, there'll just be nightmares. There won't be any rest."

She could feel Luunaiwel's eyes burning a hole on the side of her head. Darya didn't meet her gaze.

She was surprised when the elf sat down next to her.

"Blaming yourself is not going to change anything."

Darya flinched. A bitter chuckle ripped out of her throat. Luunaiwel was perceptive.

"I'm just... *I don't know,*" Darya said, grinding her heels down at the loose dirt, "I should have been home. I should have suggested you go back with me for dinner *or something,* but I didn't. And this... I don't know... I didn't *think* something like this could have happened!!!"

Luunaiwel tilted her head, "Of course you did not. You *could not have.* No one ever expects to find danger at home."

Darya wanted to say something. To argue that she should have done something. Could have prevented this from happening. Could have been more careful and not talked to that wretched fortune teller.

She buried her forehead into her knees instead. Thoughts wheeled in her mind, mercilessly prodded at her. They kept going round and round, and Darya was certain if she stayed silent any longer, she would turn mad.

"Luunaiwel?"

"Yes?"

"Being a Druid... is dangerous, isn't it?"

A pause.

"It should not be."

"Those people, the Night's Hand, are coming after *me*, aren't they???"

"Yes."

"Why... why do they... What do they want from me?!"

"Darya... I-"

"Please," She snapped her head up, ignoring the hot tears that were streaming down her face, *"please, just tell me!"*

Luunaiwel regarded her for a moment, then sighed, "Being a Druid is not dangerous. Having magic is not dangerous, at least if you know how to use it properly. It is what *other people* want out of you is dangerous."

Fresh tears fell, "H-How? What can they possibly want from *me??* I just *barely* became a Druid, I don't even know how to use a single spell, for crying out loud!"

Luunaiwel shook her head, "I do not think they know. All they might know is that you have magic. Magic can be the most wonderful, but also the most terrible tool in the wrong hands. As those who were born with magic have become so rare after the

Shattering, like all things rare and powerful, they too become desirable."

Darya's whole body froze with terror, "They want... they want to *use me???* But *how???* I don't, I don't *know...*"

"I do not know what they *think* they can do with you either," Luunaiwel said, "it is also very concerning that there are people hunting for magick-users in Flumium."

"Is this... Is this why you don't want me and Caldor to mention you to anyone?"

Luunaiwel nodded, "I am not exactly an unknown entity, unfortunately."

Darya reached out to grab her arm, "Have they been hunting for *you???"*

"They would be stupid to try," something dangerous gleamed in the elf's eyes, but it was gone in a flash, "if you are worried that those people have been following me, then no, I can honestly tell you they have not. They *know of me*, that was certain, but they also know what I am capable of. They do not have the means to deal with me."

The reassurance calmed Darya down some, "Why so secretive then?"

"I am a private person. Besides, if these people are so greedy to chase after a child with but a fleck of magic in her, what do you think they would do to the earth pulses? The glade we visited?"

Darya didn't have an answer to that. She didn't want to think about it.

Luunaiwel's eyes softened, "This is no time to delve too deep into this matter. Our main concern right now is to reach safety and get help for your sister. And for that, you need sleep."

Darya didn't want to argue. After her little outburst, she was absolutely drained. She knew she would fall face-first on the ground if she tried to ride in this condition. So without letting go of Luunaiwel's hand, Darya lay down, snuggling to Sara's side.

Still, she had to ask. Just to be sure.

"Will you still be here when I wake up?"

Luunaiwel's voice was like a song, tinkling against the night's chills, "I vowed to protect you, little bird. Rest well."

Darya let out a breath, keeping the elf's hand over her Heart Stone. Finally, she succumbed to her own exhaustion, letting sleep conquer her aching soul.

CHAPTER 11:

In contrast to her fears, Darya's sleep was peaceful. But Time didn't pause long enough for her to recuperate.

It was Sara's panicked gasping and wheezing that startled Darya awake. Her sister was clutching at her own throat, body taunt as she tried, and failed, to get air into her lungs.

Darya's sleepy haze evaporated instantly.

"Sara!!!"

Luunaiwel had propped Sara upright, but the girl's breathless inhales didn't stop. Bare feet kicked at the ground, scraping up her soles, but Sara didn't, *couldn't* stop, desperate to breathe.

"She needs to calm down," Luunaiwel said, one arm supporting the girl and the other easing Sara's grip, "she will pass out at this rate."

Darya scrambled to her sister, biting back a hiss when Sara's other hand latched onto hers, nails clamping down painfully.

"Sara, Sara! Look at me, Sara!"

Saliva spilled out of her mouth, the girl unable to control the attack. Sara flailed, panicked and helpless.

"Da-haa-Da-haaa-Dary-... haaaaah-can't-haaah-can't-haaa-bre-breatheeee-haaaaaah..."

"I know, sweetheart, I know. Just look at me, Sara. Just look at me! Count to ten. Count in your head with me. Alright, Sara?"

Jerkily, her sister nodded, her grasp on Darya's hand tightening.

"One. Two." She bobbed her head with each number, and felt her own chest easing up when Sara started nodding back.

By five, Sara's gasping slowed down.

By seven, her grip relaxed.

By nine, there weren't any of those horrible, hollowed wheezes in her chest anymore.

As Sara regained her breath, Darya gave in to the tears, and hugged her sister before she could see them.

"You're alright... You're alright, Sara."

Sara hugged her back, huffing into unkempt brown curls. Darya felt Luunaiwel's firm pat on her back before the elf stood up, giving the sisters some privacy.

Sniffling, Darya got her emotions under control, before leaning away.

"You scared me to half-death, you know!"

Sara gave her a tearful smile, voice terribly hoarse, "Sorry…"

Darya took some time to fuss about her sister, wiping off her face and brushing back her hair. Unfortunately, the silence gave Sara the time to have a good look at their surroundings.

"Uhm... Darya? Where are we?"

Always straight to the point, this one... Stumped, Darya's eyes darted to Luunaiwel, who was preparing tea.

"Oh... I…"

"Something happened in Flumium," Luunaiwel's voice was measured, "some bad people caused trouble in your neighbourhood. Your house was destroyed in the process. We did not think it would be safe staying there, so we are going to Mul Tarum."

Sara's head turned from Luunaiwel to Darya, back and forth, shock written all over her face.

"Da-Darya! Why did they-... *Where's Grandmama???* She told me to hide and... *Where is she???*"

The panic in her wide green eyes drove a knife into Darya's heart. Between fearing that Sara would get another attack and the duty to tell her poor sister the truth, Darya's words froze in her mouth. The edges of her vision burned.

"Sara... Sara, I..."

Her hesitation only served to stress Sara more, as the girl clung onto Darya's tunic tightly, pale-faced.

"What, Darya??? Where's Grandmama???"

Darya's answer came out in choked sobs, "She's... Grandmama is gone, Sara... She's... she's *dead,* Sara."

The shock, denial and *pain* in Sara's eyes shattered Darya's heart into pieces.

"No," vehemently, Sara shook her head. Tears streamed down, her eyes petrified in grief, "It... it can't be... Grandmama... Gra-grandmama t-told me t-to... She CAN'T be... No!!!"

Abruptly, Sara stood, struggling to get out of Darya's grip.

"Sara!!! No! Stop!"

"NO!!!! We have to-... We HAVE to come back!!!! D-Da... Darya!!! LET GO!!! LET ME G-GO BA-BACK!!! GRANDMAMA IS... SHE'S WA-WAITING!!!"

Darya couldn't control her own tears anymore. Taking the brunt of Sara's desperate denial was a stab in the gut, and Darya was just tired, *so tired*, she had half a mind to let go.

What kind of granddaughter was she? How dare Darya run? How dare she flee, when this was her fault to begin with? How dare she left Grandmama behind? Along with all the people who had once sheltered and cared for her family?

What kind of person would do this?

They were dead... they were dead because of *Darya.*

With each of Sara's screams, Darya's hold around her slackened further, and she would have let her sister loose if Luunaiwel wasn't there.

"Sara, if you go back there, that would be the last thing your Grandmama wants."

The elf's voice rang clear, despite being just above a whisper, and it was so firm, so *authoritative* that it rendered Sara still for a moment.

"What do YOU know??? You don't know us!!! You don't know Grandmama!!!" Sara cried, struggling futilely in Luunaiwel's iron grip.

But the elf was relentless, "Did your Grandmama not want you to hide? Did she not wish for you to get out of danger and survive?"

"I DON'T CARE!!! I WANT MY GRANDMAMA!!!! LET ME GOOOOO!!!"

And, with that heart-wrenching howl, Sara finally broke down. Loud and keening, she wailed, face skyward and tiny fists curled up by her sides.

It was unfair... So *unfair*...

Trembling, Darya scrambled to her knees, and held onto Sara. Together, they cried. For their poor Grandmama, for their innocent neighbours, for a home where they could never return to.

Bitterly, Darya thought of how she couldn't even give her Grandmama the same meagre burial she gave her parents. How she and Sara couldn't even give Grandmama and the others a proper mourning out here on the run.

It was long before their sobbing died down to sniffles, and Sara's hiccoughs turned to whistling wheezes. The sky was turning to a bleak grey. Despite the trauma they had suffered, time just continually moved forward.

It was unfair... But they still had to move, if they wished to stay alive.

By some feat of miracle, Sara didn't get another attack. Biting down her lip, Darya held her sister's face in her hands, "It's alright, Sara... We're all still together, yes? We've got each other... That's all that matters now, alright?"

Once more, tears came to Sara's eyes, "W-where would we go? Darya... Darya, I don't wanna be on the streets!"

"You won't. We won't." Darya said, but she was unsure. She still had the money with her, thank the Gods, but she didn't know how much it would take to stay in Mul Tarum. Sure, Luunaiwel might help for now, but what about after? Darya couldn't bring Sara on her travels, she had to stay with Sara. Without a job, they wouldn't hold out for long.

"You will not be on the streets. Not when I have any say to that," the elf tilted her head, approaching the sisters with a steaming cup of tea. *Real* tea, not the herb kind that Darya served her back in Flumium.

She put the ceramic cup into Sara's hand, "now, drink this. It will help you stay calm and control your coughs for a while."

"Tha-thank you, Luna."

Luunaiwel smiled down at her, "Anytime. Darya, a word, please?"

Worried, she stood, promising Sara she would be back in a second before following the elf to where the mounts were.

"They will catch up to us soon."

Blood drained from Darya's face, "That fast???"

"They can ride at top speed. Their travel beasts do not have to carry extra weight. They do not have to stop and rest like us," nonchalant, Luunaiwel listed, "Our rest was extended. They will catch us sooner than planned. Definitely before we could reach Mul Tarum."

"But..." Darya turned to look at Sara's shaken form. Her throat tightened.

Darya didn't think she would be able to deal with it. If Sara was in danger... she didn't know if she could deal with it.

"I will fight them off." Luunaiwel said, as if she was talking about chasing off a couple of scavengers.

Squaring up her shoulders, Darya pushed down her fears, and nodded, "Right... Right. What do you want me to do?"

If the elf didn't think they were in too much danger, then there was no reason Darya should lose her mind over it. She must keep her mind clear, so she could protect Sara.

Luunaiwel pointed to the distance, where the slopes of Eria Mountains began, "There are some rock formations for you and Sara to hide behind there. Tie up the horse's reign in case she startles and runs off."

Simple enough. She could do this. Darya could do this at least, "Anything else?"

"Nah," Luunaiwel shrugged, grin glinting with fangs, "you may watch, if you dare."

Her confidence brought a chuckle out of Darya. A bewildered, hysterical chuckle, "You can be such a handful..."

"So I was told. Never curbed my attitudes, unfortunately."

"Why didn't you try and fight them off earlier then? Before we had to run?"

"Ah," Luunaiwel clapped once, smiling, "it is time for a little tactical lesson. One: You never pick a fight with someone so close to their homebase. The possibility of help arriving long before you could win is far too high. Two: You do not want to attract unnecessary attention to yourself. As of now, I believe they only know of your existence, a runaway young Druid, and not of mine. If I fight and kill them, which I will shortly, they will know you are accompanied by someone powerful."

Darya looked down, "Sorry for breaking your anonymity..."

Luunaiwel patted her head, "That is fine, as long as you learn, little bird. Oh, and," her eyes gleamed, both mischievously and viciously, "three: Never reveal your trump card when there could be possible witnesses to inform your next enemy of it."

"Aren't you a treasure trope of surprises?"

"Oh, my dear," Luunaiwel's smirk sent chills down her spine, "you have *no idea.*"

It didn't take much convincing to get Sara onto the horse. In fact, if the situation wasn't so dire, Darya thought Sara would have been more than delighted to be riding for the first time.

"I wish I coulda travelled with you sooner." She said, quietly, but there was a shine in her otherwise dull eyes that had Darya's shoulders felt a tad lighter.

"Believe me, I didn't think I was gonna be able to afford a horse, much less travelling like this."

They reached the mountain side after an hour, but Luunaiwel didn't stop until they came face to face with a field of boulders. Darya was surprised that she recognised this place. It didn't exactly come with a happy memory though. When she was still working at the mines, one of the kids gave her a cruel dare. Stubborn as she was, Darya snuck out and came here on foot, just because the kid said she could have his three days' worth of his pay if she brought back a stone.

Long story short, Darya managed to come here without being lost or killed by wild animals, and brought the stone back only to be told she had no proof of its origin. She got into a brawl, almost got suspended from the mines and was cuffed on the head by Grandmama.

"Hide behind the rocks. Do not make any sound." Luunaiwel told Darya and Sara, leaving her saddlebags with the girls, "in the very unlikely event that someone reaches you... Run. Bring my bags with you to Mul Tarum. Someone will help you there if you tell them my name."

Darya blinked, mildly afraid, "Do you think we will have to run?"

Luunaiwel pretended to ponder on it. Then smirked, "Nah." Before disappearing from sight.

Rolling her eyes, Darya sat down next to Sara. It looked like they would have to wait for a while. Might as well get comfortable.

"Want anything to eat?" She asked Sara, rummaging through her own saddlebags for the leftover rations. It wasn't ideal for Sara to eat something so tough, but it was better than letting the poor kid starve.

Quietly, Sara took a piece of jerky and the water skin from Darya. Instead of eating however, her sister just stared at her lap. Making an educated guess about what might come next, Darya braced herself.

"Darya... Luna isn't really a historian, isn't she?"

Darya grimaced. Of all the questions Sara could have asked...

Darya thought about the secrecy vow. She probably should have cleared it with the elf first about the details... Maybe it would be fine to talk about Luunaiwel to the people who already knew about her existence?

"To be honest? I'm not quite sure," Darya said, opted for a safer route without having to lie to her sister, "knowledgeable as a historian, that's for sure."

Sara seemed to accept that, "She seems... highborn, though. Like a noble. Is she?"

"I... I don't know. We didn't talk about ourselves much on the road." And they didn't. Luunaiwel overheard Darya's past, and everything they talked about on the road was purely for scholarly purposes, along with some combat training.

Sara giggled tiredly, "I bet she's like... a disguised princess or something. Like that story about the princess who fell from the stars she told us."

Darya chuckled at her innocence, "Maybe," then tried to divert the topic, "how are you feeling, Sara?"

Thankfully, her sister took the bait. Unfortunately, it was just another pitfall. Sara looked away, fiddling with the piece of jerky, "I'm alright..."

Darya's heart clenched. She knew exactly where Sara's thoughts were straying.

How could one even deal with this?

She remembered losing her parents. Sara didn't, she was too young to understand. She wasn't there to help bury the dead. Not even Grandmama Clarince was.

Darya remembered crying back then. Howling to the sky like Sara did. Everything happened so fast and so chaotic. They didn't have the time to mourn the dead. They had to move on, or more people would die. Time didn't slow even if everything in one's life was falling apart.

Grandmama Clarince did the best she could with what was given to her to raise Darya and Sara right. She was the one who didn't say a word when Darya kept changing her professions. She was the one who supported Darya when Darya decided that she was going to be a bard. She was the one who sold her wedding ring to get Darya's father's lute fixed for her. She was the one who looked after Sara when Darya was away.

Grandmama Clarince was the pillar of their little world, a constant presence for them to lean on.

And now... she was gone.

"We'll be fine, I promise." How, Darya didn't even know. But for Sara's sake, she had to be strong. Darya was the eldest in the family now. The only one Sara had left. However, another part of Darya knew there wasn't anyone she could rely on. The only thing Darya could do was to trust that Luunaiwel would keep her promises. She didn't know what to do otherwise.

Sara's shaken voice pierced through her laments, "Darya?"

"Yes?"

"We can't go home anymore, can we?"

Seeing the tears forming, Darya gathered her sister into her arms, rubbing small circles into Sara's frail back, "Shhh, shh... It's alright, sweetheart. We'll be fine. I was planning for us to move anyway..."

Clutching at Darya's shirt, Sara sobbed, "To where?? We... we can't go back to Flumium, r-right? A-and I don't... Where is the next town??? I-I don't know! Daryaaaaa!!!"

She wailed. Afraid of Sara getting another attack, and also because Luunaiwel told them to keep quiet, Darya tried her hardest to calm her little sister down. But it was one of those episodes where a kid just had to be a kid, and Sara just needed to let it all out.

And she did. Sara cried herself to exhaustion. Darya only managed to get some water into her before Sara passed out, sniffling in her sleep.

Sighing, Darya covered her sister in her travelling cloak. In a way... this was a mercy for Sara. Wary, she looked to where Luunaiwel disappeared to.

Didn't Luunaiwel say she could watch?

Cautious, Darya wove her way among the rocks, stopping when she had Luunaiwel in sight. The elf was leaning against her Malla, about thirty feet away from where Darya was hiding, humming as she leafed through a book, not a care in the world.

Thank the Gods... nothing happened. Yet.

But not even half an hour later, Darya could see something stirring up dust in the distance. And it was heading towards them.

Heart hammering, Darya curled into herself, making sure she wouldn't be seen before daring to look again. She could just make out the shapes of horses, with men riding on them. As they came closer, Darya counted twenty-five, all hooded with leather armours. They were armed, too.

So this must be the Night's Hand.

Despite vastly outnumbering Luunaiwel, they kept their distance once they arrived. The leader, Darya assumed, rode to the front, shaking his spear menacingly at Luunaiwel.

"Where's the Druid?"

The words shook something within Darya.

Luunaiwel was right. These men... These *murderers...* They were looking for Darya specifically.

Fear, helplessness and anger burned within the young bard. She curled her hand over her Heart Stone, teeth-baring.

How could they???

Meanwhile, Luunaiwel ignored the thug, casually flipped her book to the next page, "Not even a greeting... My, what would your mother say if she knows you treat a lady so crudely?"

The man snarled under his hood, "I'm not gonna ask you twice, wretch!"

The rest of his men banged their spears together, a show of intimidation. Darya flinched where she was hiding, but Luunaiwel merely raised an eyebrow.

"Simmer down, boys. No need to get so worked up over a little girl. Tell you what," she snapped her book close, smiling ear to ear, "I will tell you where she is."

Darya's heart froze.

Luunaiwel wouldn't. *Would she?*

The leader grinned, tacking his horse closer "That's more like it, precious. Whadya say you tell me what you know, and we'll have a lil' fun, eh?"

Luunaiwel's malla growled. The elf clicked her tongue, "Charming. Unfortunately, you are not my type."

Before the leader could react. Before Darya's heart managed to take another beat. Before anyone could see the elf moving a muscle …

The leader's head dropped to the ground, rolling in the dirt with a fine spray of blood. His body followed, sliding off the saddle with a foot still stuck in a stirrup. Luunaiwel calmly wiped the blood off her naked blade on the headless body.

Nobody dared to breathe.

His horse reared in fear. Luunaiwel slapped its rump, sending it running with its master's corpse dragging behind it.

"Anyone else would like to try?"

Breaking out of their shock, the rest of the men roared, charging at Luunaiwel with their spears out. Rolling under the deadly points, she slid on the ground, both blades out, and sliced off the hooves of two passing horses, sending them and their riders to the ground. The elf skidded behind their lines, disappeared from Darya's sight for a heart-stopping moment, before she leapt, not giving her assailants any time to turn and brought one sword down into one of them, piercing him from skull to chest.

Yelling, the men drew their own swords. Luunaiwel jumped away before any of the weapons could touch her, landing behind them gracefully.

"And you called yourselves Night's Hand. What a shame. Your people used to make better." She taunted, eyes gleaming in the sun.

Luunaiwel was toying with these men. Just like with the Gargantuan.

The ruffians didn't take kindly to that, cursing. Instead of pressing her attacks, Luunaiwel waited for them to turn their horses. Her lips quirked up with a vicious grin as they charged her again, and called.

"Tuura. Now."

The malla let out a deep below, flailed his hooves and charged at the men's rears.

Darya couldn't believe her eyes.

At the last moment, before Tuura collided with the hunters, the Malla *changed.* Fur and scales shifted into skin. Talons into hands. Horns retracted into a rounded skull. The beast became a man that was as large as a bear and just as gruff with a wild auburn mane of hair and golden eyes. Clad in leather armours, his fists were covered with claw-like blades, shredding two unsuspecting men into ribbons. They screamed as the giant man, *Tuura,* tore them apart, sending gore flying.

Formation broken at the unexpected enemy, the men panicked. One tried to ride away, but Luunaiwel flung herself at him, splitting him in half from shoulder to abdomen.

It was a bloodbath.

Tuura was deceptively fast for his frame, and his strength was incredible, as he easily knocked over a horse on its track and tearing its rider straight out of the saddle. Luunaiwel's carnage wasn't any less brutal. Unlike with the Gargantuan, where she aimed to cause as much damage as possible before killing it outright, anyone who came close enough died in one strike. She attached and detached from her victims with vicious efficiency, swords faster than lightning, stained with blood and severed life from every man they touched.

The ground turned crimson, and the only ones moving were Luunaiwel and Tuura. Outnumbered twenty-five to two, and still they were *crushed.*

"This is bad." Tuura spoke, voice like distant thunder, rumbling and deep in his chest. Luunaiwel cleaned her swords on one of the dead men's cloaks, shrugging.

"Everything is bad nowadays, my dear. The child is alive, that is most important," mismatched eyes turned where Darya was hiding, "You may come out now."

And she did, shakily so. The sight alone was horrible to look at. It was like a butcher shop turned inside out, and the smell was nauseating. Seeing this... it was more nightmare-inducing than any story Darya had heard. Not even the Withered was as scary. They were monsters, after all and these... they were *humans.*

If she didn't witness the whole thing, Darya wouldn't have believed that this was caused by just two people. Well, an elf and *whatever* Tuura was.

Twenty-five men pursued them. Only scraps of them remained.

Not for the first time, Darya was incredibly glad that Luunaiwel was on her side.

CHAPTER 12:

"Where are my manners," Luunaiwel said, smiling as she wiped off the blood on her cheek, "Tuura, Darya. Darya, Tuura Earthenclaw. Wild-walker and Shapeshifter extraordinaire."

Hesitantly, Darya took the man's offered hand, mindful of the curved claw-blades, "Uh... Pleased to meet you..."

"Charmed," he said, unsmiling but his amber eyes twinkled kindly, "I'm sorry that our official introduction was done in such poor circumstances."

At a loss for words, Darya shrugged. In favour of ignoring the bloodied mess around them, she inspected Tuura.

He was tall. Taller than Luunaiwel, and she must be over six foot four. Tuura looked like he was made out of pure muscles. His arms were like slabs of stone, left bare with his sleeveless leather armour. Scars dotted his skin, and there was a crude mark, almost tattoo-like, on his left upper arm in the shape of a paw. With square jaws and high cheekbones, he must be quite handsome under his unkempt beard. His auburn hair, the same colour as his malla form's fur, was just as wild as his beard, with small braids woven into it and decorated with stone beads.

Normally, Darya would have bombarded Tuura with so many questions, he would run out of breath explaining. But she was in too much shock to utter beyond an awkward hum. Luunaiwel's prodding of the mangled corpses with her boot did not help whatsoever.

Eyes prickling, Darya looked away before her control slipped and let go of what little left in her belly.

"I was right," she heard the elf said, "they were Night's Hand."

"Do they bear the mark?" Asked Tuura.

"That they do," Luunaiwel spat, "we should get moving. Their remains will be found soon. And they will come back with more."

Tuura nodded at Darya once, and shifted back to a malla. The transition was like a ripple of water, a seamless blend from human to beast. Like a mirage appeared to weary travellers on the wide barrens, Tuura reared, kicking up dust and shaking his mane under sharp sunlight. It made Darya question her own sanity, if what she saw was an illusion her jaded mind made up.

Then she glanced at battered bodies on blood-darkened soil, and the wonder shattered. Shaken, Darya ran after Luunaiwel towards the rocks, to pack and saddle up.

Thankfully, Sara slept through all the noises, being so used to all the rumbles back in Flumium. She woke briefly to ask what they were doing, but didn't have any other questions when they rode off, to a different direction of the carnage, thank the Gods.

Only after an hour of riding did Darya find her voice.

"So he's not really a malla?"

Tuura snorted under Luunaiwel, prompting the elf to laugh. "No. No he is not. Tuura is a shapeshifter, one who bears the Gift of the Wild. He can change to certain animals at will."

"Is that magic too? What he does, I mean."

"Yes and no," Luunaiwel tilted her head from side to side, "he does not use magic, unlike what magi and druids do. His abilities were blessed into his bloodline, which originated from elven-kin, and manifested when he called upon it. Shapeshifters have always been a bit of an enigma even to the most learned, you see, for they are an example of wild and natural magic anomalies."

"Alright, alright," Darya waved a hand at the elf, "I'm sure if you try to explain it any more right now, my brain would explode."

"We would not want that." Luunaiwel said, all smiles.

Darya sighed, "He's that trump card of yours, isn't he?"

"That he is," Luunaiwel patted the side of Tuura's neck fondly, "and the less people know about him, the better. Speaking of which, he will shift to his human form when we near Mul Tarum's gates. The dwarves do not know he is a Shapeshifter, and I would like to keep it that way."

This got Darya a bit wary, "Would I have to make another secrecy vow?"

"No, unless you want to."

"I think I have enough of that for a lifetime, thanks. I don't fancy my throat being ripped out by thorns, thank you very much."

Luunaiwel laughed, the sound chiming like silver bells, "My apologies. The penalty for breaking the vow was simple asphyxiation. I took the liberty to add some creative flares, so you would keep your mouth shut."

Darya gasped, shocked beyond words, "Argh! That gave me nightmares, you arse!"

"And I apologise, yet again," Luunaiwel grinned, not at all sorry, "to be fair, the end result would still be death."

"Yes, but being strangled to death is still a less horrifying image!"

Mischief twinkled in mismatched eyes, "Truly."

"Just for that, you should remove the vow for me!"

"Well, I would not remove it just for some harmless jest," Luunaiwel hummed, much to Darya's chagrin, "however, I did not consider that you would travel with me when the vow was formed."

"I don't think either of us did." Darya huffed, a hand coming up to touch her Heart Stone out of instinct.

Luunaiwel chuckled, "I do suppose it is alright. I will lift the vow for you, as many in Mul Tarum know me. I do not want you to needlessly die due to my own carelessness."

Pulling out the blue ribbon used on their vow from inside her cloak, she tore it in half. The elf pocketed one strip, and put the other to her lips.

"Child of Thorns, heed my words. The Vow is lifted, for Darya. First Druid of the Shattered Age, Sister of Sara."

The ribbon darkened in her hand, turned black then ashen, before dissipating into the wind. Luunaiwel winked at Darya, "It is done. I would still like you to refrain from gossiping about me to strangers, however."

Feeling a huge weight was lifted off her chest, Darya shook her head, "Trust me, I won't be talking to strangers for a while."

Before they went past the low slope of mountains to reach Mul Tarum's gate, Tuura shifted back to his human form. Darya slowed her horse to a trot, so everyone could keep the same pace. Besides, with the danger gone for now, she would rather not have to rush.

To fill the silence between them, but also out of curiosity, Darya asked, "Luunaiwel, why didn't you use magic to deal with the men back there?"

"Because I did not want anyone to know there was another magick-user with you. Using magic sometimes leaves a residue in the elements at the place where it is used, and that can be picked up using certain methods. Not that many knew how to do it, but better safe than sorry."

Darya blinked at the elf's toothy grin, "I'm not sure if you are just paranoid, or you did that because you wanted to... uh, *get physical* with them."

With a hand on her chest, Luunaiwel mocked a gasp, "My, I would never!"

Darya rolled her eyes, "Whatever... They deserved it. I just hope they won't come after us again."

"They will. And it is not just to capture you. On our next encounter, revenge will be added to the list."

Not knowing how to respond, Darya looked away, her stomach churning. With fear, yes, but also anger and frustration.

She didn't ask for any of this, she didn't ask to be a Druid in the first place. But it was already done. The moment Darya decided to follow Luunaiwel's cloaked silhouette in Edurn, she had set something beyond her imagination into motion. She couldn't stop it now. Not as she was.

"I need to become a proper Druid."

Luunaiwel quirked up an eyebrow, "Rather early to make up your mind, no?"

"Maybe," Darya rubbed her face, tired, "but I can't stop being a Druid, can I? And I'd rather not have to rely on you or someone else when those people show up again. Not that I'm being ungrateful!"

Luunaiwel gestured for her to continue. Darya sighed.

"But I was thinking... I was helpless when they attacked. Yes, I wasn't there, but even if I was, there would be absolutely nothing I could have done. Mortia be my witness, I would have been captured, or worse! And then you wouldn't know anything until it's too late."

"You want to grow stronger then?"

Swallowing back dread, Darya nodded, "Yes. I know you said Druids aren't supposed to be on the front line and aggressive, but... I'd like to be able to defend myself at least."

Darya knew she could be slow, but she wasn't stupid. There was no telling if Luunaiwel would stick around after she fulfilled her part of the vow, whenever that might be. Luunaiwel could get tired of running, as she and Tuura were perfectly capable of handling themselves. Luunaiwel could easily decide that tomorrow or the next week Darya would have completed her first cycle of training, whatever that was, and dropped her in the middle of nowhere with Sara.

After all … the terms of the vow weren't as clear as Darya initially thought.

Still, Luunaiwel had done enough. If anything, Darya was the one interrupting Luunaiwel's quest. Darya definitely wasn't on equal terms with the elf. If they parted ways, there was no possibility of Darya surviving on her own.

"Alright," Luunaiwel said, "I shall see what I can do."

Darya smiled weakly, "Thanks. Looks like I owe you another one."

"Anytime, little bird. Ah, look," the elf grinned, gesturing ahead, "Mul Tarum, as I live and breathe."

There it was, the Gates to the great dwarven city under the mountains. Built against the Eria Mountains' southernmost tip, the gates were at least a hundred feet tall. Even at this distance, they looked seamless, like they were parts of the rocks. Smooth, symmetrical and imposing, they were simple in design, with thick runes carved into a sharp arch above the entrance, and two great dwarf statues guarding each side. Shields, round and polished to perfection, lined the statues' bases, gleaming in the late sun.

The ground under their feet slowly transitioned into a cobbled path, leading to a stone bridge over a ravine before the gates. There were eight guards posted, four on each side, all armoured in metal and armed with great axes. Their beards were all squarely cropped, and their hair braided tightly against their skulls.

"Halt," one called, voice rough under his helm, "who goes there?"

Luunaiwel looked up at Darya, winked, "Watch this."

She stepped forward, and flipped her hood down. Instantly, all eyes widened.

"Lady Luunaiwel! By me beard," a dark-haired dwarf shouted, waving his axe enthusiastically at her, "you're back! And Lord Earthenclaw, too!"

The elf laughed, shaking forearms with the guard, "Earlier than expected, Kilund."

"Aye. The Lord Whitestone'd be excited to hear yer return! And ye have company," Kilund said, leaning back so he could look up at Darya and Sara, "humans, eh?"

Luunaiwel chuckled, "Yes, they are. These girls are Darya and Sara. They come seeking asylum from the Great Halls of Mul Tarum."

"Ah, business as always," another dwarf eyed the sisters over his crooked nose, "no paperwork, I assume?"

"None unfortunately, Dali."

Dali nodded, pulling out a scroll from his belt and jolted something down, "Will you and company be staying at your quarters, m'lady?"

Luunaiwel gave him a charming smile, "I was hoping to bring them to Nathi."

"A'ight," Dali jolted down another few words, "anything else, m'lady?"

"That would be it for now, thank you."

"Of course, of course. SÍR!!!" He turned around, bellowed at the other side of the bridge and almost startled Darya off her saddle.

A blonde dwarf rushed over, eyes narrowing at the girls, huffing, "Aye?"

Dali shoved the scroll into his hand, "Bring this inside to Muira. Notify the Lord Whitestone and family, as well."

Sír saluted, waddled back past the bridge and entered the mountain through a side entrance. With that done, Dali pulled out a pouch, and gave Luunaiwel two metallic badges, each stamped with a rune.

"These are for them," then sternly told Darya, "now don't lose these, else you'll be in trouble, a'ight? They prove your visitor statuses, and don't get into any trouble, hear me?"

Gulping, Darya nodded, "Yessir!"

"A'ight," Dali turned back to Luunaiwel, saluting her, "great to see you again, m'lady. May your business be fruitful and journey safe."

"And yours. Thank you, Dali." Luunaiwel returned the gesture, then led their entourage over the bridge.

Darya was a bit disappointed that the Gates didn't open for them to enter. Instead, they went through the same side entrance Sír did. She guessed it would have been too complicated to open such giant doors every time a visitor came.

What she got to see inside more than made up for it, though.

Darya understood why the gates were so tall now. They were to scale with the buildings inside, constructed against the walls under the mountains, floor level to a ceiling so high she got dizzy just looking at it. The buildings were hexagonal, stacked together and buzzing with life. Even at first glance, Darya knew this was the main street, as the ground floors were all businesses. Shops with see-through walls that reflected the firelights off blazing braziers, services bustling with throes of clients, stalls with lines that could pack a Flumium bridge. The roads here were wide and clean, with streams of people browsing goods. Nobody seemed to mind Darya's company, despite how strange their group must look. Dwarves, the stocky bearded people, were always so busy, always having something to do or somewhere to be, they had no time to glance at passers-by.

"Wow..." So entranced by the sight before her, Darya didn't realise Sara had woken up, and she too was mesmerised.

"I know, right?" Darya said, still dazed.

"Welcome to Mul Taurum." Luunaiwel said, sounding smug.

Luunaiwel led them to a grand communal stable. A clean-shaven dwarf took Darya's horse reins when she dismounted and gave her a tag.

"One silver for one night. Two for three." He said. Darya gave him two, figuring they would be staying here for a while.

It took a bit of convincing to pry Sara away from the mallas' rounded pen. She insisted that she could walk, she did have lots of sleep after all. Though reluctant, Darya agreed, as long as they were holding hands and Sara promised to say something if she was getting tired.

From there, Luunaiwel brought them to what looked like a series of one-storied cube rooms, and a small line of dwarves standing in a queue in front of each. Before Darya could ask Luunaiwel what was going on, something happened that made both Darya and Sara drop their jaws.

A few of the rooms started *floating*, going up against the wall slowly. *With people inside of them!*

Arm flailing, Darya grabbed Luunaiwel's hand, "Wha- *what in the Gods' names are those???"*

The elf chuckled, herding them to a line, "They call it a lift. Do you see those metal bars and markings on the walls?"

Darya nodded, still in shock, "Uh-huh?"

"To put it simply, the rooms are attached to the bars, where an intricate net of steel wires are hidden and lead to a floor under us. These wires are pulled by mules. The markings on the walls are doors to a specific floor in the mountain, and only open when the lifts arrive due to safety reasons. This makes travelling in-between mountain floors much faster. Each floor is where a hall is built, catered to each of its residences' careers and purposes. The one we just came from was the Merchant Hall."

"Uh-huh..."

Darya was sceptical when it was their turn to step into one of those "lifts". Despite their size differences compared to the dwarves, she was surprised that the lift room was pleasantly accommodative. Even Tuura didn't have to crouch.

Once the door was closed, Luunaiwel rang a bell in a corner once. Gasping when she felt the room was moving *up*, Darya clutched at Sara, who giggled at her.

Darya decided very quickly she liked her feet planted on the ground.

When it finally stopped, Darya stumbled out into steady stone floor with much relief.

All the lifts led to a narrow room, which had a single entrance where another eight guards were posted. Similar to at the Gates, these guards greeted Luunaiwel and Tuura with much enthusiasm, and were happy to let them all through once Darya presented them the badges.

The Hall they entered wasn't as vast as the Merchant Hall. Not to say it wasn't breath-taking, though.

The buildings were standard but bigger than those in Flumium, and built out of stone slabs. The ground under their feet was uneven, with pebble-lined roads that led through a network of streets, lit by glowing lamps. The ceiling was unpolished, with huge, glittering stalactites hanging from above, basking the entire Hall in a pleasant dimming light. Fewer people wandered here, all dwarves, quiet but just as focused in their own business as everyone Darya had seen here so far.

"This is the Scholar Hall," Luunaiwel explained, as they climbed up a winding hill, "the person who can help us lives here."

Exchanging a look, Darya and Sara picked up their speed, eager to have a rest after the recent trauma.

They came to a stop before a three-story residence, made of red and grey stone, with a huge marbled front yard that was decorated with a grand, honest-to-good fountain with running, clean water. Luunaiwel pushed open the decorative iron-wrought gate and ushered them all to stand before the house's door.

She knocked three times. The door burst open before the elf could step back.

"Lulu! Yer lil' shite!" A dwarf boomed, his accent thick, throwing his arms around Luunaiwel's legs.

Luunaiwel laughed, crouching down to return the hug, "It is good to see you too, Brother."

Brother??? Darya blinked at the fiery-haired dwarf, whose language grew progressively fouler and fouler as he thumped the elf's arm.

Seemed like Luunaiwel wasn't done with her surprises today.

CHAPTER 13:

After the loud and explicit greetings, Darya didn't expect to be seated at the ginger dwarf's dining table, waiting for a meal with Sara as Luunaiwel rummaged through the pantry. Without really introducing himself, the dwarf had snapped something about how they came at a terrible time, and he was having patients, so they should get their "arses to the kitchen and wait there".

Like all things Darya had seen so far in Mul Tarum, the dwarf's furniture was made of stone and marble. The chairs were a bit low, but had cushions made of the finest fabric Darya had ever touched and so plush she could sleep sitting up. The table and fireplace mantle were decorated with beautiful, shiny pieces of decorative... *something*, where small white sticks flickered with fire. On one of the walls there was a large family painting of dwarves, too many to count and...

Unmistakable with a scar running down her face and mismatched blue and green eyes, Luunaiwel stood at the edge of the painting, towering above all the dwarves with a radiant smile.

She did call the dwarf here her "brother", but Darya didn't think that it was in a literal sense!

The sounds of plates being placed on the table broke Darya out of her thoughts, "You must forgive Nathi. He gets carried away easily." Luunaiwel said, giving Tuura, Darya and Sara each a fork and an empty plate.

The elf had put out quite a spread for them. Darya's mouth watered at the sight. There were cut ham and sausages, some cured meat that smelled *divine*, cheese chunks of many kinds, several small breads and pickled vegetables. The sisters were also given two flagons of purplish red liquid, almost like wine but didn't smell alcoholic.

"Sindri is not home yet, so we will have to deal with ration food for now," Luunaiwel sat down, the chair and table clearly too low for her but her smile was unwavering, "what are you waiting for? Dig in!"

Tentatively, Sara went for the flagon first. Upon the first sip, she let out a squeal of delight, and promptly chugged like a blacksmith at a tavern. Mildly concerned, Darya tried the drink too, and it took all her willpower to not copy Sara. The drink was sweet and tangy, filling her with so much *joy* she didn't know how to describe it.

Thankfully, they had Luunaiwel, "It is a blackberry and honey drink, one of the most popular beverages here, not counting anything alcoholic. Fermented berries in sealed jars, diluted in water. Add a touch of honey, and we have the famous mountainberry juice!"

"Wow," Sara breathed, having parted from the drink long enough to look at it like it was some godly revelation, "what's a honey?"

"Ah, I keep forgetting that they do not have bees on the surface anymore," Luunaiwel smiled, pushing forward a clear jar with an amber-coloured liquid inside, "this is honey. It is produced by bees, a type of insects, by collecting nectar from flowers."

She gave them a bit on their fingers to taste. Darya's eyes widened, "It's so sweet!"

"And delicious," Sara chimed in, sucking her finger, "can't believe a bug made this!"

"Yes," Luunaiwel pointed to the flickering flames all around them, "they also produce wax, which is then made into candles. They burn much slower and emit less toxic fumes than oil lamps, torches or coal. Perfect for an indoor light source. The holders are called candelabras."

Both Sara and Darya made the appropriate appreciative noises, before Luunaiwel pushed a plate of meat to them, "This is honeyed ham."

They didn't need more invitation than that. The food was *glorious*, the best Darya and Sara had tasted their entire life. The sisters ate like ravenous beasts compared to Luunaiwel's dainty bites and Tuura's rather proper pace. The two adults looked amused as the two girls polished everything in front of them in record time.

However, Sara had a slight problem after consuming two flagons of mountainberry juice.

"I need to goooo..." She whined, clutching at her belly. Luunaiwel chuckled.

"The outhouse is to the left of the backyard, on the left against the mountain wall. Can you manage by yourself?"

"Yep! Thank you, Luna!" And rushed away.

Bemused, Luunaiwel shook her head and pushed herself away from the table, stretching with a sigh. Darya also leaned back and felt her muscles uncurl. This had been a much needed break.

Unfortunately, the comfortable silence soon turned stale. The vicious cycle in Darya's mind turned back to the inevitable.

Sara was safe and fed. It was difficult to imagine what happened in Flumium would occur here, in a fortress under the mountain. They were safe. Yet, at the same time, it was hard to accept what happened. It was hard to think that they were alone in the world now. It was hard to think that they could never return to Flumium, to never pick up the pieces of what they left behind.

The inside of Darya's mouth turned bitter. Her lute was there in the debris, too. Left behind, just like Grandmama.

Darya shuddered when tears dropped onto the back of her hands.

Why did it have to be like this?

Stubbornly, she wiped her face. She had to be strong right now. Be strong for Sara, at least. Darya could wallow later, when she found the space to be alone.

She was startled when Luunaiwel made her way around the table. The elf stood at arm's reach, but not touching.

"How are you holding up?"

"Not good." Darya looked away. She didn't want to talk. She wanted to lash out, but knew that she shouldn't. Luunaiwel *didn't deserve it* after everything she had done for her and...

Darya didn't know she was crying until Luunaiwel pulled her into a hug. A sob ripped out of her. Her heart felt like it was shattered into a million pieces. It was only Luunaiwel's arms that anchored her and held her together.

The Heart Stone pulsed, soothing, calming... Darya placed a hand over it, clutching at her chest.

There was the sound of the door opening and closing. Exhausted and heartsick, Darya buried her face into Luunaiwel's armoured abdomen. With a shuddering breath, she sucked in her tears, willed her heart to stop trembling, wiped her face and turned to face Sara.

"Feeling better?" Darya asked, keeping her face neutral.

Nodding, Sara shyly kept her hands behind her back, "Mmhmm. Thanks for the meal, Luna."

"Anytime, little one. Now, let us go see Nathi, yes? He can have a look at your condition, and perhaps help you with it."

That strengthened the resolve within Darya, "Let's."

Luunaiwel took them through a small corridor that was carpeted with fibre so soft Darya had the urge to take her shoes off, and into a room double the size of the dining room. There, Nathi was sitting behind a grand marble desk, scribbling something on a long piece of parchment. Around him, each wall was fitted with great rows of shelves. There were so many books and tomes in this room, Darya bet it could make the Monks in Flumium grow green with envy.

Unlike the guards they spoke to, Nathi boasted a full, luxurious beard, impressively decorated with braids and golden beadings. The braids were carefully connected into a net over his chest, falling just above his waist. His hair was knotted neatly behind his skull, practical but elegant. The dwarf had removed his dirty apron, showing an impeccable sky blue robe, lined with gold fabric and trimmed with embroidered runes. He wore silk slippers, inlaid with stones the same colour of his eyes. And if Nathi's attire didn't speak for his social status, his straight back and unwavering gaze did the rest. He was barely above four feet, but the way he carried himself made Darya feel he was taller than her.

"Busy, as always, brother." Luunaiwel said, smirking at the dwarf.

"Some of us have ta work while yer out there, frolicking 'round," Nathi waved his quill menacingly at the laughing elf, then turned his bright blue eyes to Darya, "bah, sorry, lassies, I completely forgot ta introduce meself. I'm Nathi Sigurðrson of the Whitestone Clan, pleased ta meet ye."

Darya smiled, and went to shake his hand, "The pleasure's mine. I'm Darya, and this is my sister Sara. Thank you for letting us into your home and... uh... thanks for the food..."

She said the last bit bashfully. Luunaiwel laughed, "We helped ourselves."

Nathi laughed too, patting Darya's elbow, "Bah, don't worry about it! I'm sorry I can't give ya a hot meal taday, but stick around! Me wife Sindri would love ta meet ye!"

Luunaiwel chuckled along, but her expression quickly turned neutral, inclining her head at Sara, "We might have a need for your expertise, by the way."

Nathi barked out a laugh, "Ha! Since when do ye *not* need me expertise," then beckoned Sara over, "how do ye do, lil' lassie?"

Intimidated, Sara looked up at Darya for approval before hesitantly making her way over to Nathi's desk.

"I'm... uh... I'm alright?"

"She has a condition." Luunaiwel chimed in, taking over the conversation much to Darya's relief, and listed off Sara's symptoms, word by word.

Twirling a braid in his beard, Nathi nodded when Luunaiwel was done, "Aye. I've had patients like her. Now, let's see what yer vitals are like..."

Wordlessly, Tuura pushed out a chair for Sara.

"Aye. As I thought," Nathi hummed after a moment, then scribbled something down to another piece of parchment, "I'll need ta get a couple o' things from the Haven Hall."

Darya's anxiety reared its ugly head, "Is she alright?? We haven't been able to take her to a physician last year, so I don't know if she's gotten worse or not..."

"It's a'ight, lassie." Nathi patted her shoulder reassuringly, and rolled up the parchment, "Her condition's absolutely treatable. Ain't goin' ta be quick, but treatable."

A breath of relief sucked out of her chest. "Tha-thank you, Nathi! Thank you so much! Uh... how much do I owe you?"

"Bah! Nonsense! Yer came in here with me sister! If Lulu's willing ta take someone ta me, then that someone's a guest, and a guest ain't goin' ta pay a dime!"

Darya's eyes widened, "Re-really? But..."

"You will still have to pay for the medicines," Luunaiwel said, "but Nathi's diagnosis and treatments will be free of charge."

Tears sprang to Darya's eyes, "I don't know how I can ever thank you," she grabbed Luunaiwel's gloved hands, squeezing, "thank you. So much. For everything. I really mean it."

Luunaiwel smiled, "I believe you, little bird. Now, would you like to visit the Haven Hall? I promise, it is nothing like you have ever seen in your life."

Drying her face with a sleeve, Darya grinned wetly, "Everything you've shown me is like nothing I've ever seen in my life. I'll take your word for it. Let's go!"

"I wanna go too!" Sara, who had been quiet this whole time, jumped out of her chair. But then a sudden string of coughs forced her to sit back down, holding her chest. Darya immediately came to rub circles into her back.

"I think this has been enough excitement for you in one day." Darya said once the coughing subsided. Sara pouted, but didn't argue.

"It's a'ight, lil' lass," Nathi assured her as he poured a cup of water for Sara, "with yer condition, it'd be best ta move ye ta the Haven Hall anyway. Ye will see it soon. Just not taday."

Though still rather sulky, Sara wasn't pouting anymore, "Alright."

"Good lass," Nathi chuckled, "I'll show ye ta yer guestroom. Ye can have a rest there."

Seeing that Nathi had the situation handled, Darya thanked the dwarf once more, told Sara to behave, and followed Luunaiwel out, Tuura in tow.

"I want to get some fresh honey." He said. Luunaiwel chuckled.

"You just want to avoid dealing with Sindri alone when she gets back."

Rolling his great shoulders, Tuura offered Luunaiwel a small smile, "Can you blame me?"

"Why are you avoiding Sindri?" Curious, Darya asked as they started down the street.

"Sindri is a Master Seamstress," Luunaiwel explained, smirking, "she is incredibly talented, and is especially excited whenever someone visits. *Especially* when that someone has a body size and proportion different from her usual customers."

Darya made a noise of understanding, "So she would basically measure and pin everything she can find on Tuura when she sees him?"

Tuura grimaced, "Unfortunately."

Luunaiwel patted his forearm, laughing, "My dear, I am afraid it is a bit too late for you. She does have all your measurements already, and the moment she knows we are here, she would have something offered to us, already prepared during our absence."

Groaning, Tuura shook his mane of hair, "I don't see the appeal, honestly. While Sindri is an incredible seamstress, her garments aren't enchanted, and would be ruined if I shift. It's a waste."

Mischief sparkled in Luunaiwel's eyes, "Saying that would only pose a further challenge for her, and she would be even more insistent for you to try on more of her clothing."

Tuura made a pained noise. Darya giggled, "You should be happy. I'd kill to get a new set of clothes. There are entirely too many holes and patches on mine."

"You might just get your wish," Luunaiwel said, "Sindri would be happy to have you and your sister draped in her clothes."

Startled, Darya flailed her arms, "Oh, no... She shouldn't! I'm already indebted enough to all of you! I can't take anything else for free!"

"Relax," Luunaiwel chuckled, "sometimes, it is healthy to receive kindness along the way. Besides, it is unlikely that clothing you and treating Sara would hurt Nathi's household in any way. Sindri owns a successful business, and Nathi's head of clan is one of the Nine Hammers that run dwarfish society. He is a Lord, and also one of the Last Healing Hands Under the Mountains."

Darya's eyes almost popped out of their sockets, "He's... he's a *Lord???*"

"A Junior one," Luunaiwel grinned wolfishly, like it was a joke Darya didn't understand, "his uncle is one of the Hammers."

"Huh..." Darya said, dazed. A Lord … And she thought Luunaiwel was just making that up like the rest of her cover story.

To think that Darya would ever be in the presence of a Lord, and staying at the house of one!

That aside however, she needed to convince them to stop treating her like a charity case. While it was nice to not worry about money, it wasn't a great feeling knowing that she was indebted to someone and would be unable to repay the favours. Even though Darya was sure neither Luunaiwel nor Nathi thought of it that way, she didn't want to get used to the habit of expecting everything to be free. She certainly didn't want Sara to have that impression of the world either.

While Darya was busy with her thoughts, Luunaiwel led them to another lift, this one much higher than the last and didn't have much of a queue. Darya gulped, looking up the seemingly endless vertical wall, cutting off abruptly from the natural cavern ceiling in the Scholar Hall.

"Do these ever... fall?"

Luunaiwel's smirk made Darya immediately regret her question, "Not too often these days. There were a lot of accidents back when they were experimenting with the prototypes. But these are safe. Mostly."

Despite knowing Luunaiwel was messing with her, Darya grimaced, "Thanks. That really boosts my confidence."

Luunaiwel's tinkling laughter echoed ominously in the cavernous Hall. There too was a bell inside this lift, and a bronze plaque below it with a series of runes. Luunaiwel rang the bell three times. Shuddering, Darya braced herself, feeling the contraption ambling upward. The sound of rumbling stone on metal grated on her already frayed nerves, making her squirm in discomfort.

"Can't this thing go any faster?" She found herself asking. Luunaiwel shook her head.

"Any faster, and the tension cords would snap."

"I don't like it any more than you do," Tuura nodded at Darya solemnly, "but this is much faster than climbing stairs."

He made a fine point. With the size of each Hall in Mul Tarum, and the height of Eria Mountains at some peaks, it would probably take days to get from one place to another without these lifts.

It didn't mean Darya had to like them any better, though. Life before, she was the first to burst out when they stopped, heaving a little. Any longer, and she would have lost her stomach.

As with the Scholar Hall, these lifts also led to a narrow room with one entrance. However, this room was better-guarded, with a group of sixteen dwarf guards, and another at a table before the point of entry, all heavily armed. Like the others, they recognised Luunaiwel and Tuura right away, but weren't as jovial.

"Lady Luunaiwel, Lord Tuura," The sitting dwarf greeted, "welcome back to the Great Halls of Mul Tarum. May I ask your purpose of visiting Haven Hall?"

Luunaiwel inclined her head, "Greetings, Bork. I am here on behalf of Lord Nathi Sigurðrson, to pick up some ingredients for his patient. Here is the list."

The dwarf took the list from her, skimming through the words before returning it, "What about the human girl?"

"A guest. Her relatives are being treated by Lord Sigurðrson."

Bork turned to Darya, "Very well. May I see your paperwork?"

Darya her badge on the table, "Here, sir."

Carefully, Bork inspected the rune, "Ah, Lady Luunaiwel, this badge is only valid for general entry and does not cover the Haven Hall. We cannot let the girl through."

Luunaiwel tapped her chin, thoughtful, "Hmmm... I understand, I forgot about the procedure."

Bork nodded, "It has been a while since you've last taken a guest to Mul Tarum."

Despite the disappointment, Darya smiled at Luunaiwel, "It's alright, Luunaiwel. I can wait outside."

Luunaiwel raised a hand to stop her. Speaking to Bork, "Is there anything you can do?"

"Well... This is rather unorthodox, as the girl is human, but I do suppose I can make an exception," Bork hauled up a leather bound tome from under his desk, so big it was almost the size of Darya's torso, "this is the visitor list. Since your guest does not have a relative or friend staying inside the Haven Hall, she would have to pay an entry fee for insurance. I assume she will be paying for the items taken outside as well?"

Luunaiwel confirmed this. Bork jolted down a few runes on a page, "Perfect. The end payment will be subtracted to this fee, and the remaining balance will be returned to her in three days should there be no regulation violation. Is she staying with the Lord Sigurðrson and family?"

"That is correct."

Darya felt they were skimming over some important information, "Sorry, but how much is the fee?"

"Fifty silvers."

To her credits, Darya only *almost* screamed, *"Fifty silvers???"*

"They will be refunded once we finish our business." Luunaiwel assured her, but Darya couldn't stop reeling.

That would be half a gold!!!

Completely ignoring Darya's reaction, Bork nodded at the elf and wrote down something else before turning the tome to Luunaiwel, "Please read through and sign if you agree to the terms. The girl needs to sign below your signature."

Luunaiwel signed her name with flourishing elegance. When she passed Darya the quill, the elf whispered, "You need to see this. Sign."

Feeling like she was cutting off her own arm, Darya numbly scrawled under Luunaiwel's name. She counting each coin sullenly, before surrendering them to a small pouch Bork held out for her. He marked it with a tag similar to the one down at the stables and gave Darya a copy.

Satisfied with the procedure, Bork saluted, "May your business be fruitful and journey safe."

On the other side of the doors, the guards were doubled. There must be something incredibly precious in this hall then, if security was so tight and the fee to enter was so steep.

Trying to swallow around the sour taste in her mouth, Darya followed Luunaiwel through a long and well-lit corridor, towards a shining door.

By now, she should have known to trust the elf's words more when it came to important matters.

The sight beyond it was nothing Darya could have imagined.

It was *green*.

In any direction she looked, everything was green. It was much, *much* larger than the glade they went to back then, and so much livelier. Everything was thriving, *blooming*. This was a garden... no, a *forest* in its prime, with trees of every kind, reaching high towards a transparent ceiling, where twilight sky was dotted with flurries.

Darya gasped. They must be directly below the mountains top!

Luunaiwel grinned, smug.

"Welcome to Tarum y Fýri, the Floating Forest of Mul Tarum."

CHAPTER 14:

It was so much to take in.

The contrast against the grey and white corridor behind them was almost too much. She couldn't hold down the laughter that bubbled forth.

Something thrummed in Darya's veins. Warmth pulsed from her Heart Stone. A torrent of pure emotion coursed through her veins, making her light-headed.

Disbelieving. Giddy. Excited. Delirious.

There was a sudden, inexplicable urge to run barefoot on the rustling grass before her. So she did. Shucking off her boots, Darya ran. A whooping laughter ripped out of her throat as her skin touched cool grass.

There was green! There was green everywhere! There were trees, rustling in their own rhythms. There were flowers, delicate and radiant. There were vines, heavy with fruits and never knew the barren lands outside of this paradise. Every leaf glistened under late light as if brushed by morning dews. Everywhere in sight, everything was growing in abundance, thriving and healthy like nothing she had ever seen before.

And, by the Gods, there was *Life*.

Birds flying in flocks, singing in tunes so sweet they brought tears to Darya's eyes. There were deer and hares, curious eyes followed Darya as she rushed past. There was music, skipping in the air in harmony with every leaf and feather and heartbeat.

Darya then realised Luunaiwel was running alongside her, feet also bare and mismatched eyes alight with joy. The giddiness inside Darya increased tenfold and she sped up, running towards where she didn't know. She only knew she needed to soak this in, to breathe in this air, so clean and so sweet. To immerse in this wonder of life she had never experienced before.

A crashing sound reached her ears from beyond the trees, enticing Darya over, her heart soaring with elation.

Beyond a veil of draping leaves, stands a thundering waterfall, white like ice, falling into a lagoon so blue it could make the sky jealous. Entranced, Darya approached moss-covered rocks and sat, feet dipped in cold but gentle water.

"Beautiful, is she not?"

Luunaiwel had come to sit beside her, smiling. Breathless, Darya smiled, dreamily, "Yes. This is... incredible. How is it possible? I thought... I thought all the great forests disappeared after the Shattering... And *inside the mountains...*"

Luunaiwel chuckled, "Have you been wondering why the dwarves treat me so highly, even though I am not kin?"

Slowly, Darya nodded, eyes still glued at the incredible nature, "Yes..."

Gesturing around, Luunaiwel smiled, "This was my idea."

Darya almost fell into the water, *"You're kidding!!!* You *made* this???"

"No, I am no Druid, little bird," Luunaiwel was bemused, "it is a long story, but... The dwarves have always thrived with their trades and wondrous inventions, but they had to rely on supply sources from the outside to survive. Without sunlight, they could not grow anything under the mountains aside from fungi. Agricultural effort on the mountain sides had proven to be expensive to upkeep and harmful for their living situation, as they literally had to farm right on top of their roofs. However …"

She pointed up to the ceiling, where stars blinked at them from beyond. "Long before the Shattering, they created this material called 'glass' by melting sand."

"The see through stuff... it's called *glass?*"

Luunaiwel nodded, "Not only is it pretty, under the dwarves' crafty hands, it could withstand pressure and damage far beyond what any other material could handle. It was perfect. I suggested the dwarves try their hands at growing and farming once more, by lifting the earth to the topmost of their mountains, and building a glass roof over it to let the light in."

A spark of pride glinted in her eyes, "Of course, being dwarves, they took the idea and ran with it."

Darya was speechless.

Luunaiwel snapped her fingers under Darya's nose, startling the girl, "But I did not bring you here to talk about the past. As a Druid, you need to establish a connection with Nature. The Druids of the olden days could hear the earth and all its living beings speak to them. In ages past, young Druids would be taken to forests over a thousand years old, and meditate to spark a connection with said forests. Tarum y Fýri qualifies, despite being

… artificial. The earth here is old. Since it was lifted from its mother, it is unaffected by The Shattering."

"So... you want me to meditate? Until *the forest* speaks to me?" Dumbly, Darya asked.

"Yes."

"For how long?"

"For as long as you need to. Or until I come back to get you. I still need to gather the medicinal components for your sister, and find Tuura. Poor lad, we left him behind."

"Oh," Darya blinked, having completely forgotten about the quiet Shapeshifter, "uhm, alright. I'll have a crack at it. I'll be here, I guess."

"Good girl," Luunaiwel winked, making Darya blush a little. She stood, brushing off pieces of grass stuck to her cloak.

"See you, little bird."

Left alone with only this incredible view, Darya took another moment to soak it all in. Who would have thought she could experience this in her lifetime?

The world she was born into was dead. Earth that could barely support craggy grass. Seeds that almost never grew. Animals and humans starved everywhere, clawing at crumbling soil to survive. The weather was unpredictable and harsh, destroying more than it nurtured.

Forests like Tarum y Fýri survived in tales only. Stories that even the oldest people barely remembered and none could envision. Darya could see why the dwarves guarded this place so zealously. No treasure could amount to this. Tarum y Fýri was the true gem under the mountains, and having the permission to walk amongst these trees was a privilege.

Darya tried to send off as much gratitude as she could to the forest, hoping that it could feel what she was feeling right now.

The forest was silent, but her Heart Stone pulsed, warm and encouraging.

Darya put her hand into her collar, feeling the smooth edge of the stone. Luunaiwel told her to meditate, but she had never done it before. Life on the road didn't give her much peace for that. Meditations were for the monks of the Holy Temple, or Royals who had too much time on their hands.

Darya pulled her freezing feet out of the water, and walked around the lagoon. Maybe it would increase her chances to connect with the forest if she was next to a tree? The older the tree, probably the better?

She found one a few minutes of aimless walking, and had to take a moment.

It was majestic. The base trunk was more than five men's embrace, gnarled with age, yet still full of life. Thick branches split up four feet above the ground, forming a cradle, and fanned out in every direction.

Darya let her fingers run along the tree's rough bark. Experimentally, she grabbed hold of a branch, and climbed into the cradle. The tree canopy rustled above her, peaceful and soothing.

The Heart Stone's warm thrumming grew stronger. She must be doing something right ... right? Darya pulled her knees up against her chest and leaned back against a branch. It felt... nice. She hadn't made much progress for a connection, but she felt content here. She felt *safe*. All tension seeped out of her. All the worries, all the fears, all the sadness... just melted away.

Even for just a moment, the lifted weight was welcoming. Just for a moment, she didn't want to feel the clench of her back teeth, the tension on her shoulders, and the trembles in her hands.

Wasn't that the goal for meditation? To let go of all troubles? To feel weightless and peaceful for the moment allowed?

Closing her eyes, Darya let her head loll back.

It felt nice.

It feels nice.

She wondered what kind of tree this was.

Birch man. Birch man.

Letting out a long exhale, sleep welcomed her in a blissful embrace.

My child. My child.

She was floating. Movements sluggish, and yet she felt so free, so weightless.

My child. My sweet, late child.

Someone was singing. She spun, her hair fluttering as if underwater.

My sweet child. My late child.

Her voice was like bells. High and low like a song, despite being just spoken words.

"Luunaiwel?" Darya called.

She turned around.

Her hair was as warm as the earth, cascading in waves that bounced with every laughter. Glittering green eyes were innocent, yet spoke of enticing secrets. Her curves were lustrous, accented with sun-kissed skin and pouting lips. She was full of *life*, and her sight alone beckoned every and all mortal to flock to her steps.

My child.

She smiled, arms opened. Her lips didn't move, but words still flowed into Darya's mind.

"Where have I seen you before?"

She smiled again.

Darya blinked once. Twice.

Leaning upon an ivory arm, she smiled. Distant. Despondent. Hair draped over her shoulder, loose waves spilled from under a crown of flowers. Her eyes were framed with delicate lashes, dewy and faraway.

Darya gasped.

"Goddess! My Goddess Vita!"

She tried to bow. But her muscles were sluggish. Weighed down and suspended in time.

The Goddess of Life smiled again.

No need. My child.

Darya looked on in awe. The Goddess spoke again, voice a song.

My child. My late, sweet child.

Precious. Unfortunate.

The seed is sown for you. Your destiny awaits.

Will you bloom for me, my child?

Grow to be the strongest birch, roots embracing the world.

To restore what once was mine.

My child.

Behind you, all that once was.

Before you, all that can be.

Beware, the Night-Touched One.

My child... My young Seedling

Her hand caressed Darya's cheek. Warm. Welcoming.

She could feel her Heart Stone thrummed, in rhythm with her own heart.

Be safe.

So you may grow.

Darya opened her eyes. The starry night stared back, twinkling behind rustling leaves. She winced. Her neck was stiff and her arms wooden. Darya sat up, hands trying to find purchase against the tree branches. She grabbed onto something *soft* instead.

Darya sprang up.

She was still in the great birch's cradle. But where she sat, *flowers had bloomed.* Purple, in clusters and looking like bells. Swaying softly in the wind, delicate and magnificent.

"Well, well, looks like someone made her connection."

Luunaiwel's voice almost startled Darya off the tree. It took her a moment to comprehend what the elf just said. Darya gasped.

"I did! I did it! Did I???"

"Seems so to me. Wolfsbane is not the kind of flower to grow on top of a birch tree," Luunaiwel tilted her head, "and you probably should get off. Wolfsbane is poisonous."

That got Darya scrambling in panic. She would have fallen flat onto her face if Luunaiwel wasn't there to catch her.

"Thanks," flustered, Darya righted herself, only to blush a deeper pink when she noticed Tuura was standing there, holding her discarded boots, "ah, I-I'll take those."

Fumbling to put them back on, Darya leaned back against the birch for balance, bare hand scrabbling at its bark.

[Greetings, Seedling.]

She should have jumped out of her skin. But the voice, the *presence at the back of her mind*, was so gentle, it was like an old friend, reaching out with warmth and familiarity. Her Heart Stone thrummed, joyous, urging Darya to respond.

So she did.

Hello?

[Thank you, for the gift.]

She blinked, looking to the swaying wolfsbanes. A smile bloomed on her lips.

Thank you, for letting me rest.

[When time comes, Seedling, I would be grateful if you take me along.]

She didn't quite understand, but the request was so earnest, she hadn't the heart to refuse.

I will do what I can.

[Thank you, Seedling.]

CHAPTER 15:

Darya couldn't come off the height of her giddiness. Especially when she found out what exactly the connection could do. As she walked around the forest, Darya could *feel* each and every living being's life force that she touched with her bare skin. Even Luunaiwel was impressed. The elf took off the glove over her unscarred hand, and offered it to Darya as an experiment.

It was... it was difficult to describe, but Luunaiwel's life force was different from everything Darya had felt within Tarum y Fýri. All the trees and all the plants, they were all filled with life. Fresh, invigorating, *simple.* Their sheer presence filled Darya with the *simple joy of being alive.*

But Luunaiwel was different. Her presence was... strange. There was a vast, ancient and sorrowful feeling, and Darya for the life of her couldn't figure out why it was so familiar. She could also sense Luunaiwel's power, a circling nebula that almost overwhelmed the elf's own life force. It was as if Darya maintained the connection for too long, Luunaiwel's presence would swallow her mind whole.

Tuura was also different. His life force was like a crashing river, wild and unstoppable, and filled with life the same way the green felt to Darya. But it was more primal, crude in a sense that was both young and old.

Everything suddenly felt so fascinating, and there was a rush of happiness every time Darya touched even a stalk of grass. But it was dampened when Luunaiwel announced they had to leave. Luunaiwel assured they would be able to return again, though Darya would need to get some special permit done.

"Might as well, since we will have to take your sister here soon. I assume you would want to visit her without having to pay every single time." Luunaiwel said, on their way back to Nathi's.

"Yes, please. But why does Sara have to go there?"

"Tarum y Fýri is not just a forest. The dwarves also have facilities built there. One is for the elderly, and the other for the sick. That way, they can benefit from the sun and the environment. It aids the healing process and is healthy for the mind."

Darya was in awe, "I can see that. If I could, I would live there forever."

Tuura's chuckle rumbled in his chest, "Tarum y Fýri has that effect on people."

"I agree. The dwarves do not believe in a waste of the workforce," Luunaiwel gave them a slight smile, "as long as they live, they will find a way to contribute to the community. Most, if not all, of the residents in Tarum y Fýri help tend to the forest and their neighbours, as long as they are not contagious or bedridden. The old and disabled are given jobs at the Crafting Hall if so desired, where they seldom have to move."

"That's amazing," Darya got more and more impressed by dwarfish society as she learned, "they really are purpose-driven, huh?"

"Yes, they are."

It was late when they got back to Nathi's house. All the candles were out when Luunaiwel took Darya to Sara's guestroom. After bidding the elf goodnight, Darya stood behind the door, willing the buzzing excitement in her chest down by taking stock of the room she was in.

The floor was carpeted, plush under her feet. A fireplace crackled in a corner, dancing flames dim, but enough to cast the whole room in a honeyed glow. A few bookshelves lined the walls, a woven tapestry of a malla above them. The room smelled like fresh cotton under the sun, clean and with just a hint of the charcoal that kept it warm. In the middle of the floor, there was a rectangular pit, fitted with a mattress, fur throws and pillows galore. Sara was lying spread eagle in the middle of it, snoring with a wool blanket across her abdomen.

Shaking her head in amused exasperation, Darya tucked Sara in properly before lying down on the softest mattress she had ever felt in her life. Inhaling deeply, Darya rolled over to look at her sister, reaching out to tuck a lock of hair back from Sara's face. But she hesitated, her hand hovering. Her excitement wilted like the scraggly grass outside of Flumium.

What would Sara's life force be like?

Darya was afraid to find out. What if Nathi was wrong? What if he couldn't cure whatever Sara was having? What if Sara was destined for an early demise? What if Sara would leave Darya behind, like the rest of their family had?

Darya was afraid to find out.

But the humming thrums of the Heart Stone tingled all the way down to her fingertips, urging her to reach out. Coaxing her fears away, pushing her towards her sister.

They only had each other now.

Fingers flexing, Darya placed a tentative, trembling hand on Sara's cheek.

The moment their skin touched, Darya gasped.

Filling up the back of her mind was Sara's life force. It was shaky as it was young; a scrawny, sickly sapling. It had a few bent leaves, a few broken twigs, but it was stubborn and it was alive. Just like how much *Sara* wanted to live. Darya could feel it, as if her sister's will was the deep roots that kept the sapling from withering, that help the little sapling reach skyward with a thirst to thrive.

Darya's eyes misted over as she smoothed a hand over her sister's forehead, smiling.

Sara is going to be okay.

With that, sleep came easy. Darya's dream was full of light and life. She was back in Tarum y Fýri again, running through the greens as beautiful flowers bloomed under her feet. Tumbling water was music to her ears, the earth sang against her skin and wind combed cool fingers through her hair. She opened her Heart Stone and felt it filled to the brim with thrumming of nature. She felt full, safe and content, as her toes sunk into soft soil, soaking in all that was around. All that was alive.

It was a good dream.

Darya woke with a smile, skin tingling with a pleasant haze. The gentle floral fragrance in the air kept her rested happiness lingering for just a few moments longer.

...

Floral?

Slowly, Darya cracked her eyes open. She was greeted with the sight of white and green blooms, all over the edge of the bed.

As if struck by a bolt of lightning, she sprang up. The flowers seemed to have grown from the stone floor beneath the carpet, splitting the fibres open. Panicked, Darya looked to her left.

Sara was still asleep, *thank the Gods*.

She needed to get Luunaiwel.

Darya didn't even bother with shoes. Rushing out in terror, she bit down her lip to prevent from screaming out the elf's name. Darya climbed downstairs, hoped Luunaiwel would be there and almost tripped over at the relief upon seeing her in the dining room, having tea with Tuura, Nathi and a dwarf woman.

"Luuna-Luunaiwel!!" Darya gasped, "I need you upstairs, quick!"

Everyone at the table stood, alarmed. Darya felt herself blushing, "It's okay! I just... uh, I just need to borrow Luunaiwel for a moment! Sorry!"

There weren't any questions, thankfully, and the elf was quick to follow.

"What seems to be the problem?" Luunaiwel asked as they ascended the stairs.

"I don't know! I fell asleep, had a good dream, woke up and these *things* seemed to grow all over the bed overnight!!"

"Hoh." Luunaiwel raised an eyebrow. A hand on the doorknob, Darya added hastily.

"Sara is still asleep."

The elf nodded, keeping her face neutral as Darya pushed the door open. And promptly froze, staring at the flowers.

Anxious, the young Druid fidgeted. The problems were obvious. One: Darya couldn't control her powers in her sleep. Two: she had completely ruined Nathi's carpet, and she sure as hell wouldn't be able to pay for something so expensive. Three:

how in the world could Darya explain this to anyone who didn't know she was a Druid???

"At the very least, we know for certain that you have awakened your power," Luunaiwel said, both eyebrows rose up so far they almost touched her hairline, "I do like snowdrops, they are quite elegant."

Darya grimaced at the elf's tone, "Good to know the name of it, I guess."

Without another word, Luunaiwel swooped in to carry Sara out to the corridor, away from the incriminating scene, and gently woke her. With a sleepy groan, Sara rubbed her eyes.

"Huh? Luna? Where...? Why am I out here?"

The elf's smile was tight, "I tried to wake you up, but you were in a deep sleep. It is morning, so I figured you would want breakfast before Nathi gets to your treatments, hm?"

Yawning, Sara nodded, "Awright..."

When they got downstairs, Darya didn't miss any of the looks she was given. Ducking her head, she willed down both embarrassment and dread. Luunaiwel was unfazed however, smiling at the woman dwarf.

"Sindri, these are the girls, Darya and Sara. Darya, Sara, this is Sindri, Nathi's wife."

Sindri's hair was even redder than Nathi's, so vibrant it was almost scarlet, styled elaborately in an updo with so many interwoven braids Darya couldn't tell where one ended and another began. She smiled, green eyes glittering, the same colour as the emeralds adorning her hair.

"Good morning, Sara, Darya. My apologies, I did not have the chance to welcome you two to our home last night. I trust you had a good rest, though?"

"We did, thank you ma'am." Sindri's kind voice put Darya at ease. The dwarf had one of those faces, with round cheeks that were as full and ripe as apples and a cute button nose, but also authoritative in a motherly way.

Shyly, Sara offered her a smile, "Thank you, ma'am."

"Of course, of course. Come! Sit with us! Let me fix you some breakfast!" Without further ado, Sindri ushered them both to the dining table. For the brief moment their hands touched, Darya could feel Sindri's presence, warm like the hearth but also fierce like wildfire. She was full of life and bursting with colours, yet comforting like reddened coal on a wintry night.

Sindri went on to fix Darya and Sara a plate each, filled with fresh fruits, hot pancakes and honey drizzled on top, and a cup of warm milk. The sight and smell of breakfast was enough to break the sisters out of their timidity.

For them, fresh food was expensive, a luxury that they could never afford. Not a lot of people could either, so most produces were turned into rations, like hard tacks or jerky, which sold for a lot cheaper. Thus the two meals at Nathi's were almost too much for the girls, having never enjoyed something so amazing before. For better or worse, Sindri seemed to have an acute sense of when they were about to finish their portions, and kept discreetly refilling their plates.

By the end of the meal, Darya didn't think she could move ever again.

"Thank you so much for the food, Sindri." She managed, stuffed to the gizzard.

"It was delicious! Thank you, Miss Sindri!" Sara followed, looking at Sindri like she was a gift sent from the Gods.

"Well, I am glad you enjoyed my food," Sindri clasped her hand together, positively glowing, "if you ever get peckish, feel free to look through the pantry! I'm afraid I must head off to the shop now, but please, make yourselves at home! I will be back for dinner tonight, and I look forward to speaking with you young ladies soon!"

She came around to shake their hands, then wagging a warning finger at Luunaiwel, Nathi and Tuura, "And you three, don't have too much fun while I'm gone. Behave yourselves, you hear?"

Luunaiwel winked at Sindri, "I promise I will keep them in line."

Shaking her head, Sindri finally gave up a smile, "Yes, yes, Lulu, but who will keep *you* in line, hm? Alright, I shall see you all later."

"Tata."

"Have a great day a' work, honey!"

"Bye, Sindri."

Nathi stood up, popped his back, before beckoning at Sara, "A'ight, lassie. Lemme see ta ye."

Obediently, Sara followed Nathi over to his office. Left with Luunaiwel and Tuura in the dining room, what happened upstairs finally caught up to Darya's food-addled mind.

"So what are we going to do about … my outburst?"

Tuura was confused, "What?"

Luunaiwel sighed, "Darya grew a small carpet of snowdrop in her room during her sleep."

Tuura raised a bushy eyebrow, "That explains the smell."

Anxiety made Darya impatient, "So what are we going to do about it? What can I do about it?"

"Well, we can cut the flowers and mend the carpets for now," Luunaiwel took a sip of her tea, "but this might still happen again."

"That's not good," Darya rubbed her face, groaning, "how do I learn to control it then?"

"I am not quite sure," Luunaiwel shook her head apologetically, "I tried to tap into Druidism in my earlier days, but I never got too far with it. Not having a Heart Stone does not let me connect with life the way you can."

"Would meditation help?" Tuura suggested as he cleared the table.

Luunaiwel shrugged, giving him her empty mug, "Possibly, we will have to take her to get a permit to enter Tarum y Fýri as soon as possible then. Fifty silver a tick is too steep of a price."

Darya was both excited and dreaded, "How much would that be?"

"About a gold. Perhaps more."

That was a punch in the gut, "Right … what about Sara? Would she need one?"

Luunaiwel gestured towards the door, "Sara would have a Healer's paper, her permit will be different from what you need. Yours would take more time, unfortunately."

Dropping her head onto the table, Darya held back a curse. Everything needed time, and she didn't think that was something they had plenty of.

Moments later, Nathi called out for them. Feeling dejected, Darya followed Luunaiwel and Tuura to the dwarf's study.

"Tuura, I'm goin' ta have ye bring Sara up to the Haven Hall." Nathi said, handing the shapeshifter a satchel and a scroll, "I have all her medicines prepared in here, and that's the document needed for 'em ta admit her ta a treatment room."

"Alright," Tuura said, then he crouched down in front of Sara, offering her his hand, "I know we have not been properly introduced, but my name is Tuura Earthenclaw. I am a friend of Luna, and I will help you to the best of my abilities."

Sara's eyes went to meet Darya's. The latter gave her two thumbs-ups, which had Sara smiling. Tentatively, she put her much smaller hand into Tuura's, nodding.

"Alright, mister Tuura."

He chuckled, "Just Tuura is fine."

Darya patted her sister's back in encouragement, "I'll go see you up there soon, alright Sara? Behave yourself."

"I will! You too, Darya!"

With Sara tottering away after Tuura, Darya was left anxious.

"So? What now?"

Luunaiwel suggested, "We can go visit the Scholar Hall's library. They have some of the most valuable tomes on this side of the Eria Mountains. You can read, yes?"

Darya nodded, "My parents had me learn how to read when I was a kid."

Both Luunaiwel and Nathi seemed approving of this.

"Terrific," said the elf, offering Darya a hand, "since Nathi will have his patients pouring in soon, we should get out of his beard for now. We shall sit down and have a proper chat with everyone later."

Bobbed her head at the underlying meaning in Luunaiwel's words, Darya let the elf pull her to her feet. Bowing at Nathi.

"Thank you so much for everything, Lord Nathi."

"Just Nathi fer ye, lassie," the dwarf laughed, making a shooing motion with his hands, "now, off ye go! Behave yerselves, ay?"

Before they headed out, Luunaiwel and Darya climbed back upstairs. The young Druid felt terrible when they pulled up the flowers by the roots, wincing as she felt the tiny life forces snuffed away. It was nauseating, and after a few bulbs, she had to let Luunaiwel do the rest. She couldn't knowingly kill these plants, even if it was her fault this happened.

When they finally emerged from Nathi's home, the dim lights of Scholar Hall were soothing to Darya's nerves. However, it was difficult to tell the time here, as there was no way to see the sky. There was a bell tower, stood tall over all the houses, but the time displayed seemed wrong.

"I haven't heard any ringing since we got here. Don't they use the tower?" Darya asked, peering up at the tall construct curiously.

Luunaiwel said, "Unfortunately, no. Down here under the mountains, the ringing was deafening when struck, and after a flood of complaints, they took the bell down."

Darya wrinkled her nose, "How do people tell the time down here then?"

"By using hour glasses. They are little contraptions, made of glass and filled with sand."

The elf's attempt to explain about hourglasses was lost to Darya's ears, when she spotted something peculiar further down the street.

A giant cluster of crystals, red and glowing, protruded from the jagged earth. The size of them were as wide as any house here, while the height of the tallest column could easily rival the bell tower itself.

Gasping, Darya couldn't help but be drawn in by the gentle light they were emitting, "What... what are these?"

"They are called the Fire under the Mountains," Luunaiwel tilted her head, "the dwarves unearthed this cluster while building

Mul Tarum thousands of years ago. It is said that the crystals are imbued with magic, thus giving it light, and a warmth that keeps Mul Tarum from freezing over. The dwarves said it was a gift from their God of Flame, Lokgu."

Darya blinked, looking at Luunaiwel, "A version of Ignia?"

The elf smirked, "Yes."

Knowing that Luunaiwel might have an entirely different interpretation, Darya asked, "What is it really?"

Amusement twinkled in her mismatched eyes, confirming Darya's suspicion, "It is simply a massive growth of ægian kowach. In your language, it is loosely translated to Fire Quartz. A crystal formed in underground fire, absorbed its wild magic, and tempered by the earth."

"Wow," Darya glanced back at the crystals, mesmerised, "it's still pretty impressive. A gift of the Gods or not."

"Indeed."

Continuing up the slope, they took a left turn before going further down the road leading to the Haven Hall lifts, and into a small market.

It wasn't as grand as the Merchant Hall, but it was well-stocked. Each merchant had a square kiosk, displaying all their goods with neat signs. They were mainly selling food and certain necessities, probably to cater to this particular Hall's residences so they wouldn't have to travel too far from their homes for daily resources.

But Luunaiwel didn't stop there. She led Darya through the market and exited from a side entrance.

The sight of a grand building greeted them, with robed dwarfish statues guarding on either side of a well-decorated door. The stairs leading up to the door were polished to perfection, and each column holding up the crimson roof was carved with such intricacy, Darya didn't even know where to look.

Grinning down at her stumped expression, Luunaiwel winked, "Let us conduct our studies and business here, shall we?"

CHAPTER 16:

Even after they had sat down, Darya couldn't stop craning her neck around, staring at everything in awe.

There were *a lot* of books. There were so many books, so many titles, in so many languages and so many colours, Darya was lightheaded at the sight alone. The shelves seemed to be carved out from the same slates as the floor, lined up in neat rows from the entrance, up to the spiralling staircase, to yet *even more books*, and small, private alcoves that contained equipment for scholarly studies. The building was nine storied tall, well-lit with dangling chandeliers and glorious beyond words. Darya was no scholar, but she could appreciate this grand archive for what it was.

The alcove Luunaiwel chose was two floors up, overlooking the library. Curious, Darya opened a cupboard, and found it stocked with supplies, like scrolls, quills and ink of all kinds. Some works lay open on the desks, most unfinished, though the writings and illustrations were so vivid and precise, it was difficult to believe they were done by hand and not magic.

"This is... this place is *amazing!*" Darya breathed, finally sitting down again.

Closing the alcove's door behind her, Luunaiwel chuckled, "Indeed, it is," Unlike Darya however, the elf didn't bother to keep her voice down, "you might not have realised, but each quarter is covered in glass, ensuring privacy for the user."

That immediately got Darya up on her feet once more. Sure enough, as she reached out over the marble railing, her hands were met with a cool, smooth and near-invisible layer, "Oh my wooooooooooord!!!"

She didn't care that Luunaiwel found her behaviours amusing. Never in her wildest dreams could Darya imagine she would one day experience such wonders.

"I own this alcove," the elf said, gesturing for a bewildered Darya to sit down, "do feel free to come here and study for as long as you stay in Mul Taum."

Darya's eyes bulged, "*Really???* Are you sure??"

"I am sure. You can read everything from the public section as long as you stay inside the library. To bring a book outside, you will need a specific permission slip. If there is anything you would like to borrow, let me know."

The young Druid shook her head vehemently, "Oh, no! I'm sure... I mean, thank you, but I'm sure I can spend my time studying here! No need to bring anything out! This is beyond generous of you already!"

Luunaiwel huffed out a small laugh at Darya's antics. Her demeanour changed quickly however, shifting from jovial to serious as she threaded her fingers together and held the Druid's gaze.

"Before we start with your studies, there are few details we must go over first."

Immediately, Darya straightened up.

"Right... right," she took a deep breath, "what are we... What are we going to tell everyone?"

Luunaiwel tilted her head, "Do you wish to tell anyone?"

"I," Darya opened her mouth, stopped herself short, swallowed and started again, "I don't know if I should tell Sara."

"Are you sure that would be wise?"

Pushing against the surge of grief and bitterness, Darya sighed, "She needs to heal first before she could handle more... shocking news."

Luunaiwel nodded once, "It is your decision. I will not try to dissuade you or otherwise."

Letting out all the air in her lungs, Darya looked down for a moment, trying to compose herself. Luunaiwel, thankfully, was always patient, and she let Darya take her own time to tackle these matters.

Finally, Darya asked, twisting her hands together, "What about Nathi and Sindri?"

"I trust them with my life," Luunaiwel answered without hesitation, "but to entrust them with your status or not, that is your decision. However, I would advise to keep it a secret with the rest of Mul Tarum's population, regardless of whether you would share with Nathi and Sindri or not."

That was fair. After what happened in Flumium, Darya didn't think she was keen on talking to strangers. By the Gods, she didn't even blabber to anyone, and look where it got her. Darya fought off the onslaught of pain, and sucked in a breath to steady herself.

"Do you think I should tell them?"

There was a small pause. Luunaiwel tapped her chin, contemplating the answer, "I would say yes. Despite being a Lord, Nathi has very little interest in politics. However minor his influence is, he can still grant you permission for many privileges within Mul Tarum. Besides, you are staying in their home. It would be difficult to explain why there are fresh flowers growing every night where you sleep."

Grimacing, Darya filled that thought away for consideration, "So... uh, training. Other than reading of course, what do you want me to do in the meantime?"

"As discussed, we will try and get you an entry permit to Tarum y Fýri, where you can strengthen and test your bonds with nature. I will attempt to teach you a few earth-based spells once you have a better handle on your powers."

The prospect of learning actual magic perked Darya up immensely, "For real??"

Chuckling, the elf held out a halting hand, "Do not get too excited yet, little bird. In order to get you a permit, we will need to get you some identification."

That deflated Darya's excitement, "That's going to be difficult... I have some paperwork for my travelling, but … I left everything in Flumium."

Luunaiwel didn't need further clarification, "Perhaps that is for the best. We can create new ones that would be more beneficial for you here in Mul Tarum."

Intrigued, Darya asked, "What do you have in mind?"

"I still think it would be unwise to reveal that you are a Druid to everyone. But perhaps it would be easier if we only tell the truth... partially."

"What do you mean?"

"Magick-users are highly regarded within a dwarfish society," Luunaiwel explained, "Mul Tarum pledged to protect and preserve magick-users, as they protect and preserve many now extinct species of the surface world. You would also be granted easy access to many parts of Mul Tarum. As long as you swear to never take up arms against the dwarves, of course."

Chewing on her lower lip, Darya mumbled, "I don't think I'll ever go to war against anyone... It should be fine?"

Luunaiwel inclined her head, "I would not be too sure if I were you. There is no telling what the future holds."

Her words dropped a chill down Darya's spine, "What are you suggesting?"

"I am suggesting to register you as my disciple," Luunaiwel proposed, dead serious, "I am well-known as an Archmage, and by registering yourself as such, you would not owe allegiance to anyone but me. You will also be known as a magick-user to the authority only, as a trainee Mage. That way, we will not have to come up with lies and covers should the need arise."

Running a hand through her hair, Darya was anxious. Rightfully so.

"How much of a difference would it be then, between saying I'm a Druid or a Mage?"

Luunaiwel's eyes narrowed, "The difference is night and day. A Mage cannot hope to ever revive the world, for a start."

The alcove was buried in an uncomfortable silence. Luunaiwel did explain before, back when they were in that fateful grove in the middle of the Dead Forest, how important being a Druid was. Darya's awakening dream, along with the Goddess Vita's words also rang clear in her head. She had a terrible feeling that though the choice was hers to make, no matter what she chose to do, it would affect everything going forward.

And Darya wasn't ready for this. Wasn't ready to face such consequences.

She was a bard, a tiny, nameless bard, whose significance to the world should be miniscule. But it was her own foolish choice that got her here. Her choice that got her tangled with such a terrible mess that had cost her far too much.

Darya told Luunaiwel that she wanted to become stronger. To become a proper Druid. But Darya made that request at the heat of the moment.

Still.

She didn't realise her hand had been clutching at the front of her tunic, where her Heart Stone thrummed warm against her skin.

Even if she decided to stop involving with all things Druidism, even if she tried to deny what was given to her, Darya couldn't escape it now. She couldn't just stop being a Druid. The magic was part of her now. So was the burden.

All because of one stupid choice.

And the only choice Darya had now was to take responsibility for it.

"I... I don't want to be manipulated by politics," Darya decided, searching Luunaiwel's eyes, "and it feels like if I tell just anyone about being a Druid, that might be exactly what would happen."

The elf nodded once.

Breath sucked out of her lungs, anxiety filled Darya's veins in droves, but she still held the elf's gaze "I want to learn to become a full-fledged Druid. But at my own pace. If I decide to commit to revive this world, which I don't think I can, I want it to be my own choice. No one else's."

There was a smile on Luunaiwel's lips now. Not with the usual flippant attitude, but with a hint of approval and, if Darya wasn't being delusional, *pride.*

"As it will be."

The thrumming of Darya's heart, along with her Heart Stone's, grew stronger, "I know you have helped me a lot so far, and there is no way I can ever repay you... But would you tell me? If someone is looking to use me for their own gains?"

There was steel in Luunaiwel's mismatched eyes when she nodded, "By my honour, I swear."

Relief filled her in a rush, "Thank you."

"Anytime, little bird."

Silence filled the gap between them once more, as Darya shifted through her mind for what to discuss next. But their private bubble was interrupted when the door opened.

Startled, Darya jumped to her feet, but it turned out it was just Tuura. The man's golden eyes darted between Darya and Luunaiwel.

"Am I interrupting?"

Luunaiwel grinned, "Not at all. Sit."

Tuura went to Luunaiwel's left. The chairs definitely weren't made to accommodate his size, which led to some awkward shuffling, Patiently, Luunaiwel waited, while Darya turned away when she realised she was gawking. As nice as Tuura had been so far, she hadn't gotten to know him well enough yet. She didn't want to turn that fearsome Shifting ability against her.

Once Tuura settled himself, red above his beard, Darya cleared her throat, and prompted the next topic. One that effectively chased off whatever good mood she had left.

"Luunaiwel."

"Yes?"

"You said you would tell me more about those men... who came after us. The Night's Hand."

The elf went quiet. For a moment, Darya thought Luunaiwel would turn her down, or would try to avoid the topic. But then Luunaiwel's shoulders slumped, a shadow crossed her bright eyes. From her pouch, she pulls out a dark scrap of fabric. In white paint was a skeletal hand, holding a bleeding four-pointed star between its thumb and forefinger.

"The Night's Hand is an organisation who dedicate themselves to hunt down and capture young magick-users all over Ardent. They call these people, children really, *recruits*. The captives would either be raised to serve their purposes and further their influences, or sold to the highest bidders."

The explanation was like a physical blow. Darya clutched at the table, shock and outrage sent tremors through her body, "They *sell* people??? To who???"

Luunaiwel grimaced, "Influential people. Lords, Rulers, Nobles... A magical slave or bodyguard, trained and under forced vows to obey goes for a lot of money. Especially in this day and age when magick-born is as rare as hen's teeth."

Darya definitely felt sick, "How do they track magical people anyway? Did they know about my magic because of that fortune teller??"

"That fortune teller you spoke of must have been a clairvoyant. Clairvoyants have no magic themselves, but they can sense magic in people using certain senses. Yours happened to be touch."

"And she ratted me out." Darya felt all the strength drained out of her. She was careless with her pity.

"Don't be too hard on yourself," Tuura suddenly spoke, "the Night's Hand is good at what they do. They have infested just about every major city known to men. That's why we travel with utmost secrecy."

Luunaiwel frowned, "The Night's Hand is one of those things that unfortunately survived the Shattering"

Darya gasped, "What???"

Luunaiwel and Tuura exchanged a look. The former laced her fingers together, gaze faraway.

"They are an ancient cult. Over the years, they have changed masters and operations, but their core purpose remains the same. To accumulate wealth and power, so they would have every

King and country bow to their will. In the shadows they fester, slithering their way into every court known to men, solidifying their hold over a territory only they knew the border to. Not many stand before their expansion and survive."

Darya paled, "And they want me. Why?"

"You gravely underestimate how valuable you are," Luunaiwel said, "a new Druid is a miracle in this age. Can you imagine the power one would have if they get to influence someone who can potentially revive the world?"

"He who holds the Key to the New World will own the World." Tuura hummed.

Why did the Gods have to test her so?

Holding a hand over her Heart Stone, Darya asked, "You are... familiar with how they work?"

Luunaiwel wrinkled her nose in disgust, "Unfortunately. They have always been an infection, and it was always a headache dealing with them. They are *everywhere*. I have encountered some as far as Garstan. Recently, there have been rumours of them controlling Golden Hills, and doing deals with some Lord in Furbarst. Many of them hold high positions in human courts, some run thieves guilds and some live among commoners. All under disguises."

Tuura shook his head, "Their clairvoyants usually assume invisible roles. Nannies. Beggars. Merchants. Easy to approach people without raising suspicions."

"Have you ever had a run in with them, Tuura? With the... Night's Hand?"

The Shapeshifter smiled, but there was no humour in his eyes, "They organised an attack that cornered me against the northern side of the Eria Mountains. I killed them all, but was mortally wounded. Would have died, if Luna didn't find me."

Luunaiwel grimaced, "I made an effort to keep them off areas near dwarven territories for the last century. And they have not dared to wander near Mul Tarum and Mul Nordihr since. Well, at least until now."

"Security must have become laxer since you left." Tuura grumbled.

Luunaiwel sighed, "And they return, like flies to honey."

That explained why Luunaiwel said she hadn't expected the Night's Hand to be in Flumium. Darya buried her face in her hands.

"Are we going to run into them here?"

"Not within the halls, no," Luunaiwel said, "the dwarves detest such practices. However, you can never be too careful. They most likely know you are here."

Darya nodded. She didn't need any more hard lessons to know that. Pitching forward with her elbows on the table, the young Druid asked in a conspiratorial tone.

"So, what's the plan?"

CHAPTER 17:

The young Druid had agreed to go with Luunaiwel's initial plan, mainly because it would be easier for her to access and practice in Tarum y Fýri. Conveniently, access to the Floating Forest would help her keep an eye on Sara as well.

Luunaiwel agreed that Darya should tell Nathi and Sindri in her own time. She didn't even have to say anything at all. Darya could simply let the official paperwork speak for themselves, and none would be the wiser.

The next morning, Darya woke up to a carpet of small, white flowers filling her visions. Chamomiles. She had fallen asleep in Nathi's guest room, after a long day at the library with Luunaiwel and Tuura. When she opened the door, Luunaiwel was already there with a pair of scissors.

Guilt was an uncomfortable feeling, especially when Sindri's breakfast was so wonderful.

Once she inevitably had to leave Mul Tarum, it would be Nathi and Sindri who would be taking care of Sara in her stead. Darya was informed that Sara's treatments would take at least a year. If Darya wanted to become a true Druid, Mul Tarum would not have the resources needed for her to achieve this goal. Staying would only compromise the fragile secret she was keeping and, in turn, would compromise Sara.

Darya could choose to be selfish and bring Sara along. Luunaiwel said she wouldn't mind. But even Darya knew it would be a terrible idea. Sara grew tired easily, she required plenty of rest, and she needed medicines that would not be available on the road. Perhaps, if Darya was a trained Druid, she could produce said medicines, like how she grew her flowers in her sleep, but none of them knew how that worked yet. Darya would be damned before she condemned Sara to such chances.

Another choice would be to stay. But confidentiality would be difficult. As secure Mul Tarum could be, it was still *the* trading capital of the world. People with the right paperwork could get in, and knowing how valuable Darya was, the Night's Hand would try every trick in the bag to capture her. Being just a meagre apprentice mage on paper, she honestly doubted the dwarves would amass an army to get her back. Unless news of Darya being a Druid was revealed, which might ultimately bind her into a different kind of vows and servitude.

The safest choice was to split up. Luunaiwel told her she had the maximum amount of three months to prepare. Both for herself and Sara.

Sara wouldn't be happy. Not after what happened in Flumium. Darya wasn't alright with this arrangement either. But that was why she didn't give Luunaiwel her answer yet. Darya decided that she had to trust Nathi and Sindri about her status as a Druid first, before entrusting her sister, her only remaining family, to them.

Darya knew Luunaiwel trusted Nathi with her life. But Darya didn't have the same bond Luunaiwel had with Nathi or Sindri. She had her doubts. Why would the dwarves agree to shelter her sister out of the blue? Why would a Lord and Lady take care of a stranger for free? No questions asked?

When they gathered for dinner that night, Darya watched Luunaiwel play with the silverwares, clinking the utensils together to make a quick, happy tune as Nathi tapped along on the table. Both Tuura and Sara watched them, amused.

An idea came to mind when she looked at the dwarfish family portrait, and Darya asked Luunaiwel, knowing that it was a fine chance to glean into the elf's past.

"How did you get yourself a dwarf family anyway?"

Luunaiwel smirked, "Funny you should ask. I happened to save Nathi's Great-great-great Grandfather's life, Master Nadin Whitestone of Mul Tarum. He insisted on adopting me into his family since."

That piqued Darya's interest, "How come Nathi calls you *sister*, then?"

"Because she torments me like a sister would, and we get along much better than any of me family's members," Nathi said," 'sides, calling her me great-great-great Aunt's a mouthful, don't ye think?"

"Well, there was also that time..." Tuura began, then trailed off and wilted when Luunaiwel threw him a glare.

"Not a word."

Darya perked up, "Oooooh... I must hear this! What happened???"

Nathi's laughter boomed, almost making poor Sara drop a plate, "I found her falling off a cliff! Bwahahahahhahaha!!!!"

Darya gaped at Luunaiwel, whose withering glare was now directed at Nathi, "Fell off a cliff? How did you manage that???"

Not at all deterred, Nathi laughed even louder, "She fell off a cliff fightin' way more Withered than she could handle! I hauled her arse back home ta heal her! Was a wee lad back 'en!"

Bewildered amusement filled her, Darya giggled, "That must have been a small legion for you to be pushed that far!"

"I was distracted," Luunaiwel grumbled, cuffing the back of Nathi's head, "I used to have a talking raven, whose language was even fouler than Nathi's. She was the one who attracted so many damned Withered and got me lost to begin with. Needless to say, I never had a pet again."

Nathi crackled, "Ha! I miss that feather-brain! A funny one, that thing!"

"Only you would think Sía was funny." Luunaiwel snorted.

"Simmer down, you two," Sindri admonished them, but not without fondness, "Nathi always gets rowdy when Luunaiwel is around."

"Oye! Why am I the only one called out, woman?"

Nathi ended his holler with a yelp, when Sindri pinched his ear.

The gammon roast was fantastic. Glazed with honey, paired with braised parsnip, carrot and potato, the fragrance alone was otherworldly. There was a whole boat of gravy, browned stuffing, and delightfully puffy baked buttery pastries as accompaniments.

By the end of the meal, it was difficult not to blurt out all her secrets. Darya could have sworn Sara almost cried when they were presented with an actual pound cake for dessert.

They all retreated to Nathi's reading room for the sweet treats. Gathered around the hearth, everyone was content and full, cosying up to the warmth with a platter of cake and a cup of white tea.

"How about a story?" Sindri asked Luunaiwel. Chuckling, Luunaiwel sat up on her chaise, putting away her empty plate.

"Hmmm... Which one shall it be... ah, yes." A glint of mischief sparkled in Luunaiwel's eyes. Sara, despite her sleepiness, leaned forward in her shared armchair with Darya, eager to hear more stories from Luunaiwel.

"It was the time when Mul Tarum was first established," the elf mage hummed, "the Great Halls under the Mountain started out with just two chambers, and many, many old mine shafts left behind by the Orcs. Abandoned in the darkness, they were infested with a plethora of nightmarish creatures.

There were white shadows, the terrifying Snow Maidens, a bloodthirsty cousin of the malla. They were excellent hunters, lurking in the depths of Mul Tarum's underground lakes, and their slender silhouettes would be a careless adventurer's last sight before being torn to pieces.

There were the scoria, spider-like creatures who were more stone than animal. Bound by wild elements, they skittered along cave walls, grating against rocks as they sought out their next meals. They were just as dangerous as they were patient, and when they found an unfortunate prey, they would crush the poor soul into a paste to absorb.

Then there were the melcheil, giant, slimy worms with a maw that could grind boulders into dust. Their ravenous and eternal hunger knew no bounds, and they would feast on everything around them, inanimate or alive."

Sara gasped, curling into Darya at the fearsome descriptions. Darya, on the other hand, leaned in closer, clearly invested. If she still wanted her side gig of being a bard, it was best to remember all the tales she heard, so she could recite them later. Besides, where else could Darya listen to such a wild tale?

Luunaiwel gestured with her hands, her eyes glowed ominously, flickering with the reflection of hearth, "And yet, none of them held a candle to the menace known as the Ischkallion, the Scourge of Mul Tarum. It was an ancient creature. Older than elves. Older than dragons. Forged in the deepest bowels of the earth and so dangerous, they said the Celestials imprisoned it under the Eria Mountains, ensuring that it could never crawl its way to the surface and terrorise the world.

The Ischkallion was a creature of many monstrous parts. It had tentacles like a Kraken, but its black, slimy skin was covered with pools of pus, poisonous and flesh-eating. It had a shell like a turtle, stronger than the finest steel and larger than the mansion of a Lord. Instead of a head, all it had was a gaping maw at the gap between its shell, armed with millions of razor sharp teeth and a barbed tongue.

Its appearance was so strange and so horrifying, the faint-hearted could go mad just from a single glimpse. The stench it emitted was poisonous! Its glistening skin could not be penetrable by normal weapons of any means! And its whipping tentacles were just as powerful as they were fast!

With their persistence and resilience, the dwarves tried and tried, for they knew as long as the Ischkallion was alive, there would be no safety for their new Halls. But many expeditions journeyed down to the Ischkallion's chamber and lost. Many bands of adventurers failed to rid Mul Tarum of its terrible Keeper.

When it seemed as though all hope was lost, the Hero King of Mul Tarum, Erling, pleaded for aid from the Legendary Mage, Othelron, and the God-Touched Smith Næsla of the Elvendom. Together, they created enchanted weapons, equipment imbued with incredible magic. Objects that now are known as artefacts."

Just like the staff and swords Luunaiwel had. Not for the first time, Darya was curious of where Luunaiwel got her hands on those.

"With a chosen party of twenty-four heroes, Erling, Othelron and Næsla braved the darkness, and descended into the

Ischkallion's lair. Sensing their approach, the great beast stirred in anger. The dwarves could hear it all the way to what is now known as the Merchant Hall.

Oh, how shaken our heroes were! They had not a strategy, how to kill this terror that was sealed away by Celestials. Alas, it was something they must do, for getting rid of this menace would mean a new age for the Dwarves, and a prosperous, new alliance between them and the Elvendom for centuries to come.

And down to purgatory, they went."

Anxious, Sara blurted out, pressing Luunaiwel, "Then what happened!?"

"All the bravest and best of Ardent, against a menace that was easily more dangerous than an ancient dragon," the elf lowered her voice, making the others lean in closer, "they were afraid as they stepped into the vast cavern the Ischkallion called home. It was flooded, water came up to their knees and waists. The smell was putrid, untouched by light, of rotten flesh and of the monster itself. The water was thick like mud, forcing the heroes to leave cloaks and boots behind, unable to move with the muck dragging them down. Plans were devised, though there was no guarantee any of them would work. And yet the heroes bravely marched on, deeper and deeper..."

Clutching at Darya's arm for comfort, Sara listened to Luunaiwel with bated breaths. Even Nathi, Sindri and Tuura had no trace of sleepiness left in them. Vaguely, Darya noted all of this, impressed by how Luunaiwel was setting the atmosphere.

"Finally, the heroes could no longer advance, for the water was so deep and dark, there was no telling where the bottom lied," she paused, letting the brief silence increase the dramatic effect, "no one dared to make a sound. No one dared to even light a torch. The only light they had were of the pale, luminous crystals that formed in the deepest layers under Eria. Dancing reflections pushed everyone's tension on edge, not knowing when the creature would strike...

Then all of a sudden, the water exploded," Luunaiwel stood, her voice rang loud, making Sara gasp, "tentacles reached out from the depths, blindly grasping at the heroes! Some were caught, screaming for help as their comrades scrambled to free the captured. As the tentacles were severed, black and green blood hissed out from them, poisonous and vile-smelling, wounding those who were near.

The Ischkallion screamed, sending waves of oppressing water toward the heroes. Shouts of warnings and hurried footsteps filled the chamber, but the screeches of the Ischkallion were loudest! It flung boulders at the heroes, grabbed them and pulled them towards its enormous maw. Severed tentacles regrew, each more aggressive than the last.

The heroes knew the only chance they had was to strike at the gaping maw. The Ischkallion's arms were regenerating too quickly to keep hacking at, and its shell too tough for even the artefacts to damage. Melee fighters charged forward, while the ranged and magick-wielders protected their paths from tentacles. They, at last, found a footing upon a column of debris, piled high in front of the raging beast.

A great struggle it was! Tentacles shot out of every watery direction, some to wrap and pull, some simply to crush! The Ischkallion's body shook with anger as it thrashed, trying to snap at them with its menacing jaws! The heroes parried and shouted, slipped and dodged, hacked and slashed. All grew tired, but so did the Ischkallion. After what felt as long as an eternity, the tentacles stopped growing, leaving only nubs behind. All the Ischkallion could do was thrashing in pain!

With all the might they could muster, the surviving heroes poured their powers into one last blow, ending the Scourge of Mul Tarum once and for all!"

Sara almost flew out of her seat, cheering at the beast's demise. Everyone else clapped for the bowing Luunaiwel, having enjoyed the tale greatly.

Shyness forgotten, Sara jumped at Luunaiwel, tugging at her sleeve with wide-eyed awe, "Another! Another! Please!!!"

Chuckling at her enthusiasm, Luunaiwel patted Sara's head, "And I would love to comply, little one, but I believe it is past your bedtime, no?"

"You can't really tell here!" Sara childishly argued, but at the mention of bed, she tried, and failed, to break a yawn.

Grinning at her sister, Darya carefully peeled Sara's grip off Luunaiwel, "You're making me jealous over here. What about my stories, huh?"

"Luna's are cooler." Sara stuck a tongue out at her.

"Ouch! No hesitation! I see how it is!" Darya put a hand over her heart, feigning hurt. Her little sister giggled, but it was clear exhaustion was catching up to her.

Amused, Sindri got up from her armchair, "I am sure there will be plenty of time for stories. But how could you listen to them if you get no rest? Come, dear lass. I'll tuck you in and sing you a lullaby."

"Awright..." Obediently, Sara held onto Sindri's hand, stumbling after her.

Sindri was hardly taller than the ten-year-old Sara, but their age gap was evident just by that one interaction. Darya didn't realise she was watching this with warmth in her chest, until Nathi's wishful voice pulled her to the present.

"We've always wanted a child."

Darya blurted out before she could stop herself, "Why don't you?"

"Too busy," the dwarf physician shrugged, "Sindri's business ain't going ta run on its own, and I'm always swarmed with patients... Who's goin' ta take care of the baby?"

"No one is going to criticise you for enlisting help, you know?" Luunaiwel prompted with a roll of her eyes. Nathi snorted, clearly was just as sleepy as Sara.

"Hmmmm... Maybe, aye," he mumbled, his head lolling back against the couch, "maybe whenever Spring comes next, we'll have a child."

CHAPTER 18:

On the next morning, Nathi took Sara back to Tarum y Fýri. After telling her sister to behave and focus on getting better, Darya took care of her flowering predicament (it was chamomile again this time) before searching for Luunaiwel. She found Tuura instead, waiting for *her* outside by the fountain.

"Luna is sorting out some paperwork. She told me to take you to the training ground."

Darya didn't expect this, but nodded, "Alright."

They went down to the Merchant Hall. Darya requested to stop by the stables so she could pay for more time for her horse, knowing it would be a while until they had to leave.

The Merchant Hall was just as impressive as the first time she saw it. Business was in full swing, even this early on the day. Now knowing what the "glass" was made out of, Darya was even more in awe with how it showcased all the items different merchants had to offer. They had absolutely everything here in

Mul Tarum. Clothes, food, armours, weapons, jewellery, decorations, furniture... Everyone put their products on display, and everyone was looking to buy something. There wasn't a single beggar in sight.

"It must be nice to live in a society like this." Darya mused aloud.

Tuura chuckled, "They worked, and still are working hard for this. Dwarves don't believe in wasted workforce. Everyone has a role to fulfil."

"How do they manage to provide jobs for everyone?"

"They have a system that requires younger generations to attend once coming of age. Each dwarf would be assigned to their chosen trades when they turn twenty five, twenty seven years old."

"Whoa, that's old." Darya couldn't imagine that kind of life. If she wasn't able to work until her late twenties, her family would have starved.

"Dwarves live longer than humans. And they breed less, too. They live up to three hundred years, and only consider getting married during their eighties. They generally conceive during the middle of their second century."

"Whaaaat...? Pffft, are you telling me Nathi and Sindri are in their *eighties???*"

Indulgently, Tuura smiled down at her, "Nathi is one hundred and thirty six years old, while Sindri is one hundred and forty one."

Darya's lower jaw unhinged, "You're pulling my leg!!!"

"I certainly am not."

"But they look *so good!!!* I thought they are in their late thirties at most!!!"

Tuura laughed, "I'm sure they would be flattered to hear that. But dwarves don't age like humans do. And if you think that's unbelievable, then try to have a crack at Luunaiwel's age."

"But she's an elf," Darya flailed her arms, bewildered, "aren't they supposed to be *immortal?*"

"In a sense."

"And how old is she anyway? I don't think that ever came up in our conversations."

Tuura hummed, "You know... That never came up in our conversations either. But guessing a lady's age is rude, so I don't try too hard."

Darya laughed, "Fair enough."

It was nice to get to know Tuura finally. Considering the circumstances of their meeting, there hadn't been time aside for basic introductions. It didn't help that Tuura was such a quiet person, and Darya was going through so much in the last few days.

It was nice to just... converse. Like Mul Tarum was just another one of her journey, and she could return to Flumium whenever she wanted. Like she could send a letter home if she saved up enough for a courier. Like just any moment now, she could go tell Agnus and Cecil all about her adventures. Like her Grandmama wasn't dead.

It was nice to pretend that everything was *fine*.

"So how did you meet Luunaiwel anyway?" To distract herself, Darya asked.

"She saved my life," Tuura said simply, "the same experience with the Night's Hand I've told you about."

Darya gasped, "O-oh! That's... That's terrible! I'm so sorry!"

Tuura shrugged, "It's the past. Besides, if they hadn't attacked me, I would have still been wandering around aimlessly, without a purpose, and never would have met Luna."

"She saves a lot of people, huh?"

"She has."

"I do feel bad," Darya confessed, knitting her fingers together, "if it wasn't for my sudden... *change,* she wouldn't have to abandon her quest."

"It was an important quest. But right now, you take priority."

Darya huffed out a tired laugh, "Unfortunately, I have to be thankful for that."

The chatter turned light after. Darya did most of the talking, pointing out merchandise and shops that stood out to her. Eventually, they came to a grand staircase, width as large as a square and was at least three hundred steps tall. As they ascended, Darya finally saw how useful those lifts were. By the time they came to the top, the young Druid was wheezing.

"I... will... haaaah... never question... haah haah... those lifts... again... haaaaaah..."

Tuura, whose breaths barely quickened, laughed, "It seems like these stairs turn out to be a perfect warm up."

"Please... haaah... don't say that..."

The training field was a massive span of even ground with indented squares filled with packed dirt, lined with racks of practice weapons, and training dummies planted within. The area was entirely lit by braziers of burning coal, and the domed ceiling did nothing to lessen the echoes of clashing noises. Packed with warrior dwarves, the field was filled with the sound of spars and routines.

Warily, Darya asked, "Do I have to fight one of them?"

Tuura was amused, "No. They would beat your skull in. Dwarves pack a lot of strength, and they don't know the meaning of 'going easy'. They would treat you just like any other trainee, and you wouldn't want that."

Darya gulped, "Nope."

To an empty training patch they went. Pointing at the weapon rack, Tuura said, "We need to decide on your main weapon. During your short journey with Luunaiwel, she has taught you the basics of hand-to-hand combat. Good base, but we need to work on your main combat method."

Darya thought for a moment, "Don't you use those claw-things to fight?"

"Aye," Tuura pulled out one of them from his belt pouch to show her, "it's called a fist weapon."

The weapon bore etched marks that resembled bear paws. The edges of the plates were trimmed with golden runes and tufts of brown fur, while the metallic plates were tempered to have a jet black colour. There were three blades attached at the back-of-hand plate, gleaming in the light, menacing even as they sat there resting on Tuura's hand.

"I think I'd cut myself trying to use this." Darya said. The weapon was beautiful in its own deadly way, but it was not a good match for her.

Tuura nodded, "These are customised to my fighting skills and capabilities. You should look for a weapon that extends your reach."

Darya raised an eyebrow, "Are you calling me short?"

Tuura only grinned at her. Darya grumbled under her breath, turning to the weapon rack. Being almost-five-foot tall sucked …

"What do you recommend then, o' tall one?"

"A staff or a spear. Long reach, don't require an overt amount of upper body strength. With the right techniques, they can be both offensive and defensive. You can utilise both ends of the staff as well."

"Luunaiwel did say something about a staff." Darya went to inspect her options.

Though they were practice weapons, she didn't feel particularly keen on stabbing anyone. Perhaps it was naive of her to think so, but Darya doubted she could ever stomach killing anyone.

That didn't stop the Night's Hand from killing Grandmama, though.

She went for the staff.

"Good choice." Tuura approved.

He proceeded to instruct Darya on how to hold the weapon properly, and teach her basic stances and manoeuvres. The length of the staff, though made specifically for dwarves and barely her own height, still threw Darya off. Her only experience with fighting was with her dagger, or grabbing whatever closest to her and blindly smashing it around.

Thank the Gods, Tuura was a patient instructor. He was very attentive with his demonstrations, and managed to get Darya on course quickly.

As they progressed, Darya was surprised to find how flexible fighting with a staff could be. True to Tuura's words, she could use both ends, with moves that included a series of strikes at various angles. She could even use the middle of the staff to block!

"It's recommended to redirect the blow instead of blocking it, especially when you're fighting against someone with a blade or a blunt force weapon."

"How come?"

Tuura lifted Darya's arms up to a blocking stance, "With your force against it and an opposite force striking at it, the staff is very brittle. The more force applied, the higher chances it will break."

He made a chopping motion at the centre of Darya's staff. She grimaced, "That's not good."

"Not at all," Tuura agreed, "it's better to use a quick deflect then redirect the flow of the fight, instead of being caught in a tug of war. It's always safer to assume your opponent would have more body strength than you. Fight defensively and opportunistically."

Eyeing her instructor's mass of muscles, Darya clicked her tongue, "Isn't it nice to never have to?"

Tuura flashed her a grin, "It is."

Sometime past midday, they stopped for a much needed break. A small stall was set up at the training ground for lunchtime. Fifteen coppers for a meat pie was a bit steep, but considering a fresh loaf of bread in Flumium was about the same, Darya supposed it was fair. She insisted on paying for Tuura, much to his amusement.

Sitting side by side at the stairs, Darya thanked Tuura for training her. Tuura chuckled.

"I'm doing the best that I can. I've never had to teach anyone before."

Darya swallowed her mouthful of pie before answering, "Coulda fool me! You're a natural!"

Tuura's smile was somewhat bashful, "Thank you."

Conversation through lunch was light, mainly about dwarves and their professions.

"You can distinguish them by their hairstyles." Said Tuura.

Darya raised an eyebrow, "Really? Well, I mean I recognise guard dwarves all have square-cropped beards, but I thought that was just protocol."

"In a sense," the Shapeshifter bobbed his head, "dwarves are actually very vain creatures, don't ever tell Nathi I said that … They are all obsessed over hair. There's even a rivalry among all groups when it comes to choice of up keeping."

"Hair-obsessed." Darya giggled.

"Indeed."

Tuura proceeded to explain each group's grooming habits. Bemused, Darya listened with rapt attention.

The most prominent group was the militant dwarves. The males had square cut, full but neatly trimmed beards, while the females had one tight braided bun at the top of their skulls, held together with golden pins. The merchants were the most decorated, the men boasted well-styled, oiled beards, while the women wore elaborate hairstyles, with gemmed brooches and stylish hats. Most practical would be the crafters and miners, with cropped beards and hair, some with full-shaven heads. Scholars like Nathi had voluptuous long beards, untrimmed and braided depending on their social standing, while the women had loose single braids, adorned with beaded jewelleries.

"They bicker a lot about styles, and it's the number one cause for brawls." Tuura concluded, making Darya burst out laughing. She couldn't imagine someone prim and proper like Sindri fighting with someone over hairstyle. Nathi, on the other hand …

Her amusement was distracted upon seeing Luunaiwel however, gliding up the stairs effortlessly.

"How is everyone doing?"

"Tuura's been showing me some moves with the staff. Where have you been?"

"Why, getting you the paperwork required to enter Tarum y Fýri, of course."

Immediately, Darya was excited, "Do you have it?"

"Not yet. But it should be ready for you by tomorrow afternoon," Luunaiwel said as they made their way back to the training area, "the fee was twenty seven silvers, which I have taken the liberty of subtracting from your deposit."

Ouch. That was hefty, but still much better than having to pay fifty every time she visited, "That means I still have twenty three left, right?"

Luunaiwel tilted her head, "No. You still have to pay for your sister's medicinal herbs, which was taken from Tarum y Fýri. That would leave you with nine silver from your initial fifty."

Darya almost face-planted. *Nine silver left???* She hadn't spent that much money in *a whole year* of travelling! And that included the amount sent back to Flumium!

Hanging her head, Darya sighed in defeat. All for the greater good, she supposed...

"I'm going to have to start performing again. Are there any taverns around?"

"Let us hold off on that until we have to travel again," Luunaiwel chuckled, "as a human, you must acquire a permit to perform here."

"Why does everything require a permit here?!"

Luunaiwel shrugged, "So they can keep their resources exclusive to Mul Tarum. Why do you think dwarves are so prosperous? They open trades with other races for only goods they cannot produce, and keep the best of what they can to themselves. They are not only crafty, they are also shrewd businessmen."

"That's how they survive and thrive when everyone else is dying." Tuura said quietly. Something in Darya wilted at those words.

Sensing the sunken mood, Luunaiwel clasped her hands together, smiling, "Since you are a novice and just had a meal, you should take a longer rest. I and Tuura will spar. Perhaps you can pick up a move or two watching us."

Tuura blinked, "We are sparring?"

Luunaiwel grinned at him, fangs and all, "We are."

The big man huffed. Stepping into the middle of the training area, Tuura strapped on both of his fist weapons. Likewise, Luunaiwel slipped off her travelling cloak and separated her sword. She was wearing a simple leather tunic and breeches today, without all her armour. Knowing that this could get dangerous, Darya hastily darted to sit on the side line, watching the two combatants with interest.

Luunaiwel's stance threw Darya off however.

She was relaxed, with her upper body leaned back and her swords dangling from limp arms in loose grips. Darya's brows crept up, incredulous. Luunaiwel's posture looked unguarded and defenceless, all in all just *wrong*.

Tuura took cautious steps around the elf whilst she stood still, a small smirk playing on her lips. Luunaiwel might have brought swords into the fight, but Tuura's arms were more than enough to make up for the reach. He circled around her, in the same fashion a wild predator would a dangerous prey, closing in as he went. Luunaiwel swayed gently, to a tune only she could hear.

Without warning, Tuura sprang forward like a loose arrow. Luunaiwel threw herself backward, body bent impossibly close to the ground. Elegantly, she rolled out of his striking distance, her arms still limp, a dancing willow to Tuura's whirlwind. Diving in, Tuura struck again, one hand above and the other to her left, but Luunaiwel blocked both blows with her swords, sliding the deadly claws away, using his own force to make Tuura tumble. He hastily jumped back, only to dive in once more and lashed out with the ferocity of a giant bear. This time, Luunaiwel kept the swords and her arms flush to her body, dodging Tuura's rapid strikes so fast she became a blur.

From the corner of her eyes, Darya saw that the spar was attracting attention from the others around the training ground. Not that she could blame those who gathered. Darya herself was entranced. The way Luunaiwel and Tuura moved was wild, inebriated, and more beautiful than Darya could put to words.

Luunaiwel was all defence and no offence, while Tuura was the complete opposite. His attacks were so rapid there was no opening at all.

When Tuura brought his fist down upon her, Luunaiwel ducked and dashed in, her body flush against his as she brought both her swords to his sides, forcing him to turn defensive, blocking just before she split him in half. He flicked her away and found no resistance. Luunaiwel grabbed onto his arm, using the momentum to vault herself away. The elf resumed her stance from the beginning, grinning.

"Can't catch me, bear-man."

"Watch me, raven."

Luunaiwel winked at him. Tuura growled.

She wasn't going to attack first, Darya realised amidst the crowd's growing cheers. Luunaiwel was baiting Tuura to come to her on his own. If he charged in, he would be at a disadvantage.

Darya was surprised when Tuura did so anyway, but just before he was within striking distance, he threw himself to the side to dodge the blades that would have run him through. Sliding on the ground, he wasted no time aiming a kick at Luunaiwel's legs, but she had anticipated that and leapt, dancing away as Tuura sprung up to lash at her again.

Blows were traded, dodged and blocked, but neither of them had gotten anywhere. It already passed a quarter hour mark and Luunaiwel was getting visibly impatient. Darya could see why. Any normal man would have fainted out of sheer exhaustion. By the Gods, most of the one on one fights Darya had witnessed only lasted for minutes. *Seconds,* even.

But Tuura was strong and resilient. His moves were bolder and stiffer than Luunaiwel's, but his speed made up for the flexibility and cunningness the elf possessed. Though he didn't have the same finesse as her, he certainly wasn't taking any punishment.

Luunaiwel had also switched her tactics and was now circling Tuura instead. She sprang up suddenly, her swords slicing the air as she turned offensive. Her movements became even faster, though she never managed to land any hit. The closest she got was cutting off a few strands of hair.

Tuura went defensive against her feral attacks, using the plates of his fist weapons as efficiently as small shields. Luunaiwel seemed to be everywhere at once. Left, right, up, down, back...

Finally, Tuura caught up to her movements. Luunaiwel tried to deflect him again, but Tuura anticipated that. He turned, striking into her opening. The fist weapon stopped just a hair before her face, but at the same time, her sword was at his throat.

They stood frozen for what seemed to be an eternity.

But then laughter spilled forth from Luunaiwel, as a grin broke out on Tuura's face. They lowered their weapons in the crowd's thunderous cheers, clasping hands and bowing at their spectators. Darya cheered as well, running towards the combatants.

"That was *incredible,*" Darya yelled above the noises, "I need to write a song or two about this!"

"I say it is worthy of a song." Luunaiwel laughed, raising Tuura's hand up again at another wave of cheers, "I have not had this much fun in decades!"

Bashful, Tuura laughed.

Luunaiwel turned to Darya, eyes twinkling in mischief.

"Now, little bird, show me what you have learned."

That effectively ended Darya's excitement, and filled her with dread instead.

Oh, boy.

CHAPTER 19:

By the time they left the training ground, it was late and Darya's entire body was sore. It felt like she was put in a sack and beaten with sticks. While she understood Luunaiwel had no intention of hurting her, the elf seemed to have fun knocking Darya off her feet for the entire afternoon.

Luunaiwel's good mood persisted all the way back to Nathi's estate, humming under her breath as Darya limped grumpily after her. Before they entered the manor, Luunaiwel suddenly asked, "Have you bathed since we got here?"

Darya blinked, sores momentarily forgotten, "No. Everything was so chaotic."

The question definitely got her self-conscious though. After the training, rolling in the dirt up in the Floating Forest, and everything else before that, Darya must stink to the Ancient Five.

"Right. No time like the present then."

Following Luunaiwel, Darya sniffed her pits inconspicuously while they waited outside of the master bedroom. She gagged. Stank to the Ancient Five indeed. She was surprised Nathi hadn't kicked her out yet.

Sindri was in the sitting room, her hair out of the elaborate do while she worked on a piece of embroidery. The curls trailed down her back in glossy cascades, so vivid in hue that Darya thought they were moving flames.

The dwarf smiled up at them, "You're back! How was training?"

"They beat me up." Darya muttered, sore.

"How else would you learn?" Luunaiwel's grin had no remorse or whatsoever.

Sindri chuckled daintily behind her hand, "So it begins. How can I help you?"

The elf jerked a thumb at Darya, "I am taking her to the bathhouse. Have you finished your project, Sindri?"

Sindri's pretty green eyes lit up, "Oh, but of course! Wait here just a moment!"

"Project," Darya echoed as Sindri disappeared behind her door, "what project?"

Winking, Luunaiwel held a finger over her lips, "Patient."

Sindri returned just a few moments later, holding two bundles. Confused, and not just a little concerned, Darya peeled open a package shoved into her hands. And almost fainted at the contents.

There was a sleeveless tunic, plain but expertly tailored, dyed forest green with gold brass buttons on the front. A pair of tanned leather breeches, laced on the legs, soft and sturdy. A pair of woollen gloves and a belt were included, neatly wrapped in a knitted shawl. These clothes must have cost two years' worth of coins, maybe more, of what Darya could have earned on the road. Even the untrained eyes could see that they were impeccably made to her size, with all the care in the world put into each and every stitch.

"Si-Sindri, I … I can't take this!"

"Nonsense," She patted Darya's hand, "I made these for you! What use would I have for them if you don't accept them?"

"But-"

Luunaiwel cut in easily, "Say 'thank you', Darya."

Feeling tears pricking her eyes, Darya lowered her head, "Thank you, Sindri."

If Sindri noticed the tremble in Darya's voice, the woman gracefully didn't address it, "You're welcome, dearie. Now go, enjoy yourselves."

Darya could do nothing else but to stutter her steps after Luunaiwel. She couldn't tear her eyes away from the bundle of clothes in her arms, and mumbled under her breath once they were outside.

"I need to tell them, don't I?"

"You do not *need* to do anything," Luunaiwel put an emphasis to the word, "whatever Nathi and Sindri choose to do, it is from the heart. They do not expect any repayment, nor would they demand an explanation from you."

Frankly, that made Darya feel worse about herself, "Maybe so, but it doesn't mean I shouldn't do anything either."

"In your position, it would be wise to take all you can, for what will be expected from you would be far more than anything you might receive along the way."

"That's not an excuse," Darya said, frustrated, "I never wanted to be a … you know! And I don't want to take anything for granted just because I'm one. I wasn't born one, and that shouldn't define who I am!"

Luunaiwel watched her out of the corner of the eye. The elf inclined her head.

"How noble of you."

Darya wanted bristle, but she also sensed no sarcasm in Luunaiwel's tone. She averted her eyes instead, "I'm not. I just don't want to owe anyone anything."

"Alas, the decision is yours. I will neither persuade nor stop you."

A neutral stance, as always, "Thanks. I know you've known them for a very long time, so it must be difficult for you..."

To her surprise, Luunaiwel scoffed, "Please ... I have known them for all their lives, but that is me. And I am not you. You barely know them for five days, which hardly gives you any reason to trust them."

"But ... shouldn't your word and experience hold some weight at least?"

The looked Luunaiwel gave Darya was piercing, "Perhaps, but that does not mean you should rely completely on my judgement. You are allowed to form your own opinion about someone, regardless of how another person might think."

Confusing, but Darya understood her point, "Right. I just thought since you said you trust them with your life …"

"And I do, because of our history," Luunaiwel said, "but that is not yours."

"Is this another lesson?"

A smile cracked upon her lips, stretching the thin scar on Luunaiwel's face, "It is. Always take someone's words with a grain of salt. The moment you start blindly following someone, it would be the gravest and last mistake you will ever make."

The conversation died off. Darya didn't know what else to say, and Luunaiwel didn't seem keen on talking anymore.

Luunaiwel led them down the road towards a facility, single-story and much larger than Nathi's residence. The inside was covered from floor to ceiling with a light marbled granite. Well-lit with candled scones on the walls, the space was basked in a soft glow that immediately relaxed Darya. There was a fragrance in the air, not too strong, but prominent enough to encourage her to take a few lungful, rib cage expanding with pleasant lavender and chamomile.

There was a woman standing behind a counter at the back, dark hair rolled into an artful bun atop her head. Luunaiwel gave her a couple of silvers for a key and a wicker basket, before heading down a long, carpeted corridor.

The room their key opened was hexagonal and tiled with marble. There was a large pit in the middle, but instead of a mattress, it was filled with steaming water, and the edge was lined with soft carpet. Luunaiwel locked the door behind them, and placed all her bundles on a table by the hearth.

Stumped and a bit embarrassed, Darya turned away when Luunaiwel undressed and eased herself into the pool.

"Get in. There are soaps, towels and sponges in the basket. Relax." The elf said, undoing her long hair.

Hesitantly, Darya stripped off her dirty clothes, careful not to let them touch the new ones Sindri gave her. Even though the pool was big enough for ten people to lounge about comfortably, Darya went to the opposite side of Luunaiwel, giving both of them the much needed personal space.

An unexpected but pleased sigh escaped Darya when she finally slipped into the water. It was the perfect temperature, a warmth akin to being wrapped up in a blanket by the hearth on a cold day. It relaxed her coiled up muscles, and eased away the stress that had Darya aching in places she didn't even know could ache.

Luunaiwel seemed content to let silence rule between them. The elf was leisurely enjoying herself, water only came up to her waist. Her long, wet hair was brushed back, fully exposed her sharp-tipped ears. Her pale skin glistened with moisture, the mist from the water defined her wiry muscles and her intricate network of tattoos. They were just as mesmerising as the first time Darya saw them, pieces of art that seemed to move on their own under the dancing light.

Still, they couldn't distract Darya's eyes from the elf's scarred arm.

She couldn't help but wonder what happened. What kind of incident could possibly leave such a terrible mark? Was it the same cause that carved the scar over Luunaiwel's green eye? Or was it something different? Darya's speculations ran wild, for she remembered not much was known about the elusive elf before her. Not even her age. Perhaps even Tuura and Nathi didn't know everything about Luunaiwel.

While Darya knew the elf preferred to be secretive, she couldn't help but think Luunaiwel led an extremely lonely existence. Known and loved by many, yet never let anyone close.

Realising that she was being intrusive, Darya looked away, cheeks burning. She started scrubbing her own hair, relishing in the bubbly soap from the basket. She had only ever seen servants from the Duke of Flumium used soap before, and no other place on her travel could people afford such luxury. It was an exclusive dwarfish product, and dwarven-made products were always expensive. Darya had never felt this clean in... well, ever, and she didn't think her skin could ever get this soft or dirt free.

"Luunaiwel?"

"Yes, little bird?"

Darya's hand went up to cup at her Heart Stone, "Would there be any text about Druids in the library?"

"Likely. The Great Library of Kul'loc is an accumulation of knowledge, collected and preserved for millennia. Even I have not scratched the surface of it."

"How would one locate the needed knowledge, then?"

Luunaiwel smirked, "Why, the catalogue, of course."

Darya blinked, "Catalogue?"

"It is a register of sort. One that serves as inventory of the library's content. I believe that would greatly aid you in your quest for knowledge."

That brightened Darya's mood considerably, "Would such a thing be available for me?"

"Of course," Luunaiwel chuckled, "I must warn you that … with a library that great, the catalogue is lengthy. And most of them are in Dwarfish."

Excitement wilted just as fast as it came. Darya made a distressed noise, brushing away the sweat that had gathered on her brows.

"Our few months stay isn't going to be enough to learn a new language."

Luunaiwel's head shake was dripping with amusement, further fuelling Darya's irritation.

"I must admit, this is part of my oversight. I was too consumed by my purpose to seek the earth pulses, I did not consider a Druid could possibly play a part in the world's revival. It has simply been so long."

It took a moment for the meaning of Luunaiwel's words to settle in. Sixteen years of life seeing the barren roads, living through all the hardship she had, starving and drowning in poverty … it didn't amount to how long the world had been in this state. Half a millennium, wasn't it? And Luunaiwel had likely seen all of it.

Had she perhaps struggled like Darya had? Probably not. But she had seen much of it, and strived to fix what she could in her own way. Luunaiwel said people gave up on the hopes of a Druid two centuries after the Shattering.

Did Luunaiwel give up hope on a new Druid too?

She must have.

Biting back a sigh, Darya resumed her self-cleaning. She lifted her leg above water, and almost hit her head on the side of the pool. Slipping under, Darya came up sputtering to a chortling Luunaiwel.

"Careful now. We do not want your entry to Tarum y Fýri turned into a permanent residence, do we?"

"That doesn't sound terrible, all things considered." Darya half-joked, messily wiped off water on her face with her hands. Only to blush furiously when she saw Luunaiwel glided over, sponge in her hand.

It was easy to be mesmerised by the elf. Luunaiwel's inked skin might be a piece of art, but she was art itself, in the mysteries and incredible capability she held in her willowy form. It wasn't just her beauty, but it was in the way she moved. Even when without a shred of clothes, Luunaiwel wore her coursing experience and power like an armour, the confidence in her unwavering blue-and-green eyes made Darya stay rooted at the spot.

"I ... I can do it myself!" The young Druid squeaked, coming to her senses before the elf could reach for her leg. To prove her point, Darya lifted her own limp up again and, by some feat of miracle, didn't fumble this time.

She let out a small, triumphant cry, much to Luunaiwel's amusement.

But then ... everything shifted.

"Darya?"

There was something unusual in Luunaiwel's voice. The note sent a chill down Darya's spine, not unlike how she felt when they were about to plunge into the darkness infested with Withered.

"What's wrong?"

Before Darya knew it, Luunaiwel had grabbed her right foot.

"Wah! Hey!!!" She sputtered, struggling out of instinct, very much alarmed. The sudden flood of Luunaiwel's life force sent her head into a dizzying spiral, making Darya flail about in panic. She squirmed to yank away, reaching over to bat off Luunaiwel's iron grip, until she saw what made Luunaiwel so worked up.

Darya promptly froze, a different kind of panic bled into her.

There was a line *inked* into Darya's skin, wrapping around her calf all the way to her knee. It was fashioned like a vine, with delicate leaves fanning on both sides.

Gasping, Darya stared at *her tattoo* in disbelief, "What in the name of Vita..."

"When did you get this?" Luunaiwel's voice was strained.

"I... I don't know," Darya stammered, pulling her foot free to get a better look at it herself, "my pants are long and it's dark in the outhouse, and the last couple of days have been *so crazy I don't even know I have this thing!!*"

Luunaiwel crouched to have a closer look. In a different situation, Darya would have died of embarrassment, but she was too spooked out to care at this point.

"When you established your connection in Tarum y Fýri, you fell asleep. Did you dream?"

The girl blinked, the distant memory of a singing voice came to her, "Yes?"

"What did you see?"

"I .. I..."

Her hair was as warm as the earth, cascading in waves that bounced with every laughter. Glittering green eyes were innocent, yet spoke of enticing secrets. Her curves were lustrous, accented with sun-kissed skin and pouting lips. She was full of life, and her sight alone beckoned every and all mortal to flock to her steps.

Darya's eyes widened, "The Goddess Vita..."

"The Celestial of Life." Luunaiwel mumbled, looking like she just saw a ghost.

"Luunaiwel?"

"Did she say anything to you?"

Steadily growing more fearful by the second, Darya nodded, "Y-yes, she said... she asked me to... bloom for her. To grow? And... restore what was hers? And then something about... Sorry, it's a bit of a jumble in my head and it's hard to put into words..."

"And you have been growing flowers in your sleep ever since."

"I... Yes ..."

Luunaiwel sat back on her haunches, mismatched eyes haunted. Worried, Darya waved a hand in front of the elf's face, "Luunaiwel? What's wrong?"

It was difficult to decipher the emotions Luunaiwel wore when she looked at Darya, "Darya... You are not just the first Druid we have seen since the Shattering. You are also Celestial-Blessed, or *God-Touched,* as you might say."

Yet another new term, "What... What does that mean?"

"It means you are entrusted with a portion of a God, your Goddess Vita, to be specific," Luunaiwel pointed at the inked vine on Darya's leg, "that vine is one of the Celestial of Life's most prominent symbol. When a Celestial chooses a person, a mark will be bestowed, engraved upon the receiver's skin."

"That's..." Gaping, Darya was at a loss of what to say.

"I was wondering why you were able to grow flowers without seeds or viable soil nearby," Luunaiwel leapt out of the pool, quickly drying and clothing herself, "you cannot create something from nothing. Not with ordinary magic. Doing something like that would have killed you if you were any ordinary magick-user. No ... The only beings who could, *can,* are those who came from Nothingness itself."

Feeling her panic growing, Darya followed suit, "What does this mean???"

Luunaiwel's piercing eyes glittered, "It means that the Celestial of Life is willing to enlist a mortal to take back what was hers. She is not willing to forsake us, yet."

Darya's head spun. She stared down at her leg like the appendage wasn't attached to her.

First a Druid, now this?

Another person would probably feel privilege. Special. Important. A Chosen One. A hero that appeared on my fabled tales and myths.

But the deaths of almost everyone Darya had ever known still hang around her neck like a shackle. Fear seized her when she thought about Sara. Even Luunaiwel, Tuura, Nathi and Sindri. She knew bad people wanted to get their hands on her before, but now Darya had more power, and that just made her situation even more dangerous. Maybe Luunaiwel's paranoia was rubbing off on her, but the young Druid shuddered to think how high the stakes could be now.

Infuriatingly, she was still far from being prepared. If anything happened, Darya would still be useless and had to rely on others to get out of trouble.

"I am sorry, Darya."

Startled, she turned to Luunaiwel, and was taken aback by the remorse in the elf's odd eyes.

"For what?"

Luunaiwel shook her head, "I told you that it would be your choice, whether you would like to be a Druid or go back to your life as it once was. For the first time in this age, I cannot keep my words. This situation has escaped our grasps. And for that, I am sorry."

There was so much honest *regret* in her voice that Darya couldn't help but give Luunaiwel a hug. Feeling arms coming around her, Darya bit down her lower lip.

"It's alright, Luunaiwel... We'll figure out a way."

"For your sake, little bird, I hope we will."

CHAPTER 20:

The physical fatigues kept Darya asleep. For better or worse, she was thankful for the rest. But waking up to clusters of wolfsbane immediately hitched up her anxiety.

Just like the day before, Darya was brought to the training ground by Tuura. Her muscles were stiff, and she moved even more rigidly than the day before despite knowing the moves better. Tuura's mock spar knocked her down more times than she could count.

"Gah," Darya smacked the ground, frustrated, "I can't do this! My body feels like stone today!"

Tuura was patient, "Your body needs to get used to the exercises. Stopping now would only do you more harm than good."

Groaning, because she knew he was right, Darya rolled back onto her feet, "Fine... Let's get this over with. You're lucky it's not you who I wanna beat up."

Tuura gave her a crooked smile, "Lucky me."

Darya waved her staff around menacingly, "Don't push it, big man."

She was knocked on her rump again in five seconds flat.

"Gah!!"

In hindsight however, having to keep an eye out for Tuura and his lightning-fast moves kept Darya's mind off her most recent discovery. She wanted to put a hold over that for as long as she could.

Luunaiwel didn't show up until late afternoon. The elf brought a small bag with her this time, containing Darya's shiny new badge, a few documents and the remainder of her fifty silver.

"You may access Tarum y Fýri freely at any time with this," Luunaiwel pointed at the badge, "do not lose it. If you take out anything, herbs, flowers, etcetera, you still have to pay for the individual items. This paperwork is for your horse, so you will not have to pay extra for the rest of your stay here in Mul Tarum. You will have to have it renewed on your next visit however."

The last pieces of paperwork didn't bring Darya as much joy. It was a guardian consent to let Sara stay in Tarum y Fýri for the rest of her treatment and agreement to share guardianship with

Nathi while Darya would be away. Dwarves really had every kind of formal document for every kind of scenario.

"It would not be in effect unless you sign it," Luunaiwel said, "you have time to decide."

"I need to talk to Sara about this." Darya sighed, skimming through the words. Thank the Gods, her parents had the insight to have her learn how to read when she was a kid. Being literate had proven to be essential on so many occasions, especially here in Mul Tarum.

Luunaiwel nodded, "I would also suggest spending the night in the forest. Being a Druid, sleeping on healthy earth would help you revitalise quicker."

"I'll need that." Darya winced.

After finishing dinner at Nathi's, Darya was sent off to Tarum y Fýri with a blanket. Luunaiwel told her it would be best if she slept directly on top of the soil. Despite not asking any question, the dwarf physician did give Darya an inquisitive look upon the instruction. The young Druid could only duck her head and retreat, feeling guilt rose like bile in her throat.

The guards upstairs didn't give her any grief, professional through and through. It was a massive relief. The guards in

Flumium could be cruel to commoners, and she would rather not have to go fetch Luunaiwel when her limbs were ready to grow roots.

The moment Darya shucked off her boots and sunk her toes to the grass, a wave of soothing energy washed over her.

Her Heart Stone pulsed, warm as the forest spoke to her.

[Druid Friend.] The grass sang.

[Druid Friend.] The trees rustled.

[Druid Friend.] The flowers spun.

The tired fog in her head cleared, and Darya took a moment to relish in this gentle companionship.

Despite the huge trees, the forest wasn't as dark as it should be. There were specs of something luminescent, growing in the crevices of barks, hiding under shades of great canopies.

[Firefly caps.] A young cherry tree happily supplied. Darya smiled, smoothing her hand along its bark.

Thank you.

The tiny fungi nestled in small cracks along trees' bodies, shielded them away from direct, harsh sunlight, but still enough to absorb some to shine at night. Blue, white and green they flickered, basking the forest in a soft, ethereal glow.

Darya felt as though she was walking in a dream.

You're beautiful. She thought.

Velvety caps shivered under her fingertips, voices in a chiming chorus.

[Thank you, Druid Friend.]

Deeper into the green, she walked. Everywhere her feet touched, she felt the gentle presence of the forest at the back of her head. Darya reached out to all of them, and let their welcome ease her heavy heart.

Slowly but surely, the forest led her back to the old birch. The wolfsbane swayed serenely in his cradle, and the grass where he grew was velvety soft. Reaching out, Darya pressed her hand against the birch's bark.

[Hello, Seedling.]

The birch's ancient presence filled Darya's mind, pulling the last of her tiredness away, replacing it with a comfortable haze of sleepiness. Yawning, Darya curled up among gnarled roots, ready for a restful night.

Sleep came easy, and she dreamed a dream so vivid and tender, it was like a memory.

From darkness, she rose to light. She heard noises, words that she couldn't understand. She felt the earth around her shifted.

Small, young and afraid, she was moved to an unfamiliar home.

But gentle hands came, and with them, a gentle voice.

Druid.

He was kind. He was patient.

He brought water to her, and told her tales of the world that her young mind hadn't yet understood. But she yearned for his voice, for the nurturing hands that urged her to grow.

Bright eyes. Green as the world around her.

Bright hair. White as moonlight.

A circlet was woven into his hair. Silver and adorned with gems.

A crown fit for a Prince.

Most times, he came alone. Sometimes, he came with her, a lady with laughing blue eyes and hair dark as midnight. They would sing for her, urge her to grow, and tell her how much the world would behold her as its greatest wonder.

They came, dressed in white once. They strung her branches with silk and flowers, dancing under her canopy. They were happy, and they made a vow of eternity under her leaves.

She wished she could have sung for them.

They didn't return after that day. Not for a long, long time.

She grew as she waited. Growing and watching over the others who grew, too. Growing until she wasn't alone, growing until she was the strongest and oldest of them all.

Still, she waited.

The lady returned. Alone. With scars on her eye and in her heart. With a hand on the great birch tree, she mourned.

The birch stood, leaves rustling in the wind.

Waiting, waiting, *waiting.*

Until another Druid came to wake him once more.

Darya woke to sunlight dancing in her vision and sprawling reaches of flowers. Yellow, red, purple, pink... Each was packed full of petals, cute as a button and vibrant with colours.

[Zinnia.] The birch hummed.

The dream was his, of days gone and long past. Darya bowed her head, thanking him.

[Thank you for the gift, Seedling. Return to me, when you are ready for the journey ahead.]

Careful to not step on the swaying flowers, Darya bid her goodbye and hurried to the entrance of Tarum y Fýri. She recognised one of the guards, Bork, and he was kind enough to point her to where the treatment chambers would be, left from the front door.

Darya never looked at the paths on either side of the forest before, always too distracted by the trees. The white building at the end of a winding path had a similar structure as the shops down in Merchant Hall, with smaller glass windows and balconies arching with blooming vines. Unlike the wild growth that was the forest, the grass before the treatment building was neatly trimmed to a soft fuzz. The bushes were also tamed, dotted with fragrant flowers, surrounding a common area where inpatients and their visitors sat under the morning sun.

A nurse kindly helped Darya to find Sara, who looked pink and vibrant despite having only spent a few nights here. Something in Darya's heart tightened.

Deciding to by herself some time, Darya took Sara down to the Merchant Hall for breakfast. On the lift down, Sara suddenly giggled.

"What's so funny?" Darya asked.

"It's just strange," Sara shrugged, still smiling, "a few days ago, Grandmama was worried about not having enough for dinner, *just* dinner. And here we are, going to get *breakfast* like noble ladies. And Grandmama is..."

"Gone." Darya finished, when the silence followed grew too heavy.

Sara looked away, "Yes. *Gone.*"

For a moment, Darya thought her sister was going to cry. But Sara didn't, even though her voice was stifled when she continued.

"I thought about a lot of things yesterday. About Grandmama, about you, about me... It really does suck, but I think... It's better for me to stay here. But you... you shouldn't have to wait around for me. I'm no good travelling with you like this, and I *want* to travel with you, eventually, when I'm better. And I *am* getting better. I *feel* better with the treatment so far and the forest... The medicine is a bit yucky, but it's nothing I can't handle."

Sara paused to think. Darya didn't dare interrupt her, knowing that this must have been difficult. Gods above, Darya herself was struggling to hold back tears.

Sara chewed on her lower lip, nervous, "I spoke with Nathi yesterday. The treatment would last for at least a year. He said even if you don't pay anything... he and Luna would be happy to cover for me..."

That was unexpected. But Darya supposed she should have known. Luunaiwel never hesitated to go the extra mile, and money never seemed to be a problem for her. Still, whether Luunaiwel would handle the payment or not, it would still be Nathi who had to look after Sara while they were away. Darya just didn't think Nathi would be willing to go that far.

Guilt came in a tidal wave.

"Oh." Was all Darya could say.

Sucking in a long breath, Sara nodded, "So... So go ahead and don't worry. Alright?"

Darya was wrong. Sara wasn't the one who cried. *She* was. But the young Druid quickly wiped her tears away, not wanting

Sara to have any more reasons to be sad. Her little sister was being brave, so Darya should be, too.

They bought some fresh pastries from a bakery in Merchant Hall, and went to sit at the bottom of the training ground stairway. They reminisced about the past. Some old, some new. Most of it Sara couldn't remember. Some were painful enough for them to cry over and some made them laugh amidst tears.

It certainly didn't feel like it was the kind of conversation two young girls should have. But Darya supposed it was alright. They needed to grow up quickly. They needed to become stronger, in their own respective way.

Sara went back up to the Haven Hall before midday for her treatment. Having nothing else to do, Darya returned to Nathi's house. The dwarf was seeing a patient, so she postponed thanking him and went to the sitting room, where she found Luunaiwel.

"How are you feeling today?" The elf asked with a smile.

"I feel... pretty well, actually," Darya shrugged, "I told Sara … about us leaving. She took it better than I thought."

Luunaiwel raised an eyebrow, "You have decided?"

"Yes."

"I see. She took it well?"

Darya nodded, feeling her throat closed up, "Look, Luunaiwel, I just want you to know that I'm really, *truly* grateful for all you've done for us. I don't know if I can ever repay you. But if you don't want to carry on protecting me, I'd understand, I've been a lot of trouble and I-"

Darya didn't even see when Luunaiwel moved. One moment, the elf was across the table, the next, she was inches from Darya's face.

Staring into eyes that looked like they held constellations, Darya didn't dare to breathe.

"I still do not think you understand how important you are," Luunaiwel spoke slowly, her voice barely a whisper, "it is imperative that you are to be protected, that you are allowed to seize control of your gift."

The elf stood up, heaving out a sigh.

"This is far bigger than just you or I. It is not your fault, but someone with much higher power has forced our hands. We have to play along, but until something more deliberate is *implored*, I will do my best to spin this to your favour."

Swallowing, Darya nodded. Luunaiwel was right. This whole thing with her turning into a God-Touched Druid was important, and she couldn't risk this, risk *herself,* with the likes of the Night's Hand still being out there.

In hindsight, three months of preparation didn't seem enough.

"When do you think it would be best to leave?"

"There is a celebration in two and a half months' time, the Moondust Festival. It is celebrated four times a year, when the moon is at its peak. There will be free flowing ales, whole-roasted swines and goats, and music playing from dawn to dusk. Best of all … everyone will be blackout drunk."

Facing Luunaiwel's grin, Darya deeply regretted not being able to attend such an epic event, "It'd be easy for us to slip out then."

"Aye."

"Would that be enough? We were talking about three initially …"

Luunaiwel's grin widened, "Ample."

Her confidence fuelled Darya's own, "What do we do next then?"

Something mischievous twinkled in mismatched eyes, "My dear little bird, I believe it is time we forge your own weapon. One that is unique and answers only to you."

CHAPTER 21:

It took two weeks for Darya to make up her mind.

Whether it was the glorious mushroom omelettes Sindri prepared for breakfast, or Darya's enormous guilt, she didn't know. But Darya felt it was the right thing to do. If she left without resolving this tangle, she knew her conscience could never rest well.

It was the least she could do.

She chose to break the news after dinner one night, so they were at least high in spirit.

"I can never thank you enough for all you have done for me and my sister," Darya said, pouring all her sincerity and gratitude into those words, "and I don't think I can ever repay you. So if there is anything I can do, please let me know."

"I'm goin' ta be straight with ye," Nathi tapped a finger on the table, "I wouldn't have gone out of me way for ye if it wasn't for Lulu."

Darya nodded, having expected this, "I understand."

Nathi held a hand up, "But also, children bear no fault of their forefathers. What happened ta ye and yer family ain't yer fault, and I hate the Night's Hand as much as any other civilised person."

Blinking, Darya turned to Luunaiwel. The elf inclined her head.

"I have given them the reason why you are here with us, and that you are my disciple. Nothing more."

Flashes of the tragic events in Flumium filled her mind. Gripping at her thigh under the table, Darya willed them away. This wasn't the time.

"I just want you to know... that I am grateful. For everything. You both have been so kind to me and my sister. Because of Luunaiwel's request or not, that doesn't change. I owe you the truth, at least."

Reaching across the table, Sindri squeezed Darya's hand, "Dearie, you owe us nothing. Being decent to someone in need should be a common courtesy. You shouldn't have to feel obliged to tell us anything. We know that you are Luunaiwel's disciple, and that is enough for us."

Nathi nodded in agreement, "If Lulu thinks it's important enough ta keep quiet even ta us, then it ain't our business ta know."

Darya trembled, trying to speak around the lump around her throat, "But I... I *need* to tell you. I *want* to..."

Exchanging a look with her husband, Sindri frowned, squeezing Darya's hand once more, "Are you sure?"

Locking her jaws together, Darya nodded. Heart pounding, she took a deep breath, then let go in a rush.

"I am a Druid."

The long stretch of silence that followed was unnerving.

"Yer a *what??!*" Nathi sounded faint.

Darya opened her mouth. But Nathi held his hand up, stopping her.

"I need a moment."

Nervously, glancing at Luunaiwel, Darya wilted when she realised the elf was keeping her expressions carefully blank. Tuura was stoic as ever, but there was a deep grove on his forehead.

Sindri had gone completely quiet, frozen in shock. Biting her lower lip, Darya pulled her hand away from the dwarf woman's, feeling her heart sink when she met no resistance. Darya shrank down into her chair, wishing that she could just disappear.

By Vita... They weren't taking this well at all.

A million thoughts shot through Darya's head, none of which positive. But she steeled herself. She had thought of the worst case scenario. If Nathi and Sindri telling her secret to the authorities, Darya would have to grab Sara and run.

But … *where?*

Ice and fire runs down the back of her neck. She should have discussed this with Luunaiwel beforehand, instead of just … blurting it out. Darya twisted her hands together under the table, could only hope that her own idiocy wouldn't cost her so much this time.

When Nathi found his voice again, the dwarf's bright eyes moved between Darya and Luunaiwel, his skin several shades paler under his red beard.

"I don't know whether this' a good thing or a bad."

Luunaiwel tilted her head to the side, "How come?"

Sindri's lips were a thin line, "Lulu, the Night's Hand... They know about Darya?"

The elf mage affirmed Sindri's question with a nod. The seamstress sighed.

"She can't stay here, then," Darya shrunk further down, having expected that much, "she can't stay *anywhere* for long at that matter. They will catch up to her, and she will be in danger."

Darya blinked. *That* she didn't expect.

Luunaiwel nodded in agreement, "She needs to be capable of fending for herself first. Though she has begun her training, Mul Tarum will not be safe forever."

"If her pursuers came from Flumium, and the trail went cold half way from there, then they already know you are in Mul Tarum," Sindri pointed out, "they will be waiting for you. When you do leave, you cannot use the main entrance."

"They'd want ta catch her young. Easily manipulated." Nathi grimaced.

Luunaiwel exchanged a look with Darya, "We have already discussed this. We will most likely be leaving in two months' time, at the height of the Moondust Festival."

Nathi groaned, shaking his head, "Ye've thought of everything, ay?"

"I would not say *everything*," Luunaiwel rolled her shoulders, giving Nathi a crooked smile, "I have only presented a few possibilities, of which Darya here would decide which would be best for her journey."

Darya fidgeted when all eyes were on her. Her tongue was stiff due to the sudden wash of emotions. Fear, relief, gratitude and anxiety all mixed into one tangled knot in her chest.

"I haven't decided on where to go yet." She said honestly.

Luunaiwel squeezed her shoulder in reassurance, "We do have some time. This is something to be carefully considered, after all."

That made it a bit easier to breathe, "Thanks, Luunaiwel."

"Anytime, little bird."

Hesitantly, Darya turned to look at the two dwarves, "I'm... sorry. I understand that you might be feeling differently about me now, and I-"

"Bah, shut it, lass," Nathi grumbled, "I've said it once and I'll say it again. It ain't yer fault. I ain't no expert, but I know a new Druid's pretty extraordinary. From what I can tell... it didn't seem like it's yer choice either."

Darya grimaced, "Not consciously... No. To be fair, it's the consequence of my own stupidity, and I'm just here to deal with what's coming out of it."

The dwarf's bark of laughter lightened her heart, "Ain't that all o' us? But aye... ye being a Druid ain't goin' ta change anything. In fact, it makes it important that everyone who knows needs ta chip in as much as we can ta ensure ye'd be able ta fulfill yer mission."

"What my husband is trying to say is," Sindri smiled, shaking her head, "you owe us nothing. It is our duty to ensure that you, the first Druid of this Shattered Age, will be able to restore the world. *You* are its last hope."

Swallowing, Darya nodded, "Thank you."

Hearing that, the weight on her shoulders grew heavier. A debt was easier to bear than the hope of everyone she knew.

Luunaiwel then stood, clapping her hands together with a smile, "With that out of the way, I would like to move onto what needs to be done. Darya needs a weapon. She has been taking well to the staff as of late."

"It has ta be wooden," Nathi was quick to suggest, "she ain't goin' ta be able ta use a metal one."

Sindri hummed, "That means we will have to get it from Tarum y Fýri. Does it have to be a choice piece of wood or any can do?"

Luunaiwel said, "Supposedly, it was a tradition for a new Druid to *ask* the forest where he or she first established a connection with for a gift. A blessed link for companionship. I believe something of that degree can be formed into her weapon."

Image of the old birch flashed in Darya's mind, "I think I know what to do."

"That'd be expensive." Nathi wrinkled his nose.

Luunaiwel shook her head, "The cost of everything else needed for her staff would be expensive anyway. What she needs is no ordinary weapon."

Uh-oh... "How much are we talking about?"

"Something around ten gold."

Darya's head spun, "I can't afford that!!! And I don't want you to have to cover it for me either!"

Luunaiwel's eyes twinkled with mischief, "I do appreciate your virtues, but now is not the time for it. However, what you can do is help Nathi and Sindri in repayment. Celestials know Nathi needs those bookshelves cleaned."

Nathi glared, "Heeeeeey..."

Eagerly, Darya accepted, "I can do that!"

"You can also come help Sindri at her store."

"I would appreciate that." Said seamstress smiled kindly at Darya.

"And you can help me organise my travelling bags and polish my armours." Luunaiwel finished, looking smug.

"That's absolutely doable," Darya was more than happy to agree, some form of repayment would be better than none, "how about you, Tuura?"

"Nothing for now." Tuura spoke for the first time since the beginning of this stressful conversation.

"I am sure he can come up with something," Luunaiwel chuckled, "you are still expected to train with him every morning from now until we have to leave."

"Alright. Anything else I can do?"

"That would be it, for now," Luunaiwel said, "something else will come up eventually, that is certain. Now, since we still have the rest of the day, shall we start gathering components for your staff?"

As conflicted as Darya was about everything, she still couldn't suppress her excitement.

"Let's!"

It was overwhelming when Luunaiwel led her to a jewellery store in the Merchant Hall. Diamond, ruby, sapphire, topaz … they glittered with so many colours under dancing candle flames. Darya was afraid to touch anything, not wanting to mar the glass. Wide-eyed and at a loss for words, she looked around, completely mesmerised, and not really listened as Luunaiwel spoke to the shopkeeper. A case of loose gems were then brought out for them to choose in private.

Darya could only gawk. There must be enough gems to pay for a Duke's mansion in that box alone!

Luunaiwel explained when the shopkeeper retreated, giving them some privacy to browse the gems, "Most magick-users of higher tiers wear a lot of gemstones back in the day. As they formed deep within the earth, a primal source of magic, gems can serve as conduits or storage for excessive magic depending on the enchantment. Think of it as a coin purse for energy."

Darya nodded along, still rather stunned.

"You need to pick out two."

"Two???"

Amusement coloured Luunaiwel's voice, "Yes. Two. Quickly now. We have other errands to run."

Darya looked down at the collection again. She didn't know where to begin. By Vita, she didn't even dare to touch any of them! Even some Nobles couldn't afford most of anything here.

Luunaiwel encouraged again, sensing Darya's hesitation, "They are not as outrageously priced as you might think. Gems are common finds within the deeper reaches of the Eria, as thus even commoners can afford them in Mul Tarum. The dwarves just trade them in a controlled quantity with the rest of Ardent, making these rarer than they seem."

Another shrewd business tactic. Not wanting to waste Luunaiwel's time, Darya inspected the gems, and found her eyes caught by the rubies. Glistening under candlelight, they reminded Darya of her Heart Stone. Red, like blood. Birthed from the veins that bled to keep Ardent alive.

Darya thought it would be fitting, to have the gems of her first staff matching the stone that started this adventure.

"I … I would like those. Rubies, I mean …"

"Perfect." Luunaiwel hailed the shopkeeper.

The elf paid four gold coins for two stones, each the size of an egg. Darya almost fainted.

Looking at Darya, Luunaiwel chuckled "I believe I should hold onto these for now." And took the velvet boxes that now housed the gems.

As they walked out, Darya finally came to her senses and flailed her arms, *"Luunaiwel!!! This is too much!!!"*

"Is it? We got a good deal, actually. They are impure and the colours are not desirable for jewellery."

"They're four gold!!!"

Luunaiwel's tone was nonchalant, "And they could have gone for much higher if they were a deeper red. Loose gemstones typically come cheaper than set jewellery."

At the verge of a meltdown, Darya couldn't utter another word when Luunaiwel herded her off to Tarum y Fýri.

"You said you have a tree in mind?" Luunaiwel asked.

"Yes. He's an old birch."

Something glinted in Luunaiwel's mismatched eyes, "The same one you established a connection with?"

"The same."

"Interesting. But suitable."

When they got to the tree, Luunaiwel whistled at the patch of zinnia, "You have been busy."

Darya blushed, "It's not like I can control it yet."

Luunaiwel didn't know much about the official rituals and happenstances of how Darya could ask the forest for a blessing. But as they weren't in an exactly ideal situation that whatever Druidic protocol could be applied to, both agreed to just let Darya wing it with the request and see how it might proceed from there.

Carefully approaching the birch, Darya reached out, and was immediately soothed by the familiar presence.

[Seedling.]

Hello, Birch-Man.

[Is it time, Seedling?]

I... think so. I am here to request for a blessing.

[Take your pick, Seedling. Take me to see the world, and I will aid you with all that I am.]

The branches above her rustled, gentle and encouraging. Mesmerised, Darya let her fingers brush against fanning leaves.

Will this hurt you?

[We do not feel pain like your kind do, Seedling.]

Thank you.

Turning to Luunaiwel, "I can take any branch, he said!"

Luunaiwel raised an eyebrow, "You want to look for a healthy one. Something sturdy and not too young."

"What about the shape?"

"As long as it is not too crooked, any would suffice."

With some help from the old birch himself, Darya found a branch that drooped close to the ground, with a slight curve at the end. Luunaiwel cut off roughly six feet of it, then sheared the leaves and smaller branches off. Sending one last gratitude to the birch, Darya followed Luunaiwel out, feeling giddy about her potential staff.

The price of it however, almost made her carry the branch back inside.

"Five gold?!?!?! Are you kidding me?!!?!?!?" She hissed at the elf, eyes bulging as they rode the lift back down to Scholar Hall.

Luunaiwel gave her a grin, enjoying Darya's reeling immensely, "Healthy wood in this day and age is rarer than gold."

"But *five whole gold...*"

Luunaiwel's grin widened, "I hope you are good at cleaning, then."

"I don't think *any* amount of cleaning is worth that much gold," she then sighed, "alright, what's next?"

"You will need to carve down the bark by hand. Tuura will help you refine it. It will need to be dried, then we will add some metallic bracing to sturdy the whole structure and socket the gems. Nathi's cousin, Nadin the Third, is a metalsmith. He can help us with this process. We will also need to varnish the staff. Do you have a colour or material in mind?"

At a loss, Darya threw out something at random, "Blackberries?"

That put Luunaiwel to a halt, "Blackberries."

Feeling her cheeks heating up, Darya scrunched up her nose, "I just... I remember that drink you gave me when we first got here, and the colour is pretty..."

Luunaiwel chuckled, "I shall see what we can do."

When they returned to Nathi's, Darya did as Luunaiwel told, carefully peeled off the bark and had Tuura help fine tune the branch into a bare staff. It was then propped up by her room's fireplace to dry.

Darya started spending every afternoon going between Nathi's house and Sindri's shop. Luunaiwel was right, Nathi's shelves needed *a lot* of dusting, and there were *a lot* of books. Darya did get to read some interesting books during her cleaning time though, learning about plants and flowers that she had never seen before. It helped her identify the ones she created in her sleep. Darya mainly grew Traveller's Joy these days, clusters of white flowers that smelled so sweet it was a shame to trim off.

As for Sindri's shop, Darya mostly handled simple labours that didn't require a lot of finesse. Carrying bolts of fabric, sorting boxes, and taking care of deliveries … Sindri's trade might not interest Darya, but she was sure if given the opportunity, Sara would jump at being a seamstress. It wasn't physically taxing, and her little sister had always had an eye for prettier things.

Sara was scheduled to join them for dinner three times a week, and she had been reacting very positively to her treatments. Darya always accompanied her sister on her returns to the Haven Hall. She would sleep in Tarum y Fýri on those nights, feeling most at home among the trees.

A week passed just like that. A simple pattern, peaceful and easy to fall into. On the second day of the third week since their arrival at Mul Tarum, Luunaiwel deemed Darya's staff dry enough.

"I will be taking this to the Forge Hall," The elf said, "you should come and choose the design for your staff."

The Forge Hall was at the end of Merchant Hall, up one floor and into the stifling heart of the Eria Mountains. The stonework here was cruder than the other halls Darya had seen, fitted together in giant slabs and marked both by heat and constant collisions. This Hall was a long rectangular structure, with huge forges lining the walls. Their red flames never went out, and the central forge at the very back of the room was said to be heated with lava. Trailing the length of the hall was a great pool, where they cooled their forged creations. Workshops were set up in between forges, each had their own specialty.

The dwarves here wore very little, just breeches and sleeveless tunics, their beards and hair trimmed short or tightly braided. As with the Merchant Hall, everyone was busy with their own projects, occasionally shouting over the thunderous clanging of the forges.

Down the hall they went, to the workshop of a chestnut-haired and blue-eyed dwarf. He was stout and muscled, but Darya immediately noticed that his left forearm was covered with a metallic brace, and where his hand should be was a clamp. His toothy grin glinted with gold when he saw they approached.

"Oye! Lulu!"

"Cousin Nadin," Luunaiwel crouched down for a hug, mindful of the giant tongs Nadin was still holding, "I brought the materials."

"Straight ta bus'ness, as always!" His laughter was booming. Turning to Darya, he greeted, "Hello, lassie!"

"I'm Darya, pleased to meet you." Darya offered Nadin a hand, and almost stumbled when Nadin pulled her into an enthusiastic hug.

He gave her two thumps on the back that knocked the air out of her lungs, "No need ta be so formal! We're all friends of friends here!"

A bit dazed, Darya wrinkled her nose at a discreetly chuckling Luunaiwel. She handed over the branch to Nadin. The dwarf flipped it this way and that, inspecting the curves and pulling out a tape measurement.

"Hmm, hmm... So ye want ta add metal? An' sp'cific kind?"

With Luunaiwel's help, Darya quickly ran down the necessities, what she absolutely needed to have on the staff, the metal she wanted (red brass), where the sockets for the ruby should be and what design she wanted for decoration.

Nadin seemed happy with the information, "Th'rough, I like ye, lassie."

"When would you be able to have it done?" Luunaiwel asked. Nadin counted on his finger joints.

"Come back in eight days. Should be ready by then."

"That would be perfect. Thank you, Cousin."

Nadin laughed, "No sweat. Send Nathi me regards! Nice ta see yer lassies! Now, get outta me face! Got work ta do!"

Darya had an excited skip in her steps as they exited the Forge Hall,

A one of a kind weapon. Something made for her and her alone. Even though she knew there was much danger waiting ahead, Darya couldn't help but compare herself to the heroes she knew in legends and myths.

Perhaps one day, a long time after her quest was over, a bard would sing epic songs about her, as Darya did for the heroes she knew.

CHAPTER 22:

Darya thought that all they had to do before leaving Mul Tarum was to prepare for the trip ahead, but trouble came in the most unexpected and heinous way.

Four days before her staff was finished, a frantic Guard burst into Nathi's home at breakfast.

"Lord Whitestone, Lady Luunaiwel! We need you at the Gates, at once!"

Everyone at the table froze, except for Luunaiwel who slid out of her seat immediately.

"Magic-related problem?"

"I... Aye, milady," The Guard said, his dark eyes wide, "the scout found something... disturbing due South West of Mul Tarum."

"Do they need us to bring anything?"

"Gloves, and something to cover your nose and mouth."

Luunaiwel's scarred eyebrow almost touched her forehead, "Understood."

It wasn't difficult for Darya's mind to immediately jump to the Night's Hand.

"Can I come?" She blurted out without much thought. The look Luunaiwel gave her made Darya want to take back what she just said.

"Very well. But be careful."

With the guard leading the way, neither Nathi nor Luunaiwel spoke a word. There were plenty of exchanging glances between the two however, which only added to Darya's anxiety. Perhaps she was being foolish again. If this was a ploy to draw Darya out, then hadn't she just fallen right into it?

Curse her stupid curiosity.

There were military mallas waiting for them at the Gates of Mul Tarum. They rode for five miles, towards the mountains' southernmost edge where a group of dwarfish guards came into sight. One intercepted them, his face covered with a piece of cloth and though only his eyes were visible, terror was clearly written on them.

"Milord, Miladies! Cover yer faces! We think 'tis necromancy!"

Loudly, Nathi swore. Both he and Luunaiwel wrapped up their faces with their travelling cloak. Darya scrambled to pull up the shawl Sindri gave her.

Necromancy?

When they passed through the semicircle of guards, Darya finally understood why everyone they had seen was panicking. Nathi swore again. For once, Darya had to agree.

The sight was nothing short of awful.

The creature... it must have been some sort of small bear before it died. Matted fur was dirty, bald in patches. Where skin was supposed to be were globs of warts, pulsing with yellow puss and red-rimmed. The bear was all hide and bones, one hind paw missing and the remaining ones were blistering with infection. Its lower jaw was unhinged, and it was unclear whether that happened before or after its head was severed from its body. Nauseatingly, the bear's body was still twitching, and showed no sign of stopping.

Oh, and the *stench*. Everything reeked of *rotten death,* even through Darya's shawl. It took all her willpower to not vomit, because throwing up meant she would have to breathe in more of the air here, and Darya certainly did not want to do that.

None of that seemed to faze Luunaiwel however. Swinging off her saddle, the elf ordered everyone to keep their distance.

"Give me a dagger." Luunaiwel said, eyes glued on the corpse.

A guard threw a sheathed dagger towards Luunaiwel. The elf wasted no time. She went to the bear's detached head and, much to Darya's queasy horror, flipped it over, her gloved fingers searching its throat. Clumps of fur and rotted flesh fell off at the slightest of pressure. Puss and sores broke at the softest prod. This went on for what seemed like painful forever, before Luunaiwel finally found what she was looking for, and cut off a chunk of something that looked like grey flesh with fungi growing on it.

Darya gave up. She tacked her malla away and emptied the content of her stomach.

"Burn the remains," Luunaiwel ordered, putting the sample taken from the bear into a leather satchel, "make sure that nothing is left but ashes. Report to your Captain. We will determine the cause of this before notifying the Council."

After a chorus of "Yes, m'lady", she led Nathi and Darya back to Mul Tarum.

"So what in Mortia's name was that thing???" Darya exclaimed as soon as they were out of hearing distance.

"Funny you invoked the name of your Goddess of Death," Luunaiwel said, but there was no hint of laughter in her voice, "this, little bird, is the work of a necromancer. Low-tier and sloppy, but dangerous nonetheless."

Darya scrounged up her knowledge of epic tales, trying to remember why that term was familiar, "Are those magick-users who can control the dead?"

"That's what they're known for, aye. Nasty bunch." Nathi spat, now that they were far enough away to remove their face covers.

"Not necessarily," Luunaiwel said, carefully peeled off her gloves, "ugh, I need to burn these... Anyhow, contrary to popular belief, true necromancers are highly skilled physicians, and they are well-versed in the arts of healing. Their ability to cure fatal illnesses and deathly wounds are uncanny. But that is not to say a necromancer would help you if you ask. Everything is an exchange for necromancers, and the price is often too hefty to pay. But... *yes*, they can control corpses."

"Like I said. Nasty bunch." Nathi grumbled.

Still curious and also a bit sick, Darya asked, "And the *stuff* back there wasn't made by a true necromancer?"

Luunaiwel wrinkled her nose, "That back there would be a shambler, and it was a poor imitation of what a necromancer could do. Instead of magic, the creature was infected with special parasitic fungi that inject a compound of poison into the host's bloodstream. The fungi can cause abnormal infections all over the host's body, as you saw, along with strange behaviours. The fungi also eat the host from the inside, causing flesh to decompose while it is still alive."

Nathi grunted, his accent grew thicker as he became more upset, "They use many types of fungus. And there're worse things. One type imitates the transition ta a Withered, just wit' more infections, crazed ferocity, immunity ta sunlight an' shor'er lifespan."

Darya felt like she was going to vomit again, "Nasty. Is it... contagious?"

Luunaiwel sighed, "Depends on the type of fungi. We will need to conduct some tests. But that is not our main concern."

Darya paled, "Do you think the Night's Hand is involved?"

"Possibly."

"They might be tryin' ta draw the lass out?" Nathi asked, bushy eyebrows scrunched up.

Luunaiwel tilted her head, "It is not the first time they employ such techniques."

The ride back to Nathi's house was quiet. Sindri was waiting for them in the sitting room, worried beyond her wits.

"Is everything alright? Is everyone alright??" She jumped to her feet the moment they came through the door.

Luunaiwel shook her head, "We are not sure yet."

Quickly, Nathi explained what happened to his wife. Sindri's lips tightened.

"The Guards won't be making any statement?"

Nathi shook his head, "Not till we have t' result. They're tryin' ta avoid mass hysteria."

Sindri sighed, "As expected … Alright, I will be at the shop if you need me. Make sure you got all of that rinsed off."

"Aye."

Once she had left, Nathi ushered Luunaiwel and Darya into his office, "Lassie, grab me a pot, me dissecting kit and ta cloth gloves."

As Darya hurriedly fetched the items, Luunaiwel handed Nathi the fungus bag. She gathered everyone's cloaks and shawls in a wicker basket to disinfect.

"We should go scrub ourselves off, too."

"What about Nathi?" Darya asked, when Luunaiwel guided her out.

"La'er," the physician said, not looking up from his desk, "I need ta concentrate on this first."

With much weighing on their minds, Luunaiwel took Darya to the bathhouse. Soaping up a sponge, Darya asked.

"This threw a wrench into the plan, didn't it?"

Luunaiwel sighed, "Unfortunately."

They sunk into silence, both absorbed in their own worries. Darya went over the options given to her.

Luunaiwel's first suggestion was Evenmoor. There was once a Druid-established town beyond the vale, and it was the most populated Druid grove back in its time, according to the library's text. But they would have to go through Flumium first.

The second option gave them the same exit point. Its destination would be the famed Mount Amun, sitting to the far West of Ardent, North East of Apricum.

It was no surprise that Darya wasn't at all eager to return to the River City. Now that there was the possibility of a necromancer working for the Night's Hand... she didn't think both options were still worth consideration. She didn't want to run straight into an ambush.

"I don't think it'd be safe to go to either Evenmore or Amun."

Frowning, Luunaiwel nodded, "If the Night's Hand is desperate enough to hire a necromancer, they would be watching every open entrance to Mul Tarum. And while I have no qualms against tearing through a small army or two, I do not wish to involve innocents."

Darya winced, "Damn. But you don't like our third option all that much... right?"

Luunaiwel winced. She did say she wouldn't even consider it unless there was no way they could make it to Evenmoor and Mount Amun.

"Yes. The Island Nation of Imirra."

"I still don't remember seeing that on any map..."

Luunaiwel explained, "Because most common maps, especially in recent centuries, do not record Imirra, as they closed trades with other human nations and cities before the Shattering, as King Sollos the Second refused to go to war. Naturally, feelings were hurt, but since it would be a huge waste of resources to attack an island so remote, mainland kingdoms decided to erase their existence out of their written history instead."

"That's awful! They deny a whole nation's existence just because its people didn't want to go to war???"

Luunaiwel shrugged, voice dripping with sarcasm, "Such is the nature of powerful men. Ultimately however, it serves Imirra's favour. The island managed to escape the brunt of the Shattering, and still retains many lifeforms before it."

Darya's eyes brightened at the prospect, "Imagine that... Why you don't want to go there then?"

The elf sighed, sinking into the warm water of the pool, "It has nothing to do with Imirra. It is more to do with the one who we must ask to teach you."

"Oh," Darya said, feeling her anxiety simmering to the top, "who is that?"

Luunaiwel's face scrunched up again, "Euryle the Mirage."

"Why wouldn't that person want to teach me?"

"Not exactly a person," it seemed like the elf's mood worsened more and more as they spoke, "Euryle is a Dragon."

Darya's eyes widened, "A Dragon?!"

Vaguely, she recalled the fear upon seeing Luunaiwel's elf-ears the first time. The fear upon potentially seeing a Dragon dwarfed meeting a scary elf by a hundredth. It was a terror that ate into humans' veins. The terror of spotting ginormous sails of wings in the sky, so large and powerful they could blot out the sun. It was the dreadful scorch marks that still marred the earth till this day, all around Sorrow Shards, despite hundreds of years having passed since their disappearance. Their hatred towards mortals was legendary, and it was said they once treated humans like wolves slaughtering livestock.

Elves were ruthless in the Great War, but Dragons alone almost wiped the whole Ardent off existence. With flames that drowned cities and talons that tore fortresses apart, Dragons dominated the world, until the elves and the Shattering drove them away.

Darya's distress was on a physical level, prompting a gentler tone from Luunaiwel.

"You should have no fear. Euryle is not like many dragons depicted in stories."

Still, Darya couldn't keep the grimace off her face, "I'll hold you to that. Why would she be a problem then?"

Luunaiwel's sullen mood returned, "Because she has a problem with me."

Taken by surprise, Darya blinked, "How come???"

The elf's face could put a prune to shame, "We have a... history."

After a moment of shocked silence, Darya blurted out before she could think it through.

"Were you two together?????"

Suddenly, Luunaiwel completely smoothed out her expression. Darya's breath died in her throat. She was painfully reminded of how secretive Luunaiwel was about her past, and could only hope that the elf wasn't going to neck her out of spite.

"Everything is irrelevant until we reach Imirra. We must get to Mul Nordihr and board a ship at the harbour"

Glad for the change of subject despite her curiosity, Darya asked, "And where is Mul Nordihr?"

"Under the Blade of Mortia."

"Isn't that just a five days ride from Mul Tarum?"

Luunaiwel tilted her head back, "Yes, but that is not where the entrance to Mul Nordihr is. The only way to get there is either by boat or via the tunnel connecting the two Great Dwarven Halls."

"Can't we just use that tunnel then?"

Luunaiwel shook her head, "Unlike Mul Tarum, Mul Nordihr is not open to other races. It is, after all, where the Nine Hammer, the dwarves' Supreme Council, reside. Entry is restricted, as you might imagine."

Darya felt rather defeated, "Isn't Nathi a nephew of someone there? Can he help?"

"You would still need clearance to enter."

"Great ... More paperwork?"

Luunaiwel's lips quirked up, "That is correct. On the bright side, if we want to avoid further confrontations with the Night's Hand, going through Mul Norhdir is the safest route."

The conversation left Darya feeling downtrodden. One they returned, she spent the rest of the afternoon helping Nathi with his reports on the undead bear encounter.

The discussion over Darya's departure was the main topic around the dinner table that night. Sindri was understandably worried.

"Would there be a boat to Imirra though?"

"There are always a few Imirrian vessels at the dock," Tuura said, passing the ham along, "they would be happy to sail for the right price."

"That can be easily arranged," Luunaiwel said, playing around with the peas on her plate, "I have a contact there. He would be happy to help out as long as we make it out there before the Moondust Festival."

Nathi hummed, "That means ye'd have ta stick 'round till the Festival."

"Not quite. We can wait it out in Teda."

Sindri raised an eyebrow, "The Imirrian settlements?"

Luunaiwel confirmed with a nod, "My contact has family in Imirra. He sails in between rather frequently."

The seamstress seemed a bit perplexed, "Wouldn't you rather stay here with us? We wouldn't mind, you know."

Luunaiwel gave Sindri a reassuring smile, "I know, dear one. But getting Darya her paperwork will take some time, and I would rather head straight through Mul Nordihr once that is done."

"Would cause less attention that way." Tuura added.

Biting her lip, Darya reached out to hold Sindri's hand, "Thank you for offering though. I'd have loved to stay …"

Gently, Sindri squeezed back, "How long would it take to get Darya a permit for passage, Nathi?"

Said physician frowned at Luunaiwel, "Hard ta say. I've never requested passage for anyone before. There'd definitely be questions though, since ye abruptly returned ta Mul Tarum with an apprentice, and now want ta go ta Imirra all the sudden despite havin' a predetermined course."

Being so occupied recently, Darya had forgotten all about Luunaiwel's quest from before. A new wave of guilt surged within her as Luunaiwel frowned at this new snag in their plan.

"That is fair. I have not reported to the Council since I got back either. If we are going through Mul Nordihr, they will definitely inquire after it."

The table sunk into silence. Everyone either swished their mugs of blackberry juice around or picked at their food, deep in thought.

"We can get a boat from Pompi and sail there? They are not as strict about the docks, as long as you don't cross Mul Nordihr." Tuura suggested. Luunaiwel shook her head.

"I would rather not have Darya travelling out in the open. While I know that both you and I do not mind fighting, they would be more cautious now after their failed pursuit from Flumium. There are too many places between here and Pompi that they can set up an ambush to snatch Darya away in the chaos."

Sindri frowned, "She's right. And even if you all make it to Pompi, the Council has no jurisdiction over it. In the unfortunate event that the Night's Hand already has influence over there, there would be no help from Mul Tarum."

"Besides," Luunaiwel said, eyeing Darya, "there would be even more questions, should I decide to go around Mul Nordihr instead of straight through to Teda."

"Politics is stupid." Tuura grumbled.

Nathi sighed, "Aye, but without it, we'd all be barbarians."

They sunk into silence once more, food all but forgotten.

At last, Sindri spoke, "You can tell a partial truth about Darya."

Both Nathi and Darya stared at her, dumbfounded.

"Ye want ta out the lassie ta the Council??"

"Not necessarily," Sindri said, "the Council also detest the Night's Hand, and know that Lulu has been making an effort to ward them off Mul Tarum as well as helping those who were affected by them. You can always say the reason why Darya is here with you is because she and her family were attacked. You accepted Darya as a disciple only to escort her safely to Imirra."

Luunaiwel nodded, but there was a note of reluctance in her voice, "I have thought of such an option. I simply do not wish for them to look too far into Darya's case and link her to the attack in Flumium. That aside, escorting a refugee and abandoning my quests … That is not how I usually operate."

Nathi snorted, "Aside from bus'ness, the Council ain't too bothered about other problems in a human city."

A faint smile quirked up the elf's lips, "You cannot be too careful nowadays."

Tuura hummed, "Doesn't hurt to try."

Darya swallowed dryly. Mentions of Flumium did nothing to quell her churning mind. Quietly, she pushed her plate away.

"We can try … it sounds like the easiest solution."

Luunaiwel inclined her head, but didn't argue, "As my disciple, Darya would not be allowed inside the Hall itself. But she can wait with Tuura outside the Hall, as Tuura was not present when we dealt with the bear. Nathi will accompany me inside. He can be testament to any question regarding Darya as well."

Simple enough. A collective murmur of agreement came from everyone.

Tuura then asked, "What about the staff?"

Confused, Darya blinked, "What about it?"

Slapping his forehead, Nathi grimaced, "It's too expensive ta be given ta a mere apprentice."

"Can it be for Luunaiwel instead of me?" Darya suggested, hopeful.

"No. Nadin knows it is for you." Luunaiwel chewed her bottom lip.

"And it would be too short to be Tuura's." Sindri added.

Damn it. Another snag.

Curious, Darya asked, "Can we afford to let Nadin in the loop?"

Sindri grimaced, "Unfortunately, his father is one of the Nine Hammers. He and Nadin are not exactly close, but we cannot risk it, I'm afraid."

Nathi made a noise, "It can be a gift then. Ta a noble in Imirra."

The elf blinked, "That... can work. Yes. And we asked Darya to have the details etched on because the noble is a girl the same age as Darya."

"Perfect." Sindri clapped, raising her mug, "I like it when a plan comes together well."

With excitement and anxiety warring in her heart, Darya toasted with the others, silently praying to whichever God was listening that the plans would go on without a hitch.

CHAPTER 23:

Somehow, the remaining days were passing both too quickly and too slowly.

At least that was how it felt to Darya. Everyone else seemed busy with their own tasks. A preparation here, an errand there, some loose ends to tie up, etcetera.

The highlight of it was when Luunaiwel finally, *finally* accompanied her to Tarum y Fýri, and taught her some basic earth magic.

Sitting cross-legged facing each other, the elf told Darya to discard her gloves.

"In contrary to popular belief, spells work best when they are spoken in the weaver's mother tongue," Luunaiwel held Darya's hand and pressed the girl's palm onto a patch of soil, "or whatever the weaver is most fluent with. Not some complicated spell-words or a lost language. It helps immensely if the weaver has in depth understanding of the language."

Darya's eyes fluttered closed as she felt the grass' young and lively presence in her mind, as Luunaiwel continued.

"The core rule of magic remained the same with every type of magick-user. You cannot create something from nothing. You cannot summon fire without a spark or air. You cannot call upon tidal waves in a dessert. You cannot call upon the earth in the middle of the ocean."

Digging her gloved hands into the ground, Luunaiwel chanted, "Soluma, wæ shuuröl siech, orchrani wæbi."

To Darya's awe, the earth around Luunaiwel shifted, rising from the ground and stacking together into a shield before her. Rumbling, they smoothed out and turned into stone, completely blocking the elf from view.

"This is a slower spell. You must tell the element exactly what you wish it to do, then visualise in your mind how it would manifest physically."

"Uh, do I have to say the same thing you said?"

The mage chuckled, "Yes, but perhaps not in the same language."

Darya let out a relieved sigh, "Oh, great, because my tongue would twist around and break off if I have to repeat the same thing. But you did invoke the God of Earth, Soluma, right?"

"Yes. Just as I invoked Ignia before. You must call for the Elemental's name when performing its magic, to ground your energy, no pun intended, and aid your visualisation."

Darya nodded, "Alright, I think I can manage that. Does it have to be the specifics like you've told me before?"

"Depends on your situation," Luunaiwel grinned, pleased that Darya had paid attention to her stories on the road, "however, I do think it is wiser to train with your given Element, Earth, for now."

"I'm not too greedy. Earth is great." Darya shrugged, despite thrumming with excitement. She was going to do magic! Darya! A nameless bard from Flumium, was going to perform *magic!!!*

"As a druid, not only do you possess your own magic, but you may call upon the strength of the earth."

That excited Darya more. However, she soon wilted, "I might have a problem... I can feel the trees and the plants' life forces, but I can't seem to feel the earth itself."

"That might have to do with how Tarum y Fýri was formed," Luunaiwel inclined her head, "the earth here was indeed lifted from an earth pulse point, but that does not make it an earth pulse. It is not the same as the glade where you were gifted your powers, for it does not hold the same memories the earth pulses share with their Druids."

Darya blinked, "I think … I've read something about that in the library. The earth can share memories with Druids?"

A finger under her chin, Luunaiwel hummed, "Yes. What have you learned?"

Feeling a bit more confident, Darya recited, "In the books, it said the Earth remembers everything, for it carries the memories of all those who live and die. The Druids of old used this to etch their own experience into the earth pulses they tended to. That way, they can easily train the younger generations and transfer their knowledge along, ensuring that nothing will ever be lost."

Luunaiwel smirked, "I see your time has been invested properly."

The praise brightened Darya's enthusiasm for a moment, but she then completely deflated, "But … As only Druids can speak to the earth, their secrets remain buried after the Shattering. So I can only rely on my own magic for now, I think …"

"Yes."

Darya sighed. She knew that was too good and easy to be true, "Alright... Where should I start?"

"You want to tell the elemental a task first. The phrase I used meant 'Soluma, I beseech thee, protect me'. I visualised a shield in my head, and shifted the components into stone."

There was no surprise that putting her magic into practice was tougher than Luunaiwel made it look. Darya didn't have trouble speaking the spell, nor visualising it in her head. Her problem was in holding the image together until it was physically formed.

In her first attempts, she got distracted by the sight of the earth forming by her magic. That resulted in sad, misshapen clumps that did nothing but drain her strength. It was soon apparent that Darya was too easily distracted, and her concentration kept slipping randomly. By the time she managed to form a shield resembling Luunaiwel's (without turning it to stone like the elf), the young Druid was out of breath.

Luunaiwel wasn't all that disappointed, however.

"You withstood longer than I thought."

If there was one thing to be glad about, it was that Darya didn't make flowers bloom in her sleep that night, as her magic was completely depleted.

Darya's schedule during their preparation remained more or less the same. Practice with Tuura in the morning, helping Nathi or Sindri with their work in the afternoon, and learning magic with Luunaiwel after dinner until late evening. Darya spent most of her nights in Tarum y Fýri, after a good session in the library, and accompanied Sara down to Nathi's place for breakfast every other day.

Admittedly, the most difficult task was telling Sara the departure date.

Brave as she was, Sara swallowed back her tears, "I was hoping we could celebrate the Moondust Festival together … It sounds like so much fun..."

Shaken, Darya pulled her sister into her arms, "I was hoping so too … But at least … At least you'll have Nathi and Sindri, right?"

Sara made a noncommittedly sound, lips quivering, "I wish Grandmama and Cecil could see it too …"

Thorns that crept into Darya's heart and seized her insides until she could no longer breathe. Crouching to Sara's eye level, Darya was painfully reminded of how small, frail and young her little sister was.

"Would you like me to stay?"

Green eyes, wide and wet, held her gaze. The twist of pain and impending regret was like nothing Darya had ever felt before.

She almost wished Sara would say yes. Damn the world, damn the Gods and damn being a Druid. What kind of saviour could she be, if she broke Sara's heart? If she left her own sister, the very last of her blood behind to strangers that they barely knew? Would Darya really be alright with leaving Sara behind, to embark on a journey that she didn't know when she could return? This was nothing like her past travels, when she could come back home on a whim. There was no home to come back to, there wasn't a soul she had known all her life to entrust her family to.

They were all dead. Just because Darya was careless, because she left them behind for something new.

She wasn't going to make that mistake again.

"You have to go, don't you?"

Darya badly wanted to cry.

"I don't have to, if you tell me not to."

Droplets gathered around Sara's eyes, glistening dangerously, but the brave girl refused to let them fall.

"I know … I know there are things that you don't tell me."

Breath dying in her throat, Darya opened her mouth, but Sara pinched her arm, stiffened up her lips.

"I don't need to know. I … I know you have things you can't tell me. Grandmama has… *had* things she couldn't tell me either. And you don't have to. I know you've been preparing lots of things for your trip with Luna. I know the trips must be very important that a Lord like Nathi agreed to take care of me so you could go. So … so you have to go."

Trembling, Darya shook her head, "I don't- … Sara, I- … I can't leave you like this, I can't!"

At the sight of her tears, Sara's face crumbled.

"But Darya … I can't go with you …"

Darya broke down.

It was probably a good thing that they were in the middle of Tarum y Fýri. That way nobody could see her falling to her knees, holding onto Sara. Nobody needed to see her wail, soundless in its high pitches, over the choice she had to make.

A voice in her head, a voice that sounded suspiciously like Luunaiwel, told Darya that everything had a good and a bad side. That leaving would be the best thing she could do right now.

And Darya knew that. *She knew that.*

But why did it have to be so difficult?

Why did she have to lose every familiarity for this duty that was imposed upon her? Wouldn't it be enough for just Darya to bear the consequences, and not those who she cared for?

The unfairness of it all left a bitter taste on her tongue, even when her tears died down into sharp, stifled inhales. And Sara … her brave little Sara, stood there in silence, hugging Darya through the worst of her sobs, tiny hands rubbing soothing circles into her back.

Darya was ashamed. She should be the one to comfort Sara. Not after everything that happened.

She peeled herself away, blinking off the remainder of her tears, "Sorry …"

Bright green eyes peered up at her, glossy with water, but Sara still managed a shaky smile, "It's fine, Darya … It's good to cry it out sometimes, you know?"

Darya knew. Because Sara, for all her illnesses and frailness, was resilient. But a kid was still a kid, and they, Darya and Grandmama, always told Sara to let it out when it was too unbearable. The reminder was too much, and Darya swallowed back a fresh wave of tears.

"I'll write back as much as I can on the road," Darya promised, squeezing both Sara's hands in hers, "I asked Nathi and Sindri to help you learn to read, so... when I come back for you, you'd better be able to read all my letters!"

Sara nodded, "I'll be more well-read than you, you'll see!"

Though wet and shaky, a laughter bubbled forth between them, "I'll look forward to that."

In hindsight, perhaps two months of preparation was not enough.

One afternoon, Luunaiwel returned with Darya's staff. Or rather, the coffer that contained Darya's staff.

"Officially, this is a gift," Luunaiwel said, pointing at the wax-sealed lock, "you cannot open it until we pass Mul Nordihr."

Bummer.

Still, by all accounts, Darya was very fortunate for the time allowed, plus she had supportive people in her corner.

Yet, she still felt like it was impossible to handle all the worries she had.

"Would it be possible for Sara to learn a trade while she's living here?" Darya asked Sindri one afternoon, while she was watching the dwarf woman embroidering a piece of silk.

"Isn't she a bit too young for that?" Without looking up from the needlework, Sindri asked.

Darya grimaced, "Not quite? In our society, it's normal for kids... younger than her, to start learning a trade and bring some sort of income to the family. But Sara's always been sick, and she's much smaller than kids her age, so we didn't dare let her do anything strenuous. Even if we did, no-one in their right mind would take her, even for apprenticeship and-... "

Realising that she had been rambling, Darya closed her mouth with a click, ashamed.

That finally had Sindri's full attention. Carefully, she put her square of silk away, "Ah, I often forget humans have a much shorter lifespan than dwarves. My apologies."

Biting her lips, Darya bobbed her head. Wouldn't it have been nice to be born as a dwarf? Into a world that gave them the time to grow, and provided them with the means to earn their way through life?

If she and Sara were born as dwarves, perhaps none of the tragedies they experienced would have struck. They would probably still have their family. Still enjoying their adolescents without having to worry whether or not the next meal would come. Sara wouldn't have to suffer with her sickness, and Darya wouldn't have had to leave home for money.

And Grandmama wouldn't have to die.

"If you would like to," Sindri prompted, breaking Darya out of her reverie, "I can take Sara in as an apprentice during your time away?"

Darya's eyes widened, "You would?? But-"

Misunderstanding Darya's surprise, Sindri quickly added, "If you are worried about the strains, have no fear! I assure you, she would only be assigned the less laborious tasks. Like sewing and embroidering. She wouldn't need to move much, and I'm sure Nathi would be happy to monitor her work hours. Besides…"

Sindri smiled, reaching out to pat a dumbfounded Darya's shoulder, "I would be missing your helpful presence. Your sister would be of more help to me then I'd be to her, I'm sure."

Darya didn't know what to say. She probably didn't have to say anything. The hug Sindri gave Darya told her that the dwarf woman understood.

As for Nathi, Darya had also taken to assisting him with his patients, once they deemed his book collection was spotless. While she didn't have the extensive healing knowledge he did, Darya was efficient with the more physical tasks, like milling and grinding medicines. All things considered, her occasional bursts of flower-growing sleep was considered most fortunate in the doctor's notes.

"This would save lotsa money for the patients. Thanks, lassie." Nathi grinned as he sheared the chamomile in Darya's room one morning. She snorted out a laugh.

"Yeah... I'm just sorry you have to replace the carpet after I'm gone."

He waved a clump of flowers at her, "Bah! Nonsense! Sindri's always looking for an excuse ta redecorate anyway!"

The longer she stayed in Mul Tarum, the more Darya grew reluctant to leave. She became accustomed to her routine. She enjoyed the tasks she had every day, and she loved her interactions with everyone. Darya knew she and Sara were safe here.

Darya thrived in her training with Tuura, exhausting they might be. She was fond of the sessions with Sindri, though she couldn't even sew a straight line. She delighted in helping Nathi with his work and their trips to the library together, regardless of his tendencies to swear at nonsensical things. She loved studying magic with Luunaiwel, despite the elf still eluding topics about herself.

Darya was becoming greedy, and two months were far too little.

It was a week before the Moondust festival when a messenger, a lady dwarf whose hair bun was the tightest Darya had ever seen and lips pressed so firmly together they were almost invisible, came bearing summons for Nathi and Luunaiwel to Mul Nordihr. Despite all the time dedicated to preparing for this moment, Darya didn't want to go. Especially when she looked into Sara's teary eyes.

When Darya carried all her belongings out of Nathi's home, she felt her heart plunged into her stomach. This was it. Even though she knew this safety was temporary, it was still difficult to leave it behind. With the little time they had, it still felt like a proper household. It was warm, it was safe and Darya was still able to smile despite all the tragedy that struck.

But she couldn't stay. She was never meant to.

Sindri and Sara had come to see them off, by the rail connecting Mul Tarum to Mul Nordihr. Darya embraced her sister, arms shaking. The normally chatty siblings now rendered speechless, both doing their best to bite back their tears. They had already spoken what needed to be said. Did what needed to be done.

Still, the child in Darya wondered if she could stay. If she *should* stay.

With titanous efforts, Darya finally pulled away from her sister, eyes misty, "Be good, you hear? Be good to Sindri. Be good to Nathi. I don't want to hear a single complaint from them when I come back for you, alright?"

Sara sniffled, "You be good too. Don't give Luna too much trouble..."

Choked up, Darya leaned down and kissed her sister on the cheeks, bumping their foreheads together, banking tears burning her vision. Turning to Sindri, Darya gave her a hug.

"Thank you so much for all you've done."

Sindri petted her hair fondly, "No need, dearie. *When* you succeed on your quest, you will be saving all of us. What we did is insignificant to what you can do. Here."

Sindri pulled out a pin from her scarlet hair, gold with a cluster of tiny pearls and emeralds, and put it on Darya's ponytail, "To remember us by. Be brave, sweet Darya, and take care of yourself."

That broke Darya's resolve, and she started crying, "A-alright, Sindri. You take care too..."

"I will," the woman gave her another tight hug, "may your quest be fruitful and journey safe."

"And yours. See you, Sindri."

Drying her eyes, Darya threw on her travelling cloak, gave Sara one last hug, and turned away. Tuura and Luunaiwel were now waiting for her with Nathi by a passenger cart. There was a savage grin on the doctor's face.

"The first step o' no return!"

Luunaiwel rolled her eyes, "You are as dramatic as ever."

The dwarf barked out a laugh, "Lil' shite... If I could, ye know I'd go with ye."

Tuura chuckled, "Maybe one day, when the world is alive again."

Mismatched eyes met Darya's, a smirk played across Luunaiwel's lips, "Let us see how far we can go."

Darya gulped, "I'll try to live up to the expectation."

"Let's go!" Nathi hollered, and threw the door open.

As the rail carts shuffled along, Darya looked back until Sara and Sindri's waving silhouettes disappeared from sight.

A year. Darya prayed, to the Gods and Goddesses. *Keep her safe for a year. Until I return.*

CHAPTER 24:

The journey was relatively silent, aside from the coal-fuelled machine that the others called a *train*, with only some occasional exchanges between Luunaiwel and Nathi.

If Darya had been in a better mood, she would have been beyond curious about their mode of transportation. It ran on the same rails she often saw back in Flumium, with the same kind of carts. But the one they were sitting in had installed benches for passengers, and the cart for their mounts looked just like a mini stable. All carts were chained together, and the contraption that pulled everything was a strange shape, made of giant metallic tubes and squares, hissing out smokes as it ran and with giant wheels linked together by metal bars. And, as with all dwarfish structures, it was painted deep crimson and polished grey.

Despite having ridden on this cart for what must have been a whole day, Darya didn't feel tired. There was an itch to look back every now and again, but she fought against it. There was an urge to talk to Luunaiwel and the others, to ask more about where they were going. But Darya didn't say anything, in fear that she would ask to return to Mul Tarum.

To be with her sister.

So Darya did what she did best, before all of this chaos changed her life. She started singing, a familiar song that trembled under her breath.

"Five thousand men and their thousand horses

Sunlit road paved to glory

Kingdoms rise under gold-maned banners

Till the end of earth, they cry.

Five thousand men and their thousand horses

Ride bravely unto sunrise

Kingdoms fall before silver-tipped blades

War horns howl, the end is nigh

Five thousand men and their thousand horses

Fearsome troops reduced to one

The land be his, earned by blood, by tears

Over yonder, forever more."

So wrapped up in her own singing and anxiety, Darya didn't notice Luunaiwel's staring.

"What an interesting song." The elf said, eyes glimmering in the torches that danced along stone-lined walls.

Darya managed a smile, "Isn't it? It's about a hero who fought in the Great War, and helped end it."

"Truly? Do you know this hero's name?"

Frowning, Darya shook her head, "I don't know. Nobody does. Legend says, due to his part in the war, he was cursed by an elven witch, who removed his name from history."

Luunaiwel looked away, "Ah, what a shame. Thus was the misfortune of many who fought. It was a dark time."

Curious, Darya asked, "Did you... go to war?"

The elf's eyes sparkled, "Do I look that old?"

"N-no! I just thought-..." Panicked, Darya flailed her arms, not wanting to offend Luunaiwel of all people.

"D'aw, give the lass a break, Lulu!" Nathi laughed, prompting a chuckle out of Luunaiwel.

She hummed, a gloved finger on her chin, "I would not say I fought *in the war*. Rather, I fought *to prevent* the war from happening. Needless to say, I failed on that aspect."

Darya sat up straighter in her seat, "Huh... In the history I was... uh, taught, the elves were all out for blood back in the Great War. I guess not all elves wanted war..."

Bitterly, Luunaiwel huffed out a laugh, "Nobody wants war. Only those who do not know better do. And those who wish to profit from it."

Darya grimaced, "I've read about some of it back at the library. The Great War was sparked by the events at Mount Amun, right?"

Nathi huffed, "Aye, Goes by many names. The Beginning of End-time, War of Blood, Cinder-end, etcetera. Regardless o' fancy names, human historians didn't want ta record that one. Didn't want ta admit it was largely their fault the whole fight started."

"It wasn't much of a fight between three sides, and more of a power-induced temper tantrum," Tuura said, "to be fair, the dragons didn't make things easier by being so judgemental over the hierarchy of Dragon Priests."

"I've heard about Dragon Priests before, but there was never much details." Always eager for more information, Darya looked to Luunaiwel.

"Dragon Priests are those who are tasked to watch over a Dragon's territory and den. They are also tasked with raising dragon hatchlings after the eggs were hatched by Orcs."

"What? So the dragons have nothing to do with their children??"

Tuura shook his head, "Dragons are nothing like humans, dwarves or elves. Strength and power are valued above all. Their core belief can be condensed down to survival of the fittest. Before Dragons Priests and Sanctums were a thing, they were almost driven to extinction due to the brutal conditions their youngs had to face."

"Bah, there ain't many of them left now," Nathi spat, "ye can say they reaped what they sow."

Luunaiwel rolled her eyes at the dwarf, but didn't respond.

Hesitantly, Darya asked, "And what did the Priests hierarchy have to do with the events on Mount Amun?"

The other three exchange a look. Finally, it was Luunaiwel who spoke.

"Dragons tend … *tended* to look down upon mortal races, especially humans and dwarves. They found no joy in including humans to their Priests' ranks, and often treated human Priests poorly compared to their elven counterparts. And even the treatments given to elves were debatable...

When a poor acolyte was killed for a simple mistake, outrage almost drowned Mount Amun whole. The human Priests threatened to raze the Amun Dragon Sanctum to the ground. The elven Priests tried to mediate the situation, knowing nothing good would come out of this. Agitation turned to violence and, before anyone knew what was happening, twelve elven Priests were fatally poisoned.

Chaos ensued. A member of the Sanctum, a great green Dragon named Jormun the Bright took matters into his own claws. Young and violent, he tore into the mass of Priests, killing humans and elves alike."

Horrified, Darya let out a shocked gasp. Luunaiwel nodded grimly.

"Everything went terribly wrong from that point onward."

The rest of the ride sunk into a heavy silence. Before the Great War, there was already tension among all races. The event at Mount Amun shredded an already delicate truce to pieces.

Glancing over to Luunaiwel, Darya couldn't help but wonder how much of that the mage had witnessed.

They arrived at Mul Nordihr early in the next morning, or so Darya estimated. It was always difficult to tell the time under the mountains.

The entry to Mul Nordihr was not as spectacular as Mul Tarum. The hall they entered reminded Darya of the narrow room after every lift in Mul Tarum, just wider and looking more like a military camp. The staircase leading to the main floor ended with stone barricades. There were two armoured guards every three steps, standing still as statues and armed to the teeth. The hall was lit with a giant brazier in the middle and torches along the walls. There were even more guards on the main floor, and a group of eight standing before two giant doors that must lead to the inner Halls. Nine dwarf statues stood above them, hooded and each held a war hammer, looking down with solemn authority.

One of the guards went to greet their entourage, thumping her breastplate.

"Lord Tuura, you and the apprentice must wait here. Only the Lady Luunaiwel and Lord Nathi are summoned."

"Understood." Tuura nodded, a hand on Darya's shoulder, "How long will the meeting be?"

"That is up to the Council." The woman said and bowed at him curtly, before leading Nathi and Luunaiwel inside through the main doors.

Darya only managed a glimpse of gold and crimson carpeted floor and hanging braziers before the door swung shut. Letting out a sigh, she helped Tuura herding the mounts off the train to a stable for replenishments.

When Luunaiwel and Nathi didn't come out after a whole hour, Darya felt her eyelids start to droop. It was getting harder to stay awake, especially when the Mallas and her mare's presences were so soothing. She couldn't communicate with them the same way she could with the trees, but she could still feel their life forces, as with all living things. These travel beasts were so gentle and calm, they were making it difficult to not just crash right then and there on the hay bed.

Still, Darya wasn't dumb enough to do so. The others had gone through a great deal to keep her secret. She would be a disgrace to out herself with a nap. So Darya turned to Tuura instead.

"How long do you think it will take?"

Tuura, who had been leaning against the fence all this time, eased his stance and shifted his weight onto another foot.

"Another hour or two. Meeting with the Council tends to be long."

"Have you ever been to one?"

"No. What I handle usually aren't big enough to concern the entire Nine with."

Nodding, Darya copied his stance, "How did you become a Lord with the dwarves anyway? I know it's not a title they just throw around."

Tuura gave her a crooked smile, "Stick around with Luna long enough and you'll get a title too."

"I'm starting to get that feeling." Darya chuckled.

"She does a lot of work for the dwarves. Nathi's long line of family, to be specific. She sees them as her family and they see her as their own," he folded his arms, then flicked his chin at the doors, "since Nathi's family, the Whitestone clan, has a seat in the Nine Hammers, it makes everything Luna does a service to dwarf-kind."

"Ha... That must be nice."

Tuura chuckled, "It is."

"What about her *real* family? I mean, she obviously wasn't born a dwarf." Curious, Darya asked.

The dark look in Tuura's amber eyes made her regret asking.

"She has none. Not alive. Her family was betrayed during the Great War. She lost everyone in one night."

Darya couldn't help the gasp that escaped her, "By Vita... I'm... I'm sorry, I shouldn't have asked..."

Tuura shook his head, "Don't be. And better to hear it from me than Luna. She doesn't deal with pain well. Elves live for a long time, longer than dwarves, longer than the flame-forged orcs. And like dragons, their memories do not fade."

What could Darya possibly say to that? No wonder Luunaiwel always averted from speaking about herself. How could anyone deal with loss when they knew the wounds would never fade?

"And," Tuura cleared his throat, "since I know you're curious by nature and you're bound to ask eventually... My family is gone, too. My entire village, actually."

Her heart clenched painfully, "I'm so sorry, Tuura, I-..."

"It's alright," he rolled his shoulders, "at least I didn't have to witness it."

Covering her mouth, Darya looked up at him with wide eyes, "What happened?"

"Avalanche."

Darya definitely didn't need any help staying awake after *that* conversation. She knew her companions had seen tragedies in their lives. But not to this degree.

Much to Darya's relief, Nathi and Luunaiwel emerged soon after. Stopping herself from hugging the elf, Darya stood up straight and asked.

"How did it go?"

"Well enough," Luunaiwel shrugged, "the Nine Hammers agreed that the necromancer poses a possible threat, and would be restricting entries to Mul Tarum for now, as well as increasing scouting parties."

"What about the... " Darya cleared her throat, then leaned in with a whisper, "Night's Hand?"

"They will negotiate an investigation with the Duke of Flumium, as there was no proven connection between the Night's Hand's activities and the necromancer yet." Luunaiwel fixed her

Malla's saddle, then swung on, "The Council will keep an eye out, but not going to get close unless forced to."

Darya didn't know whether she should be relieved or disappointed, "I see..."

"Politics." Nathi said, climbing onto his saddle as well, "Always give me a headache. Are we getting outta here or what?"

Luunaiwel grinned, "Let us go."

When they trotted past the guards at the front, Darya's heart thumped madly in her chest. She couldn't find herself calming down until she saw the light of day, and the distinct sound of waves crashing against the rocky shore.

And was that...?

"Trees!!!" Darya gasped, staring at the rows of pine, scruffy and scrawny, *but alive*, against the mountainside.

"Welcome to Mortia's Strand." Luunaiwel chuckled, "Rather lively for such a name, is it not?"

Darya rode close to the pines, immediately taken, "How did this happen?"

"This was once a Druid's grove. My self-assigned mission started here."

"Wow..." Darya was in complete awe, "Has this always been here?"

Luunaiwel chuckled, "No. The pines started growing only after some ... creative problem solving. It is not quite like a proper earth pulse connection, but it is something."

"And... on that note, I'm getting outta here," Nathi's booming laughter drew Darya out of her daze, "it's been fun running 'round with ye, but home awaits!"

Darya turned her mare around, and tried to give Nathi as much of a hug as she could on the saddle, "Thank you for everything, Nathi. Please send my regards to Sindri."

He laughed, thumping Darya twice on the back, "Will do. Behave yerself. I know Lulu can be a pain sometimes, but she does know best."

Luunaiwel smirked behind him, "Can I have that embroidered on a handkerchief or something? A tunic, perhaps?"

"Don't let that go to yer head, it's fat enough as is," Nathi wagged a finger at her face, before hugging Luunaiwel anyway, "take care of yerself, ye hear? Don't get inta too much stupid shite when I ain't 'round ta stitch ye up!"

Laughing, Luunaiwel squeezed Nathi in return, "I shall do my best. You should behave as well. Do not make Sindri too angry while I am away."

"Bah! Women! They always take each other's side!" Nathi complained jovially, then shook forearms with Tuura, "Watch her back fer me, would ye?"

Tuura chuckled, "Always. We will be in contact as soon as we arrive at Imirra."

"Ye'd better!" Nathi slapped his elbow, then, finally, let go, "May yer quest be fruitful and yer journey safe!"

Luunaiwel smiled, leaning over to kiss Nathi on his brows, "And yours. Goodbye, brother."

With one last wave, Nathi rode back into Mul Nordihr, disappearing behind stone gates.

This was it.

Darya didn't even realise she was tearing up until Luunaiwel spoke again.

"The dock is at the bottom of this slope. Let us meet my contact, and then we may arrange for rooms in Teda."

Quickly wiping her eyes, Darya tacked her horse after the mallas. The mountains' curved path opened up to a gentle cliff, from where the ocean was in full view.

Darya could see the blue sea, endless over the horizon, and waves that were silver with foam. There were ships along the coast, flags and sails full of wind. There were people, dwarves and humans alike, busy atop the docks. Cool morning wind soothed the sting of departure, bringing in the fresh scent of pines, green along the mountains, rustling their needles softly.

The sense of *freedom* and the thrill of a new adventure that ripped a whoop out of Darya. She heard Luunaiwel's laughter ahead, tinkling amidst thundering hooves and talons. They galloped down the stone-paved road, edges sprawling with green, eager to start the next chapter of their journey.

Luunaiwel's contact was Captain Ascott Silas. Robust, having a bit of a belly but with muscular arms, he would have been mistaken for a dwarf if he wasn't six foot tall and completely bald.

"We'll be ready to depart a day before the Moondust Festival." Captain Silas told the elf, teeth white against sun-beaten skin, "There's an inn, the Nautilus Wheel, in town if you're looking for a place to stay for the next few days. Food is good. Price's a bit steep though."

"Are you and your men staying there?" Luunaiwel inquired.

"No, m'lady. We need to get all the cargos sorted, have one last check up and all that junk. We'll be on the ship. Either me or my first mate is always on board if you need anything."

They went over some other details, like departure time, travel beast capacity, and sleeping quarters, before Luunaiwel bid the Captain a good day, and led them further down the beach.

It wasn't the first time Darya had seen the sea. The first day she became a bard, Darya had travelled down the Flumin to the coast. Pompii was where she made her first copper, and decided that truly, a life of travels was her calling.

The strand soon broke into a bay, followed by a sea canal. The town of Teda was split into two by the canal, the east side was nestled in the growing pines and connected to the west side by a stone bridge.

Imagine Darya's disappointment when Luunaiwel told her the inn was on the west side.

Chuckling at her longing look towards the pines, Luunaiwel said, "We can visit tonight if you would like. But some rest is in order."

The Nautilus Wheel was probably the cleanest tavern Darya had ever been to. The walls were covered with white paints, bright and welcoming. The windows were all glass, offering a beautiful view to the sea. Wooden beams were free of cobwebs and dust, instead, there were strings of herbs and roots hung to dry. The counter practically sparkled, void of dubious stains or drunken sailors. A delicious smell wafted from the back kitchen, making Darya bounce on the balls of her feet, excited as Luunaiwel purchased a shared room for the two of them, and one for Tuura.

When they got to their room at the inn however, a concern arose.

"What if I make flowers grow here? It's easy to conceal them at Nathi's, but..."

"That is why I am here," Luunaiwel assured, tossing off her cloak, "I will teach you how to channel your excess magic into gemstones."

Darya was immediately excited, "Are we finally opening up my staff?"

"No, little bird, we are yet outside of dwarfish territory, and I would rather not have rumours flying about. We will be using this."

She tapped at the pin Sindri had given Darya. Blinking, Darya pulled it out of her ponytail. The craftsmanship of this bauble was superb, giving the illusion of silken petals despite the shine it gave off. Darya ran her thumb over the gemmed clusters of flower, silently thanking Sindri for being so kind.

Carefully, Luunaiwel pried it out of Darya's hands, "The gems are unenchanted. I am more familiar with earth crystals rather than pearls, but they might work better for you than me"

"How come?"

"Pearls are formed by inside mussels, clams or oysters. They are organic materials, and thus might have a better connection to life forces, just as the core of your powers."

"Huh? That's interesting... How come we didn't pick up pearls for my staff instead then?"

Luunaiwel wrinkled her nose, "Because it is trickier to enchant, as it is not exactly a stone. Earthbound gems react better to magic due to their connection with earth pulses, especially if mined near one. Besides, can you imagine how terribly expensive a pearl that size would be?"

"I see," Darya nodded, peering down at the pin in Luunaiwel's hand, "should I learn how to enchant then? If the pearls might work better for me, then I might as well have a crack at it."

Luunaiwel chuckled, "You can work on that during our trip. There is not much else to do otherwise."

The elf shuffled through the contents of her bags, poured some water into her travelling cup, pulled out a jar full of a rich, dark brown substance that Darya strongly suspected was soil, and brought everything over to the hearth. Luunaiwel put the jar and the cup on either sides of the hearth, then put the pin down before them.

With her palms cupping the gems, Luunaiwel kneeled on the floor, eyes closed, *"Toe i Ignia, i Ær, i Soluma, i Aqua, wæ, Ysol sa Ævesta, obdarz na siech sono moch doe zæweich mæ orchrani i mægia ætin doe siech sæ siæch mistre."*

Luunaiwel's Elvish tongue was always interesting to Darya's ears, gentle like a hymn, yet unyielding like a command. By now, Darya could pick up a few words here and there, noticeably the four chief elemental Gods of Fire, Air, Earth and Water. She would have to get the rest of the chants translated later though.

Luunaiwel repeated the phrase three times, until her hands glowed a soft blue, and the light seeping into the gems. They glint under dancing hearth fire, as if winking at Darya.

"There. That should work." Luunaiwel said, putting the pin back on Darya's hair.

Touching the jewels, she expected to *feel* something different about them, but found none, "Okay? Uhm... So what's next?"

The elf guided Darya to sit down on the bed, "What needs to be done here is fairly simple. You need to imagine the gems as containers. Imagine your excess power as a stream of water, flowing into the gems. Once you have that image in mind, say aloud: I trust you to protect what is mine safe."

Luunaiwel made everything sound so simple sometimes. Licking her lips, Darya shifted into a comfortable position, closed her eyes and visualised what Luunaiwel told her in her mind.

"I trust you to protect what is mine safe."

Darya wasn't sure if it was just her imagination at work, but she could have sworn the gems pulsed with warmth for a split second. Cracking an eye open, "That's it?"

Luunaiwel smiled, then patted her head, "That would be it. Now, get some rest. Exploration awaits when you wake."

Yawning, Darya curled up, feeling exhaustion steadily catching up to her, "I can't wait."

CHAPTER 25:

Waking up to the sun was a feeling Darya hadn't had in a while. The young Druid stretched luxuriously. Then the strangeness of where she had woken up to hit, and Darya sprang up, flailing around in a heart-stopping, sleep-addled attempt to hide the flowers that she must have unconsciously sprouted in her sleep.

Only to find none.

Seemed like the pin worked!

There were, however, find two red flowers on the floor when she got up.

"Poppy, right?" Darya squinted at the bright petals and dark centre.

"That would be correct." Luunaiwel swooped in from nowhere, uprooting both in one quick motion. Darya winced as the elf carefully put the flowers into her bag.

"So it still happened..."

"True, but this is a massive improvement, do you not think so?"

Darya shrugged, standing up, "Can't argue with that. And I didn't have to exhaust myself with magic practicing this time... What time is it?"

"Mid-afternoon. The bells just rang."

"Oooooh... Can I go see the town?"

Chuckling at her enthusiasm, Luunaiwel tossed Darya's travelling cloak to her, "Go ahead. But wait until nightfall to explore the grove. I shall accompany you."

Reasonable enough. After so much stress, Darya was absolutely famished anyway. Since they weren't at Nathi's anymore, it was time to feed herself.

After all the endeavours in Mul Tarum, Darya was left with two gold and thirty-nine silvers out of the six she got from Luunaiwel. The fees for her badges and random payments aside, she had bought herself a dwarf-crafted lute. She left one gold and some loose coppers for Sara, just in case, despite her sister's protests. While what Darya currently had was still a small fortune, she knew if she didn't watch her spending, she would be left without a copper to her name. Besides, Darya didn't know when it would be safe to start performing again.

With that in mind, Darya went straight to the market instead of grabbing a meal at the inn. People were happy to point her in the right direction, and Darya soon had a loaf of bread and some liver terrine to munch on as she walked around.

Much like the towns she visited before, Teda was mainly built with stone. The townsfolk were a mixture of humans and dwarves, most were fishermen. There were some farms and gardens scattered about, small but thriving, much to Darya's excitement. They seemed quite self-sufficient, with merchants from Mul Tarum to fill up stalls in the market and ready natural resources.

It was a nice town. Wishfully, Darya thought that maybe, one day, she could bring Sara here. Get a piece of land, build a life. Live close enough to visit Sindri and Nathi. Perhaps Luunaiwel and Tuura would drop by every once in a while too…

Yes, Darya would love that.

Finishing up her late lunch, Darya wandered across the bridge to the eastern side of town. Her Heart Stone thrummed yearningly towards the woods, but she fought back the urge, and settled on people-watching instead. There were more farms on this side than the other. There were even some livestock, chickens, cows and goats that wandered about the hills. Shrubs were growing most abundant, most being blackberries and salmonberries. Among the crops, Darya recognised potatoes, yams and parsnips, with a few tall in the mix corn stalks.

Back in Mul Tarum, Darya hadn't the time, nor did she have the authorization, to visit the Farm Hall. It was further down the Eria Mountains, with the same structural base as Tarum y Fýri. As wonderful as Darya imagined it must be, she didn't think it held the same beauty as these tiny patches, growing in earnest under the sun.

As the sun fell red over the ocean, Darya doubled back to the Nautilus Wheel and found her companions at a table, engaged in a serious game of dice. Luunaiwel was winning by three points, grinning ear to ear as she enthusiastically shook her cup.

Luunaiwel crowed upon seeing her, "Afternoon! How was your day?"

"Pretty good! The town is beautiful. I wonder if I can come down to the docks and watch the fishing boats tomorrow."

"Should be fine," Tuura said, taking the cup from Luunaiwel, "as long as you don't slip into the water. It's cold this time of the year."

A moment of silence followed when Tuura rolled.

Snake eyes.

"Ha! Pay up!" Triumphantly, Luunaiwel cried out as she won the last round, holding her hand out.

Huffing, Tuura slapped a folded piece of parchment into the elf's palm. Luunaiwel blew him a kiss, pocketed it and then winked at Darya, "What a good day, hm? Hungry? Dinner is on me."

Never one to turn down free food, Darya grinned, "I can eat."

The inn served a thick stew, warming and hardy. Not as excellent as Sindri's cooking, but was much better than the stuff Darya had on the road. It was a good way to tide over the evening, spending most of the time conversing about nonsensical things that had absolutely nothing to do with their journey. Like how to properly brush a malla during shedding season and when Flumium might run out of coal to trade with Mul Tarum.

It was good reminiscent about her past travel, albeit missing was the light strumming of her lute. Though Darya had to admit, she enjoyed the company more than a few lonely notes. Being a bard sounded romantic, but it did not feed anyone well. When your own patrons were also starving, they had little needs for anything other than to fill their bellies. Occasionally, Darya would get lucky, and someone with spare coins to line their pockets would be amused enough to flick her a chipped copper. If her luck shot through the roof, a silver.

Being a bard wasn't the best profession, but it was the only thing she could do. Darya was too weak for the mines. As a town crier, she couldn't shout over the noises of production. There was no field to work on, and the noble, richer households would not hire anyone from out of town.

Being a bard hadn't gained her much, after all.

Still, Darya missed the music. She hadn't played much since she met Luunaiwel. Since she became a Druid. Perhaps Captain Silos and his crew wouldn't mind her playing a few songs on their voyage.

As night-time approached, the patrons started dissipating. Luunaiwel discreetly tapped Darya's wrist. They made their way back to the room, bidding Tuura goodnight. As they rounded the corridor, Luunaiwel gestured to Darya to stay quiet. Together, they snuck out the back door.

They weaved in and out of the shadows, avoiding the few people still on the streets. In the darkness, navigating through alleys and following Luunaiwel's fluttering blue cloak, Darya was vividly reminded of her first encounter with the elf. It was barely two months ago, and yet it felt like a lifetime had passed. If she wasn't so conscious of their stealth, Darya would have let out a few hysterical giggles.

Who could have possibly imagined this would be the kind of adventure she had ended up with? Certainly not her younger self, wide-eyed and desperate to support her family. How could a simple bard even dreamed of being part of a story another bard might sing about?

"I feel like a burglar." Darya whispered as they stopped under a bridge, waiting for a cart to pass.

Luunaiwel chuckled, the sound rich and playful in her ears, "Exciting, is it not?"

When they finally approached the pines, Darya wanted so badly to reach out and make contacts, but Luunaiwel suggested they went further in.

"I thought fortune favours the bold?" She huffed, impatient.

Luunaiwel's eyes glittered, "Now, my dear little bird, the bolds hardly ever survive, do they?"

She had a point.

They ventured on, until the town's flickering lights disappeared. Unable to wait any longer, Darya ripped off her gloves and placed both hands on a young pine. She had expected an experience like Tarum y Fýri. Full of awe and wonders and gentle, peaceful whispers. This was anything but.

The tree's presence was... sluggish, as if it was in that state between sleep and wake. It was strange, and Darya was unnerved. But she could feel her Heart Stone's quiet encouragement, to reach out more. She felt an inexplicable urge to connect with the earth, curling around the warmth of her core, pushing her forward for *more.*

So Darya followed the impulse, kicking off her boots and sinking her feet into the stubbly needle carpet, digging her toes into the soil.

The change was...

It was *explosive.*

All at once, she could hear the calls, *feel* them all at the back of her head.

[Druid.]

[Druid!]

[Young Druid.]

[New Druid!!]

[Druid!!!]

[New Druid!]

[Druid.]

[Druid!]

[DRUID!!!]

It was overwhelming to the point of being painful. A tidal wave of voices and presence crashed against her consciousness. Her mouth opened, as if to let out a scream, but no sound came out. She tried to bring her hands up to clutch at her head, but her muscles stiffened, refusing to obey under the shocking onslaught. Her eyes rolled to the back of her skull.

And there was light. Blinding light.

In an instance, she was no longer in the grove of scrawny, sleepy pines. But in an ancient forest, where the green was all that she could see. Green below and green above. Before her stood an old tree, bark and roots twisted together under moss and earth.

In its cradle, there was a heartbeat.

Instinctively, she reached out.

But something. *Someone.* Got hold of her hand first.

There were whispers. Of many voices and many memories. Memories of those that came before her.

Those who were once Druids.

They were ancient. They were trapped. They were overwhelming. With touches of memories that were both beautiful and terrible.

They were supposed to be *familiar*. For Druids inherited their memories from the earth. And the earth passed it on. But they were strange and twisted and writhing in a disjointed echo of *loss*, like a torn-apart painting that was never completed.

They were like spring rain. When spring used to be gentle and nurturing.

They were like a summer's breeze. When summer didn't destroy all it touched.

They were like autumn's golden sun. When autumn was once bountiful and kind.

They were like winter's first snowflake. When winter used to bring wonders and kindled warmth in all hearts.

But they also felt the scorching tongues of destruction.

They also saw the incoming Shattering. When the earth pulses were torn asunder. When Life's hand was ripped away from her creation.

They scattered as the trees withered and fell.

They screamed for salvation as life crumbled away from their fingertips.

It was *madness*.

And in all of that, Darya saw what the world once was. What it *could still be*.

She could see it. When dragon wings used to fill the skies.

Beloved Child. They called for her.

She could smell it. When flowers once bloomed in every corner of the lands.

So incomplete, so *loved.*

She could hear it. When Druid-songs used to dance in the woods, urging the trees to grow.

This burden now falls to you.

She could *remember* it. When the world had not drowned in strife.

She wanted to see it all again. *She wanted it all back.*

So that her children and the children of her children would never have to know this suffering she knew.

Come to us.

She reached out. Past the memories. Past the singing voices of those who once were.

Seedling.

Come to us. Come back to us.

She felt her soul ache with their loss. With their memories of both pain and joy.

Still, she reached.

Please, she pleaded, *I need to know. I need to learn. I need to be complete.*

No. They said. In whispers that clawed at her soul and threatened to pull her to pieces. *You must come to us. Come back. To where you belong. Where there are those who loved you.*

There were faces. Flashes of memories. Memories of her own. Of those she had lost. Of those she might lose. Eyes that she could not look away from.

Her heart felt like it would break. What she would not give to have a family again?

But there was something else. A warmth. Small, weak, but persistent and refused to give out. No matter how loud the whispers became.

Her Heart Stone pulsed, hot upon her chest, urging her to brave the storm. To move forward. To block out the cries of the dead.

No, she shouted to the voices, *I am where I am needed to be. I do not belong to you, for you are only what once was. I am what will be. I am where I am supposed to be.*

So she pushed and pushed. Against the broken memories. Against the pain of loss. Against those who tried to pull her into their abyss.

She reached for it, for the heartbeat encased in roots and earth.

Until the light was in her hands.

It was...

It was gentle.

It cleared her head, cleared her pain.

Like a spring of thawed ice, it washed away the maddening presence, calming her wounded mind. It cooled her Heart Stone, returning it to its soothing thrums.

[Young Druid.] Another presence greeted her. Singular. Deep and old as the Earth itself.

It *was* the Earth itself.

[I am weak. I am dying. But you arrive.]

She reached out further. To try. To *heal*. But the Earth spoke again.

[You bring change. You are changing. But so is the world. By the hands of those who broke what was given to them.]

What am I supposed to do? She asked. Desperate. She had the powers. But she had no idea how to use it. No idea how to control it.

[You are learning. You fight. In the eternal struggle of life, you control what you must. Let it control what you cannot. Move forward. Follow the God-Touched. For Life and Death must always be in balance.]

I don't... I don't understand...

[You have the will to see it through. Just as you have the will to fight your way to me. Keep it close. Let it guide your power.]

She could feel the voice fading. She could feel the edge of consciousness in her mind.

Thank you.

[You have the Power to right what was wronged, Seedling. Never forget.]

She came to, staring up at blinking stars and Luunaiwel's mismatched eyes.

"Darya?" The elf asked, worried.

She blinked, huffing out a breath, "That was... *wow*. That was *crazy!*"

Tentatively, Luunaiwel helped her sit up, "Well, I do hope you learned something useful, because we have a problem."

Alarmed, Darya jumped to her feet. She immediately regretted it. Dizziness hit her like a frying pan to the head, and Darya would have face-planted if Luunaiwel wasn't there to hold her steady.

"What's... what's the problem?" She asked, gasping.

Luunaiwel didn't answer. She pointed instead. Darya's eyes followed, and she almost fainted at the spot.

The small, scrawny pine tree she was grabbing onto before the vision was now at least two hundred feet tall and the size of a small house.

"Shit."

CHAPTER 26:

When Darya slipped into Tuura's room, she almost got a heart attack. She didn't even notice anything until the man's fist weapon was half an inch from her face.

"It's me!!! It's me!!!" Facing the sharp blades and his eerily glowing amber eyes, she let out a stifled screech.

Slowly, Tuura retracted his claws, "Should have knocked. Where's Luna?"

"She, uh..." Darya paused, hesitating.

After what happened in the pine grove, Luunaiwel had told Darya to sneak back to the Nautilus Wheel and stay with Tuura. The elf had to go back to Mul Nordihr and prevent whatever mess that could have spawned from what Darya unintentionally did.

All Darya could do was frantically racing back to the Nautilus Wheel. Fortunately, no one caught her, because she sure didn't have the mind to watch out where she was going. It was also nothing short of miraculous that she didn't stop and empty the content of her stomach. The thrumming *pain* of what she just went through clawed at her insides like a ravenous beast. Darya was clammy and anxious, her skin crawled with the residue power-rush, and her head was spinning. If she wasn't so worried about Luunaiwel, Darya would have already given up and collapse.

"Well?" Tuura raised an eyebrow.

Rubbing her face, Darya recalled what had happened. Minus that part that her spirit was sucked into the earth pulse and almost got buried by the tormented souls of the past Druids. Darya didn't want to think too much about that just yet.

Tuura's eyebrows were steadily climbing higher up on his forehead, "So now there's a giant few-hundred-years-old-looking tree in a clump of saplings?"

Darya winced, "Yes. Sorry..."

Tuura sighed, "It's not your fault. None of us has expected this. Did Luna say anything else?"

Swallowing, Darya fidgeted a little, "She told me to break the seal on the staff and hold on to it. She also said if she doesn't return by sunrise, we must do everything possible to leave Teda."

Tuura's every muscle seemed to freeze. The room sunk into a tense silence, before Tuura let out a great exhale, visibly forcing his body to relax.

"Go get your staff."

"But what about Luunaiwel? She isn't going to get into trouble, is she???"

His hardened expression did nothing to reassure Darya, "She might. She might not. But even if she got into trouble, she's not the one who will have problems getting out of it."

"But-"

"Go get your staff."

There was no room for argument in Tuura's tone. Biting down her retorts, Darya slipped out and into her shared room with Luunaiwel. Seeing the elf's bags on the floor and no sign of her made Darya's heart clench. To Darya, Luunaiwel had always been powerful and unstoppable, a force to be reckoned with. She always had a solution to everything, always ready to face whatever might come next.

It was disconcerting, to not have that presence around. To know that it was her fault, again.

The edge of her vision blurred, Darya gritted her teeth, refusing to let any tears fall. If she had time to cry, she might as well surrender to the Night's Hand. So she grabbed her bags and Luunaiwel's, along with the staff's case, and hauled them all back to Tuura's room.

Seeing Darya walk in with all the luggage, Tuura stared, his gaze carried silent questions. Darya squared her shoulders.

"If we have to leave, she'd want her stuff when she catches up."

It was tiny, but Darya had been around Tuura long enough to notice the corners of his mouth turned up under his beard. He didn't say anything, but went to rekindle the hearth and poured Darya some water.

For a while, they sat staring at the fire, Tuura on the bed and Darya on the floor. Two hours passed at a snail's pace. Darya's fatigue was rapidly catching up to her, her eyelids and entire body felt like lead, but she refused to fall asleep.

Another full hour passed like that, with Darya swaying where she was sitting. Then Tuura finally spoke.

"You're not going to open it?"

Startled out of her own thoughts, Darya looked down at the case in her lap. She didn't even realise she was holding onto it. Gripping to it so tightly her knuckles turned white. Sucking in a breath, Darya carefully let go, wincing when her fingers creaked.

"I... I don't know..."

Just a few hours before now, she was dying to see the staff, *her* staff. She had imagined Luunaiwel would be there when Darya broke the seal, seeing her first reaction, pointing out how to use it in sync with her magic...

Darya didn't expect to open it without Luunaiwel. She didn't want to open the case like this. Without any of the excited anticipation and with all the fearful uncertainty.

She glanced over to Tuura, quietly imploring. He nodded once.

The wax seal snapped without much resistance.

Lying against dark fabric, the staff was of the finest craftsmanship Darya had ever seen. The birch had been polished and stained into a deep red, almost purple. A delicate vine, made of brass, coiled around it in the same fashion as the God-Touched tattoo on her leg, glimmering in a pale gold under firelight. The staff's end was covered in brass, a simple globe with brass studs all around. The slight curve at the top was fashioned into a bird head, its eyes glimmering red with the rubies they bought in Merchant Hall.

Tentative, Darya placed her hand over the staff. She could feel the energy thrumming through it, the power imbued within the rubies and the faint, but familiar presence of the old birch. She couldn't communicate with the staff as she did with the Old Birch, but the presence was there, and it comforted Darya, slightly.

"It's... exquisite." She finally said, running her fingers down the staff.

Tuura nodded, "Nadin is the master of his trade."

Carefully, Darya lifted the weapon out of its case. It was heavier than the practice staves, sturdier and felt like the proper weapon it was. She could feel her magic responding to it, intertwining with the enchantments Luunaiwel had woven. Despite having not cast a single spell yet, she knew magic will come easier to her, with this staff acting as a focus.

Tightening her grip around the staff, Darya trembled with the urge to rush out for Luunaiwel, and struggled to dismiss the though. She had to believe the elf could handle herself, just with everything else they had encountered.

Darya wouldn't know what else to do if Luunaiwel didn't come back. She didn't want to think about it.

The hours ticked by. Quietly. Slowly.

"It's almost dawn."

Tuura's words were like a whip to Darya's frayed nerves. Her hands tightened around the staff again.

"Just a few minutes, I'm sure-"

Tuura stood up, his whole bulk was almost threatening, "We can't afford to wait."

"But Luuna-"

"Can take care of herself. You cannot. And we need to get out of here." Tuura's tone was final, picking up his bags and Luunaiwel's.

Frantic, Darya took a foolish stance before the man, who was easily three times her size and endlessly more dangerous, "Aren't you even *worried* about her??? She could have been *killed* and-"

The look in Tuura's eyes stopped anything else that might have come out of Darya's mouth, "I care about her more than you could ever know. I also know her better than you do. It will take more than a dwarfish council to hold her down."

As the first rays of dawn filtered through the window, the air in the room could be cut by a knife.

Darya's lower lip trembled, her body seized with both fear and stubbornness. She didn't budge an inch.

And cut it was, but not by a blade. By the easy swing of the door, and the light as featherfall footsteps.

"While I appreciate the sentiment, I can assure you I would have appreciated it more if you had followed my order."

Luunaiwel strode in. Right as rain and smirking.

The staff fell, clanging onto the floor as Darya threw herself into Luunaiwel's arms.

"By the Gods!!! Are you okay??? I mean, you're here but... I was so worried, I... Is everything okay? Is the Council onto m-I mean us???"

Immediately, Luunaiwel hushed, "Not safe to talk."

Over Darya's head, Tuura inquired easily, "Breakfast?"

"Sure," Said Luunaiwel cheerily, "bakery? Then down the docks for a stroll?"

"The weather is nice." The big man answered, almost nonchalantly. But Darya didn't realise how tightly his hand had curled into itself until Luunaiwel gently patted it.

"Wrap your gift into a cloth, little bird." Luunaiwel threw a smile at Darya. Nodding, Darya gladly complied, swinging the weapon over her shoulder.

When they exited the Nautilus Wheel, Teda was at the brink of waking. And at the brink of realising that they now had a giant tree.

Tuura whistled, "Nice."

"I know, right?" Luunaiwel said cheerily.

Squirming, Darya wished the earth would open up and swallowed her whole. Though, with her powers, wishing for that might be a bad idea.

They mingled with the gathering crowd, presenting appropriately shocked reactions as people made all kinds of speculations. Pinpricks of anxiety ran along Darya's skin, and she tried to hide under Luunaiwel and Tuura's shadows, blearily averting her eyes and biting back a yawn. Now that most of the stress was gone, exhaustion came back with a vengeance. Darya fought a losing battle to keep her eyes open, as Luunaiwel bantered with a group of strangers.

Maybe she could nap standing up, just for a few minutes.

The arrival of a group of dwarfish guards rode down from Mul Mordihr interrupting their moment of respite. Eyes snapped open, she watched as their leader, a dwarf riding on a grey-coated malla, announced to the crowd.

"This is the work of our associate mages and sorcerers. Do not be alarmed. They are working to restore the Strand back to its former glory."

As he droned on, Darya leaned close to Luunaiwel, whispering, "You told them that?"

Still smiling, the corner of her mouth barely moved as Luunaiwel whispered back, "My apologies, I took credit for it. I have been working on the earth pulses for a while, and the Council knows."

Darya blinked, "Ah, so it'd make sense that something you did finally works. Smart."

Luunaiwel's grin was smug, "Thank you."

They stayed with the crowd as the guards answered questions, and drifted away along with the flow of people. Luunaiwel bought them breakfast rolls from a still bewildered baker, and down to the docks they went.

Dawn made the waves sparkle, pretty and joyous even in Darya's haziness. They headed to a far pier, where Luunaiwel and Darya sat with their legs dangling above the water, while Tuura stood leaning against a stake. For a while, Darya was content to enjoy the blissed sound of gentle waves lapping beneath them, and watched as fishing boats bobbled their ways towards the open sea. If Luunaiwel realised Darya was leaning a bit closer than usual, the elf didn't move away nor did she address it.

It was so peaceful Darya could fall asleep right there and then. And she almost did, if not for Luunaiwel's voice, clear above the wind and water.

"Last night, did you learn something from the earth pulse?"

Sleepiness once again ebbed away, Darya hummed, "I … believe so? It has something to do with my will to control it. My powers, I mean."

"I see … Did you see some kind of vision? Images in your head when you connected to the earth?"

Darya blinked, "Yes. It's difficult to explain, but … I did tell you about the living presences that I feel, right?"

"Via touch, yes."

Fidgeting, because the memory of everything still sent her a sharp pang of headache, the young Druid picked her words carefully, "Last night, when I made contact with the... earth pulse, there were images in my head. Like a dream, almost. A really vivid dream."

"Has this happened before?"

"When I received my power, when I first established my connection, the one with the Goddess Vita. And my first night sleeping in Tarum y Fýri."

"What did you see, then?"

Darya wasn't sure if it was her place to divulge it, so she said instead, "Memories. Of the earth and the old Druids back at the grove and here. And the old birch tree's memories, in Tarum y Fýri."

"So you have tapped into the store of memories in this earth pulse."

Darya winced, thinking about the discordant screams and the curling tendrils of power that urged her to forsake everything, "Something like that... It was definitely different from the birch."

Luunaiwel's eyes gentled, "Perhaps you were able to access that particular tree's memories because it has lived an incredibly long life."

That made sense. Darya pondered about it for a moment, but felt her pounding headache coming back.

"I want to test it out, but that's probably not going to be the greatest idea, isn't it?"

"Unfortunately," Luunaiwel said, sympathetic, "I am sorry for dragging you out here so early. The power surge must have tired you greatly, but I do not wish for others to notice your absence after such a night."

"It's fine." At that, Darya finally caved and yawned so hard her jaws clicked. She slumped over, giving up the pretence. She leaned onto Luunaiwel, relishing in her solid presence. A dull thump of relief and joy swirled in the pit of her stomach when she wasn't pushed away.

"It is impressive. I was worried, but it appears the earth pulse has absorbed your excess magic instead of your own life force. It is a blessing in a way."

Darya had to take a moment to fully comprehend what Luunaiwel was talking about, "So that means … I'm not going to be sprouting flowers in my sleep for a while?"

The elf chuckled, "Yes. And perhaps with the new knowledge you have acquired, you may now harness your God-Touched abilities and control them much more efficiently."

That perked Darya up, hope in her eyes as she looked at Luunaiwel, "Really?"

The smile she received was kind, and it warmed Darya in more ways than one, "Really."

It was enough for Darya to let out a content sigh, nuzzled against Luunaiwel and drifted off to sleep.

CHAPTER 27:

As they no longer had Mul Tarum's protection, Darya's magical training came to a temporary halt. Though Luunaiwel did explain to her how the staff's enchantments work.

"One of the rubies is similar to your pin. It will store any and all your excess magic in your sleep, but with a much larger capacity. Just repeat the same chant before bed, and keep the staff close. The other one is imbued with the fire of the Great Forge of Mul Tarum. It will shine in the darkest of nights, and warm when the cold encroaches."

In awe, Darya touched the gem, delighted when she felt the rolling heat under her fingertips, "Would I be able to use fire spells?"

Luunaiwel shrugged, "In the past, Druids could only use earth-based magic. But, who knows, you might be an exception."

She went on to teach Darya a new skill.

"I did have a few Druid friends back in the days. Like you, they can sense other living beings' presence, but they can also communicate with those who did not come from the earth." Luunaiwel said, taking off a glove.

Wide-eyed, Darya glanced at Luunaiwel's offering hand, "How did they do that?"

"It has to be a two-way communication. The person who you want to communicate to also has to reach out to you. However, that person needs to also feel your presence."

"So we need to establish a connection sort of?"

Luunaiwel smirked, "Correct, little bird. Which was why this method had not been popular, considering the requirements. Most people without magic cannot detect a Druid's mind presence. But I am certain this can come in handy in some situations."

Darya grinned, "Can't hurt to try!"

The spell worked faster than Darya had thought. The presence within Luunaiwel shifted, accommodating Darya's sliver of thought as the elf coached her along. Luunaiwel's constellation of magic no longer overwhelmed Darya's senses, instead, it was fluid, like an underground river. Something that she was aware of but couldn't *see*.

Hello, Darya.

She startled when Luunaiwel reached out for the first time. It was nothing like when the Old Birch Man or the earth pulse spoke to her. She wasn't seeing images nor feelings. Luunaiwel's way of communicating was simple words of thoughts. Simple and far more straightforward than the Druids of old memories here in Mortia's Strand.

Luunaiwel?

Seems like it works.

How long can we maintain this?

As long as we maintain physical contact.

That's amazing!

Indeed.

It wasn't anything spectacular, but this new ability to communicate filled Darya with joy. They practiced for the rest of the day before the departure, and Darya was giddy to find out it didn't take as much time to master as regular spells. She even had the opportunity to try it on Tuura, though the connection wasn't as strong as with Luunaiwel.

"His magic is more dormant," Luunaiwel explained, "it does not manifest with spells like yours and I."

"Ah … and you need someone with adept control of their magic, right?" Darya asked, the quickly added sheepishly, "Not that your magic isn't adept, of course!"

Tuura chuckled, "I'm sure something will work out if we put in enough practice."

"Perhaps that would be something for you to do on our voyage."

Darya grinned at Luunaiwel's suggestion, "Anything to stave off the boredom!"

Morning came with little fuss. There was no flower growing through the floorboard, giving Darya a bounce in her feet as they started loading up on the ship. Darya was in charge of their mounts, which only added to the high. It was always pleasant to interact with the beasts, their life forces gentle under her fingers, their quiet huffs and nuzzles dulled the ache of departure in her heart.

Darya mulled over the names she could give to her mare, and wasn't surprised when everything she came up with was a flora. Without knowing it, she really had taken to this whole druidic theme. Chuckling, Darya backed out of the stable, pushing back her horse's searching sniffs, and bumped right into a woman in the hull, knocking a bucket out of her hands. The water splashed all over her dress, startling her into a yelp.

Gasping, Darya quickly picked up the bucket, "By the Gods! I'm so sorry!! Are you alright???"

Flustered, the woman took back the bucket and held it in front of her like a shield, "Oh... yes... Yes! I'm... I'm alright! Oh... oh no... That... that was supposed to be the stable beasts' drink for... for the day..."

Feeling terrible, Darya fidgeted, "I'm so sorry! Here, I'll help you refill!"

Startled, the woman blinked wide blue eyes at Darya, "I'm... uh, I am fine, it's … it's alright..."

"Are you sure? I'll-"

"Metzan, what's wrong?" A voice came from the stairs cut in.

"I'm... I'm alright!" Blond hair falls out of her head scarf as the woman turned around, her voice betraying the reassurance.

Darya looked over to the man who came down. Strange, if she squinted this way, he looked almost like...

Her eyes widened in realisation, "*Caldor???*"

At a loss for words, Caldor, the last person Darya had expected to ever run in again, gawked back, "Darya??? What are you doing here???"

"I'm sailing on this vessel! What are *you* doing here???"

"What??? *You're our passenger???*"

"What do you mean *your* passenger???"

"I'm a sailor on this ship!"

The woman, Metzan, followed the steadily shouty conversation in growing concern, "Wha-what's going on??"

Before either of them could answer, a fourth voice joined in, making both Caldor and Metzan jump,"Well, well, well... What a nice surprise this is, Mister Caldor..."

Immediately, Caldor growled, *"Elf."*

"Polite as ever, I see." Luunaiwel drawled, leaning against the railing with a taunting grin.

Darya rolled her eyes. She strode over to stand between Luunaiwel and Caldor, in case someone (most likely the latter) decided to be uncivil and someone (most likely the former) would escalate the situation into a bloodbath.

"We've been travelling together since we parted ways with you," Darya said, mustering up a reassuring smile, "how have you been?"

"Better, until I saw *her,*" Caldor groused at Luunaiwel, but did crack a tiny smile at Darya, "it's good to see you alive."

Feeling the tension in the air was ebbing away, Darya beamed, "Same! I can't believe we ran into each other like this!"

Caldor huffed, "Small world."

"Tiny." There was a smirk in Luunaiwel's voice. Nevermind, the tension had returned, "And who is this charming young lady you are travelling with?"

Caldor's switch to a protective stance was instant. Squaring his shoulders, he glared at Luunaiwel, "None of your business."

To Darya's surprise, the previously timid Metzan rolled her eyes at Caldor. The young Druid bit back a chuckle. Perhaps Metzan knew Caldor's huffy proneness to anger better than most.

"My name is Metzan, pleased to meet you." She said, aiming a tentative but polite smile at Luunaiwel.

The elf smiled back, tilting her head to the side, "I am Luunaiwel. The pleasure is mine," a pause, "Mister Caldor seems to attract magical folks to himself, does he not?"

At first, Darya was confused. But then, when the colours steadily drained from Metzan's face and Caldor's turned a purplish hue, the young Druid realised what Luunaiwel was implying.

"I don't know what you're talking about." Caldor said. His tone was careful. Guarded. Unlike his thunderous expression.

Luunaiwel scoffed, "Please, child. My green eye permanently sees in the magical spectrum. She has magic, and judging by your expressions, you both know it," tilting her head the other way, "and both are too *noble* to lie convincingly about it, too."

If Caldor gritted his teeth any harder, they would crack. But Metzan was the one who spoke next.

"Please... please don't tell anyone about me... about us..." Though pale, her voice was firm, and she stood straighter, a fist upon her chest.

Darya sighed. At this rate, Luunaiwel was going to either make Metzan cry or Caldor attack her. Or both.

"This is hardly the place to talk." Darya raised her hands, offering a smile towards Caldor and Metzan, while also throwing a pleading look at Luunaiwel, "We still have... uh, five hours until we set out, right? Why don't we grab something to eat and have a chat down by the piers?"

"I don't have anything to say to-" Caldor began, but Metzan put a gentle hand on his arm.

"Our break is in another hour," her smile was a bit shaken, but her voice was sure, "we will be there."

Luunaiwel looked especially pleased with herself, ignoring Caldor's seething glare, "Delightful. We will be waiting."

Darya smiled at Caldor and Metzan, "It's nice seeing you again, Caldor. And nice to meet you, Metzan. Sorry about your dress!" She added sheepishly.

With one last wary exchange of glances, Caldor and Metzan took their leaves.

And Darya didn't wait until they got off the ship to voice her displeasure with Luunaiwel, "Why did you have to do that?"

Luunaiwel's grin was positively *blinding*, "Whatever do you mean, little bird?"

"Caldor. I mean *Caldor*. Why did you have to rile him up?"

The elf's chuckle was airy, "Mister Caldor is a fine young man, and his quick temper is simply amusing. Once in a while, you ought to create your own amusement, no?"

Before Darya could retort, Tuura spoke, having appeared by Luunaiwel like a shadow, "Caldor? That thief-Knight is here?"

"He was never a thief!" Darya hissed under her breath. Oh... these two were impossible! "And yes, Caldor is a sailor here now."

Raising a finger, Luunaiwel said cheerily, "With a magick-wielder, I might add!"

Tuura cocked an eyebrow, "Isn't that interesting?"

Palming her face, Darya heaved out a sigh. Fine. If they were going to behave like that...

"Luunaiwel, you said your green eye sees permanently in the magical spectrum? How do you do that? And what's a magical spectrum?"

Immediately, Tuura looked down at her with a frown. Luunaiwel's smile turned sharp. Darya gulped, but held her chin up stubbornly. It was unfair how only Luunaiwel could have all the fun all the time. Besides, it was Luunaiwel's fault for bringing up something so intriguing in the first place. If she could leak something personal to spite Caldor, then Darya had every right to ask.

As Darya expected, the answer she got was vague, "It was the one fortunate result in a chain of unfortunate events. The magical spectrum is similar to what you can feel with living beings. But instead of presences or life forces, I can see traces of magic in the air. An aura, if you will."

That instantly piqued Darya's curiosity, "Really? How does m-"

"This is hardly the place for this kind of conversation." Cutting in, Tuura grumbled. Stopping, they looked at the crew, each busy with one task or another on deck. Darya gulped.

"You're right..."

Luunaiwel grinned, "Have we finished loading?"

"All the bags are in our designated cabins." Tuura said.

Darya nodded, "I've stabled my mare and the mallas."

Luunaiwel clasped her hands together, "Perfect. Does pie for lunch sound good?"

The pies were nice. Hot, flaky and filled with gravy goodness, but Darya was too distracted to enjoy them fully. She kept her mouth shut though, until they were at the end of the piers. Only then did Darya eagerly fill Tuura in about the encounter in the hull.

But Tuura didn't seem concerned about the same things as Darya did, "Metzan is her name?"

Darya blinked, not expecting that question, "Uh... yes. She said her name is Metzan."

Luunaiwel grinned, "Interesting, right?"

"I ... don't follow..."

"The Count of Edurn has, or had, a daughter. Her name is Metzania." Tuura said bluntly.

Darya was glad she was already sitting down, "Wait, *what???* You think Metzan is..."

Luunaiwel smirked, "The same person Caldor was accused of 'defiling'. Among other charges. I say he has scored himself something big."

Scouring her memories, Darya thought of everything she had heard about Caldor's false crimes, what he told her and what she heard about Metzania. He was accused of breaking into the

Count's manor, and Metzania reportedly fell ill after he did. Metzania was supposed to be married to some lord, and she was sent off despite kicking up a fuss a day before Luunaiwel and Darya left town. When Darya and Luunaiwel parted ways with him, Caldor did say something about having previous arrangements.

 The Metzan she saw in the hull, though definitely dressed too poorly to be a lady, was too frail for labour work. Her voice was too soft, and she was well-spoken despite her stuttering, though that was Darya's fault for startling her to begin with.

 And she had *magic*??? Caldor definitely knew that, judging by his reaction. But he was protective of her instead of being terrified like he was with Luunaiwel when *she* used magic.

 It was a good thing that Caldor and Metzan walked up to them only half an hour later, otherwise Darya's curiosity would burst where she stood.

 Upon seeing Tuura with them however, Caldor stopped with an arm before Metzan, cautious. Darya called out, "It's ok! Tuura is a friend! He's been travelling with us."

 After a moment, the pair continued, but not without Caldor's distrustful glances at Luunaiwel and Tuura. The five of them stood on the pier, face to face. Darya wasn't sure what to say, and it didn't look like either Caldor or Tuura knew what to do either. Luunaiwel seemed like she was having the time of her life, her grin brighter than the sparkling sun, while Metzan bit down her lower lip, anxious.

Surprisingly, it was also Metzan who spoke first, despite looking like she was close to fainting, "Caldor refused to talk about you at all... I ... apologise, I do not know your names…"

She trailed off, then shrunk to herself when Luunaiwel spoke around a smile, "Do not blame Mister Caldor, for he was bound to never speak of my name. I am Luunaiwel, and these are my companions, Darya and Tuura."

Blinking, Metzan gave them a hesitant smile, "I am Metzan, pleased to meet you..."

Darya gave her a small, encouraging wave. Caldor didn't seem at all relaxed though. He glared at Luunaiwel.

"Does this mean I won't die if I speak about you now?"

Next to him, Metzan flinched. Luunaiwel grinned, "I am glad you have kept your end of the bargain. Very well, since we will be travelling together for the time being I would be glad to release you from your vow."

Flabbergasted, Metzan whispered, "Caldor, what *vow...?*"

She stopped short when Luunaiwel's glimmering gaze moved to her, "*If* you let us know why you are travelling with a magick-wielder."

Metzan immediately went pale. Caldor growled at Luunaiwel, "You're an arse."

Luunaiwel inclined her head at him mockingly, "I must uphold my reputation."

"Luunaiwel, *please.*" Darya was exasperated.

Shaking her head, Darya looked to Metzan with the utmost sincerity, "It was a very complicated situation. I don't think either me or Caldor knew what we were getting into. Uhm... Please don't be afraid, me and Luunaiwel are just like y-"

A sudden squeeze on her shoulder stopped Darya short. Luunaiwel leaned forward, chin hovering above the young Druid's ear, her pose exuded pure intimidation, "Hush, little bird. We do not know if dear Metzania here is Night's Hand or not."

If it was possible, Metzan's face dropped many shades paler, "Oh... Gods... How did you... how do you know my name??"

Caldor's reaction is different. His sword was immediately drawn, and his face was drawn with rage, "How dare you accuse us of associating with those scums?!"

Great.

Darya covered her face. This was getting out of hand too quickly.

CHAPTER 28:

"Luunaiwel was passing through Edurn when Caldor was falsely imprisoned for breaking into the Count's manor. She was the one who bailed him out and bought his service to lead her to the glade of herbs. Luunaiwel wanted to keep her journey to herself, thus the vow of secrecy. Darya was accompanying them, that's why she knows. The story about the Count's daughter's involvement was widely discussed in Edurn."

Up until this point, Darya had never been as grateful of Tuura being around as she was now. Folding her arms, Luunaiwel pouted.

"You are no fun."

Tuura rolled his eyes, if not rather fondly, "And you're having too much fun."

"I *was* until you ruined it!"

"Hold on a minute!" Caldor waved his sword around, looking just a tad mad, "How do you know about the Night's Hand then?!"

Darya sighed, supposing that it was her turn to step in before Luunaiwel took this opportunity and ran with it, "They were coming after me. Massacred my neighbourhood. Broke down my home, killed my grandmother."

Metzan's hands flew to her mouth, "Oh, Gods above! I-I am so sorry!"

Ignoring the bitter pang in her stomach, Darya forced a smile, "Don't be sorry. It's not your fault. How about you? How do you know about them?"

Caldor tensed. Metzan looked away.

"They were coming after me." She said after a long moment.

Darya froze, "How come?! I'm sorry if I'm prying but... why were they coming after you? I thought you were supposed to marry some lord..."

She trailed off, seeing the fury in Caldor's dark eyes. To her surprise, he sheathed his sword, "Not by choice. Metzan was practically sold by her father when he discovered she had magic. She was only ten when this deal was struck."

His voice lowered to a hiss at the last part. He only relaxed by a margin when Metzan touched his elbow.

Metzan's blue eyes were pained, "To the public, it was a prestigious proposal. He was not just any minor lord. The man who offered to take my hand in marriage was the Duke of Furbarst, the second largest city in the North."

Body visibly shaking with how much anger he was holding, Caldor spat, "He wanted to make Metzan a slave."

Metzan's hands twisted together, "My half-brother, Aragni, was against this. But he was in Apricum and had previously entered a bound servitude. Thus, he had no way of interfering. Until he grew desperate and confined to his best friend, Caldor."

Said man nodded curtly, "I left Apricum before I completed my training, at Aragni's behest. I built a life in Edurn, biding my time and secretly bridging communication between them. The night I broke into the manor, I was supposed to take Metzan away to Apricum and meet up with Aragni. You know what happened next."

Metzan sighed, "The wedding was planned to be two weeks from then. However, my father decided to send me off immediately after Caldor's escape."

Darya was liking this Count less and less. What sort of father willingly sold his daughter into slavery?

"Knowing that there was no way I could stop this alone, I rode to Apricum for Aragni," Caldor continued, his face grim, "we intercepted Metzan's entourage just before they entered Furbarst territory. However... it did not come without a cost."

Tears came to Metzan's eyes, "Aragni perished trying to save me."

A soft gasp escaped Darya. She clamped her mouth shut immediately, eyes and ears training on the two people in front of her.

Caldor sighed, pain flashed in his eyes, but his voice was steady, "We rode nights and days along Mount Amun, hoping to hide our tracks along the mountainside. Our horses collapsed after a week, and we were left stranded at a village due west. We hoped to lay low for a while, just enough so we can figure everything out."

Luunaiwel raised an eyebrow, "Let me guess. The Lord of Furbarst was not all too jolly about his bride-to-be being snatched away right under his nose."

Metzan shook her head, "No, he was not. He sent the Night's Hand after us."

"Long story short, we've been running ever since," Caldor said, "I didn't know where else to go. Having nowhere left to run to, we went to a fishing village east of the Desecrated. That was where we heard rumours about this place. I used my gold to buy a boat and got ourselves here."

Luunaiwel smirked, "Looks like your investment worked out. Are you two settling in Teda, then?"

Metzan shook her head, her lips a thin line, "We cannot stay in the mainland. There are rumours about the Night's Hand's presence in Flumium. I... *we* will be sailing to Imirra, where I hopefully can find shelter from their influence."

Caldor narrowed his eyes, "If you people are here, then I suppose that Night's Hand rumour is true."

Darya shrugged, "You can say that."

Luunaiwel clasped her hands together, smiling as if she hadn't heard one of the saddest stories Darya had ever come across, "And now we are all on the same boat! No pun intended. I do suppose I should lift your vow now."

Tuura raised an eyebrow, "You're not going to verify?"

The elf shrugged, pulling out the strip of ribbon she used for Caldor's vow, "If they are lying, it is not like there is anywhere they can run from us."

Caldor stared at the strip of ribbon distrustfully, "Why is it torn?"

Luunaiwel smirked, "Why, I had to lift the vow on Darya first. You cannot travel with someone halfway across the continent and not have *some* form of trust now, can you?"

Before Caldor could make any scathing retort, Luunaiwel put the strip of ribbon to her lips, "Child of Thorns, heed my words. The Vow is lifted, on one named Caldor. Wayfinder. Knight of Stars."

The ribbon darkened in her hand, turned black then ashen, before dissipating into the wind. Darya had to admit, she felt a bit smug that her initial reaction to that process was a lot calmer than Metzan's. The blonde's eyes were wide, staring at Luunaiwel's hand.

"Did you just... I am sorry, pardon me, but... *was that magic???*"

Luunaiwel smiled indulgently, "That was, Lady Metzania," mismatched eyes then moved to Caldor, leering, "how did you dolts figure out she has magic?"

Caldor glowered, but Metzan was quick to supply, "When I was a kid... I could make the hearth burn whenever I was cold. I could light torches without touching them, or ignite the stove without being near."

Luunaiwel tilted her head, "Ah, an affinity to Ignia. I can respect that. Now, since this party is over, shall we board our beautiful vessel and head out to the open, treacherous sea? I do believe we have an hour left before one of us got horribly seasick and donate food to the fish below."

Darya didn't know whether she should laugh or be disgusted at that image. But as they, herself, Luunaiwel and Tuura, made to leave, Caldor asked, incredulous.

"Wait. That's it??"

Luunaiwel's grin was sharper than a knife, "It is. Unless you want more. I still remember you owing me a barrel of the finest wine in town, by the way."

Darya could tell Caldor was going to yell something, due to the increasing wrinkles on his forehead, the way he unhinged his jaw and how puffed up his chest was, but Metzan beat him to it.

"Milady Luunaiwel... You... You are a magick-wielder, correct?"

"And what if I am?"

Metzan slightly staggered, by the way Luunaiwel's mismatched eyes were boring into hers. But she didn't back down. Her grip was knuckle-white on her apron, "Are you teaching Miss Darya?"

Luunaiwel stood up straight, her height towering over the petite Metzan. She repeated "And what if I am?"

Metzan opened her mouth and closed it. Sucking in a startled breath, she bowed, golden hair spilling over her shoulders as she did, "Would you please teach me as well, milady?"

Surprised, Caldor turned to her, "Metzan! You don't know what you're asking for!"

Metzan ignored him, speaking to Luunaiwel with a shaken but determined voice, "Please, milady! I can learn from you... I would *love* to learn from you!"

For a moment, there were only the sounds of lapping waves and creaking docks around them. Darya didn't even dare to breathe. Luunaiwel's face was void of emotion as she regarded the still bowing Metzan.

"No."

A rush of air escaped Metzan. Startled blue eyes looked up at the elf. Darya looked away, unable to stomach the creeping despair in them.

"Why?"

"Unfortunately, Lady Metzania," Luunaiwel's smile did not reach her eyes, "I happen to have my hands full already, and I would rather not concern myself with the whims of a noble woman. You have nothing to offer me, nor do I have any interest in you beyond a fellow passenger. Now, if you will excuse me, I believe all of us have elsewhere to be."

It was clear that Metzan was trying her hardest not to cry. With another swift bow, she hastily walked away, a glaring Caldor in tow.

Despite knowing that this was in no shape or form her fault, Darya still felt guilty as they walked back to the ship, keeping a distance from the other two, "If I wasn't in the picture, would you have mentored her?"

"Of course not," Luunaiwel raised an eyebrow, "I have no interest in having a disciple. And, before you ask, I would not have had you around if you had not turned out to be a Druid. At the same regard, I do believe you would not have wanted to stick around with me either if you did not become one."

Out of instinct, Darya wanted to argue. But she closed her mouth in the end and quietly followed the elf. Luunaiwel was right. They wouldn't have associated with one another for this long if it wasn't for Darya's current status as a Druid. Even back then, with her careless curiosity, Darya knew it would be dangerous to follow the elf.

Feeling bad for Metzan didn't change the fact that this journey was dangerous. And Darya wasn't selfless enough to let go of Luunaiwel for a complete stranger, even if the elf allowed Metzan a chance.

To kill what little time they had left, they milled around on the deck. As Luunaiwel conversed with the Captain, Darya busied herself with looking at the ship's details, as she hadn't time before.

The ship was named Valiant Will, a grand name for a grand ship. With two great masts and many sails, it was nothing like the small fishing boats Darya saw on her mornings here in Teda. The Valiant Will was definitely bigger than Nathi's manor, the deck itself was double the size of his front yard. Though there was a slow bobbing underneath as the waves moved, Darya wasn't at all unnerved.

On a ship this big, there was no way she needed to be afraid of anything.

Right?

Darya didn't know her answer was coming down the slopes of Mortia's Strand, in the form of thirty military dwarves on horseback.

Curious, she leaned over the ship's railing to watch them. She didn't expect Luunaiwel to grab her elbow. With a bare hand.

Something is not right.

Flinching at the sudden mind connection, Darya almost yanked away. But she took a deep breath and willed her heart to calm down.

What's wrong?

Luunaiwel narrowed her eyes. ***I do not know yet. Stay put and out of sight.***

The elf's presence was gone before Darya could respond. Luunaiwel slipped off the boat and went to stand at the front of the dock, waiting.

Too soon, the dwarf troop stopped twenty yards in front of Luunaiwel. The leader rode to the front, his voice was loud enough to carry above the waves.

"Lady Luunaiwel, the Council of Nine Hammers have issued a formal order. Do you accept it?"

With hands clasped before her belt, Luunaiwel answered with a smile, "I have never accepted an order before hearing it. What is this about?"

"You are hereby relieved of your duties as Mage of the Nine Hammers, and to surrender the refugee Darya of Flumium into our custody."

If she wasn't holding onto the railing, Darya would have collapsed right there and then.

What???

She thought... She thought Luunaiwel had it handled... How did they...???

Around the ship, whispers started to buzz. But Darya couldn't hear anything. Every ounce of focus she had was on Luunaiwel.

Luunaiwel didn't even react to the dwarf. At least not from what Darya could see.

"Is there a reason for this?"

The dwarf ignored her, "You are to surrender without question."

Luunaiwel tilted her head, "And if I will not?"

"Then there will be consequences. Men."

Three horses were led to the front, each had a sack over the saddle. Two dwarves, axe in hand, kicked the sacks off and ripped them open.

Darya's heart froze in her chest.

Nathi, Sindri and *Sara,* Nathi was still in his travelling clothes while the girls were still in their nightgowns, bound and gagged. Instantly, there were blades at their necks.

A muffled screech escaped Sara, her eyes wide in terror. Both Nathi and Sindri were dishevelled, but defiant.

Darya wanted to scream. She would have. If not for Tuura's big hand around her mouth.

"Hush." He whispered, face hard, "If you let them know you're here before Luna could negotiate, everyone would be dead."

Darya bit down her lip, tasting blood.

No... *Nononono...*

They were supposed to be *safe* in Mul Tarum. They weren't supposed to be here, being held *hostage*.

To trade for Darya.

No...

"This is not how the Council typically operates." Luunaiwel's voice rang clear, cutting through the haze of panic in Darya's mind, "I cannot comply unless you show some identifications."

What the...

Darya wanted to yell out. To snap at Luunaiwel to quit it, to *stop posturing* while the others, *her sister*, was in danger of *death*.

But she couldn't squirm out of Tuura's hold, no matter how hard she struggled.

The dwarf in charge bellowed, "You have no authority to ask for our identification! Give up the refugee, or they all die!"

Luunaiwel tilted her head. The air seemed to be strung on a thin string, and could snap at any sudden movement.

"Fine. Darya. Come down. Slowly."

Both Darya and Tuura froze at that. But the young Druid came to her senses first and yanked herself out of Tuura's grip. Feeling like her heart was going to give out, Darya made stuttering steps down the plank. She almost ran towards her sister too, but Luunaiwel reached out and grabbed her by the elbow with her bare hand.

Do not do anything stupid.

Darya froze. Then tried to pull away "They have my sister!!!"

And they would kill her if you act rashly. Your sister does not have any value to them aside from being a bargaining chip.

Darya froze again. Luunaiwel used her body to shield her from sight when the dwarf leader tacked his horse forward. Despite every nerves in her body's protests, Darya forced herself to breathe. Forced herself to speak through their connection.

What now?

Luunaiwel pinched her elbow. The sharp pain cut through her panic.

Kick off your boots.

What?!

We are on a sliver of land. There are berry bushes behind them. Try to connect with them via the earth. Grow the thorns around the horses' hooves.

I... I don't know if I can do that! That's too far away!!!

Try it. Will it to happen. Do you not want to save your sister?!

It was like Luunaiwel had physically slapped her.

Hadn't Darya promised herself to get stronger? Hadn't she told herself that she would do everything in her power to keep Sara safe? Why wasn't she willing to *try?*

As discreetly as she could, Darya shucked off her boots behind the cover of Luunaiwel's body.

"My patience is running thin! Luunaiwel, give up the girl!" The dwarf boomed, baring his teeth.

Darya sucked in a breath when she made the connection with the earth. *Please.*

"There is no guarantee that you would not kill the others if I do give her over." Luunaiwel held her head high, unwavering.

It was slow. The earth's presence here was slow. Like the pine sapling before, the earth was sluggish, sleepy.

She was too far away.

Darya's entire being quivered.

Please.

The dwarf leader snarled, "If you do not give her over now, I will start slitting their throats for every minute of your dawdling."

The edge of her vision burned. A tear dropped to the dry mix of soil and sand below.

PLEASE.

Luunaiwel's eyes narrowed, "Are you threatening me?"

The dwarf pointed his axe at her face, eyes bulging with rage, "Know your place! You *serve* the Council!"

[... Druid?]

Behind the dwarf leader, Nathi sputtered, pushing past the gag through his struggles.

"LULU!!! THEY'RE NIGHT'S HAND!!!"

Time seemed to stop.

Darya didn't know exactly what happened. She didn't know *how* the reaction came so quickly and so slowly at the same time.

The power in her Heart Stone thumped once. Painful.

Darya saw red.

It was Night's Hand.

It was Night's Hand that threatened her friends and the sole surviving member of her family.

Night's Hand.

[Night's Hand.]

They must pay.

[Destroy.]

Behind the line of Night's Hand dwarves, thorns burst forth.

KILL THEM!!! KILL THEM ALL!!!!

*[BURY THEM. DRINK THEIR BLOOD. **GROW**.]*

It was so quick, so *brutal*, that neither dwarves nor horses could scream. It was a maw *of thorns* that impaled through a full row of enemies, leaving them no time to react. Blood rained upon the remaining dwarves, their horses rearing in fear.

A shadow swooped from above. A giant eagle, with knives for talons, gorged on the faces of those holding Nathi, Sindri and Sara hostage. The bird shifted into Tuura as his enemies thrashed in death, quickly snipping off the ropes around them.

"Run!" He snapped, fist weapons already flying to parry incoming blows. The enemies were maddened with the sudden provocation, and was now lashing out at everything in reach.

Luunaiwel didn't waste a second. With bounds and leaps, she chased after the leader, who had turned tail, and grabbed onto his head before he could get too far. Her blade's swing was almost invisible, and her eyes were feral.

Meanwhile, Darya felt her mind slipping away. Into a blank state of pure fury

She couldn't think. She couldn't feel.

Nothing aside from *kill, kill, KILL*.

Luunaiwel flew into battle, dodging and slashing at impossible speed. At both Night's Hand and Darya's frantic thorns.

Something came whistling out of the air and into the earth beside Darya. The enemies had pulled out their crossbows.

They wanted to kill Darya.

"Someone needs to stop her!!!" The elf yelled, slicing off a lashing strand of thorn in her way, "The earth will drain her dry if she doesn't stop!!!"

Her Heart Stone *burned* on her chest.

[PROTECT!!!]

The earth *exploded* with thorns. Darya's ears were filled with screams.

More arrows came. Most of them missed. One pierced through her shoulder.

She didn't feel the pain.

Just rage.

[PROTECT DRUID!!!]

"Darya!!! Stop!!!"

It was Sindri.

Hands grabbed onto her arms, the dwarf woman's face was pale and tears-stricken, her green eyes dilated with fear.

Green eyes.

Just like Sara's.

Save Sara. Kill them all.

"Darya!! Please!!! Snap out of it!! Or you'll kill us all!!!"

Kill.Kill.Kill.Kill.Kill.Kill.Kill.Kill.Kill.Kill.Kill.Kill.Kill.Kill.K
ill.

"DARYA!!!"

She felt like flying.

For a second, she was.

Something, or *someone*, knocked her onto her back.

Ripping her feet away from the earth and onto the wooden docks.

Her glazed eyes turned skyward. Blinking.

She saw red.

Was it Sindri's hair?

Darya closed her eyes.

Darkness came, silencing the screams and the rage.

CHAPTER 29:

Darya woke up feeling like her entire body was bruised and beaten. Her right shoulder especially. It felt like it was hammered.

Everything felt like it was swaying, and Darya was afraid she would slide off whatever she was laying on.

Darya forced her eyes open, and instantly regretted her decision.

Her eyeballs hurt so bad they could pop out of her skull. There was light, Darya was sure of it, but her vision was filled with white spots. She was feverish. Darya squeezed her eyes shut. But the pain didn't go away.

Something was heavy on her chest. It was her Heart Stone, throbbing dully.

She shouted, but all that came out was a croaking groan.

Suddenly, something pleasantly cool draped over her forehead. Someone said something, but her ears were muffled.

Darya forced her heavy eyelids to open again. The white spots were still there, but they were slowly dissipating as she blinked.

There was someone there. Yes. Someone she knew... maybe.

Blue eyes and blond hair...

She was pretty, Darya squinted. She was saying something too. But Darya still couldn't hear it.

Metzan ... right?

She tried to talk to Metzan, but only a dry moan came through.

Metzan raised a finger, gesturing for Darya to wait, before leaving. Darya tried to stop her, but her arm felt like it was chained down with iron. The effort alone was *painful.*

What happened?

She wondered, lying there, staring up at an unfamiliar, swaying ceiling. Her memory was both foggy and a jumbled mess.

She remembered being on the dock with Luunaiwel and Tuura. She remembered bumping into Metzan and Caldor down at the ship's hull. She remembered speaking to them. She remembered having pies with Luunaiwel and Tuura...

Chapter 29

She remembered fear. She remembered rage. She remembered...

The screams.

She wanted to cover her ears, but she couldn't. The screams rolled from one ear to the other. They were *unstoppable*.

She squeezed her eyes shut.

Please, stop!!!

"Darya."

All at once, everything was silent. As if all the muffled, chaotic noises in her head were sucked out, leaving behind blessed silence.

Daring to crack an eye open, Darya almost cried when she saw Luunaiwel.

"Luuu..." She wheezed out, "... Huuurts..."

There was a frown on the elf's face, a gloved hand smoothed Darya's hair back, "Hush, little bird. Sleep. Rest."

Something cool was placed on her lips. Gently, Luunaiwel pried her mouth open, pouring a sweet liquid down Darya's throat.

Slowly, the pain slipped away. Replaced by sleepiness.

Darya let it take her, sinking into darkness once more. This time without pain.

Chapter 29

Her sleep was deep and dreamless. But Darya could have sworn someone was reaching for her hand. Calling out to her. She tried to reach out, but it was like catching steam.

Darya let it pass, and let go.

When she woke up once more, it was to a flickering light and the gentle sound of lapping waves. She felt heavy, with a faint headache, like she had been sleeping for much too long. But the pain was gone, and she only felt an overwhelming thirst.

Darya realised she was on a cot, with a candle on the side table and, *thank the Goddess Vita,* a pitcher of water. Leaning on her elbow, Darya gulped down as much and as quickly as she could, heedless of splashing herself in the process. With her thirst sated for the moment, she felt a stab of ravenous hunger, so strong that it made her dizzy.

"Darya?" Someone called out, sounding startled.

Darya squinted. It was Metzan again, pale-faced.

"You're awake! Let me... Let me go get Luunaiwel!"

She left before Darya could get a word out. Groaning, Darya tried to sit up, but felt so weak and fatigued, she slumped back down.

The headache was growing stronger, throbbing at the back of her eyes. Darya rubbed a shaking palm over them, registering a dull ache on her left shoulder. The constant movements around her didn't help at all.

Darya was sure of one thing. She had never been inside this room before. Not that she could remember it anyway. It was sparse, with her own cot and another on the opposite wall, where Metzan had been, with a table between them. There was a barrel of something in a corner, and an oil lamp hanging above it. She saw a clump of bags on the floor by the door, some of them her own, and her wrapped up staff leaning over them.

Where in Mortia's realm was she?

Before Darya could think any harder, Luunaiwel entered. Under the dim lighting, the elf looked haggard, and her eyes were glowing eerily. There was relief in them however, when Luunaiwel's gaze landed on Darya.

"You are awake. Good."

With quick strides, Luunaiwel came to sit by her, easily lifting her head up to prop something behind Darya's back. As soon as she was in a sitting position, a wave of nausea hit Darya so hard, she pitched forward and would have fallen to the floor if Luunaiwel hadn't caught her.

"Easy there. You are still weak."

"Luuna... I'm... hungry... so hungry..." Darya managed between wheezes.

"Understandable," Luunaiwel sighed, slowly easing Darya back to the pile of blankets behind her, "you exhausted yourself. Every ounce of your power was drained, including what little you stored in your gems."

"What... what happened...?"

Luunaiwel frowned down at her, "Can you not remember?"

Brows knitting together, Darya shook her head. Luunaiwel studied her for a moment, but didn't say anything. Before Darya could ask, Metzan walked in with a huge tray full of food. Darya was immediately distracted by the mouth-watering smell.

This was a feast for three, from hot mushroom soup to a whole steaming kidney and ale pie, with a warm mug of berry cider and a small wheel of cheese. It looked better than anything Darya had ever seen in her life, and she dug in before Metzan even managed to place the tray down on her lap.

"Whoa there! Slow down! You might choke!" Surprised, the blonde chided, but Darya couldn't stop.

She didn't know what she crammed into her mouth first, the pie, the cheese or even the hot soup, and she definitely didn't think she chewed all that much, only stopping to wash it down with the cider from time to time. It was delicious, but Darya couldn't even comprehend what anything tasted like, as she polished her meal in record time, even sticking her finger into the pie pan for the last few crumbs.

She had chowed down a whole feast, and yet...

"I'm still a bit peckish." Darya admitted, biting back a belch.

Metzan looked a bit mortified as she left with the tray. Luunaiwel rolled her eyes, "You can have more later, your stomach would burst otherwise."

"That was so good!"

"Of course it is," Luunaiwel huffed, "Tuura made it. Be thankful the ship has a kitchen."

Blinking, Darya stared up at Luunaiwel in confusion, "The ship...? But..."

Something painful jolted deep within her. Darya clutched at her head, doubling over as memories rushed back like an unstoppable tidal wave.

There was...

There was so much blood.

So much *screaming*.

As if hit by a bolt of lightning, Darya sprung up, gasping, "Sara!!! Where is Sara???"

Luunaiwel's hands were immediately on her shoulders, "You need to sit down."

"Sara!!! I need to see her!!! Where is she?!!??!"

"Darya! You need to calm down!"

"No!!! Where is Sara?!?!? Is she hurt??? *Where is she?!?!*"

Luunaiwel's slap was hard enough to push her back to the bed. The shock of it and the stinging sensation on her cheek rendered Darya speechless.

"You are not going to see her in this condition," the elf's voice was devoid of emotion as she stood, looming over Darya, "You have been unconscious for eight days. You have a fever. You are depleted of strength thanks to the stunt you pulled. You are in no condition to leave this room, much less seeing your sister."

"Eight days...??? I've been out for eight days???"

Luunaiwel nodded, sharp eyes unwavering. Holding a hand to her swelling cheek, Darya shifted to sit upright, "How is... how is Sara, then?"

The elf sighed, rubbing her forehead, "She is alive. Unwell, but alive."

That worried Darya greatly, but at least... at least it didn't seem like Sara was beyond saving. *Not like Grandmama Clarince.*

Sucking in a deep breath, Darya nodded up at Luunaiwel, "Sorry... sorry for that outburst... I didn't mean to..."

Luunaiwel sat back down on the cot, pulling out a vial of shimmering blue liquid from a pouch on her belt, "No need. I should have expected it. Here, drink this. It will speed up your magic's restoration."

It was the same cool, sweet stuff that she was given before. Darya downed it in one go, smacking her lips, "Thanks."

They sunk into an awkward silence then. Darya didn't know what else to say, especially after her little tantrum. Now, after that full whole meal, and knowing that they were relatively safe, Darya just felt... tired.

There was no longer that throbbing pain all over her body when she woke up the first time. Darya was simply exhausted, and there was still an ache at the back of her head. She was overall fine, at least physically. Well, her shoulder was sore, but if she remembered correctly, she did take an arrow through it.

Darya sighed. If she closed her eyes, she could still see the utter *chaos* back there.

"How did they still allow us to board after what happened?" The young Druid heard herself asking aloud.

There was a frown to Luunaiwel's fair brows, "It did not take much convincing. There is another reason why I specifically picked Silos' ship for this trip. He helps ferry many victims of the Night's Hand to Imirra. Be it a fleeing magick-user, or the relatives of one. After seeing the stunt on Mortia's Strand... he pulled the anchor up the moment we all boarded."

Darya's eyes widened. That might also be why Metzan was here too.

"I need to thank him."

"Make sure you do."

A pause. "How come, though? Why is he so interested in helping Night's Hand's victims?"

There was no joy in Luunaiwel's smile, "Because his younger sister was one."

Something cold squeezed Darya's heart, "What happened to her?"

"She was captured and forced into a vow of servitude. Threw herself off a bell tower to escape her imprisonment."

The simple explanation caught Darya by surprise. Tears pricked at the corners of her eyes, "Oh..."

"His family stayed in Teda to help reach out to as many victims as they could. Many of the crew members are family of those who were once harmed, or escapees in Imirra."

Her vision became blurry, but she refused to cry. Darya's hands wove into the blanket over her, twisting the fabric in white-knuckled fists, "This is wrong... How could they...? How could the Night's Hand be so cruel...?"

A sneer twisted Luunaiwel's lips, "It is all about profits for them. It is ironic how many of the leaders are magick-users themselves. The world is dying, so they hoard as much as they can."

The elf tilted her head. There was something dark, something ancient and cruel and bitter in her eyes, "Little do they know... Death takes all, but never riches."

Darya bit her lower lip, looking away, "You can take money to the grave, but never with you to the afterlife."

Huffing out a laugh, Luunaiwel asked, "Did they teach you that at the Holy Temple?"

"It's what the monks always yell to the rest of Fluminum when they're looking for donation." Darya chuckled wetly.

It all seemed so far away now.

Sighing, Luunaiwel patted Darya's knees, then stood with a slight wobble, "I must go tend to the others. Metzan will bring you dinner later. Try and get more rest. Your body is depleted of magic now, so no flower will be growing in your sleep."

"Alright ... Thanks, Luunaiwel. For everything. Again."

"Anytime, little bird."

As she sank back down into the cot, Darya had one last question before Luunaiwel left, "Oh yeah... How are Nathi and Sindri? Are they alright?"

Luunaiwel's hand paused on the door, "You may see them when you are well."

"Alright."

CHAPTER 30:

It took Darya two more days to get out of bed without help, and another half to just get out of the door by herself without feeling faint. She blamed it on the churning waves.

At least Darya wasn't seasick. It would have been a waste to puke out all the amazing food Tuura cooked.

The moment she was able to get out of her cabin, Darya demanded to see her sister. Not even Luunaiwel's scowls could stop her. In fact, that only made Darya more anxious.

She certainly did *not* expect to see what she was led to.

"What the... *what in the name of Vita is this???*"

In a stable stall, at the very end of where the travel beasts were kept, there was a giant tangle of thorns. Twisted together with all its sharp needles out, the mass of vicious vines nearly took up the entire stall.

Panic welled up in Darya's chest.

"Luunaiwel, if this is a joke, it's not funny! Where is my sister???"

There was a mixture of feelings dancing in the elf's mismatched eyes. Discomfort, hesitance and *pity.*

"Your sister is in there."

Shock knocked Darya to her knees.

"W-what?!"

Luunaiwel crouched down next to her, voice filled with sympathy, "I am not sure what happened, however..."

Tentative, the elf grasped at Darya's hand with her own bare one.

Darya sucked in a breath, not expecting the connection. She felt Luunaiwel's usual presence at the back of her mind, but something was trying to push forward.

What are you trying to do???

Hold on. I cannot explain this. I need to show you.

Darya was baffled. *What...?*

And there it was.

Mortia's Strand.

"My patience is running thin! Luunaiwel, give up the girl!" The dwarf leader boomed, baring his teeth.

She finally was able to place why he looked so familiar. This dwarf's name was Sír. The same dwarf who was tasked to send missives to Luunaiwel's family back at the Gates of Mul Tarum.

Startled, Darya almost pulled her hand away.

This was the same event that happened. But this wasn't Darya's...

This was Luunaiwel's memory. And the elf was sharing her perspective, through their connection.

Nothing happened yet. She had expected this. Darya was a novice. The child might not be able to help at all.

Luunaiwel glanced skyward. Nothing. Tuura needed more time. There were too many people on the ship. If they saw him shift, the commotion might cause one of the hostages' lives.

"There is no guarantee that you would not kill the others if I do give her over." Luunaiwel held her head high, unwavering.

*They expected her to do something. They knew what she was capable of. Well, not **all** of what she was capable of, but they were keeping a cautious distance. Enough to kill Nathi, Sindri and Sara before Luunaiwel could take action.*

Sír snarled, not at all the low-ranked, timid guard she remembered, "If you do not give her over now, I will start slitting their throats for every minute of your dawdling.

Luunaiwel's eyes narrowed, "Are you threatening me?"

There was a shadow on the ground. Circling.

Wonderful, Tuura was in position.

Sír pointed his axe at Luunaiwel's face, eyes bulging with rage, "Know your place! You serve *the Council!"*

Oh, that did it. This bastard was going to pay.

Behind Sír, Nathi sputtered, pushing past the gag through his struggles.

"LULU!!! THEY'RE NIGHT'S HAND!!!"

Damn it, Nathi!

Luunaiwel must admit, the explosion of thorns surprised her almost as much as it raked terror and death into the dwarves. Almost. She did not waste her time yelling and flailing at it however, and neither did Tuura. Luunaiwel charged at Sír as he turned his horse, trusting Tuura to break the hostages out. Clumsy and slow, the traitorous dwarf left his back exposed and could not even let out a scream as her blade glided through his neck.

Shame. She had wanted him to suffer.

"I serve no one." *She sneered, taking pleasure in the one-liner no-one would hear instead.*

Around her, everything was absolute chaos.

Luunaiwel swung herself to stand between Sara and an incoming axe, decapitating the dwarf who was going after the poor child. By the looks of it, Sara was petrified and at the edge of having an asthma attack.

In their panic, the dwarves had rushed towards the docks, trying to escape the murderous thorns chasing them. Luunaiwel and Tuura were the only ones standing between them and Darya.

There was no way unarmed Nathi and Sindri could have gotten to safety on foot. Sara had even a lesser chance.

Luunaiwel reached for Sara, but cursed when an arrow whistled past the narrow space between them. The bloody idiots had busted out their crossbows. Which, unfortunately, amplified Darya's blind fury.

Sara's scream was shrill when a lashing thorn whip missed her face by a tenth of an inch. Luunaiwel chopped it off, yelling, "Someone needs to stop her!!! The earth will drain her dry if she doesn't stop!!!"

A blur of red rushed past. Armed with a bloodied axe, Sindri valiantly fought her way towards Darya. Nathi and Tuura tried to follow, but the rush of thorns, arrows and panicked Night's Hand dwarves stopped them. Luunaiwel tried to reach for Sara again, but ended up having to stand over the kid to fight off a pair of dwarves that were trying to take her head instead.

Damn it. Militia dwarves actually knew how to fight, unlike those blithering morons from Flumium.

And the waves of relentless thorns definitely did **not** *help.*

"Darya!!! Stop!!!" It was Sindri's voice. Somewhere behind the madness. Good, she had reached Darya then.

Weaving between the two dwarves, Luunaiwel decapitated one and stabbed the other through his chest. She cursed again. The struggle had lured her away from Sara, whose rolled back eyes and desperate gasping was ill-boding. Luunaiwel rushed back to the girl's side, but in her haste, she was distracted.

*"Mother of a half-troll!" Luunaiwel snapped as a spike of thorn burst from below, piercing through her left foot. She **knew** she should have invested in foot armours!*

Partially immobilised, Luunaiwel gritted her teeth, pulled her foot up and hacked off the vine under it. Darya was so going to get a slap for this one.

When Luunaiwel looked up however, it was too late.

In a circle around Sara, roots and thorns burst forth. Reaching skyward, they twisted together, interlacing and braided together into a deadly cocoon, locking a screaming Sara inside and out of sight.

"No!!!" Luunaiwel yelled, hobbling over to bring her sword down unto the mass of thorns. Her blade bounced away harmlessly.

Around them, the thorns seethed, gathering up what was left of the corpses and attacking whoever was left alive. Including Luunaiwel, Nathi and Tuura.

"Darya!! Please!!! Snap out of it!! Or you'll kill us all!!!"

Oh, no...

"SINDRI!!!" Luunaiwel shouted, running over to where the dwarf woman was trying her hardest to shake Darya out of it.

Unaware of the cluster of thorns forming behind her.

"NO!!!"

The force of that impale was so powerful, it knocked Sindri's entire bulk into Darya. Uprooting the girl from where her feet were sinking into the ground and onto the wooden docks.

"SINDRI!!! NO!!!"

Screaming, Darya ripped her hand away from Luunaiwel's. She couldn't stop it, couldn't stop the screaming nor the image of Sindri's lifeless body on top of her.

What have I done???

Luunaiwel reached out to her, but Darya shrunk away. How could she... how could *anyone* ever forgive Darya for what she had done?

Not only did she *kill Sindri*, she had also wrapped Sara up in this... in this *monstrosity*...

What kind of monster had she become?

"Darya. Little bird," Luunaiwel's voice was firm, and so was her hand on Darya's shoulder, "this was not your fault. You could not control it."

Darya tried to shrug the elf away, "I should have!!! I SHOULD HAVE!!! It's-it's MY power!!! I should have been able to control it!!! I shouldn't have put *anyone* in harm's way!!! Not you!!! Not Sindri!!! Not Sara!!!"

Luunaiwel didn't relent to her struggling, "This power was not supposed to be your burden. You have no experience, no time to prepare for all that it can do. Everything that happened was also my responsibility. I should have taught you better."

Incredulous, Darya thumped at Luunaiwel's shoulders, shouting, "It's not YOUR fault!!! It's MINE!! It's MY power!!!"

She didn't know how Luunaiwel was still able to keep her calm. Wasn't Darya the one who hurt her? Wasn't Darya the one who killed her friend?!?!? Wasn't Darya the one who made everything more complicated and dangerous?!?!?!

"Shifting the blame around is not going to bring Sindri back," Luunaiwel did not let go, "it is not going to get your sister better, and it sure is not going to fix anything. All you can do now is draw experience from it and move forward. So that everything you have done and all the others' sacrifices would not be in vain."

Those words hit her hard. Before Darya knew it, she was bawling, hands gripping at Luunaiwel's back.

"Why, Luna???" She sobbed, shaking like a leaf, "I didn't want this... I DON'T WANT THIS!!!"

"I know... I know, little bird." The elf cooed, a gentle hand on her head, smoothing down her hair. The motion only upset Darya more, reminding her so keenly of what her mother used to do when she was a child. What Grandmama used to do when she and Sara were upset.

Hiccoughing, Darya yanked at Luunaiwel's cloak to emphasise her point, "It's not fair!!! It's *not* r-right!!! I didn't as-ask for this!!! I was... I was perfectly CONTENT the way I was!!! I didn't want this!!! Grandmama didn't have to die!!! Sindri didn't have to die!!! And now Sara might d-die too because I COULDN'T DO WHAT THE GODDESS WANTS ME TO DO!!!"

"I know," Luunaiwel said, a deep sadness in her voice, "it should not have been your responsibility to put this world back together. It is not your fault. It should not have been you."

"Why... why are the Gods so CRUEL???"

Darya didn't know how long she sat there, on the rocking floor clinging to Luunaiwel, crying until she couldn't anymore. When her tears finally dried, Darya couldn't help how oddly familiar this situation had become, with her drowning in her own sorrow while desperately holding onto Luunaiwel as an anchor. How Luunaiwel had been there for her, through every hardship that was thrown her way.

How if it wasn't for the elf, Darya would have died or, worse, fallen into the Night's Hand's clutch many times over.

Darya knew Luunaiwel was bound by the vow to protect her, and that Luunaiwel might just be doing that anyway because Darya was the only existing Druid that she knew. But the elf didn't have to stick around when Darya was being an emotional mess. She didn't have to try and save Sara. She could have left Darya's sister to her fate. But Luunaiwel tried, and brought Sara, or at least Darya *hoped* that it was Sara all wrapped up in that cocoon of thorns, onto the Valiant Will.

Luunaiwel didn't have to do more than what she vowed to do, but she did anyway, much more than what Darya could ever ask for.

When she finally spoke again, Darya's voice was hoarse, and she couldn't even bear to peek at the bundle of thorns over Luunaiwel's shoulder, "How did... how did you bring... *Sara* up here?"

Luunaiwel sighed, "We tried to break her out. None of the weapons worked, and I did not dare to use magic, fearing that it might kill her. But we managed to chop off the roots and dislodged the whole bulk of it off the ground. We put a blanket over it so it would not stab us, and brought her aboard."

That was a lot of effort. Once again, Darya was grateful that Luunaiwel and everyone else didn't just leave Sara behind. Especially when she was being wrapped up in *that*. "Thank you."

"Anytime, little bird."

Sucking in a breath, Darya sat straighter, but didn't let go of Luunaiwel. Staring at the thorns, she was afraid of this next question, "How do you know Sara is... well, *alive?*"

"I can hear her breathing."

The answer was simpler than Darya thought, "Oh." She said in a rush of exhale. Relieved.

"There is another indication."

Darya blinked, "Oh?"

Luunaiwel tapped on the left side of her face, by her left green eye, "I can see in the magic spectrum. That cocoon... it is emitting magic. *Healing* magic."

"What?!"

Nodding, Luunaiwel turned to stare at the clump of thorns, "Whatever you have covered your sister with, it is healing her and keeping her alive. It sounds like she is in a deep sleep, too."

Standing up, Darya looked at the bundle of thorns in disbelief.

What in Mortia's realm had she done?

CHAPTER 31:

Darya couldn't find the courage to touch the cocoon of thorns until the day after. And when she did, it was both a relief and another weight on her shoulders.

Luunaiwel was right. Sara was alive. Darya could feel her sister's presence, the same presence of a sapling that was a bit too frail and a bit too scrawny, but still full of will to live. But there was something else now.

The thorns.

They were not exactly alive, per se. But neither were they sapping at Sara's strength, which the young Druid was sure of.

It felt like the thorns were melding onto the sapling that was Sara's presence, straightening up her spines and giving her needles so sharp they could puncture armours.

Might not be such a bad thing, considering their situation.

How to wake Sara up though... that Darya didn't know, and neither did Luunaiwel. The elf was certain that it had to be Darya to wake Sara up, or Sara had to wake by herself.

But Sara wasn't the only cause of worry for Darya.

Ever since she woke up, her Heart Stone had been feeling... different. It wasn't a constant, radiant warmth as it had always been before, and it wasn't glowing softly like it always did either. It was dull, the red of it dark like blood, and the stone was heavy on Darya's chest. Luunaiwel didn't know the reason for these changes but, as always, the elf had some theories, and none of it reassured Darya.

"As far as I know, Druidic magic has never been aggressive," there was worry in Luunaiwel's eyes when she inspected Darya's Heart Stone, "Druids avoided taking lives as much as they could, be it from more intelligent species, or flora and fauna in general. Their source of power comes from the earth and the Celestial of Life, thus all life is sacred to them."

Darya's eyes widened, "But those Night's Hand were trying to kill me! And all of you!"

"I understand that," Luunaiwel was patient, "your circumstances are different from all of the Druids I knew. You are different. Most of the rules cannot be applied to you."

Heaving a sigh, Darya dropped down to sit on her cot, "I sense a 'but' here."

Luunaiwel frowned, "But the most basic ones still apply."

"You can't make something out of nothing, right?"

"Yes. I suspect that because you are too new to magic, the magic you inherit from the Celestial of Life is so excessive, it urges certain things to grow depending on your emotion while you are asleep."

Rubbing her forehead as if that would chase her incoming headache away, Darya looked up at Luunaiwel in pure torment, "But that *is* making something from nothing, right?"

The elf shook her head, "Not necessarily. At first, I thought it was simply the energy from the Celestial that allowed you to create something from nothing. However, the magic you possess is not produced by you, therefore, the excessive amount of magic from the Celestial is used as a catalyst for the plants."

"Fine. Sure. What does that have anything to do with my Heart Stone's recent wonkiness then?"

"I am not entirely certain," Luunaiwel glanced at Darya's chest, "but I believe that as you urged the earth to kill the Night's Hand dwarves, not only it used your magic as a toll, but also took their bodies as compensation."

That made Darya feel a bit sick, "The earth did say something about drinking their blood and grow..."

Luunaiwel didn't seem all that fazed, "Ah. Life for life. It was an equal exchange."

It went without saying that if Sindri, or what was left of her, didn't knock Darya away, the thorns would have consumed Luunaiwel, Tuura, Nathi and even Sara as well.

The elf cleared her throat, "Back to the topic at hand... The way you and your magic operates are different from what the Heart Stone's intended purposes. As I have told you before, the Heart Stone is a piece of Earth Magic itself, formed by and within an earth pulse. It is gifted to a Druid, so that he or she may connect with the earth and those who were born by and upon it. It also acts as a conduit to help funnel the earth's magic into the Druid and nurture life."

Darya thought over what Luunaiwel said for a moment. What she realised made the young Druid groan, "So what you're trying to tell me is that while my magic doesn't function as any normal Druid, my Heart Stone is the same as everyone else's, therefore creating a conflict."

Luunaiwel smiled, but there wasn't much joy in the curve of her lips, "You are a bright one. But yes, unfortunately, I believe your Heart Stone is, in simple terms, in shock."

Darya buried her face in her hands, badly wanting to scream.

Luunaiwel advised her not to try and get Sara out, or perform magic in general, until they figured out how to get Darya's Heart Stone back to normal. Darya knew they didn't have a chance of finding a solution anytime soon, considering there was no Druid expert on the ship, much less a freak case like Darya.

Last, but definitely not the least of Darya's problems, was how to face Nathi after what happened.

Darya hadn't seen much of the dwarf since she was well enough to walk about. She didn't know who was avoiding who, she or Nathi, but he often wasn't around wherever she was and neither could she bear to seek him out. Darya knew she was a coward, and she couldn't blame him for not wanting to see her.

He and Sindri were kind to Darya and Sara, and did far more than they needed to in order to help her. And Darya repaid them by killing Sindri.

She had no right to seek Nathi out. The most she could do was to apologise, and that would *never* be enough. There was nothing Darya could do to make it right with him, she knew that. She just wished she had enough courage in her to at least find him and say sorry.

On her fourteenth day on the Valliant Will, Darya finally came down to the mess hall for lunch with everyone else. Mostly because she was finally well enough, and she felt like a slob for bothering Metzan and Luunaiwel to bring her food, especially with the latter's foot being screwed up by Darya's outburst.

The ship's hull was separated into two levels. The bottom was the stable and cargo hold. The top was the kitchen and mess hall, along with the crew communal sleeping quarter. Guest cabins were on the deck, just below the captain's wheel.

The mess hall was just the size of one big room, and at first glance, Darya didn't know where to sit until she spotted Caldor, alone in a corner. Hesitantly, she stood at the door staring until Caldor rolled his eyes and waved her over.

"I don't remember you being coy." Caldor commented when she came to his table.

"A lot has changed since we parted ways." Darya forced out a laugh.

Eyeing her, Caldor took a gulp of his beer, "So it has."

Darya focused on her food for a moment, letting the mess hall's buzzing fill the silence between them. She didn't know what to say to the man in front of her. Any question she had for him had been asked, and she didn't feel like prying for more. Darya had to admit, she was curious about the relationship between him and Metzan, but that *definitely* was none of her business. Seeing that she and Metzan were currently rooming together, it would be even more inappropriate to ask.

Besides, Darya already had enough on her plate as it was.

"I also remember you being a lot chattier."

Darya grimaced, putting down her slice of cheese, "Honestly? I don't know what to say."

Caldor shrugged, leaning back against his corner, "That hasn't stopped you before."

That pulled a chuckle out of her, "That's true."

"So how was travelling with that crazy woman?"

Her chuckle turned into a surprised huff, "Crude as ever, aren't you? Luunaiwel isn't that crazy. Between me and her, I think I have a few more screws loose."

Caldor raised an eyebrow, "Uh-oh. What has she done to you?"

"Stop it," Darya flicked a breadcrumb at him, "in human standards, Luunaiwel is a bit eccentric, but she's taught me far more than I could ever ask for."

"Heh... I saw that."

The reminder of Mortia's Strand had Darya shrunk down in her seat, her appetite ebbing away, "Yep."

They sank into another awkward silence, and Darya would have left, if a familiar voice didn't draw out from behind her, "My. I felt my ears itching. Were you fine lady and gentleman talking shite about me?"

Caldor's eyes immediately narrowed when Luunaiwel perched on the empty seat by Darya's side, "Seat's taken."

"Too bad," the elf said cheerily, "how are you today, little bird?"

"Better now," Darya cracked a smile, "how are you?"

Luunaiwel smacked her lips together, "Chipper. How about you, Mister Caldor?"

He glared, "Broody."

The corner of Luunaiwel's lips curled up, "Shame. And here I thought we have finally found the cure to your condition."

Caldor rolled his eyes, "Woe is me."

Wait, was that ... *banter?*

Eyes wide, Darya asked, "Am I missing something here?"

"Not much," Luunaiwel chuckled, artfully arranging cured meat and cheese on a slice of bread, "we simply found out that we see eye-to-eye on certain matters."

Curious now, Darya implored, "And that would be...?"

Blunt as ever, Caldor butted in, "We both hate the Night's Hand. And we agreed that ferrying refugees from mainland to Imirra is not a long term solution."

Darya's eyes bulged, "*What?* Are you two going to start a crusade or something??"

"To an extent," Luunaiwel hummed, "my apologies, little bird, but there have been many discussions during your semi-coma."

Sometimes, Luunaiwel's way of speaking could be a little too much. "And what would they be??"

For once, the elf and Caldor exchanged a look that didn't end up with the latter fuming. Caldor sighed, tapping a finger on the table, "We think that it is best to hunt down and eliminate the Night's Hand as soon as possible would be everyone's best interest. It's not going to be easy, but I've been asking around the crew, and a lot would be down to band together."

"It is not going to be easy, nor would it be a matter of days." Chewing thoughtfully, Luunaiwel added.

Caldor nodded, "There've been attempts at quelling the Night's Hand's atrocities. But they were all started by individuals, and thus weren't very successful. But with our number... I think we will have a chance."

"Alright." Darya nodded. These bastards were due for a payback, "When do we start?"

The other two went silent. There was that strange wordless exchange again. Luunaiwel sighed, "After we dropped off you and everyone who is a refugee in Imirra."

Everything around them seemed to fade into nonexistence. Darya gaped, at a loss for words.

"What?!"

"It will be safer that way," Luunaiwel tilted her head, "the Island Nation of Imirra is not just an unreachable fortress. It also houses the last Dragon Sanctuary in the world."

"You're not going to stay??? I thought you were supposed to *teach me!*"

The elf shook her head, deepening the shock that was squeezing at Darya's heart, "I have nothing left to teach you. All I could do was instruct you on the basics of magic, and prepare you for your next cycle of study. A Dragon, whose connection to the primal magic of this world is second to none, is more suited to guide you than I could ever be."

Darya couldn't believe it. This... *this was it?* After everything that happened, Darya thought that... Darya thought that Luunaiwel would be there with her in Imirra too. To help. To teach. What, Darya didn't know, *but.*

After losing her Grandmama and Sindri, plus with Sara in her current state, having to part ways with Luunaiwel... it was *unthinkable* to Darya.

The sense of sudden loss was a blow to her chest, hollowing out her heart.

She couldn't be around Luunaiwel.

Not right now.

Darya made to stand up, but Luunaiwel's steel grip on her arm prevented her from moving.

"The circumstances are not ideal for us to stick together," The elf said, voice urgent, "you need to understand this."

Caldor quickly added, "When I was on the run with Metzan, we've seen and heard terrible things. More than ever the Night's Hand has been scouring the world for magic-users, no matter the potency of their magic, no matter how strong or weak. We didn't think much of it at first, assuming that they've just been desperate for more riches. Until we stumbled across something terrible."

Honestly? Darya wanted to yank away from Luunaiwel, to run away and ignore everything they were saying because she was *hurt*.

But she wasn't a child anymore, and they were attempting to explain this to her instead of leaving in the dark. And, after everything Luunaiwel had done for her, the least Darya could do was to listen to what the elf had to say.

So the young Druid stayed, biting back her tears.

Seeming relieved by her decision, Caldor leaned in, continued in a low voice, "While we were hiding out at the village due west of Mount Amum, we thought of settling down in the Golden Hills for a while. It's remote, but has self-sufficient resources and the earth can sustain some form of farming. As we went looking for a patch of land to call our own, we came to this ruins, hidden among the hills."

"The old foundations of Amun's Temple." Luunaiwel supplied quietly.

Caldor sighed, closing his eyes for a moment. Whatever he had seen must have been painful. But when he looked at Darya again, there was fury in his dark eyes.

"It was horrid. Bodies strewn everywhere, men, women, even children, from every walk of life. Some were fresh, some were left to rot for Gods knows how long. There were strange symbols drawn in blood, and a foul altar that was formed with decapitated heads of both humans and animals."

Luunaiwel hummed when Darya flinched, "That would be a ritual ground. A construct of dark magic that is used to either imprison primal forces or summon something wicked."

Caldor snarled, "Either way, it's *vile*. We left as quickly as we could, as you could imagine. When we made our way south, we encountered another one, just as terrible, near the Desecrated. Whatever they've been doing, they aren't exactly trying to hide their trails. There's no one to stop them. No King or Queen or Noble who cares enough to do so."

"In fact, those Kings and Queens of yours might be funding them." Luunaiwel took a sip of her water.

"Aye, and no commoner has the power to defy them. In fact... That's the reason why I and Metzan didn't go back to Apricum. The King hired services from the Night's Hand multiple times in the past, and he was never discreet about it..."

Luunaiwel tapped on the rim of her cup, eyes distant, "All the good people can do is run."

Bewildered, Darya exclaimed, "Then why leave me in Imirra??? I can help!!! I have the power to do so!!!"

"Little bird, it is *all* about what *you* can do," Luunaiwel's eyes bore holes into her, "*we* may fail. We may die trying to stop them. But the impact of such an event would have little consequences. But if *you* die, or fall into the wrong hands... that would be the end of all."

Darya slapped the table, frustrated, "Well, I can't just sit by and *watch!!!* Not after everything that's happened!!! Do you think I'd feel alright about that??? Knowing that all of you are out there, possibly *dying* and needing help while I'm... while I'm *frolicking* on some island???"

Luunaiwel and Caldor exchanged another look. Darya was getting fed up with that. What else weren't they telling her??? What else had they already decided for her???

Sitting up, Caldor swished his beer around, looking haunted, "Feelings are impertinent to situations like this."

Darya opened her mouth to argue, but Luunaiwel's hand on her shoulder silenced the Druid.

It had been a while since she looked straight into the elf's eyes this close, enough to count each curved lash and see the constellations in her strange eyes.

"Something looms over the horizon," Luunaiwel whispered, her voice so quiet it brought chills down Darya's spine, "something terrible. Something dark. Each of us has a role we must fulfil. Each of us has a path we must follow. And if we go astray, there will be nothing waiting at the end of our path."

Luunaiwel's eyes glowed, eerie and ancient.

"Tell me, little bird, are you prepared to shoulder that consequence, should you choose to forsake yours?"

CHAPTER 32:

Even though she had been performing on a stage since she was barely a teenager, Darya could never control her anxiety. Especially when it came to the more important matters of her life.

Her feet were twiddling together, and her hands worked the front of her tunic into a crumble. Heart hammering, Darya felt sweat built up in her palms, while the back of her neck felt ice-cold. Her nerves were in shambles, and she had to remind herself to breathe several times. She recited what she wanted to say, and should have said as soon as she woke up, but she couldn't even grasp the words in her head. But Darya didn't think that would matter.

Not really.

Seriously, what could she possibly say? Nothing Darya could say would make any of this better. Nothing would bring Sindri back.

Darya didn't know how long she stood there, staring at Nathi's cabin door. It took the last of her resolve to not just run away. Because she knew if she didn't at least apologise, then she would regret it for the rest of her life.

"What yer doing here?"

Feeling as if her stomach had dropped to the ground, Darya slowly turned around to face Nathi.

He didn't look well. There were bruised circles under his eyes. His normally neat braids had all unravelled, tangled in matted clumps. His breath stank of alcohol, staining the air despite standing a few feet away from Darya. Gone was the jovial, somewhat inappropriate physician from Mul Tarum. The Nathi before Darya was a broken man.

And it was Darya's fault.

She wanted to cry, but she knew she didn't deserve to. She caused this ... this grief, this devastation.

But she couldn't do anything about it.

"Nathi, I ... I- How are you?"

He didn't say anything, staring back at her with empty blue eyes. It was heart-breaking, and Darya was shaken to the core.

She would feel better if he had reacted, with sadness, with fury, with... anything. Anything but this depressing lack of reaction.

"Nathi... I... I..." She hesitated, tripping over what she planned to say and wanted to say.

Nathi didn't even blink at her. Darya swallowed dryly.

"I'm ... I'm sorry, Nathi," she finally chokes out, "I didn't mean to ... I never wanted this to happen, I- ..."

No response. The edge of Darya's vision burned.

"I didn't mean to h-harm S-Sindri. I-," she fought back a sniff, grinding her teeth to force back her tears, "I lost control, and I'm so, *so* sorry! I didn't know- ... I don't know how to ... how I could ever atone for what I did but I- ..."

She couldn't stop it. She lost her voice at the end, hot tears tracking down her cheeks. Darya tried to talk through it, but all came out were blubbering noises. Angry with herself, she tried to slap the tears away, only for more to come.

"I'm- I'm sor-sorry, I- ..."

"Stop."

That single word froze Darya at the spot. The look in Nathi's eyes was just as empty as before, but it was now directed at the floor. His fists curled by his sides, shaking as the dwarf forced his words out.

"I can't talk ta ye right now. Please, leave me be."

It was like being sucker punched. Darya's breath escaped in one painful gasp. Her heart sank as low as her bow before Nathi, biting back sobs even when water dripped down the tip of her nose. Keeping her head down, she walked past Nathi's rigid stance, before breaking into a run.

Darya ran out from the hull, along the length of the ship, and didn't stop until she was at the back of the ship. Gripping at the railing, Darya cried to the crashing waves, and let the wind drown out her anguish. Out here, nobody could hear her, and even if they could, she couldn't bring herself to care.

She had lost whatever semblance of peace she had left in this world. She had ruined her family, her friends, with these powers that she didn't ask for. She didn't know whether Sara would live or die, she didn't know if Nathi or even Luunaiwel and Tuura would ever forgive her for what she did.

Luunaiwel was certainly eager for them to split up.

Darya had to bite down on her lips to stop a scream from ripping out.

Even her Heart Stone was still cold to the touch. It no longer pulsed with the reassuring warmth that she never realised she needed. That instilled a fear within Darya, a fear that her now only valuable asset, the very reason that got her into this mess, was no longer with her. It made her cry even harder.

Why did it have to be this way?

She wished they didn't have to leave Mul Tarum. She wished she had taken Sara along. Maybe then Nathi and Sindri wouldn't have been involved. Maybe then Sara wouldn't have been dragged into this. Maybe then Sindri wouldn't have to die.

Why was Darya given the power of life, if all it could bring was death to the people she loved?

"Y'know ... Beating yourself up isn't going to make anything better."

In a more normal circumstance, Darya would have jumped when Caldor snuck up on her out of nowhere. But all she could muster up was a wet glare.

"Go away."

Of course, Caldor wasn't going to come out all this way to be dismissed so easily. The former Knight-in-training came to lean against the railing, far enough so she couldn't lash out at him, but close enough to stop her from doing anything stupid. Angrily, Darya sniffed and turned away.

There wasn't any exchange between them, just the sound of rolling water and Darya's attempt to stifle her storm of emotions. This was something private, and she was mad that Caldor decided to butt in. He wasn't the one who Darya wanted to come around for her but, at the same time, she didn't think she deserved to have anyone for comfort. She wanted to yell at Caldor, to tell him to get lost, but couldn't find the strength to.

In the end, Darya just stayed quiet, her sobbing reduced to stilted huffs.

"Why are you even here, Caldor?"

"I made a promise." He answered without hesitation, hands clasping over the sea, "Even if the person I made the promise to is dead, I must still uphold my words."

He was purposely misunderstanding the question. Darya let out a bitter chuckle.

"Knight Code?"

Caldor smirked, "Knight Code."

"Metzan is lucky to have you."

He paused for a moment, "And you are lucky to have that crazy elf and her giant friend."

Darya stiffened. Her fingers dug into the wood railing, leaving indentations on its weathered surface.

"I'm not going to have them. Not by the end of this. Thanks to you."

It was unfair of her to say so. It wasn't even close to the truth. But Darya didn't care anymore.

The silence that followed was uncomfortable. Not that Caldor's company was wanted in the first place. Darya contemplated walking away, but couldn't find the strength to.

Where else could she go? Back to the cabin that she shared with Metzan? To the mess hall where she could bump into Tuura? Or any strange corner that Luunaiwel might have disappeared to?

Or down at the hull stable where Sara was cocooned up in that nightmare?

"Regardless, you'll be safe." Caldor suddenly said, clumsily trying to continue their conversation. Despite his effort, Darya only felt worse.

"Where have I heard that before?"

She was being irrational. Mul Tarum had been safe for the entire duration that they stayed there. It wasn't until they left that something terrible happened.

Darya knew she shouldn't be blaming herself. The Night's Hand's timing was impeccable. Sindri and Sara must have been captured the moment Darya and the others left, and Nathi as soon as he returned to Mul Nordihr. They didn't attacked Luunaiwel, because they knew that would have alerted Darya to run. It was meticulously planned, it was an inside job, and there wasn't anything Darya or even Luunaiwel could have done about it.

Still, the Night's Hand only went after Darya because of her power. If it wasn't for her, none of the others would have to be in this predicament.

She dropped her head to her hands, wanting to scream at the vicious cycle that raced round and round in her mind.

"You're doing it again."

Caldor's rough hand fell onto Darya's shoulder, the squeeze was enough to snap her out of her thoughts. Darya wanted to cry again, but she didn't want to in front of Caldor. She was ashamed didn't shrug his hand away.

"Blaming yourself isn't going to make anything better."

"I'm not sure if anything can make things better at this point." Her voice came out hoarse.

"It might seem so, but-"

"If you're gonna say it's only going to get better from here, then I'll throw you overboard." Darya hissed the words out from behind her teeth.

Instead of being intimidated, Caldor barked out a laugh, "You've been around that elf for too long."

"At least she's not irritating! Would you just shut up for once?!!" Whirling to face Caldor, Darya snapped, glaring daggers at him.

Caldor didn't even flinch, staring right back with a raised eyebrow. Chest puffing and hands balled to fist, Darya felt a hot surge of anger coursed through her, feeding off the utter helplessness and guilt that had been festering since she woke up on this ship. It was dizzying, and Darya was a hair away from being reduced to a hostile mess.

By the Gods, what had become of her?

She stumbled backward, and would have fallen over if her scrambling hands didn't grab hold of the railing.

Darya took a long inhale of air, filling her lungs with the salt-heavy scent of the ocean and the musty, sweet rotting smell of the wood's varnish. Once upon a time, they would have been completely foreign, something that she would only hear of from collected tales, and never would experience. But it had become a constant, and would be so for the next few miserable months.

Gods ... Darya wished she could come back to the days in Flumium. Life was difficult, but it was so much simpler. The only thing she had to worry about was the next meal and not the safety of everyone around her.

"I'm ... sorry if I pushed you too far."

Darya looked up at the inquisitive Caldor, who seemed concerned for once. He stepped back, scratching the back of his neck.

"I'm really not good with this kind of stuff ..."

So he *was* trying to cheer her up. Clumsy and crude, just like himself. And Darya would have laughed, but she couldn't find it in her. She was exhausted with all the emotional turmoil, and with the physical reality.

"I wasn't going to say it's going to get better from here, just so you know."

Darya looked up, confused and tired. Caldor simply shrugged.

"You being you, it's likely you're going to have to face far more difficult trials and tribulations. If you can't bounce back from this, then you won't survive."

She wanted to say something sarcastic, but Darya turned away instead. He was right. Everything that had happened after she received her Druidic powers, Darya had Luunaiwel by her side. Plus Tuura, Nathi and Sindri. After this journey, upon arrival at Imirra, they would all be gone. Darya would have to depend on some strangers, and she would have to figure out how to save her sister by herself. And that was still without counting the hope everyone had for her to save Ardent from its withering demise.

Caldor was right. It would only get more difficult from here.

"What if I don't want to bounce back anymore?"

He raised an eyebrow at her. Darya looked to the foaming waves. Her gaze darkened.

"What if I want to give up?"

"Then we will persevere."

Not expecting that, Darya turned to stare at Caldor's stony visage, eyes widened. But the shock wore off quickly. Her lips pulled back into an ugly sneer of a smile.

"I guess it's true. Everyone's better off without me."

Caldor's eyes narrowed, "You're mistaken. Look, I'm not too clear on all this magic stuff, and I'm still not sure about your whole Druid business, but ... Would this world benefit from you helping out? Yes. But there are too many possibilities that you might not be able to get there. In the scenario that you can't, we'll simply have to go on without."

His words drew out a grimace from her, "You're still a pessimist."

"The world is cruel. It always takes more than it gives. You and I both know this," Caldor paused for a second, then sighed, "what I'm trying to say is ... whatever happens, don't think about what you have to do for everyone else for now. Just focus on what matters most to you."

Darya blinked, "I didn't think I'd ever hear that from a Knight."

Caldor opened his mouth, as if he was going to correct her on instinct, but threw a hand up, "You weren't sworn in. You shouldn't shoulder any duty that's not yours."

Shouldn't she, though? Darya's palm went to cradle her cold Heart Stone, and thought about the brand on her leg.

Perhaps she didn't ask for this, and maybe Caldor was right, in a sense. But Darya knew, in the depth of her heart, that what she wanted no longer mattered.

CHAPTER 33:

Darya spent the next week of their voyage under the hull, staring at Sara's cluster of thorns.

Honestly, Darya knew she was being a coward and a brat. But it *hurt*. Travelling bard or not, she had always been on the road, content in knowing that there would always be a home to return to. Now not only did she no longer have a home, she also didn't have any family left.

With the condition her Heart Stone was in, Darya didn't have a chance to even try getting Sara out. Darya was no longer growing flowers in her sleep, without the interference from the gems. Luunaiwel confirmed it. Back in Mul Tarum, that would have been a relief, but now...

Out here in the open ocean, there wasn't a sliver of land in sight for her to find reassurance.

Darya didn't want to admit it at first. That what Luunaiwel said was true. That the elf could only teach her the most basic knowledge about magic. Even with the addition of Tuura's self-defence lessons, they wouldn't benefit much from each other by sticking together. With her powers and knowledge, Luunaiwel would be much more useful elsewhere. With Darya's lack thereof, she needed to become more competent by finding a more suitable mentor.

But, still.

Darya's heart clenched at the thought of parting ways with Luunaiwel. Before all of this, she wouldn't have dreamed of getting so attached to a person after so little time. But after becoming a Druid and knowing how much danger came with it, Darya didn't know if she could trust anyone without Luunaiwel being around.

People either respected her boundaries or they just didn't bother. Nobody came to fetch her since Darya started her brooding. The only people Darya had seen since were the few crewmates who came down to feed the travel beasts, the ones she passed at the mess hall, and Metzan when she came back to their shared cabin to sleep.

Imagine Darya's surprise when Tuura of all people came down to see her.

She didn't acknowledge him at first, curling into the corner outside of Sara's stall. Tuura didn't didn't say anything either. He just sat down a few steps away from Darya, waiting.

Darya didn't mean to be rude. She really didn't. But Darya was hurt that they had already decided everything for her. Tuura definitely knew. Probably even before they spoke to Darya.

"What do you want?" She grunted out, glaring at the floor.

Tuura has never been one to beat around the bush, "You need to keep training."

"What good would *training* do if I'm going to be stuck on a safe, paradise island??" Darya huffed, kicking at a few strands of straw, "What good would *physical combat* do if they're going to send a troop for me every time???"

"Well, at least then you'd go down fighting." He deadpanned.

That had Darya snapped her head up to glare at him, *"Really???"*

Looking slightly guilty, Tuura raised his hands, palms up, "Sorry."

Darya opened her mouth, the urge to lash out almost overtook her. Instead, she picked up a piece of hay, and snapped it in two. Tuura had gone quiet again, cautiously watching her.

"Is that why Luunaiwel wants to drop me off at Imirra and leave?"

"What?"

Darya snorted, throwing the hay away and picked up another one, "Because of what happened to Sindri."

There was pity in Tuura's eyes. Darya looked away, unable to stomach it. She didn't *deserve* it.

"Let me be perfectly clear," the steel in his voice made Darya look back up. She almost flinched at the sharp glint in his golden eyes, "if you were anyone else, I would have killed you for what you did."

That did make Darya flinch. The intense, burning gaze in Tuura's eyes made her stomach twist into knots, and she was seized with fear. But then he closed his eyes. When Tuura looked at her again, he just seemed... *tired.*

"But the circumstances aren't normal. I know it was out of your control. Luunaiwel knows that too. And so does Nathi. He just needs to come to terms with it in his own time."

Swallowing, Darya looked away. Because if she kept staring at him, she wouldn't be able to bite back the tears.

"I'll go get the staff."

Tuura stood, "I'll be waiting on the deck."

Tuura was right. Safe or not, Darya would be alone on Imirra. She should at least prepare herself for bad scenarios. Luunaiwel wouldn't be there to bail her out, and Darya had no reason to believe anyone there would be as generous as the elf had been.

Feeling somewhat lighter, Darya went back to her cabin. They still had a long way to sail. She wasn't doing herself nor Sara any good moping around. Might as well do something to keep her mind from wandering.

Though, Darya didn't expect to see Metzan in the cabin holding her staff. Judging by the blonde's surprised expression, she hadn't expected Darya to come back at this time either.

"D-Darya! I-..."

Speechless, Darya held out her hand. Metzan stared at her for a moment before, flustered, passing the staff to her.

Metzan stammered, hands twisting at the front of her dress, "I... I'm sorry! I was just... I was curious and I... I'll just-I'm sorry, I'll just leave."

Out of impulse, Darya stepped in front of the door before Metzan could run out, "You said you want to learn magic from Luunaiwel, right?"

Wide-eyed, like a deer before a hunter, Metzan took a few flighty steps back and forth. Hesitantly, she nodded.

"How come?"

Squeezing at her dress again, Metzan looked like she wanted to be anywhere else but here. But when Darya was about to relent, the blonde sighed, shoulders drooping with a long exhale.

"I just... I just want to make something out of it..."

Biting her lips, Darya wondered if Tuura would mind it too much if she made him wait a little longer, "You mean your magic?"

Metzan nodded, "During my time running... I truly felt useless. There was not a single thing I could do to help Caldor, even though he was risking his life to protect mine. And I am supposed to be the one who was born with magic, supposed to be the one who possesses something *dangerous.*"

The blonde sighed again, dropping down onto her cot. Long, slender fingers that never knew a hard day of work curled around frail arms, and Metzan leaned forward, looking lost in her own thoughts.

"All my life... that has been the only valuable thing about me. A pawn for my family, arranged to marry a man I have never met, and to end up being his broodmare... or worse, a slave, eternally bound to serve. I was born to my father's mistress, you see, and the only reason I was treated better than a servant was because I have magic."

Horror churned in Darya's heart. There was pity too, towards the poor woman, who wasn't much older than herself. Darya didn't know what to say to what she was being told. Anything sounded superficial, compared to Metzan's horrid experience.

So Darya stayed quiet, listening to what Metzan had to say.

"Even though he was the first born and the heir, the rightful child, Aragni was always kind to me," tears welled up in Metzan's eyes, but she wiped them away quickly before they could fall, "my brother could have been cruel. He could have treated me with coldness and indifference like everyone else, but he did not. He never put a hand on me, nor had he ever raised his voice. He even risked everything to give me a chance at a better life."

This time, a sob did rip out of Metzan. Quickly, Darya sat down next to her, a hand on her shaking shoulder, offering what little comfort she could give.

Metzan covered her mouth to stifle another cry of anguish, "If I had known better... if I could use my powers beyond little party tricks... then perhaps I could have... maybe I could have... *Maybe my brother didn't have to die!"*

She broke down, wailing. Biting her lip, Darya put an arm over Metzan's shoulders. It didn't take a genius to figure out that Metzan had been bottling this up for a while. A Lady, no matter how low in rank, was always taught to conceal her feelings. Just as Metzan had when Luunaiwel turned her down. The shock of Darya catching her sneaking a look at the staff must have startled Metzan into spilling her guts.

There was nothing Darya could offer to comfort Metzan. She doubted Metzan spoke to her in hopes Darya could alleviate her pain either. They were in the same situation, Darya realised.

Running and hopeless. Powerless to stop others from harming they ones they loved.

So they sat in companionable, if not miserable, silence, until Metzan excused herself. As a result, Darya showed up to where Tuura was waiting much later than either of them had expected.

"Thought you were going to be a no-show." Tuura raised an eyebrow at her when Darya ran up to him, flustered.

"Just got... carried away with talking to Metzan." Darya said, a bit sheepish. Twirling her staff experimentally, "When do we start?"

"Not like that, you won't," the big man barked out a laugh, "that fancy little trick would get you killed."

The combination of slacking for the last few weeks, rolling sea deck, recently healed shoulder and a new, heavy staff got Darya stumbling everywhere for the following few hours. The sailors' staring and commenting every time she fell absolutely didn't help. By the time Tuura allowed her to stop, it was past lunch. Darya lay sprawled on the wooden deck, groaning.

"Waking up tomorrow is going to be *fun.*" She complained when Tuura offered her a hand. Begrudgingly, she took it, deciding to ignore the fact that he was sparring with her unarmed.

"You're out of shape. It's to be expected," he said jovially, "stay, and stretch your legs. I'll be back with food."

Darya didn't feel like moving for a whole month, but even sitting down hurt. So, with much contempt, Darya decided to walk around the deck while waiting. Whatever, it was a chance to explore this side of the ship properly, since she was too wrapped up in her woes the past week to do so.

The clear sky made the wooden masts shine and the sails gleam. Darya had to admit though, as she watched the waves sparkling under the sun, that the sight was pretty. However, with how tall the ship was, leaning over the railing gave her vertigo after a while.

At the bow of the Valiant Will, something caught her eyes. It was a statue of a dragon head, looming towards the sea with its curved neck and proud horns. Weathered and chipped with marks of past voyages, figurehead was prideful, as if it was the one leading the journey.

"Pretty, is she not?"

The sudden question, carried down by the wind, almost startled Darya if she didn't recognise the familiar voice. Squinting upward, she saw Luunaiwel, sitting with her feet dangling on the dragon's neck.

"What're you doing up there?"

"The view is better here." The elf answered, teeth sparkling. With elegance Darya could only dream to possess, Luunaiwel pitched forward, grabbed onto a horn and swung herself down to the deck, landing with a fluid crouch.

The young Druid rolled her eyes, masking the fact that she was very much impressed, "How long have you been up there?"

There was mischief in Luunaiwel's mismatched eyes, "Enough to count how many time Tuura had you on your arse."

"Thanks." Darya grimaced at her.

"Lighten up, little bird. We are all glad you have decided to get out and do something," chuckling, Luunaiwel threw an arm around her shoulders, then gestured up at the dragon figurehead, "majestic, is she not?"

Used to the elf's rapid change of topic, and somewhat relieved that her attitude remained the same, Darya sighed, "Yes, she is."

"Her name is Euryle." Luunaiwel hummed.

Blinking, Darya glanced up at the figurehead, "That's the dragon who'd teach me?"

"Hopefully so." Luunaiwel said cheerily, "Dragons can be flickering creatures, you know?"

Again, Darya rolled her eyes, "So is some elf I know."

Said elf was amused, "My, you wounded me, Bard of Flumium."

A faint, surprised smile plastered on Darya's lips, "It's been awhile since I was last referred to that title."

In silence, they stood, side by side, regarding the figurehead in the likeness of Euryle, each lost in her own thoughts. Then Tuura came, bringing enough food to feed five people. Darya didn't even realise how famished she was until she caught a whiff of the fish pies and gravy. The three of them sat nestled at the bow, a bit squeezed due to Tuura's bulk.

And yet Darya hadn't felt this content in so long.

They were like an odd vision of a family, Darya decided as she tore into the pie. Regardless of how they saw her as, this was what Darya saw them, as she leaned into Luunaiwel every time the ship rocked. She enjoyed their company, more than she could any of the few friends she had in Flumium. She didn't ache for her little community every time she had to leave for her journey, not in the way she ached knowing that she had to part ways with these two soon.

"Luunaiwel?"

"Yes, little bird."

"What do those tattoos you have mean?"

Pausing mid-chew, the elf went quiet. Darya almost apologised for asking before Luunaiwel began to speak.

"Magi use incantations to invoke magic. Many of them lengthy and winded, to ensure that the elements understand exactly what needs to be done. In normal circumstances, that would not be a problem. All you need is a little time."

Luunaiwel smiled, then, with one hand, lifted her heavy veil of hair up to reveal the back of her neck. The skin there was covered with tattoos, the same as the rest on her body, "A battle mage cannot afford the same luxury. A fraction of a second can be all that is between life and death. So we carve spells onto our skin. When the need arises, we only have to invoke the element's name and visualise the spell in our mind."

"Wow," was all Darya could say. She stared, unblinking even after Luunaiwel let her hair down, "you have a lot of spells done, then."

The elf chuckled, "Yes. But a normal battle mage does not need to go to such extremes as I have."

Curious now, Darya met Luunaiwel's eyes, "How come?"

The elf tilted her head, "Those who are born with magic are blessed with a specific element. Like our Lady Metzania, who has an affinity for fire. And that element would always be the strongest in the hands of those it blessed. While a mage can eventually learn to control elements other than the one he or she was born with, those elements would never reach the same height as the original one."

Darya thought about it for a moment, "So for example, my base element is earth. If I could have been a mage, that would be my elemental base, and I can learn other elemental based magic, but they would never be as strong as my earth magic?"

"Correct, little bird."

"You've mastered all the elements then? Is that why you have so many tattoos?"

"She is a bright one, is she not?" Luunaiwel nudged Tuura, who laughed in agreement. Turning to Darya, the elf's eyes sparkled, "I was born to an Archmage and a great Warrior, on the darkest hour of a moonless and starless night. They said I am blessed with the knowledge and power of the Void Beyond, where all Celestials and Elements came to be. And so I am. I can control not only the elements of the Land that birthed me, but also touched by the Sky above."

Darya whistled, "I knew you were powerful, but I didn't know you are *that* powerful."

Luunaiwel's chuckle was light, "Power can be both a blessing and a curse. You should know that well by now," clapping Darya on the shoulder, "now finish your food. More training awaits."

The reminder brought a groan out of her.

Darya proceeded to spend the rest of the afternoon being knocked around by Tuura, while Luunaiwel watched from her perch on the figurehead. Darya couldn't tell whether the food helped her or weighed her down.

When Tuura's very precise swipe at the back of her knees had Darya doing an epic but painful face plant, she decided that it was definitely the latter.

Rolling onto her back, the young Druid aimed a very colourful curse at the gathering clouds. Great, even the weather seemed to be mocking her now.

"Strange," Luunaiwel's voice rang above the whipping wind, "the Captain said we should have at least another week of clear weather."

Crawling back onto her feet, Darya grunted, "You can never tell with weather though. Besides, it might be just some clouds."

From where she was, it was difficult to tell what kind of expression Luunaiwel was wearing. Especially when she only regarded Darya for a short moment before turning her gaze back to the sea.

"You are right, little bird. You are right."

CHAPTER 34:

It seemed like Darya was wrong after all. Before she knew it, they were being pelted mercilessly by the rain. Tuura ushered her inside before going off to help the crew, and the last she saw of Luunaiwel was the elf running towards Captain Silos, her words lost in the roaring waves.

Stepping into the blessedly dry cabin, Darya found a pale Metzan, clutching onto a bucket.

"W-why is the... why is the sh-ship shaking s-s-so much???" The blonde wheezed, looking like she was about to lose her lunch.

"There's a storm brewing," Darya said, stripping off her wet cloak, "I thought you aren't seasick?"

Swallowing dryly, Metzan was doing her hardest to not hurl, "I'm... I'm o-okay with the n-n-normal... hrgggnn... movements... But this... *this* is too m-much!!!"

Darya rushed over the table to pour her some water. Grateful, Metzan was reaching for the cup when a particularly nasty wave slapped the ship, pushing it too far left before the Valiant Will righted itself. That was enough for Darya to stumble, splashing water everywhere, and it was also the last straw on Metzan's fragile control.

Vomit was always nasty and often could cause a chain reaction. Darya had performed at enough taverns to know that. So she turned away as soon as Metzan started making gurgling noises to protect the content of her own stomach.

"I'm... uh, I'll just step out for a moment." Darya said quickly. She couldn't tell if Metzan had heard her or not, the retching sounds she was making were still rather intense when Darya shut the door.

A splash of icy water in her face made the young Druid reconsider her decision. The ocean was angry, seething with rain and waves and thunder. The ship was churning, and sailors were scrambling around, shouting orders that were mostly lost to the raging elements. The only thing that kept Darya upright was her staff.

"What are you doing out here?" Out of nowhere, Luunaiwel's voice asked, startling Darya.

"Metzan is puking everywhere. I don't want to add to it."

"Wonderful," Luunaiwel made a face, though most of her expression was blurred in the rain, "you should go down to the hull then. Get away from all this madness."

Another sudden tip had Darya grabbing onto Luunaiwel's arm for balance. She yelled, howling wind and crashing waves made it impossible to hear anything else.

"I don't think I can make it there without a concussion!"

Luunaiwel sighed, "Fair. I have something that can help Metzan."

"Oh, good! Because she might pass out at this rate!"

"Might be a blessing for her, all things considered."

With much begrudging on her part however, Darya was assigned to clear out the cabin as Luunaiwel went to fetch whatever potion she had.

Thank the Gods Metzan had somehow managed to not miss the bucket. For the most parts. The poor blonde had some *remnants* of her lunch on the front of her dress, and part of her hair was suspiciously matted. The cabin did smell horrible, and Darya had to suppress the urge to gag.

"You're done?"

Dishevelled, Metzan blinked up with glazed eyes, tears and snot ruining what little impression of a Lady she had left, "I... I think so... I... didn't eat much for l-lunch... "

"I'll take that." Darya grabbed the bucket, holding it as far away as she could. Kicking the chamber pot over to Metzan just in case, Darya bit back a shudder and opened the door again.

Braving the storm, she used whatever was left of her flexibility after training to get to the edge of the ship. The contents of the bucket sloshed dangerously with each step, and at one point Darya almost toppled over. Miraculously, she managed without spilling anything on herself. However, as she struggled to hold onto the railing and dump the bucket into the sea, a particularly powerful wave shoved the ship forward and, out of instinct, she let go to grab onto the railing.

Only daring to look up once everything calmed down a little, which wasn't by much, Darya looked to the dark, angry water.

Whelp, no one was going to miss a bucket of vomit.

Making her way back inside, Darya had to force the door closed, only to have it pushed back open by Luunaiwel. The elf wrinkled her nose.

"We need to get her out of those clothes."

Weakly, Metzan gestured at her cot, "I have a nightgown..."

"I have something for your nausea, Metzania." Luunaiwel said, peeling a sleeve off Metzan's shoulder.

Metzan's voice was stifled, "Oh... Thank you... that would be... that would be great... S-sorry... for all this trouble..."

As Darya looped the nightgown over Metzan's neck, the ship suddenly lurched to the side, throwing them both onto Metzan's cot in a yelping heap. Darya's head collided with the wall hard enough for her to see stars, and Metzan's *very* sharp elbow digging into her ribs as she fell face-first onto the hard mattress.

"This couldn't get any worse, could it?" Groaning, Darya tried to sit up when Luunaiwel straightened Metzan.

When she gathered her bearings, the look on Luunaiwel's face made Darya immediately regret her words.

"Luunaiwel?"

"When did you get this mark?" The air in the cabin just dropped several degrees colder. Luunaiwel's piercing eyes were on the back of Metzan's shoulder, her gloved hand held the blonde's arm in a deathly tight grip.

Immediately cautious, Darya sprung up and away from Metzan, standing behind Luunaiwel to look at what got the elf so riled up. It... looked like a scar. A burn mark in the shape of a skeletal hand. Glossy and bright against her pale skin.

As if she was *branded*.

Darya felt faint.

There was panic in Metzan's eyes as she struggled, in vain, to escape Luunaiwel's grip, "Please... *please* don't..."

Luunaiwel's yank on her arm was merciless, bringing a terrified Metzan face to face with her, "You are marked by the Night's Hand, foolish child."

Fangs baring, Luunaiwel shoved the blonde away, looming over her as Metzan tumbled onto the cot with a yelp. The mage hissed, eyes wild.

"You have doomed us all."

A violent shove from the ship had Darya sprawled on the floor, but she could hardly register the pain through her shock.

Luunaiwel's mismatched eyes were feral as she swung the door open.

"Darya, come."

Throwing one last glance at the sniffling Metzan, Darya grabbed her staff and scrambled into the storm.

She could barely see Luunaiwel through the merciless storm. She could barely stand with every dip and push of the ship. But Luunaiwel's hand around hers kept Darya steady and, together, they trudged their way towards the hatch for the hull.

Thunder boomed overhead. Lightning flashed too close to comfort. Dark clouds blotched out the sky. The ocean roared in fury, sending wave after wave to assault the Valiant Will. The crew pushed and pulled with each precarious movement, fighting to keep their ship in one piece.

The ship rammed forward as they ran, sending even Luunaiwel sliding. But at least they were at the hatch.

"Get down there, and keep still!" Luunaiwel yelled, "Stay with Sara! Do no-"

She stopped abruptly, pulling at the hatch. It didn't budge.

"It's locked?!" Darya gave it a pull, affirming her own question. Luunaiwel looked beyond pissed now. But it seemed their problems did not end there.

"Luna!!!" Tuura swung down from a mast, soaked through and battered, "Something's wrong!!"

"I will tell you what is *wrong!*" The Battle Mage snapped, whirling around with a snarl, "Metzania is marked by the Night's Hand!! That is why they have been able to chase her down while she ran with Caldor!!! And now they know we are here!!! Out on the open sea!!!"

If it was possible, Tuura became paler than the cold already made him. Darya felt as if her stomach had dropped onto the rolling deck, *"What?!* They've been *tracking* Metzan?!!?"

"Did I not just say that?!" Luunaiwel sneered, "I should have inspected her when I had the chance! Now we need to get Darya down there and away from that child!"

Tuura shouted, "We can't! They locked it down to prevent flooding!"

"Son of a whor-" Luunaiwel's curse was lost in an echoing *thunk.*

A wave had slammed against the ship so hard it reared.

For a heart-stopping moment, Darya thought the Valiant Will was going to capsize. Scrambling, she threw herself into Luunaiwel, who in turn held onto Tuura. The Shapeshifter's huge arm came around them, bracing for the incoming impact.

But then, the ship lurched, smashing back into water as it regained balance. Cold water engulfed them for a second, washing away what little air Darya had left. Gasping, they stood trembling together as the wave pulled away. Darya could feel the deafening thunder deep in her chest. She clutched at both Luunaiwel and Tuura, fear eating away in her bones.

Out here, on the open sea, all were in its mercy.

A bolt of lightning struck much closer than the rest, whitening Darya's vision. Panic seized her, and she desperately cried out for Luunaiwel, despite still being in her arms. But when her vision cleared, Darya thought Mortia had taken them.

She didn't believe her eyes at first. She thought the lightning was making her see things.

But the screams of sailors, clamouring away from their post, told her that this was real. For they were all screaming the same thing.

"KRAKEN!!!"

Tentacles, bigger than the masts and armed with teeth the size of lances, crawled up, up and *up*. They latched onto the sails, pulled at the woods, shredded chunks of everything and cast it into the raging sea. Pale, purplish and slimy flesh writhed as its clawed suction gnawed down on the ship.

What kind of horror... was *this?*

How could they possibly fight against such monstrosity?

Is this the end?

"FIGHT!!!" Luunaiwel hollered, breaking Darya out of her stupor. With sword and staff, the Battle Mage sprang forth like a loose arrow, "FIGHT!!! FOR ANOTHER DAY!!! FOR SURVIVAL!!! *FIGHT!!!"*

Her staff ignited with light and fire, sizzling away at the kraken's flesh, and her sword followed, sinking above its claws. Blood, black as tar, gushed forth, and the tentacle shuddered with trembles, lashing out, only to be stabbed again and again.

But it was *wounded* and, horror or not, the kraken bled just like any creature did. And so the sailors took arms, in a Great War cry that rose above the thunders. Darya joined them, following Tuura's fist weapons' slashes with her own strikes.

They dodged when the claws flared, stepped back when a smaller tentacle lashed out. Then back again to hack and slash at whatever flesh they could reach. It was a maddening dance, and all the intensity of Darya's focus was on this.

There was nowhere to run. Nowhere to hide.

Might as well go down fighting.

Perhaps their attacks were as insignificant as flea bites to the kraken. Perhaps they could never kill such a terrible creature. But their cuts made it thrash, their battering made it churn. The sea howled with its shudders. And they kept on fighting despite more and more of the crew being ripped away.

Stabbing. Chopping. Batting.

But … Mortals like them... how could they hope to drive something so dreadful off?

A tentacle, bigger and with teeth sharper than all others, wrapped around the Valiant Will's main mast and *pulled*. The wood groaned, creaking and breaking with the crew's panicked shouts. Under its monstrous strength, the ship swayed dangerously, threatening to finally topple.

Hopelessness consumed Darya like a wildfire. Above terror, above desperate rage.

"NO!!!" She shouted, rushing back with Tuura and Luunaiwel to fight for the mast. But she could see it, even through the salt burning in her eyes.

The wood would give. It was made to hold up sails, not the grabbing hands of a titan.

When it went down, it would bring many of them with it. The ship would crack. Broken and sunk with all of them on it.

Even Luunaiwel. Even Tuura. Even herself. Even Sara.

With a cry of maddening desperation, Darya held onto the mast with both hands, bracing against it with her staff.

Hold!!!

Please!!!

Goddess Vita!! I beg of you!!!

If you can hear me.

Please...

Give me the strength to hold this ship!!!

Upon her chest, her Heart Stone was cold. Darya's eyes stung, her breath hollowed and raspy.

Everyone would die…

Please!!!

She searched and prayed and begged. Frantic thoughts desperately held onto the image of the mast, upright and not crumbling upon what was left of her family.

This ship needs to hold!!!

PLEASE!!!

"HELP ME HOLD THIS SHIP!!!" Darya screamed. Against the roar of the sky and ocean. Against the cries of the crew. Against the kraken's wrath.

The entire world shuddered in its cold wrath. But her veins ignited.

From her skin against long-dead wood, vines and branches burst forth. Intertwining around the mast, they grew and grew, so fast and so vicious they pushed both Luunaiwel and Tuura away, wrapping themselves around even the kraken's tentacle. Roots, thick and unyielding sprouted from the floor, anchored the base of the mast. The tentacle squelched, being squeezed and squashed by the climbing branches until it burst.

Sticky, thick and vile blood mixed with rain, pouring over Darya. Something twisted over her chest. Pain, like a million shards of glass, dug into her heart. She felt it when the magic drained out of her. She felt it over the burning of hot blood ran down her face, filling her mouth with a terrible stench of death. Every nerve was on fire, emptying everything she had into this.

She felt as if her heart, her Heart Stone, was going to shatter.

But stubbornly, Darya held on.

Even as the kraken screamed in the deep. Even as she felt all her power rushed away. Drained into the mast, making it grow again.

Her vision blurred. Because of water, blood or fatigue, Darya didn't know. All sounds began to fade away. Even the rocking of the ship seemed... distant.

By the Gods... she had gone and done something stupid again, hadn't she?

Darya just really...

She just really didn't want *anyone else to die...*

Something squeezed around her shoulders. Was it a tentacle? A hand? Darya was too weak to fight back.

It ripped her away from the mast.

Luunaiwel's startling bright eyes were all she could see. The elf's hand was on her face. Luunaiwel's lips were moving, but Darya couldn't hear.

Something glinted in those beautiful eyes. Something that made Darya reach out. Something that made Darya want to tell Luunaiwel to *stop*.

Luunaiwel stood, midnight hair whipped wildly in the wind. Sheathing her sword and buckled down her staff, the Battle Mage grabbed onto the gnarled vines and climbed.

Dazed, Darya could only watch, as Luunaiwel went higher and higher. As Tuura hacked off what was left of the tentacle around the mast. As the storm pelted them mercilessly.

Darya watched as Luunaiwel stood tall on the crow's nest. Raising her swords above her head.

Everything seemed to stand still.

Out of the corner of her eye, Darya saw Tuura's amber eyes widened in terrified realisation. She saw his fangs bared, forming a desperate shout.

She caught Luunaiwel's eyes, looking down upon them. A gentle smile bloomed on her pale lips.

Above the wind, above the sea. Over the storm and over the kraken's scream.

Luunaiwel's spell resonated as if without a sound. And yet so loud, as if her words were thunder.

"RALACH SA AMUN, ZNÆZCNÆ!!!"

Lightning struck her crossed blades, drowning out Tuura's grievous cry for her name with sparks so bright they brought tears to Darya's eyes.

No...

Luunaiwel...

No...

Eyes white, charged lightning, Luunaiwel swung her crackling swords, and dove into the sea.

Darya's eyes filled with tears. From pain, from the sudden light, and from the terrible dread that consumed her entire being.

She didn't know what she saw next was real, or if it was a hallucination her exhausted brain made up. Her eyelids shuttered, one image after the last filled her dying vision, chopped to bits with flashes of darkness.

The sea below raged. Lightning, white, sharp and spreading like veins cackled along hooked tentacles. The shadow of the Kraken was a mass of darkness against the light, its head half the size of the Valiant Will and its eyes were glowing pits of despair.

But the crawling lightning snapped like a thousand whips, circling around the monster in a white vortex that had it thrashing in torment. Electricity even climbed and sparkled on its tentacles, ripping them away from the Valiant Will. Its blood sprayed thick and warm and putrid. The ship bobbed dangerously, threatening to throw them all into dark water.

Desperately, Darya held onto what was left of her consciousness, but she knew she was fading. It was too much. Her body was shutting down, buried under the tide of exhaustion.

The last image Darya saw was the elegant arc of Luunaiwel's body, charged with lightning, rushing into the horrid mass of the Kraken, and disappearing in the shadows that consumed all.

END OF BOOK 1

EPILOGUE:

"AAAAAAAAAAAAH!!!!"

Screeching, Anga shoved the marble basin away. It shattered on the stone floor, spilling blood over her ritual ground.

"That wretch!!! That absolute *wretch!!!*"

In a whirlwind of crimson robes and white hair, Anga rained destruction in the vast chambers, throwing and smashing everything she could get her jewelled hands on. The proxy clairvoyance, gurgling in his own blood, snagged at her embroidered slippers in a desperate attempt. Unfortunately for him, that only enraged the witch further. Shrieking, Anga stomped on his face, and did not stop even after the fool's head was reduced to a smear.

Duke Dunstan Baines watched her placidly in his chair. There was no stopping Anga when she threw a tantrum. He had learned a long time ago to just let it run its course. Anga would calm down. Eventually.

Quietly, Dunstan poured himself a cup of wine. They suffered a great loss today. They wouldn't have if Anga did not insist on summoning her beast. Now, all they had left were strung up corpses, drained of blood and magic.

Not even necromancers would buy these.

They should have waited. They knew where the ship was heading off to. They knew where the Druid would be. They truly struck gold with their seemingly worthless runaway merchandise, and had uncovered far more information than they could have ever dreamt of.

They could have had, not only the new Druid, but also eyes on a Dragon, a living, breathing *Dragon*, in Imirra.

Oh, Dunstan could feel the sweet buzzing in the pit of his stomach, thinking about how much a King or Queen would pay to have a Dragon as a bound slave. Or how spilling the blood of such a fearsome creature would have furthered their cause.

But Anga was too hasty. Too eager to claim all the prizes for herself.

The witch's rampage died down after three cups of wine. Mostly because she had run out of objects to thrash about.

"Are you done?"

Seething red eyes glared at him with all the hatred in the world.

"Go fuck a cow."

That almost made Dunstan chuckle. But he held it back. Unhinged, foolish and crippled she might be, Anga was still a witch. A dangerous, temperamental witch.

"I would, but then who would help you explain this to Lord Voronda?"

Perhaps his own mouth was foolish as well. The high-pitched hiss coming out of Anga made all the braziers flare up, licking the ceiling and threatening to burn the whole place down.

By Mortia...Must all witches be pyromaniacs?

Heedless of the heat, Dunstan stood with a groan. Old age had not treated him well, despite all he had accomplished. Not only did he have arthritis, two missing fingers and three brats for grandchildren, he had to oversee this literal hole in the ground and babysit this hellion of a witch.

Vita loved testing the patience of a mortal man.

"Now, now, dear Anga. You know very well that the price of fixing these chambers is worth a gaggle of slaves. Which you have gone and wasted, I must add."

Another screech had the fire searing towards him. Dunstan sighed.

"Ær, shield."

Invisible, air whirled around him, redirecting the flow of fire back to their braziers.

"Must we do this every time, sweet Anga?"

She spat in his direction.

"If only you would calm down, I can show you how this might still benefit us."

By the way she was looking at him, Dunstan knew Anga wished for nothing more than his death. But even her, rash and violent as she could be, was smarter than that. He could see it in her eyes, how she calculated and schemed and warred with her unbidden violence.

Finally, hatred was suppressed in her eerie red eyes. Anga gathered herself into a more dignified pose, as dignified as her twisted back allowed her to anyway, and asked.

"What do you want?"

Dunstan pulled his thin lips back into a smile.

It seemed that she, too, had learned.

Afterwords:

Hi everyone, thank you for reading The Last Druid!

This book was conceived after 8 long years of planning, with several drafts, a briefly entertained idea of a TTRPG campaign and an attempt at turning it into a Visual Novel! But in the end, I think the story is best told in its intended form, a book. I hope you've enjoyed following the first part of Darya, Luunaiwel and Tuura's journey, and look forward to the next instalment of the book!

About the Author:

Nei is a writer/author living in Wokingham, England with a knack for descriptive words. She has penned a Visual Novel, several short stories and essays, proof-read and translated journalism articles, and even ghost-penned a novel once. Aside from writing, she enjoys gardening, her two cats, and is quite a notorious TTRPG Dungeon Master!

Printed in Great Britain
by Amazon